THE LAST BEEKEEPER

SILENT SKIES BOOK I

REBECCA L. FEARNLEY

LIGHTNING HYENA PRESS

WANT TO SEE A MAP OF ALPHOR?

Head to the back of the book to find out more about the world of *Silent Skies*. You'll find links to a web page with maps, character interviews and more content about this trilogy.

Enjoy!

CONTENTS

ONE

SOLMA'S HEART SINKS AS she scans the withered trees. Orchard Six is almost dead, a disaster the village can little afford. The carefully cultivated rows of apple trees, which yielded meagre fruit last year, are now twisted and black with disease.

And on top of last year's poor harvest ...

"It's worse than last time," Piotr points out, wiping his hands on his uniform of blue overalls. He looks tired. He's been orchard master in the village for nearly two decades and he's fought disease and dwindling crops for most of it. It's a wonder, Solma thinks, that he's managed to keep going for so long. But the years clearly weigh on him. He wipes the back of his sleeve repeatedly across his watery eyes and Solma can't tell if he's despairing or getting sick. Either is possible. Or both. "Some sorta disease. It's confined to this orchard for now, but ..."

He wafts his hands in front of his face as if there's something buzzing around it. But there are no buzzing things. Not anymore. The sky has been a silent, barren place for as long as anyone can remember. Longer. Poor man's just slowly going crazy. It'll only get worse as the heat reaches its summer peak.

Piotr shakes his head. "Some of them ain't producing buds. Pollinating is gonna be tough this year."

Solma frowns. "You sure?"

Piotr's face darkens. "I'm an Oritch," he growls, as if Solma might have forgotten. "Always was. I been tending these orchards all my life, like my parents and their parents. I've always been Piotr Chen Oritch. Never had no other name. I know these trees better than anyone."

Solma can't think of anything to say to that. No sense arguing with the orchard folk. They're grumpier than the Fei Field Workers and easier to offend. Still, she's not sure what Piotr expects her small squad to do about this. The Gatra—the village Gathering Guard—have one job, protect the territory from all outside threats. From redbears and wildwolves and the ever-present danger of raiders who plunder villages for what miserable supplies they might have. But they can't fight this, they can't put a bullet in a disease.

Still, he's doing the right thing by reporting it, and his orchard is on their patrol route. It's just not the news she'd *hoped* to get on her first day as Sergeant. She notes down what he says on her wax tablet, already compiling her report.

Looking up, Solma reaches towards the nearest tree and pinches a blackened twig. It disintegrates, coating her fingertips with powder. She grimaces and smears the dirt on her trousers, before trudging to the edge of the orchard and shielding her eyes to scan the horizon. There is nothing but tough, yellow grass and barren soil for miles. Spring is coming, with the usual promise of a furiously hot summer, but for now the morning air is full of winter chill. Solma leans on the rickety fence that marks the boundary between the orchards and the unmanaged wilderness. She squints at the horizon, past the line of watch towers in the distance, and tries to see the detail on the ragged line of distant trees. Is there death on those, too? Has this disease blown in on some wind, or has it been lurking in the soil all winter? She can't tell. She marches back to where Piotr waits. The other Oritch have stopped to watch her, too, their reed hats pulled low over their eyes to keep out the sun. Solma can't tell what they're thinking.

The Orchard Master stares up at her expectantly. Solma reddens, hating how almost everyone in this village has to look *up* into her face. Just one of a host of daily things that remind her how different she is. She hunches her shoulders.

"When d'you notice?" she asks.

Piotr's jaw twitches and his gaze hardens.

"Reported it as soon as I realized," he says. "I know the law."

Solma touches Piotr's shoulder. "Meant no disrespect," she says. "I know you follow rules."

Piotr digs his bare toes into the dry soil. "There's a few saplings on the border that're still healthy."

He wafts absent-mindedly at the air in front of him again and Solma looks away. Hunger does this to everyone eventually. She's seen old women in the village do it, and mutter to themselves before succumbing to starvation.

But Piotr keeps glancing at her left leg, too, as if he's never noticed that it's prosthetic below the knee, though it has been for years. Solma shifts uncomfortably, the curved blade she uses as a foot churning up dirt. She's losing patience.

"Right," she says, making the old man jump. "Show me." She turns to where the other four members of her squad linger at the edge of the orchard. They're all dressed in Gatra-black and look bored. Warren, her little brother, squats between them. He's Yuen-caste—a youngster, still—so he has no uniform, only whatever threadbare remains can be spared to clothe him, and these are almost worn through. He prods the dirt with a stick, clearly bored. Solma frowns but leaves him be. Instead, she addresses her squad.

"I'll check the edges while one of you reports to Blaiz." she says. "Maxen?"

The tallest boy, and Staff Sergeant of the squad, nods. He takes a wax tablet from his belt and begins scratching on it with a stylus. Solma bites her lip and looks away. She's more than capable of writing her own report, but it's not a skill she flaunts often. It's not a skill many people in the village have. It's different for Maxen though, because of who his father is.

Eventually, Maxen looks up, smiling. "Good idea," he says. Solma beams back before she can stop herself and has to wrestle her face back under control. Behind him, a girl with a fiery red braid and freckles splashed across her pale face rolls her eyes and glares. Solma glares back.

"Problem, Olive?"

Olive's jaw rotates around a wad of sugar cane. She holds Solma's gaze. "No," she sneers. "You?"

Maxen either doesn't notice the tension or doesn't care. He hands the wax tablet to another boy, who heads off towards the village and the grand house of Maxen's father, the Steward. Solma watches him go and hopes the report will reach Blaiz Camber before any rumors do. Blaiz does not like to be kept waiting.

Solma stretches and feels the muscles strain under the weight of her rifle. She turns her back on Olive. Wretched girl's just sore Solma made Sergeant and she didn't. The thought of it makes her stand a little taller. *Sergeant.* How long has she fought for that privilege? Long enough for it to feel sweet, now, when she hears others address her by that title.

A sharp animal cry in the distance and the squad is on alert. Solma's rifle is ready in her hands and she shoves Piotr behind her, scanning the horizon. Olive and Maxen are back-to-back, their pistols drawn. Solma squints against the low sun and swears with shock when a skinny deer clambers to its feet, its head only just visible above the long grass. It shudders, lets out the same, plaintive cry, then collapses.

Solma lowers her rifle and swallows the lump in her throat. The game is already starving ...

She turns back to Piotr. One thing at a time.

"This won't take much longer, will it?" She asks. "Only, we ain't finished setting the chemical barrier yet and we got the rest of our patrol to do by the start of planting—"

She lets the sentence hang, heavy with implication: the chemical barrier is what keeps redbears and wildwolves away: a ring of foul-smelling substances around the village, laid by the Gatra every day. if her squad miss their patrol, if the chemical barrier isn't laid, it leaves the village vulnerable. Neither Solma nor Piotr want to be responsible for dangers slipping through.

Piotr shakes his head vigorously and wafts his hands again. "No, no!" he insists. "Not long! But I want you to see everything! I know the law. Wouldn't want you to think I was keeping anything back ..."

Solma forces what she hopes is a reassuring a smile. Piotr's watery eyes shine with that fear she often sees in villagers making land reports: fear that Blaiz will accuse them of secrecy, that they will be considered traitors to the village and exiled. But Blaiz isn't like that. Blaiz is fair, and a good Steward. As leaders go, Solma thinks he's one of the strongest. He only demands candor because, without it, the village will die.

Solma wishes so much that everybody could see this, instead of flinching whenever he walks by. He's a protector, not a tyrant.

"Ok," she sighs, turning back to her squad. "Back in a minute. Come on, Warren."

Her little brother glances up from where he's squatting in the dirt, drawing shapes in the dry earth. His eyes are huge and meadow-green, but sunken with starvation. He shouldn't be on patrol with her, but it was either under her watchful eye or out tilling the fields with the other kids. He's weak enough as it is and Solma doesn't trust the other youngsters to be gentle with him. He blinks at her, his lower jaw hanging slack.

"I'm alright here," he murmurs. Solma frowns.

"No, Warren, come with us, please."

Warren doesn't protest again, just sighs and wipes his tiny hands on the ragged remains of his shorts. He plods after his sister.

Piotr glances back to Warren, frowning. "You know," he says quietly, "he's not a kid anymore. He's got to get used to guns some time."

Solma hoists her own rifle higher onto her shoulder. "He's seven," she growls. "That's still plenty kid enough for me. And I'll be damned if he's going into the Guard."

Piotr raises an eyebrow.

"There are worse places than the Guard, Sol," he says gently. "Your Ma was in the Guard, eh?"

Solma bites down on a host of retorts to that. "It's *Sergeant*, now," she snaps, and her heart twangs as Piotr's head dips in deference. "Look, I know," she says, softer now, "but—"

She trails off. How can she possibly explain it to him? She's not sure she understands herself. She was so proud to be drafted into the Gathering Guard four years ago, just after her twelfth birthday. She left the caste-name of Yuen—youngster—behind and became a Gatra. *Solma El Gatra.* Soldier. Protector. Following in her Ma's footsteps. But the truth is, she was just another kid with a rifle. Guards don't have the greatest life expectancy. Their job is about stepping into the danger zone, defending the village from raiders, protecting planters and orchard workers while they get on with generating the year's harvest. They also hunt the wild, powerful game in the managed forest to the south. Ma was in the Guard, and Solma remembers the pride on her face whenever she put on that uniform. But she also remembers Ma's agony as she'd died, the way her eyes slid out of focus as the blood drained out of her. Ma had lived for the Guard and she'd died for it, too.

Solma bites her lip. "He's not grown up enough for that, yet. I hope they'll give him a few more years."

...Or all his life. Solma doesn't want Warren in the Guard.

Her little brother deserves better.

So many little brothers and sisters deserve better.

Piotr guides Solma to the northern edge of the orchard, where the trees are still young and supple with life.

"Right," she says. "These should flower?"

Piotr shrugs. "We hope. But what good is it?" He leans closer. "Everyone's heard about the damaged pollenbots."

Solma's heart tightens. Great. She throws a dark glance over her shoulder at the rest of her squad. Whoever let that one slip is in for serious hell. They've enough to worry about this year without extra panic.

The pollenbots are old tech from before, when humans still thought they were in charge; headsets controlling squads of miniscule drones that work like insects and pollinate the crop ready for harvest. The Fei-caste planters know how to use them, but the knowledge for fixing them disappeared from the village long ago. Their loss is another disaster. She places a hand on Piotr's shoulder and tries to look reassuring. It's ridiculous. She's sixteen and he's an old man, gazing up at her in the hopes she'll tell him it'll all be ok.

But she can't. Because it won't.

"We still got some left," she says, which is true. "Enough to pollinate these trees if they flower," Possibly true. "And we should manage to stock the storehouse at harvest." Probably not true. "No reason to worry." Outright lie.

But Piotr's face relaxes. "Okay," he says. "Thanks." He laughs nervously and scratches the back of his head, lifting his eyes skyward as if in the vain hope that some little buzzing thing might come to his rescue.

But that hope died a long time ago. The sky remains silent.

"Any sign of disease here?" Solma asks, just so she doesn't have to think about any of that.

Piotr shakes his head. "Not that I can see," he admits. "We'll cut back the damaged trees and test the soil, but it might not be something we can treat. Prob'ly it's just dead earth, poor pollination, no rain ..."

The worried furrow in his brow is back. Best to end this conversation now.

"Well, do your best, Piotr," she says. "The Earth Whisperers'll help when they arrive. Some have a way with the pollenbots. I reckon they'll be here soon." Another lie. The biggest she's told today. Solma finds it worrying how easily the lies come nowadays. She ducks her head to hide her frown. Earth Whisperers. Like those layabouts will turn up any time before summer. They're supposed to offer their growing gift to everyone but they're a sneaky lot. Not to be trusted, Blaiz says, and Solma's never had reason to doubt him on that. They're a sanctimonious bunch of scammers and tricksters, who only get away with it because Alphor needs them. Solma so wishes this wasn't the case, but there's not a lot she can do about it.

"I'll move you up the pollenbot schedule," she suggests, wondering how she might swing that with Blaiz. "See if we can't save some of this crop."

She holds out her hand and Piotr shakes it.

"You're a good kid, Sol," he says. "Your Ma and Dja would be proud."

Solma fights the kick of sadness in her gut and forces a smile.

"Yeah," she says. "Thanks."

"You know I worked with your Dja?"

Solma presses her lips together. Of course she does. It wasn't a secret. And Piotr tells her every time her squad patrols his orchards. Piotr waits for her to speak, but she doesn't.

"You look like him, you know."

Solma can't help it, she lifts a hand and runs it over her dark hair, touches the lids of her deep, brown eyes and hunches her shoulders to disguise her height, all of which screams *foreigner* amidst the freckled pallor, reddish hair and stocky stature of the locals. She looks like her father and he came from somewhere else.

It hadn't mattered when Dja was alive because he was respected. Needed. It matters now.

"I know," Solma whispers.

She hitches up her rifle again, eager to be gone. "Sorry, Piotr, we got a long patrol today. Come on Warren—"

But when she turns to cajole her brother along, he's gone. There's a patch of scuffed earth where he'd been standing, with nothing but an abandoned stick dropped in it.

TWO

Solma's body throbs with panic.

"Warren?"

She whirls to face Piotr. "Did you see where he went?"

Piotr shrugs. "S-sorry, no—"

Solma doesn't wait. She races to the edge of the orchard, reaching the rest of her squad in a breathless frenzy.

"Where's Warren? Did he come back?"

Four faces stare at her with alarm. It's Olive who speaks first, rolling her eyes again as her jaw works around that ridiculous sugar cane.

"Earth's sake, Solma. We ain't got time for this!"

Solma glares, ready to utter something scathing, but Maxen is between them before she can draw breath. His white-blue eyes are full of calm.

"Alright, alright," he fixes Olive with a stern stare. She huffs and stalks aside, unholstering her pistol and examining the magazine.

"He's probably just got bored and headed home," she calls over her shoulder. Solma clenches her jaw, not trusting herself to speak. She meets Maxen's gaze.

"I gotta find him," she says. "Please. I won't be long. Meet you at the western edge in half an hour?"

Maxen searches her face, a frown forming on his. He's a reasonable boy and a fair Staff Sergeant. He and Solma have known each other since they were in their cradles, their birthdays only months apart. He's got to let her search. But he shakes his head.

"We need to finish patrol, and you got to pick up your ammo ration, still."

"Please," she whispers again. "Warren ain't like other kids. He'll—"

She can't say it, but the images buzz around her head like the wasps that once swarmed these meadows. He's too gentle, too soft and unassuming. He'll get lost. He'll trigger a snare. He'll fall and hurt himself. He'll wander too far and be eaten by a redbear ...

She looks away and shakes her head. Maxen sighs and Solma fixes him with a pleading look. He's not Gatra—not technically, anyway. As the Steward's son, he doesn't have a caste. He and Blaiz are the only people in the village allowed a sire's name. He's not Gatra like the rest of them. He's Camber.

But he's Gatra in his heart. She sees him relent.

"Half an hour," he says. "No more. Clear?"

Solma nods, turns and plunges away before Maxen can say anything else. Olive's protests drift after her on the still air but Solma ignores them. She must find Warren.

She hurtles down the path back to the main village. Her breath catches on her panic.

Where is he?

"You seen my brother?" she calls as she passes, barely stopping by the gate of each orchard. A few of the Oritch workers look up and one points south, towards the village with a shrug. Solma's off immediately, desperate for another sign of him. That little footprint could be his ... or he might have kicked that pebble.

Children's laughter drifts from the cluster of mud-and-stone houses ahead and she lengthens her stride. She mustn't give in to panic. But he's so little, so clueless.

Please, please, please ...

"Have you seen Warren?" she shouts as she pounds down the dirt road. The Aldren-caste elders, dressed in brown and hunched in their rocking chairs, barely look up, just shake their heads and return their attention to the youngsters in their care or the cloth they're mending.

Where could he be? Despite her fear, Solma marvels at his stealth and speed. He managed to slip away under the noses of a whole Guard squad and has somehow made it a long way before Solma noticed.

If Aunt Bell ever finds out she's lost him ...

Solma cuts between two houses and onto a smaller path to avoid passing her own house. Warren *might* have wandered home, might even now be sitting at the table while their aunt fusses over him, exclaiming, *just you wait 'til your sister gets home!*

But if Solma can't avoid having her ear torn off by an irate Aunt Bell, she'll at least put it off for as long as possible.

The blade of her prosthetic leg rings off the stones as she hammers up the main path, out towards the planting fields. The landscape changes around her, from run-down houses and huddled old women to tough, clustered grasses fringing bare fields where Fei-caste planters scatter meagre seed.

"Seen Warren?" Solma cries, pausing to catch her breath by the first field. One of the enormous bay workhorses, tethered nearby, flattens his ears as she skids to a halt beside him. The nearest Fei shake their heads. Solma shoves her dark hair out of her face and pushes on, scanning the desolate landscape in the hopes she might catch sight of her brother's red-blonde hair, his vivid freckles.

There!

Solma skids to a halt by field four, peering along the fence. Yes! A flash of bare-soled feet, that familiar giggle. She grabs hold of the fencepost and swings around the gate.

"Warren!"

He's just standing there. What's he looking at? If he's hurt ... Solma forces herself on, though her lungs scream for relief.

"Warren!"

He glances round. His green eyes meet hers, dancing with mischief. What's he doing? He smiles but doesn't come when she calls. Instead, he puts a little finger to his lips and points towards his feet.

Earth's sake! The last shreds of Solma's ragged fear knot into anger. How could he do this to her? He *knows* how much energy it takes her to run! She's going to give him a piece of her mind when she reaches him! Ridiculous kid.

"Warren!" she shouts, her knee giving out so that she staggers the final few feet, flushed with rage. "What was that? You can't just run off—"

She stops, peering at her brother. He hasn't even looked up. The usual wide-eyed remorse whenever he disappoints her is nowhere to be seen. Solma drops to the floor, massaging her right knee—the one not supported by a prosthesis—gasping for breath, and follows his line of sight.

"What you staring at?"

Warren says nothing, just points again, kneeling and peering at a tiny mound of earth. A mound that's moving.

And despite Solma's desperate lungs, despite her anger and fear, she gasps as the mound of earth pops open and the tiniest, strangest creature scrambles free.

THREE

THE FIRST TIME SOLMA saw an insect, she was four.
She remembers the bright spring sun, the echo of her
father's voice.

"Look, Sol!"

He'd spoken softly and she'd leant into the bristles
of his beard, half terrified, half fascinated, as she stared
at the marvel on his palm. It couldn't fly, of course. All
the flying insects disappeared long before Solma was
born, and even seeing a ground insect was unusual.
Solma watched it, transfixed. Six restless legs, an iri-
descent carapace, antennae ceaselessly searching.

"Why's it doing that?" she asked.

"It's smelling," he told her. "It don't know what we
are."

Solma scoffed. "Silly! How come it don't know?"

Her Dja smiled at her. "Do you know what *it* is,
little Sol?"

That shut her up. It was amazing to think there were things in the world she'd never seen, creatures she'd never known. It was a beetle, Dja told her. *Carabidae.* A species of ground beetle.

"What's the point in it?"

Dja held her close. "It helps the world go round," he told her. "It burrows in the ground and eats decay. Helps the world stay clean. They're caretakers of the Earth, Sol. Very important."

"Very important," she'd echoed, and held her hands out so the little insect could crawl across her palm.

Solma remembers the strange, not-quite-there sensation of that beetle's feet as she sits beside Warren and holds out her dirt-encrusted hand. The insect—for it can only be an insect—wanders groggily over the mound, seems to contemplate her fingertips for a moment and then clambers aboard.

Its feet are so light, she can barely feel them. She holds the creature up to her face, frowning as it waggles its antennae. Its gold-and-black striped body gleams in the sun, fuzzy to the point of ridiculous, with delicate gossamer wings and antennae that twitch curiously. Solma stares.

"What is it, d'you think?"

It isn't a beetle. Solma knows that much. Warren's pulling at her fingertips, straining to see. Solma suppresses a smile and holds the creature out so he can get a better look. Warren's eyes widen.

"That's a bee!" he whispers. Solma scoffs.

"No it isn't," she laughs, ruffling his hair. "It can't be, can it? There ain't no more bees."

No one has seen one in over a century. This can't possibly be a bee.

Still. What's the harm in letting her brother hope?

She watches it wriggling on her finger. She can feel it now if she concentrates. The lightest brush of life against her skin. It buzzes its wings half-heartedly and Warren grins with delight. Solma can't help grinning, too. It's been such a long time since she's seen him smile.

"Why don't it fly away?" Warren asks. "You think it's sick?"

Solma gently cups her other hand over the insect and draws it close to her chest. Could it be sick? The thought makes her sick, too. The summer skies have been empty of flying things for such a long time that suddenly she can't bear the thought of this one falling ill. It buzzes against her again, shuffling down her finger and into her palm, as if accepting the safety she's offering. Its little body thrums, begging protection.

"Maybe it is sick," Solma concedes, then balks at the stricken look on Warren's face. "We'll save it," she says without thinking.

It's a daft thought. She doubts they can save it. If it really *is* a bee, it's the only one she's ever seen. Where can it possibly have come from?

Warren scratches his head, "It's probably thirsty," he says. "And we should give it some sugar. That'll cheer it up!"

Solma smiles despite herself. "It ain't about cheering it up!" she points out. "It's about making it better."

Warren shrugs. "It won't get better if it's sad. Come on, let's take it home."

Solma raises an eyebrow. "What are we supposed to carry it in, eh?"

Warren fumbles in his pockets. They are so grubby and full of holes it's a wonder things don't fall out of them. At last, he pulls a little box out and holds it up in triumph.

"We can't use a matchbox!" Solma exclaims. "What would Aunt Bell say?"

Warren shrugs. "It's nearly empty," he points out, popping it open to show a single match remaining. "It won't mind sharing the box with one match."

Solma frowns. But her pockets yield nothing better. In fact, they're grubbier than Warren's. Holding the little bee Solma is painfully aware that both their hands are thin and pale and cold, their bellies swollen with hunger and, though Solma's flesh-and-bone foot is laced into her Guard-issue boot, both Warren's feet are bare. They can't possibly nurse the little insect back to health. There isn't even enough food at home for her and Warren.

She opens her hands and peers between her fingers at the small, stripy life humming between them.

It does look like it *could* be a bee. Solma cradles the precious creature close again. She watches its abdomen pulse with life, its fluffy body bristling against her fingers.

"It would make Olive properly jealous," Warren says, and Solma laughs.

"Yeah," she agrees, marveling (not for the first time) at how easily her brother reads her. It would make Olive wild with envy. Not that she'd be able to tell Olive. Not before they tell Blaiz, anyway. But Olive's one upped her enough times that to be the one who

found this little thing, to be the bearer of such news …
Olive's face would be a picture. And really, that's what
settles it. That and the hope on Warren's face.

"Alright," she says. "Bring the box here, then."

They persuade the little creature into the matchbox
and carefully slide the lid closed. Solma flexes her right
leg a couple of times, testing the joint. For the first
time, Warren notices she's on the ground and looks
sheepish.

"You ok?" he asks. "Does your lucky leg hurt?"

Solma smiles despite herself. Lucky leg. It hadn't felt
very lucky when she'd lost it, but trust Warren to see it
that way. "If Roseann hadn't taken it off, you'd have
died!" he'd said as she'd recovered at home. "It's a *very*
lucky leg!"

She shakes her head at him. "The lucky leg's fine,
Warren," she says. "It's my right knee. Running like
that makes it hurt. So, don't run off like that, ok?"

Warren makes his best guilty face. "Ok," he agrees.
Solma ruffles his hair again and heaves herself up with
the help of the fence post. Her right knee holds. She
stares at the matchbox in her hand and marvels again
at the tiny, miraculous life it contains.

Warren wants to keep it in his pocket all the way
home, but Solma isn't having that.

"I'll be careful," he protests.

"I know," Solma says. "But what if you fall and squash it?"

The thought horrifies Warren enough that he concedes immediately. Solma keeps her hand in her pocket, loosely cupped around the matchbox and its treasured cargo, as they pick their way out of the pollinating fields, between the milling clusters of planters. There are barely enough seeds this year to keep them busy. And as Solma scuffs her blade against the dusty earth, the topsoil gives easily, curling into the air in little dust clouds. Not good.

She glances across the fields to where the distant watch tower is a grey smear on the horizon. Maxen and the rest of her squad will be meeting there shortly. Half an hour, Maxen said. She's going to be late. Well, Warren can't come on the outer patrols anyway. She's just doing her duty, walking him back to the village before she rejoins her squad.

The path back to the village is a depressing one.

The territory's meagre fields and orchards are all but barren. The Earth Whisperers did their best with the soil last year, but even their mysterious talents weren't enough. The rains came late and left early, so the village remains in the grip of a long drought: cold in winter and sweltering in summer. Solma knows, too, that at least a third of the village's pollenbots were damaged during the winter and with limited pollinating kits, it will be a miracle if their feeble seeds yield any crop. They barely have enough to last until the next harvest, which will be pathetic anyway, and last year's province-wide crop failure means even the poorest villages are now at risk from Raiders. Solma's good mood doesn't last long as she stares at the dry fields. She may only have lived sixteen years in this wasteland, but it's long enough to have choked the hope from her heart.

She places a hand on Warren's shoulder and hugs him close. He's desperately skinny, his legs bowed from rickets, his green eyes watery and his red-gold hair lank and thin. Her little brother is already malnourished. The truth is, he won't survive another crop failure. He'll go the way of so many other younger brothers and sisters.

Solma's heart trembles at the idea.

Hold onto the bee, she thinks. Hold onto the little creature whose ancestors once made fields of fruit flourish, whose slender legs and furry bodies once carried the hope of vast cities from flower to flower, ensuring the food supply of millions. There are no cities anymore, of course. They collapsed a hundred years ago, when the insects died. And Solma would be surprised if there were even a million people living in the whole of Alphor nowadays. No cities, and no bees.

Until now.

FOUR

THE FIELDS AND ORCHARDS fade into the background as the village comes into view. Modest, is how Dja would have described it. Tragic, is what Ma would have said. The mud-and-stone structures bear the weight of winter damage, with many windows missing glass. Frost has warped the beams and roofs. The village wasn't really designed, it just sort of sprang up, with houses built as and when they were needed. Years of repairs only make it even more patchwork and haphazard. From the roofs, washing lines criss-cross between windows, hung with ragged clothes and faded sheets. At this time of day, only the very young and the very old are in the village. Everyone else is working in the fields, or out on Gathering missions, so toothless old women and men huddle in rickety old chairs, cradling infants or yelling at toddlers to get out of whatever it is they've climbed into.

Warren's excitement bursts out of him every so often and his little feet skip along the path. He runs forward, desperate to reach home, then runs back, remembering that Solma has the bee.

"I wanna catch Bell before her planting shift!" he gasps, his smile almost too big for his face. "She's gonna to be so pleased!"

"Everyone will," Solma agrees. She runs her thumb over the matchbox and feels the bee buzz within. "It's a miracle."

And it is. Hope with gossamer wings. But Solma can't shake a dark, nagging feeling at the back of her mind. What can one bee do? Solma might never have grasped the complex biology her Ma tried to teach her but even she understands the principle of species reproduction. One bee is no real hope at all, just a splash of beauty in an otherwise bland landscape. The poor thing won't last long.

And yet ...

Warren laughs and rushes ahead, calling for Bell. Solma hesitates. Everyone *will* be pleased. The Steward will be delighted the bee was found on his patch, the pollinators might not have to work so hard this year, the seed produced may even be enough for a decent harvest.

But the voice of despair still mutters at the back of her head. It's just one bee. It seems cruel to bring such an impossible hope to so many desperate people.

Solma finds herself casting furtive glances to see if any of the villagers suspect the bee's existence. She could cry its presence to the skies, hold it up for everyone to see.

But she doesn't. And she can't explain why.

A memory starts pulsing in the back of her mind, long-hidden and shrouded in fear. A girl. A flash of red hair. A flower (how can that be when the wildflowers are all gone?) and a feeling of terrible regret ...

Solma pushes the memory to the back of her mind where it belongs. Whatever it's trying to tell her, though, it's as if the truth has been corralled at the back of her throat. She can't bring herself to mention the bee.

The Aldren—especially the old women—smile at her as she passes. One lifts a gnarled old cane in greeting and grins, her lips dry and chapped but her eyes still full of mischief. She cradles a sleeping child.

"Morning, Sol!" the old woman calls. "Good planting?"

Solma shrugs, "Hi, Gerta," she says. "You know how it is."

Gerta grins, showing six grubby teeth and blistered gums. Solma can't help but smile back. Gerta Lo Aldren is still the same as she had been twelve years ago, when four-year-old Solma, a Yuen too young to be of use, played under her rocking chair.

"And the leg? It's ok?"

Solma nods and taps her fingers against the prosthesis. "Good as ever," she says.

Gerta grunts, satisfied. Solma's got no idea where the old woman found this remarkable leg, but after Solma's accident three years ago, Gerta had packed a burlap bag, taken her walking stick and disappeared for two weeks. Everyone thought she was dead until she'd come back with the shiny black limb, made of some lightweight material, that Solma now wears. Gerta, in her strange way, had tinkered with it until it fit snugly to Solma's knee and matched the length of her flesh-and-bone leg. Solma never asked where Gerta found it, didn't want to spoil the magic of learning to use it. But there are stories of the crumbling, overgrown city ruins to the west, now reduced to scavenging sites. They're supposed to be full of all sorts of wonders from the old world—before the insects died and the cities fell and the surviving humans worked to carve out the scrap of life they now live. Whatever the story, Solma's gratitude to Gerta runs deeper than she's ever told anyone. The old woman rocks the child she holds as the little one begins to stir.

"You come to me if you got any issues."

"Yes, Gerta," Solma says.

Gerta nods and turns her attention back to the sleepy child.

Solma could tell her. Right now. She's found a bee. Look! It crawled right out of the dirt like the rising of some tiny god.

But the words catch in her throat and Solma says nothing. Instead, she waves to Gerta as she ducks inside her own house. Her stomach twists uncomfortably. This is not good. There are no secrets in Sands' End Village. Trying to keep one is treason. The Steward must know everything so he can make decisions, so he can plan for the future, so he can ensure that the village survives. That's the law. And breaking it would see both her and Warren exiled. So why can't she bring herself to say anything?

This is madness. It won't matter anyway. The tiny, shivering life won't last the spring, will it? There's no need to fuss. Or hope. Or tell anyone. It isn't a secret if it means nothing in the first place.

Maybe that's best.

She hurries inside, ready to hush Warren before he can announce the news. But to her surprise, Warren sits patiently at the table, his legs swinging beneath him, his mouth clamped closed, as Aunt Bell bustles at the fireplace with various oversized pots and finally manages to pour some soup into a clay bowl. She's still wearing her day dress, but she's got her Fei-issue sandals on and her reed hat is ready on the table. Bell's always been Fei-caste, just like Dja. Neither of them liked it when Ma became Gatra. Bell detests violence. Or so she says. She seems to enjoy thoroughly telling Solma off whenever the opportunity arises.

"Look at his fingers!" she proclaims as soon as she sees her niece. "White as death! And you didn't even wrap his feet up before you took him out this morning!" In her indignation, her hair—the same red-gold as Warren's—flies loose from her bun and forms a halo around her flushed face. "What's wrong with you, girl? Don't you think of your poor brother?"

Solma bristles. "It ain't even that cold," she mutters. "He's fine, right Warren?"

Warren, who has hungrily tipped most of the bowl of soup into his mouth, splutters agreement. Bell isn't convinced. She folds her short arms and glares. For such a tiny woman, she's terrifying when she wants to be.

Solma rolls her eyes and flops down into a chair beside Warren, still holding the bee in her pocket so she doesn't accidentally crush it.

"There was trouble at the orchards, Bell," she says, hating the whine in her voice. Why does Bell always do this to her?

"Nonetheless ..." Bell says, in that sanctimonious way she always does. She never bothers finishing that sentence, only lets it hang in the air so Solma can feel the weight of her unspoken disappointment. Solma shrugs it off.

"Any soup for me?"

Bell mutters but doesn't hesitate to fill a bowl for her niece too. She sits opposite them, nursing a mug of hot tea. She hasn't served any soup for herself. Again. But she watches Solma sip the hot meal with this strange, determined look in her eye, as if she'll insist that every drop is licked clean.

So the pantry's running low already. Solma's heart kicks. She only drains half her bowl and, before Bell can protest, gives the rest to Warren. He accepts it readily, with a murmured, "Thanks, Sol," before he tips the bowl back and gulps down the watery meal.

He's messy in his hunger, droplets trickling down his chin, which he then wipes away with back of his hand and enthusiastically licks off. Solma risks a glance at Bell and their eyes meet. There's worry in both. Solma's fingers reflexively search her pocket for the matchbox again.

The bee. The bee ...

It stirs in its sanctuary. Its wings vibrate. Solma fidgets on her chair to cover the sound and tears her eyes away from Bell's before the worry can take hold. Worry won't do. Worry solves nothing.

But the bee ...

"Warren's got something to tell you," Solma blurts out. Absently, she reaches out a finger and wipes the last of the soup from Warren's chin. She smiles at him, trying to push all the warmth she can into that smile. Warren stares up at her with big, green eyes. Occasionally, she's struck by how different they look. Warren's red-gold hair, his pale, freckled skin, and his meadow-green eyes are just like their mother's and Bell's. Warren could easily pass for Bell's son. But Solma's dark hair, the color of fresh soil, deep brown eyes and freckle-free, white skin are much more like her father's.

When Warren stares at her like that, filled with all the innocence in the world, Solma wonders how her parents could have produced two such different children.

Warren licks his lips and stares nervously from Solma to Bell and back.

"I have?"

The bee stirs again. Solma feels it shifting, searching. The girl ... the flower ... the guilt ...

"Yeah," Solma nods encouragingly. "Go on."

If Warren shares the hope, it'll be a child's hope. If Warren shares it, everyone will forgive him when it dies. Solma finds herself leaning forward in her chair, desperate to hear him speak the words, to make this hope real. *There's a bee.*

Warren clenches his little fists on the table and frowns at them. His little tongue pokes from between his teeth. What's wrong with him? He'd been so excited about the bee, desperate to tell Bell. All he's got to do now is speak the words.

But when Warren finally looks up, a nervous grin on his mucky lips, he says, "I helped the planters with their seeds this morning, Bell, and I didn't even drop any!"

Solma stares at him and can't stop her mouth from falling open. Bell smiles, the skin around her eyes crinkling like their mother's used to.

"That's wonderful, Warren!" She shuffles out of her chair and scurries round the table to hug him. She holds him close and Solma watches her face harden into a frown. Solma doesn't need to ask why. She can feel it when she hugs Warren too; his swollen belly, his prominent ribs, the ribbony sinews in his arms. She looks away as that familiar lump rises in her throat.

Not her brother. Please, she thinks, don't let it be her brother this year.

"Sol's got something to tell you too," Warren says, his voice muffled within Bell's unyielding hug. Bell releases him.

"Well, we are full of news this morning, aren't we?" She turns expectantly to Solma.

Now. Tell her now. After all, what harm can it do? Excitement swells in Solma's heart, despite the nagging voice at the back of her skull. The hope has its hooks in her, even though she knows its false.

The words gather in Solma's mouth, ready to be spoken. *We found a bee, Bell. A real bee!*

But if she says it to Bell, she will have to say it to Blaiz. And Maxen. And everyone else.

Would that be so bad?

The girl ... the flower ... the memory bursts in Solma's head again, so strong it's almost painful.

She opens her mouth, hoping that the words will rush out without being bid. But as she draws breath, the bee stirs in her pocket. It doesn't make a sound, but Solma feels its pattering feet. She presses her fingertips to the matchbox, relishing the vibrations of the life inside.

And when the words come, they're not the ones she expects.

"I been promoted to Sergeant in the Gathering Guard," she says, and has to stop herself clapping a hand over her mouth. Where had that come from?

She'd been given the news the previous evening. Olive was livid, and Solma marched home with pride swelling in her chest. But then Warren had a sore tummy and took ages to soothe to sleep. In the fuss, Solma completely forgot to mention it.

Except, it isn't what she'd wanted to say.

Warren frowns at her. Bell, however, lets out a squawk of delight and flings herself at Solma, who barely has time to gulp down a breath before she's engulfed in a hug.

"About time!" Bell cries, squeezing Solma so tightly that Solma thinks she hears a vertebra crack.

She releases her niece and begins whizzing around the kitchen, talking at a hundred miles an hour.

"Extra ration a week! Make all the difference, that. Solma, I'm so proud of you! Your parents would be, too …"

Solma isn't listening. In her pocket, the bee wriggles and Solma's head is a-whirr with strange thoughts, the weight of the secret. But *why* is it a secret? Why can't she speak it though she desperately wants to? She stares at Warren and he stares back. Neither of them says anything.

"Oh, Solma!" Bell says, brandishing a ladle in her niece's direction, "Maxen came by ten minutes ago. A boar's been spotted. You're needed on a hunting mission."

Solma flops her head onto the table and groans. *Another* hunting mission? That's the third this week. If Maxen organizes many more of these, there won't be any game left by the time winter comes and Solma's fed up with shooting things. Still, she won't say no to Maxen.

"When?" she sighs.

Bell frowns out the window, checking the sun.

"Oh!" she exclaims, "Now! Hurry, Solma! And Warren, get to Gerta's. I should'a been out that door five minutes ago. Quickly. Quickly!"

She rushes them both in mad circles, wrestling Warren back into a chair so she can wrap his cold feet in cloth. The house is a flurry of mad activity as Bell sheds her dress and wrestles on the grey shirt and breeches of her Fei uniform. She shoos them both out of the house with a stern instruction to Solma to *make sure Warren is looked after!*

They both stare at her as Bell slams the rickety old door and marches up the path towards the fields, ignoring their protests.

FIVE

FOR TWO MONTHS BEFORE Warren was born, Solma remembers, there was no rain. The topsoil hardened and hot, harsh winds whipped it into dust devils. The seeds wouldn't take. Nothing grew.

Solma's mother cradled her swollen belly, tears misting her eyes.

"Little one's got no chance in a world like this," she said. "I can feel it."

But on the day Warren was born, rainclouds gathered in the sky as if they'd been waiting for him to show himself to the world. Solma remembers, at nine years old, running from her mother's side straight into the deluge, lifting her face to the roaring heavens as fresh rain fell against her skin. It soaked her ragged dress and plastered her hair to her face, but she'd never felt so glorious.

Her brother was here at last, and he'd brought the rains.

She doesn't know why she thinks of that now, as she rams one fist onto her hip, the other hand curled around the matchbox with the bee inside, and scowls at Warren.

"What was that?" She demands, "You run all the way home and then don't even tell her? I don't get it—"

She stops as she feels the bee shivering, flexing its delicate wings, as if asking for calm. Solma scowls harder. Because that's ridiculous. It's a bee. Bees don't *ask* for anything.

Although, how would Solma know? She's never seen a bee, doesn't know anyone who has. For all she knows, bees might possess some ancient magic no one really understands. She forces those thoughts aside.

"Why'd you not tell her?" She demands. "After all that fuss?"

Warren shrugs and frowns at his feet.

"Why didn't you?"

Solma folds her arms. "Because—"

But why didn't she? Why has it become a secret? Solma searches her mind for answers, but all she comes up with is that murky memory from before. A girl with red hair ... a flower ... Solma clenches her jaw.

"I dunno!" she snaps, frustration mounting. She throws both her hands in the air, glaring. But as soon as she meets her brother's wide, green gaze, the anger and confusion evaporates. "I don't know," she says, more softly this time, "It just didn't—"

"—Feel right," Warren agrees, thrusting his fists into his pocket. "I think ... she don't want anyone to know about her yet."

Solma blinks. "Who don't?"

"The bee."

Solma can't help herself. She laughs, a short, cynical bark that echoes inside her own head. "That's ridiculous!" she chuckles. "How can it want anything? How would you even know?"

Warren works his lips together, trying to find the words. Solma wills herself to have patience. He is only seven, just a baby, a boy barely out of infancy with such big, beautiful thoughts in his head. Don't shout at him.

"Well?" Solma demands. Her voice sounds harsher than she meant it to and Warren jumps. Guilt floods her and, when she speaks again, she keeps her voice measured. "This is serious, Warren. Secrets're forbidden. We share everything with the Steward 'cos that's the law."

She stares at him, wondering if he truly understands. Blaiz is a fair leader but he's not above exiling people. Solma's seen it before: a girl, under ten, with flame-red hair and a splash of freckles across her nose. Solma feels her breath catch at the thought. Was this what she was remembering earlier? But that has nothing to do with the bee, surely? The girl was exiled five years ago. Or maybe six. She'd taken something from the storehouse, Blaiz said. Quite a lot of somethings, actually. Solma remembers the mother howling, the silence of the other villagers as they witnessed her exile. The girl walking out of the village, tentative steps at first, then with growing confidence, her head held high.

She'd only looked back once, and Solma can't remember her face. The memory stirs a strange queasiness in her gut. That girl is probably dead, now.

What was her name?

Solma can't remember. For a moment, her name is dreadfully important. She must have known it at some point. But it evades her and the memory fades into darkness. Solma shakes away the flurry of anxiety in her gut.

"And if it survives," she continues sternly, "this could save our village. Which means we got to tell Blaiz. Or ... or ... You get this, right?"

Warren's eyes sparkle with seriousness. "I know," he whispers. "I in't playing. And I in't imagining. Don't you hear ... Didn't you *feel* her talking to you?"

"I—" Solma hesitates. What's he talking about now? She stares at her brother, wondering if the hunger has finally got to him, but he gazes back at her in earnest.

"She needs us," he says. "Can't you see? Life's hard for her."

"Life's hard for all of us, Warren!" Solma retorts, losing patience. Warren scowls, his little hands curling into fists.

"You don't get it!" He hisses. "She's a special bee. We got to keep her safe. We ... it's important." He stops, clearly wanting to say more but not knowing how. "We can't tell anyone, okay?"

Solma splutters.

"Where's all this coming from?"

Warren shrugs again. "I feel it. She's telling me."

"Warren—"

"I'm telling the truth!" Warren bursts, stamping his feet hard against the dusty earth. "I know what it means, Sol! I in't a kid! I in't!"

Solma holds her hands out to hush him, glancing behind her to see if anyone is listening, but the toothless old Aldren in their rocking chairs either aren't interested or are too deaf to hear.

"Okay, okay," Solma says. The bee buzzes frantically in her pocket. "But Warren, you know the rules. We got to report everything and anything that might change the land. Secrets mean exile from the village. You *know* that!"

Warren flushes. "I know that," he mumbles. "Just... not yet, okay? Give her a chance."

Solma sighs. This conversation is not going smoothly. "Look, I got to go," she says, "Maxen's waiting. We'll talk later."

"Yes," Warren agrees, and holds out his hand, "Gimme the bee."

Solma gapes at him. "No, War, what if you hurt it—"

"I won't hurt her," Warren says, his voice steady and true in a way Solma hasn't heard it before. "Anyway, she can't stay in your pocket. She needs sun and food or she'll die."

Solma hesitates. She reaches into her pocket again, cradling the matchbox. The bee hums and buzzes and pushes against the box, impossibly alive.

"Solma," Warren murmurs. "The bee."

At the sound of his voice, the little life in Solma's pocket calms. Solma feels it fall still and frowns. Why would the bee respond to Warren's voice like that?

This cannot be happening. And Solma doesn't have the time. The village needs food, her squad is waiting and she can't deal with this now.

She lifts the matchbox out of her pocket and holds it flat on her palm. "Alright," she says, "But you got to promise to be careful."

"I'll be the carefullest I ever been with anything ever," Warren promises, and Solma can't help but chuckle. She gives him the matchbox and ruffles his hair.

Warren's whole body relaxes as he pushes open the matchbox and the tired little bee clambers out. Its antennae search, its bulbous, fluffy body vibrating with joy at being in the sun again.

It should fly away, Solma thinks. But it doesn't. It clings to Warren as if he's a flower full of promise and it needs nothing more than to be near him.

But she must be just imagining that. She watches her brother gently cup the bee in both palms and hold it up to the light.

"You said it needs food," she says, skeptical again. "D'you even know what bees eat?"

"Sweetness," Warren says. "She needs sweetness."

Without taking his eyes off the bee, he coaxes it into one palm and, with his now free hand, reaches into his pocket, producing a fistful of sugar. Solma stares.

"How d'you get that without Bell noticing?"

Warren grins. "Snuck it while she was all excited about you being Sergeant."

Solma knows she should tell him off. Sugar is a scarce thing and they've only got a little left from last year's Eastern traders. They can't spare it.

But the bee ...

Solma chucks him under the chin with her finger. "Alright," she says. "I reckon she'll fly away when she's better. Be careful."

"I will," Warren agrees. The bee trundles across his fingers, running its furry, black legs over its face. Warren smiles and the bee is reflected in his eyes.

"A real bee, Sol!"

Solma nods. "Yes," she says, grinning at his enthusiasm. "Let's hope she lasts the spring."

Warren glances up, his little brows drawn together in consternation.

"She will!" he insists. "We're going to look after her!"

Solma laughs, "We don't know the first thing about looking after a bee," she whispers. "Warren, I hate to break it to you, but one bee ..." she trails off and gazes out to the north, where the planters are milling about in the fields. One bee is nothing at all. But Warren's little face only hardens with determination.

"She won't die," he insists. "She can't."

Solma pinches the bridge of her nose and takes a deep breath.

"We got bigger things to worry about, Warren, we can't spend all this time on a bee," she says, as gently as she can. "Feed it and put it somewhere sunny when you're done, 'kay?"

Warren's eyes shine with his silent plea. His little mouth trembles as he gazes from Solma to the bee and back again.

"But Sol ..."

Solma can't bear it. She shakes her head. "No, Warren. That's that." She hitches her rifle higher onto her shoulder and rubs at her prosthetic leg. She always has a phantom itch before a hunt.

"I gotta go now," she says. "Be good."

She turns away, trying not to feel the wrench in her heart as she walks away from the bee. But the village needs feeding and there is hunting to do. She strides south without looking back.

~ BEE ~

SUN ON MY FUR, at last. Paddle my feet against the boy's palm, probe him with my antennae, learn his smell. With the sun warming me, the last of the winter sleep slips away. I'm alive. Wing-muscles shiver to life. I ignite them, trying to warm myself. The air around me vibrates. Still weak, though. I need food. Need to fly. To nest. To lay.

But his palm is comforting. I trundle across it, tongue flicking, hunting for food. He tastes of salt. I recoil.

"Don't worry, bee," he says. "I'll feed you."

He says it with his voice, which I don't understand. It's a rumble that sets the air a-quiver. I remember this from the memories of my long-dead sisters. Humans are chaos. Even the way they talk disturbs everything.

But then he says it a different way, one I understand. Not sure if he means to. I don't think he realizes he's talking. But it's a calmer language. Subtler, more *bee*.

Don't worry, bee. I'll feed you.

It's a gentle change of the scent on his hand, a shift in his body, the way the air moves around him. Don't know how he does it. My sister-memories tell me humans are too clumsy to talk bee. But he's doing it. How?

And then he lifts something up beside his palm. A great, shiny pool that glistens thickly in the high sun. Smells glorious. I am cautious. Caution is key. My sister-memories hold flashes of drowning in sticky puddles, being snatched from succulent flowers by the catching claws of spiders.

Crushed under the chaotic feet of human larvae, out of malice or ignorance.

And if I die now, it isn't just me ...

Eggs stir in my body. Must find a nest. Must lay.

But the winter sleep plagues my muscles. And the silver pool at the edge of his palm smells sweet. I creep towards it, tongue flickering.

"Come on, little bee," he says in that awful way that humans talk. His hurricane breath flattens me against his palm for a moment.

Come on, little bee, he says again, in sweet scent and soft vibration. When he speaks like this, he seems honest. I creep further forward, dip my tongue into the silver pool and hope.

And oh, it tastes glorious! I drink and drink. It's not perfect, not real nectar, but it'll do for now. I drink until I am beyond sated and then I drink more, directing it into a different stomach. I am drinking for my daughters now, too.

"That's better, in't it?" the boy booms.

His voice is a thunder. I turn in panicked circles, trying to get away from the chaos of it. Wait for the vibrations of his talk to settle before I return to feed.

That's better, in't it? He says again, in bee this time.

Yes, I tell him, in flutter-and-scent. *But not so loud!*

There's a shift in his body. His palm judders as the silver pool is drawn away and he sits heavily on the ground, holding his hand (with me on) up to his face. Has he understood me? Didn't think that was possible. I search my sister-memories:

Dug up hives; crushing feet; deserts of green with no flowers as far as the eye can see; poison in the nectar; fire and machinery; war and war and war …

I shudder and withdraw from the memories before they overwhelm me. My air-sacs pump, trying to calm my quickened heart. Humans are chaos. This is the law of bees. Humans are chaos, keep them away. They raze the land, they cut the earth, they kill the flowers.

And they don't speak bee. At least, not as far as my sisters knew.

Where did this one come from?

He cups his palms together and holds them out so the sun falls on me. I turn so I can get a good look at his face. Human faces are difficult for bees. They are landscapes. It's like mapping a small forest or memorizing a valley. But I look anyway. Eyes a vivid green tinged with blue. Puckering mouth. Cheeks sun-touched and freckled. Hair corn-gold and fox-russet. Smells of honesty.

Can you hear me? I make my scent as strong as possible, powering it with a shiver of my wings. His eyes change, brows drawn together. What does that mean? Confusion, I think.

YES! Comes the reply, so overpowering I take a few steps back, my antennae stinging.

No shouting!

There's a pause, then a stilting reply. *I'm … sorry. Strange … to talk like this.*

I flicker my antennae with amusement. He is like a larva, wriggling and clumsy. I move my feet across his palm.

Bee talk, I tell him.

He doesn't answer, but I feel the change in his scent. Confusion, but happiness, too.

What you need? He asks. His scent is still clumsy and stilting, flying out in all different directions. But I can just about make out what he means. I buzz again.

A home, I tell him. *Somewhere sheltered and underground, with flowers nearby to feed on. Somewhere we can hide from moonbadger teeth, where human machines won't find us.*

His scent becomes thoughtful.

Will help, he says, *My sister'n me. We'll help.*

Sister. He has a sister. There's a thing I can understand. Sisters are to be trusted. Sisters mean life. I turn a circle on his palm.

Good, I say, and open my wings to soak up the sun.

SIX

SOLMA'S SQUAD ARE WAITING for her south of the village, on the edge of the managed forest. Maxen waves as he spots her, she waves a reply and lengthens her stride. He comes to meet her. His brows are drawn together but his eyes are gentle, questioning.

"That wasn't half an hour," he says. Solma frowns.

"Yeah. Sorry." She swings her rifle off her shoulder and slips a cartridge into the chamber, mainly so she doesn't have to look at Maxen. His disappointment is palpable, but he's softening.

"Did you find him?"

He reaches out a tentative hand. Solma stays perfectly still as he brushes her shoulder.

"Yeah," she says, offering a smile. "He's fine. Typical seven-year-old. Running off without thinking about how it scares his big sister."

Maxen chuckles. He's about to say something but Olive appears by his elbow, scowling. She glances from Solma to Maxen and her eyes narrow.

"Are we done?" she demands. "'Cos Solma's already made us late. I don't fancy wrestling pigs all day."

Solma flushes as Maxen's hand falls away from her arm. Olive is such a pain. Solma's convinced she does it deliberately, and that the pink bloom in Olive's cheeks is nothing but jealousy. Earth! She annoys Solma beyond belief.

Maxen sighs and runs a hand through his golden hair. A film of sweat coats his forehead and his neck and forearms are flushed where the sun, already high and strong, has caught his skin. Spring is well on its way if the sun is already starting to burn. It's going to be an uncomfortable day. She follows Maxen to where Ilga and Aldo are lounging beside the path, talking in low voices.

"Right," Maxen says, folding his arms. "Up, you two. Let's go."

The sun falls behind the trees as they trudge in single file. The path transforms into a slim animal trail as it slips between the trees. The canopy fragments the sunlight and Solma turns her face up to catch the pockets of light. The wood is silent save for the skittering of small animals through the undergrowth. No birds in the trees anymore. No buzz of insects. Just the sharp panic of rodents, the occasional squeal as a weasel snags a mouse, the distant grunt of boar. And the incessant crunch of sugar cane between Olive's teeth. Infuriating.

Solma's heart bucks like a frightened horse. Her leg aches, as it always does when she enters these woods, with the memory of boar tusks goring her flesh. She remembers being pulled from beneath the raging creature, watching her ruined leg dragging behind her at some obscene angle. She closes her eyes.

A hand lands on her shoulder hard enough to make her start. It's Olive's. She shoves it off.

Olive scowls. "Focus, Solma," she growls. "We need you on form."

"I know that," Solma hisses through gritted teeth.

Olive shrugs, "I don't want to pull anyone out from under a boar today," she says. "You forgot—"

Solma holds up a hand, bites her tongue on a string of insults and turns back to the front. She strides away from Olive, ignoring her protests, until she's caught up with Maxen. He casts her a sideways glance.

"All ok?"

Solma breaths heavily through her nose. "Olive's doing my head in."

Maxen snorts. "She's always doing your head in."

"Yeah, well ..."

Maxen touches her arm. "Cut her some slack, Sol," he says gently. "Life's been hard for her since ..." he trails off, reddening. Solma raises an eyebrow at him.

"Since her Dja died of the same sickness as my Dja? Seriously? That's what you was gonna say?"

Maxen bites his lip. "I know it's been years, but—"

"That ain't the point," Solma says, shaking her head. "We both lost our Djas. I don't gotta put up with her crap just 'cos've that. At least Olive still got *one* parent, even if Roseann is just as annoying as Olive."

Maxen snorts a laugh. "Yeah, alright," he mutters. "Just ... take a deep breath."

Solma grunts acknowledgment, if only to end the conversation. But Maxen's hand on her arm melts away her remaining frustration. He smiles and his ice-blue eyes hold her gaze for a beat longer than necessary.

The sound of the boar draws nearer. Solma feels how the ground trembles. Her stomach tightens and those curved tusks flash behind her eyelids whenever she closes them. She touches her prosthesis. Maxen frowns.

"You don't have to come on these missions if you don't want, Sol," he says. "I can have it arranged—"

"No," Solma says, more roughly than she'd intended. "I'm Sergeant now, it's my job. I can handle it."

Maxen shrugs, but his face is soft with sympathy. "Whatever you need, yeah?"

Solma clenches her fist to steady the tremble in her fingers. "What I need is for Olive to shut up and leave me alone!"

Maxen raises his eyebrows. "She did save your life, Sol," he points out.

Solma scowls. "And won't never let me forget it," she mutters. She softens with one look at Maxen's concerned face and sighs, touching his shoulder. "Look, let's just get it done, ok?"

Maxen squeezes her hand and signals for the others to pull close. Olive comes to stand at Solma's side, apparently oblivious to how Solma tenses. Ilga and Aldo stumble up, both breathing heavily. Solma rolls her eyes and catches Olive doing the same. She's not impressed either.

Both around thirteen, Ilga and Aldo joined the squad together at the start of this year's planting season. Solma can't help feeling they're more of a liability than anything else. Ilga's long hair is so lank with sweat and dirt Solma's surprised the boars haven't smelled them yet, and Aldo looks like he's constantly on the verge of tears. As recruits go, this year's are a sorry lot. They're only here because they make up the numbers. Olive seems to be thinking the same. Frustration tightens her face and hardens her green eyes. Solma looks away, refusing to engage. Olive might be a good soldier, a strong shot and exactly who you'd want in your squad when you're being gored alive by an enraged boar, but she's still annoying.

Maxen delivers their orders almost entirely in hand gestures. He and Ilga will move round to flank the boars on the left, Olive and Aldo will do the same on the right. Solma will move ahead towards the clearing they pinpointed during their last recon mission. Wire mesh has already been nailed to the trees in the clearing, creating a makeshift corral. (Olive did this, apparently. Maxen claps her shoulder in praise. Solma feels a kick of anger and then a flash of shame.)

Solma, Maxen says, will take up position behind the dead tree and wait. It means going inside the wire mesh corral. It's risky. She'll have no protection from the boar, but it's the best position from which to get a shot and as long as the wind doesn't change, the boar shouldn't spot her. The others will drive the boar through the undergrowth and trap them in the clearing, giving Solma a clear shot. She can't hesitate and they've got to get the job done quickly and cleanly, keeping hidden until the remaining animals break out of the corral. The pigs are smart, they'll figure out the trap eventually and either gore the mesh until it breaks or turn and charge their attackers, which could mean someone else losing a leg, so everyone is to keep out of sight. Ilga whimpers. Olive smacks her on the arm and tries to catch Solma's eye. Solma ignores her.

Everyone clear? Maxen signals. Nods all round. They split into their teams. Maxen gives Solma's shoulder one last squeeze, eyes full of concern. Earth, she wishes those eyes would never leave hers.

"Go carefully," he mouths. She nods, warmth creeping through her.

She turns before fear can stop her and heads deeper into the forest, following the path as the others get into position. She has exactly ten minutes to get where she needs to be. It isn't long. Already the timbre of the boars' snuffling has changed. They sense something. Solma quickens her step, scanning the ground as she moves with practiced silence through the leaf litter.

Already she can tell this is not going to be an easy hunt.

SEVEN

THE BREEZE WORRIES THE canopy as Solma follows the trail of marks cut into the trees. She tests the wind with a finger and grimaces. Wrong direction. Not good. The pigs'll smell her as soon as they're in the corral. They'll panic. She'll have to take the shot quickly and make sure the other animals get clear before panic turns to rage.

Absently, she reaches into her pocket and feels bereft for a moment when the matchbox that held the bee isn't there.

That bee.

Something rustles to her left and Solma snaps to attention, dropping to her knee and taking aim. A scraggly, black squirrel, mostly skin and bone, skitters amongst the leaves. Solma curses it. She pushes on, hating the way the forest taunts her, hating that she must shoot a panicking animal, hating that if she doesn't, people will go hungry.

If only that bee ...

She shakes her head. It's madness, what Warren suggested. You don't keep secrets from the Steward. Blaiz is a good leader. He'd help, Solma's sure of it. So why does she have this tugging feeling every time she considers telling him?

She could kid herself it's about managing hope. One bee has next to no chance of surviving, after all. But it isn't that, is it? Earth knows the village has lived with hopelessness for long enough. No, it's something else.

The girl ... The flower ...

The thought looms out of reach. It's a memory, Solma's sure of it, but she doesn't know *what* memory, nor why the thought of it hurts so much.

The snapping of branches makes Solma freeze, rifle raised and aimed. She scans the line of trees for signs of movement. But everything is quiet and all she can hear is her own heartbeat. The trees sway and sunlight flickers between their leaves. Solma squints, checking the branches for redbear cubs, which hunt from the trees until they get too heavy to do so. But there is no flash of russet fur, no warning growl. Solma lets out her breath but keeps her rifle ready as she heads on.

Her mind drifts again to that memory and the bee. To Blaiz, and what he would say if he knew about the secret.

The thought sends a cold shiver through Solma's body. She hits the flat of her hand against her head a couple of times. This is ridiculous. She'll get home after this hunt and go straight to Blaiz. She'll tell him they just didn't know what it was at first but they do now so they're telling him. It's best for everyone. It's the right thing to do.

She stops. Ahead of her, the forest thins into a clearing, surrounded by wire mesh. A dead tree lays just within the corral in a patch of sunlight, a few fungi blooming on its blackened trunk. Solma trudges over it, finds a place where she can get a good shot when the pigs come charging in. She tests it. It's damp, but not uncomfortably so. She'll cope. There's no sign of a stampede yet so Solma walks the perimeter of the clearing, checking the mesh corral is secure. It won't keep the pigs in forever, but it should confuse them long enough that she can make the shot. She hopes.

She heads back to the fallen tree and settles herself against it, laying her rifle out over the trunk and peering down the sight. She waits. Silence and patience.

She's a Sergeant, now. Supposedly, she's an expert at this.

Sergeant. She rolls that round her brain for a bit and smiles. The Gathering Guard might not have been her first choice of career but survive long enough and there are advantages. Better rations, favor with the Steward. One more promotion and she might be able to keep Warren from having ever to join.

She hopes.

The air in the woods changes, stretched taut like the skin of a drum. It's full of fear and Solma can barely breathe. The ground rumbles. A distant shout that sounds like Olive followed by the panicked shrieks of fleeing boar. They're flushing the animals already.

Solma swears under her breath and steadies her rifle over the trunk, lowering her eye to the sight as she brings it round to face the path. Her fingers feel slick with sweat and she wipes them on her shirt. She's behind the long barrel of a hunting rifle, all the power of humanity's most precious invention held in her hands. She can do this.

The first animal bursts from the undergrowth with such force the trees either side of it bend. Solma swears again and ducks further down behind the dead tree. It's huge. She'd known the boars around here had been getting big, but Earth! Look at it! It's easily as tall as she is, shoulders like a battering ram, corded with muscle. Its furious eyes narrow and froth hangs in ropes from its open mouth. The coarse bristles that cover its body stand on end. And those tusks! They're the length of Solma's forearm ... longer perhaps. That thing could skewer her in a second and, judging by the wild anger in its high-pitched screams, it's looking for something to kill. What on Earth has it been eating?

Solma stifles that thought before it can answer itself. The village bury their dead near the woods. No one talks about why, but everyone knows. The boars need feeding if they're to feed the village in turn.

Solma hunkers down behind the dead tree and clicks the safety off her rifle. The furious boar is followed by another pig, then another and another. They're not as big as the great boar, but still big enough to do some damage. Infected by their panic, the enormous boar bolts to the end of the clearing, clashing with the mesh. He screams. More pigs barrel into the clearing and fear curls in Solma's gut. This herd is enormous. She straightens a little so she can peer over the dead tree, but all she sees is writhing, terrified bodies. How's she supposed to shoot cleanly in this chaos?

Think, Solma. Find the biggest, the one that will feed the village for the longest. She turns her rifle a fraction, staring through the sight to find the great boar. There he is, at the front of the herd, goring the mesh. But the herd is so tightly packed Solma can't get a decent shot. The animals jostle, blinded by panic. But they're clever. They'll figure out an escape soon.

Solma shifts her weight, turns the rifle a fraction. No room for error. Ammo is precious.

A breeze picks up behind her, sweeping overhead towards the squirming mass of pigs.

Amidst the chaos, Solma sees the big boar freeze, lift his snout, test the air. Solma feels the breeze chill her cheek and her gut freezes. The wind's changed. The boar turns his ferocious head and his glinting eyes meet hers. Solma's mouth goes dry.

He charges before she has a chance to react. His scream is so primal it galvanizes the other pigs. Suddenly their movements are less panicked and more purposeful, testing the corral mesh, biting and goring.

But the big boar has his eye on Solma.

Shrieking, he hurtles towards her, kicking up dust. Solma pulls the trigger.

The shot is good, scoring a deep groove in his shoulder. Fur and blood fly. The boar shrieks, but he's so flooded with rage it doesn't slow him down. Solma's palms are clammy with panic.

Not again. Please, not again.

Stay calm.

A second shot catches him in the flank. It should have brought him down so she can bleed him out with her knife, but his hide is so thick he doesn't even feel it. Solma sees the red shine of blood from the bullet wound as he surges towards her. Earth! What is this creature? She squeezes the trigger again, almost reflexively. Nothing happens.

She swears, her voice ringing across the clearing. Stealth doesn't matter now. Solma pulls the charging handle and fumbles on her belt for a new magazine.

He's meters away, closing the space between them with furious ease. A pre-emptive pain screams in Solma's absent leg.

Where's her magazine? It should be here ... but it isn't. She forgot to collect her ammo ration. No, no, no!

Solma glances up to see the boar less than ten meters from her. Suddenly the dead tree seems too fragile to stop this thing barreling through it and stamping Solma's brains all over the forest floor.

She opens her mouth to scream. The boar's eyes bulge.

A shot rings out across the clearing from behind Solma. The great boar barely reacts. He keeps flying at her for almost a full second before he realizes he's dead, then his footing falters and he tumbles, slamming into the fallen tree. Thrown backwards, Solma lands hard on her back, winded but alive.

For a moment, the noise of the panicking pigs is muted and Solma hears nothing but her own breathing. She stares at the dead boar, at the bullet hole like a third eye in the center of its forehead. Solma almost feels sorry for it. But then her absent leg throbs and the feeling fades.

A hand lands on her shoulder and she jumps. Olive's shadow falls across her.

"Get up!" she growls. "Bleed it! Quick!"

Solma bites back a retort and scrambles to her feet, unsheathing her knife. She vaults the dead tree stump, grabs one tusk to hold the boar steady and slices across its throat. The ground blackens with blood.

The sounds of the herd have changed now. They've worked out how to break through the mesh and their grunts and squeals have purpose. There's a sudden snap, the mesh recoils and the pigs are through. They charge out of the clearing and disappear.

Solma flops back against the dead tree, rifle clasped loosely in her hand, and tries to control her breathing. Olive stands over her and drops two magazines into her lap.

"You forgot these, you utter fool," she says. "Just piss off the biggest brute of the lot, why don't you? And you're welcome, by the way. Again."

Solma grits her teeth, glaring. "*Thank you*," she snaps, and tucks the magazines into her belt. Olive scowls.

"Ridiculous waste of ammo," she mutters. "Bullets don't grow on trees, y'know."

Solma glares but says nothing, mainly because there is nothing to say. She knows ammo is precious, but she wasn't exactly thinking about conserving bullets with that monster charging towards her.

"Solma!" Maxen skids to a halt beside them with Ilga and Aldo stumbling after him. He drops to his knees beside Solma, holds her shoulders, her hands, her face.

"You ok? You're ok. Earth's sake! That was close."

Solma manages a weak smile. "Yeah, I'm fine. Sorry. Just ..."

She braces against the tree and hauls herself to her feet. "I'm fine, honestly. Stop fussing!" She punches him lightly in the arm. He feigns hurt, then smiles. Olive rolls her eyes. "Yeah, alright," she says. "When you're done, can we get this thing back to the village? I hate the stink of pig."

Solma glares. The air fizzes with loathing. Maxen touches Solma's arm and draws her round to face him.

"Olive's right, Sol. Let's get it done."

Solma sighs. "Fine."

She can never refuse Maxen anything.

Maxen beckons Ilga and Aldo over. Together they lay the pig out, tying its ankles to a carrying pole with twine. The creature's thick muscle makes it almost immovable. It takes all five of them to shift it so that it will drain properly and by the time they're done, they're all sweating profusely.

Solma mops her brow with the back of her sleeve. "How are we going to get this monster back home?"

Olive wipes her bloody hands on her trousers. "Two at the front, two at the back," she says, as if it's obvious. "And one with a rifle ready just in case another pig decides to attack you."

Solma ignores the steely glare in Olive's eyes. "Whatever. I'll take the front."

"I'll help," Maxen says. They reach down together to lift the front of the pole. He catches her eye and smiles, winks. Solma feels her anger draining.

"Hey," Aldo says vaguely. "What's that?"

"What's what?" Olive snaps. "Stop wasting time, grab the pole—" she stops, listening.

"Oh," she says. "Oh no ..."

They can all hear it now, the piercing whine drifting over the trees from the village, punctuated by the barking of the watchtower dogs. Solma stares at Maxen, whose face has drained of color. They freeze, all five of them, hoping there's been some error, hoping it's been set off by accident.

But the whine goes on, getting louder and higher and more desperate. There's no mistaking it; it's the Raid Siren. The village is under attack. Solma's breath catches and she reaches for Maxen's hand. He takes it.

"Warren," Solma whispers.

EIGHT

"Leave the pig!" Olive screams. Ilga looks horri-
fied.

"What? But we need it—"

Olive grabs her by the collar and pulls her face close.
"There'll be no village to feed, pig or not, if we don't
get back now!" she snarls. "Move!"

She releases Ilga, spitting out her sugar cane as she
grabs her rifle from the ground. She sets off at a run
back towards the village. There's no time to argue.
They all follow. The whine of the siren reaches a
painful pitch and Solma swears, running so hard her
lungs scream. She overtakes Olive just as the five of
them burst from the woods, her blade-foot clanging
against stones.

"Warren!" she shrieks. Where is he? She scans the
horizon, feels the fear in the air. A thin ribbon of

smoke rises from the edge of the village. Solma pulls away from the rest of her squad, surging up the path.

"Oi!" Olive yells after her. "Sol! Stop! The orchards are burning! *Solma!*"

Solma isn't listening. Her head is full of Warren and terrible possibilities: torn limbs, smashed skulls, his little body twisted and still—

She battles her brain into silence and tugs her hunting knife from its sheath.

The village is in chaos. Children cower under upturned carts or in smashed doorways. Broken belongings litter the street. Several of the able-bodied villagers have taken up arms—shovels and axes, kitchen knives, the odd rifle—but none of them really know what to do. The Guards posted on the watchtowers have swarmed into the village and the watchdogs run loose. One lies dead in the middle of the path with its guts spilled free. Another streaks past Solma, snarling. Amidst all this, tall figures in grey uniform sweep across everything, lighting fires, swinging blades, firing pistols.

For a moment, Solma stands, staring at the horror around her. Nausea seethes in her gut, until she bites down on the inside of her cheek. The pain brings her back to her senses.

She's Sergeant now. This is her job. Protect the village.

She can do this. She *has* to do this. Or a lot of people will die.

Panic squeezes her throat. *Where is Warren?* She presses through the smoke and noise.

An old woman in Aldren brown defends her house with the end of a broken broom handle, battering the face of the burliest man Solma has ever seen. He swears, grabs the handle and pulls it from the old woman's grip, then backhands her so hard she bounces off the door frame as she falls. Solma stares at the woman's still body. It's Gerta, who greeted her this morning, with a gap-toothed grin and a cheery wave from her rocking chair. The chair now lies in pieces outside the house. The burly raider sweeps Gerta's legs aside with one foot and makes to enter the house. Someone screams from inside.

Solma doesn't even think.

"Hey!" she yells, and he turns just in time to receive her knife in the eye. His head jerks back and Solma's knife pulls clean out, leaving a vivid, red hole where his eye had been. He teeters, his undamaged eye blinking in surprise, and falls backwards like a board. Dead.

Solma stares for a moment at the corpse, horror curling in her gut.

His blood pools in the dirt and Solma chokes down a sob, kicking the dead raider for good measure. She crouches by Gerta. Her fingers tremble as she feels for a pulse. There! She's alive. Solma whispers a quiet thanks to Earth-knows-who and shelters the old woman under what's left of her door.

Someone rushes by, firing a gun, but Solma can't tell if they're a villager or a raider. The air fills with smoke. She splutters, reaches into her pocket for a bandana to tie over her face.

Maxen appears out of the smoke like some ghastly miracle. There's a bloody gash across his left cheek and a bruise blossoming on his temple. He pulls her to her feet.

"Come on!"

"Where are we going?"

"To find the hoses!"

Solma wrestles free. "No! I gotta find Warren!"

"I found him!" Maxen yells. "He and Bell are in the bunker. Let's go!"

Solma hadn't realized, until that moment, just how afraid she'd been. They're in the bunker. Her little brother is safe underground in Bell's arms, sheltered from the raiders. He's ok.

She wilts with relief, but there's no time for that. Maxen grabs her hand and they battle through the smoke and chaos to reach the storehouse at the center of the village. There comes an animal scream and an enormous, bay horse with feathered hooves charges past. Solma barely dodges out of the way in time. The horse is followed by three field planters, all pointing after the panicking animal and shouting. "Stop her! Catch her!"

Solma's heart kicks. If the village loses its two plough horses, the field preparation will be ten times as difficult.

"Maxen ..." she cries, staring after the fleeing horse, but Maxen grabs her arm.

"Not our problem!" he shouts. "Someone else'll get it!"

He pulls her after him and they press on.

The rest of their squad, along with two others, are already there. As Solma and Maxen struggle through the chaos to reach them, Solma sees Olive dodge a knife swipe from a huge attacker. She yells as she feints to one side and thrusts the heel of her hand into his elbow. It pops free of its joint with a sickening crack.

There's a grunt of pain and the raider drops his knife. Olive knees him in the nose and leaves him slumped in the dirt while she readies her rifle.

Solma grins to herself. Olive might be excruciating, but there's no-one she'd rather stand beside in a raid. Olive fights like a redbear.

"Situation?" Maxen yells as they take their position by the storehouse. Olive swears at Aldo, who trembles beside her.

"Lift your gun, you sniveling child!" Olive roars. "Stay alert! Aim for the head!"

Solma remembers the gaping hole she'd left in the raider's eye just minutes before and swallows down bile as she readies her own rifle. Much as she hates to admit it, Olive is right. Aim for the head, or the village will burn.

"Olive!" Maxen yells. "Situation!"

They join the other two squads surrounding the storehouse, their backs to the corrugated-steel structure that houses their food—their survival—until next harvest.

"No idea how many," Olive reports. "But a lot. Squads five and seven are putting out fires in orchard one. A glasshouse got smashed and Rhona's house is on fire."

"Village support?" Maxen demands. Solma glances at him and she sees the fear tightening his jaw. Olive shakes her head.

"Most are in the bunker," she says, her voice obscured by screams and gunshots. "Some of the Fei stayed to help. Not enough though."

"Is Dja below?" Maxen asks, a quake in his voice. Olive scowls.

"'Course he is," she says. Solma stiffens against the contempt in Olive's voice. Now is not the time to argue about the merits of their village Steward. Below ground is exactly where he needs to be. She's vaguely aware of Maxen barking orders: Aldo and Ilga to grab the hoses and help the villagers putting out fires (which are popping up everywhere), three members of another squad are to help defend homes, everyone else must defend the storehouse.

Solma's mind is elsewhere. She squints through the haze of smoke, her eyes following the trail until they snag on the dark smudge of watchtower eight, standing sentinel in the center of the village. At its base is the mound of dried grass and weeds that no one ever touches: the hidden entrance to the bunker. Solma stares at it, willing those inside to stay quiet.

"Sol!" Olive snaps, and Solma jumps to attention in time to see the huge raider barreling towards her. She lifts her rifle and fires. One. Two. The first shot hits him in the leg, the second in the chest as he stumbles. He slumps to the floor. There's a roar from her left and she just manages to reload her rifle in time to fire into another attacker. She hits his shoulder and he keeps coming at her until she fires the second cartridge between his eyes. Warm blood flecks her face and Solma fights the urge to retch.

Even in all this chaos, she hears an echo of her mother's voice, speaking words that have haunted her since she was drafted into the Guard.

There is no joy in killing, Solma. But it is necessary.

"Solma! Reload!" Olive bellows. Solma swears under her breath and obeys. Why is it that Olive always manages to take charge, even though *Solma* is Sergeant now? Is the girl made of stone? Does firing guns into other human beings not unsettle her?

Solma relives the raider's face exploding at least three times in slow motion before she manages to reload. Olive has killed two more and injured a third by the time Solma raises her rifle.

"Who are they?" she cries over the din. They're like no raiders she's ever seen before; their faces twisted with determination, corded muscle rippling across their shoulders, taller than everyone Solma has ever met and, though their clothes are torn and ragged, they seem to be wearing a uniform. They're not from this province, that's for sure.

"Don't know, don't care!" Olive snarls, emptying her rifle into one man's stomach. She shoulders it and unsheathes her hunting knife instead. Olive is ferocious in close combat and, as she said, bullets are precious.

Solma turns so that she's back-to-back with Olive, peering through the thickening smoke. Something darts in front of her and she yelps, swinging her rifle round to trace the movement. A small figure kneels at the corner of the storehouse. Solma aims her rifle at it, but hesitates. The silhouette is tiny. A child? That's impossible. Even the most desperate raiders don't bring their children to attacks.

The little figure disappears into the smoke before Solma can approach. There's no time to think on it further because a cry drifts from the back of the store-house.

"Fire! It's on fire!"

Solma's head snaps round. Smoke billows from the back of the structure and the thick scent of burning stings Solma's nose. She swears. How did the fire take so fast?

"Defend the doors!" Maxen yells. "Where are the hoses?"

Olive scowls at him. "You deployed them to the village," she says. "Remember?"

Maxen's face drains of color. He glances at Solma, eyes reflecting the orange glow of fire. Solma's heart constricts.

"The water stores!" She yells. "We'll make a chain, bring 'em round in buckets and douse the fire!"

Olive glares. "That's our drinking water!"

Solma's irritation flares. "It'll be vapor anyway if we don't put the fire out!" She snaps. "That's an order! Organize the other squads!"

Olive's eyes flash with fury. She's about to say something but Maxen's voice cuts through the din. "Obey your superior officer!" he roars. "Buckets! Now!"

Olive presses her lips together and turns without another word.

The raiders converge on the storehouse, appearing out of the smog with weapons raised. They don't move quickly, they don't need to. They know they've got the squads surrounded and so they advance with that hideous swagger of a predator tormenting cornered prey. Solma shoots one in the throat and winces as he falls to the ground.

Earth! They're like an army. She's shot four or five already and yet the raiding party is still bigger than any she's ever fought. Ten ... twenty ... thirty of them. She doesn't have enough bullets. Nobody does. Something twists in her gut. This is not a regular band of outlaws. There's something different about them. Something about their black uniforms, their numbers ...

Solma can't get her head round it. Who are they?

A shot from behind her and one of the raiders slumps to the floor. The others quicken their speed, weapons raised. They're silhouetted against the growing fire, silent against the distant screams. Solma lifts her rifle, lowers her eye to the sight, lines the cross-hairs and fires.

One shot. Two. Three.

The men crumple and fall. Why are they all men? That's not normal, either. A fourth shot, a fifth.

The sixth that rings out comes from the attackers and Solma feels a jolt in her prosthetic leg. She swears, glances down. There's a tear in her trousers and a long, pale scratch against the black material of her prosthesis, but the bullet only clipped her. She swings her rifle until she finds the man with his pistol aimed at her. She fires. He falls.

Olive's voice drifts back through the chaos, sharp and impatient as always, but a line of Guards now snakes around the storehouse, ferrying buckets of water. The glow of the fire slackens, but not enough to call it a victory. Solma lowers her rifle, pulls the charging handle, which flings the empty shells to the ground. She shoves a new magazine in just in time to fire a round into a raider with a hammer. He falls with a grunt, his head snaps back. The hammer falls from his grip.

But there are more. So many more. Where have they all come from?

On her left, Maxen edges towards her, rifle raised, firing and reloading.

"Who the hell are these people?" he roars.

Solma doesn't answer. In her periphery, a movement catches her attention and horror blooms in her belly. She turns, rifle now hanging uselessly in one arm.

"No ..."

The clump of grass that hides the bunker has moved and a little figure is crawling out into the chaos. Through the smog it's almost impossible to see, but

Solma knows. She'd know that little outline anywhere. And she has a horrible feeling she knows what
her little brother is doing. That damn bee has disappeared and he's crawled into the middle of a battle to
look for it.

NINE

FOR A FEW TERRIBLE seconds, Solma just stares.
Smog churns in the air. Warren has ash in his hair and
soot coats his feet. His brows draw together in consternation, but he's paying no attention to the chaos
around him.

He's scared for the *bee*. The bee that will probably
die in a week anyway. And Warren will be dead in a
minute if Solma does nothing.

"Sol!"

Maxen's voice startles her into action. She ducks
so that Maxen can fire a neat shot into the chest of
the raider only meters from her. The raider grunts
and falls. Maxen meets Solma's gaze, fear, anger and
disappointment mixed there. Solma's gut tightens.

"Sol, they need you round by the fire!"

Solma shakes her head before she knows what she's
doing. "I can't! I—"

Maxen looks furious. "If they don't put out the fire, our food is gone! Do it, Solma!"

His white-blue eyes flash, the blood on his face now peppered with ash. Sweat coats his collarbone and brow. He looks wild. He looks like his father. Not like a Gatra, but like a *Camber*. Like the son of a Steward. And you don't defy a Steward. Even if he's not a Steward yet. Automatically, she turns to obey.

But a shout from behind stops her. She whips round, rifle raised.

"Get going, Solma!" Maxen roars, but Solma barely hears him. She's listening to the muffled echo of that little shout, the one that sounded so much like triumph, so much like her brother. She peers through the murk and there he is, stood up in the middle of all this, little hands cupped over that damn matchbox as he peers anxiously between his fingers. He's found the bee.

But the raiders have spotted him.

A few looming men turn and look straight at the little figure stood in the smoke. Solma sees one of them grin, a knife gleaming wickedly in his fist.

"No ..."

"Solma!" Maxen yells. "That's an order!"

Solma neither hears nor cares. She runs, straight for Warren. Maxen's voice drifts after her on the fire-fueled winds.

"Solma!"

She ignores him. She has to get to her brother. Her blade catches on debris and she stumbles. One knee lands heavily on something sharp and she curses at the burst of pain.

Then comes the cry that freezes her heart. Her head snaps up, her breath ragged and desperate. No! The raiders circle Warren, snarling. Warren's green eyes sparkle with fear. His little mouth trembles. He stares from raider to raider, recoiling from their wild faces. He shakes his head fiercely and says something but his voice is so small, Solma can't hear it.

Then a raider snatches Warren around the waist and lifts him from the ground. He cries out and flails his legs. But, dammit! He's still holding that bee! He's got it cupped in both hands, clutched to his chest, refusing to let go.

One raider reaches out towards his hands.

Solma roars. She has no idea where that terrible sound comes from, how she conjures something so monstrous from her own throat, but it bursts from her as if she were the epicenter of an explosion. All three raiders pause. Solma charges, unslinging her rifle from her shoulder. She doesn't bother to aim it. She simply raises it and brings the butt down as hard as she can on one raider's face. His nose explodes and his head snaps back.

She pulls her hunting knife from its sheath and jabs him twice in the gut. He doubles over, crumpling to the ground. She doesn't wait to see if he's dead. No time. The second raider swears in some language Solma doesn't know and raises a battered pistol. Instinctively, Solma drops to one knee. She doesn't have the time or ammo to reload her rifle. It's too big and clumsy.

She throws her knife instead.

It somersaults through the smoke and hits the raider in the chest with a dull thud. He staggers, dropping the pistol. She advances on him as he falls to his knees, braces her foot against his shoulder and wrenches the knife loose. It judders free with a wet crack, gore clinging to its blade. The raider's eyes widen for a moment, then the life goes out of him.

The raider holding Warren backs away from her, turning to run. Warren kicks and screams.

"Solma! *Solma!*"

The sound of his panic wrenches something inside her. She surges after Warren's captor and thrusts her foot into the back of his knee, jabbing her elbow into his head as his legs give way. She presses the blade of her knife to his neck as he falls. He stiffens, turning his face towards her. His eyes are a bright, fierce violet and his hair is cropped close to his scalp. Through the blood and soot on his face, Solma can just make out the tattoo of a small flame inked above one eyebrow. He bares his teeth.

"Let him go," Solma snarls. "Or I'll bleed you like a pig."

It would be so easy. She feels it in the sureness of her hand, just a flick of her wrist. She wouldn't hesitate. She'd kill him without a second thought like she killed the others. And that scares her.

"I don't wanna kill you," she says.

The raider meets her eyes, his own deep and unfathomable. "Yeah," he growls. "I know."

He opens his arms and Warren stumbles away. At last, Solma feels the tremble of fear in her hand. She grits her teeth, her blade cutting a fine line in the raider's skin. He winces but doesn't cry out.

She could kill him anyway. What's he going to do? He won't wander off into the sunset, will he? He'll rejoin his fellows, set fire to things, smash houses, steal food. What would Blaiz say? Blaiz would say cut his throat. She's a Sergeant, a protector of this village. She can't just let him go.

"Sol!" Warren cries. "Sol, no!"

Her eyes flicker towards him. He's standing only a meter from the raider who'd held him, the matchbox containing the bee still cupped in his hands.

"Don't, Sol," he whispers. She can't hear it through the madness, but she seems to feel him talk inside her head. His voice switches off that barbaric part of her. Her knife drops from the man's neck. The raider keeps utterly still, watching her.

"Go, then," Solma snaps. "Go! Leave!"

He presses his mouth closed, gets to his feet and trudges off into the yellow mist without a backward glance. Solma watches him go, then turns on Warren.

"What on Earth are you doing!" she demands, kneeling in front of him and shaking both his shoulders. "What's wrong with you? You crawl out of the bunker in the middle of a fight! Earth's sake, Warren!"

Warren wriggles free. "Don't!" he says, his eyes accusing. "I had to find her! I had to keep her safe!"

Solma clenches her fist in frustration. "Get to the bunker!" she growls, snatching his elbow. She half drags him back towards the watch tower. He stumbles, tries to fight her.

"Sol, you're hurting me!"

She relents and lets him go. "Alright, but get moving! Honestly, Warren, you risk your life for that bee? You think any of them would have noticed her fly away in this chaos—"

She stops suddenly, remembers the raider reaching out towards Warren's cupped hands.

Is it possible ...?

No. Coincidence. No one has seen the bee, have they? No one knows it's there. How could they be trying to take it?

"Warren," Solma says, hands on hips. "Bunker. Now."

He pokes his tongue out, eyes full of hurt, then turns and walks with defiant slowness through the battle. He peels back the grassy mound and descends into the bunker without a backward glance, that damn bee still cupped to his chest. She'll have some making up to do later, but at least he's safe for now.

She turns away from the bunker just as a raider cracks Maxen on the head with a colossal fist. Olive lies unconscious and the storehouse burns.

TEN

"You left your post, Sol,"

Maxen doesn't look angry, just dismayed. His head is turned away from her so that Dr. Roseann can clean his wound. Every so often, he winces. Otherwise, his pale eyes scan the devastation the raiders left in their wake.

The storehouse flames burned until the raiders had taken what they wanted and disappeared. Solma joined Ilga and Silo desperately trying to douse the fire, but with only three buckets and a host of incapacitated friends, there wasn't much they could do. Ilga sustained a nasty injury to her head and couldn't keep going, leaving Solma and Silo to deal with the damage.

The raiders ignored their efforts to douse the fire, smashing the storehouse open and shouldering bags of grain, dried meats, and any jars of food that hadn't exploded in the heat. Then, they'd stalked away into the smog.

Solma blinks the memories away.

"I know," she whispers, scrutinizing the dirt.

"We needed you, and—"

"I know!"

She can't stand it, but shouting won't help. She kicks her blade into the ground.

"I'm sorry, I—"

What can she say? Is that how a Sergeant should act? Solma suppresses the many *but-he's-my-brother* protests surfacing in her throat and tries to consider it objectively. The village was burning. A child of Warren's age probably won't last the next winter (her heart gives a painful kick). But they'll all die if the food is stolen.

They'll all die.

If she were the Steward, she'd strip her of her rank. So much for extra rations for the family. They'll be lucky, now, if they even get regular rations. But every time Solma relives the horrifying sight of Warren clambering up from underground, she knows she'd always do the same thing. Of course she would. It's all for him, isn't it? It's always been for him. She'd promised their Ma as she'd bled to death, promised their Dja as that disease had wasted his body. Sergeant or not, she'd rescue Warren every time.

Does that count as a betrayal?

The thought makes her sick. She's turned her back on her village: the one thing she promised herself she'd never do. The village keeps them. No one survives alone …

"Sol?"

Solma starts and looks up, meeting Maxen's gaze.

"You ok?"

Solma realizes she's been muttering under her breath. She shuts up.

"Yeah," she says, then, "no. Maxen, I'm sorry. I couldn't leave him, I—"

"Hush, Sol." He doesn't say it unkindly. "Where is he now, anyway?"

"Home," Solma admits. "Ilga walked him back before she came to Roseann. He's fine."

No one says anything for a bit.

Roseann finishes bandaging Maxen and he probes the gauze, wincing. Roseann smacks his hand away and, despite everything, Solma suppresses a laugh. Roseann has a good bedside manner, but every so often, her impatience shows. Solma can see where Olive gets it from. There's that critical, intelligent gleam in both their eyes. Like mother, like daughter.

"We'll need to change that every few days," Roseann says. "I'll look at your knee, Sol. Then, I'm going to see to Olive."

Solma's gut twists uncomfortably. Olive saved her life only that morning and what had she done in return? Run off and left her to get clobbered over the head by some passing raider. No, not the behavior of a Sergeant.

"She ok?" Solma asks, hating how small her voice sounds. Roseann meets her eye and there's a faint smile. A not-your-fault smile. Solma isn't exactly reassured. Roseann and Olive have always been mavericks. The only reason Blaiz tolerates them in the village is because Roseann is an exceptional doctor and Olive is terrifying in battle. Usually.

"She's fine," Roseann says, gently flexing Solma's right knee and testing the joint. "Awake with a sore head and cursing you to the skies. But fine."

Great.

"Take it easy for a few days, or this one's gonna give out," Roseann says. "And strap it up at night, yes?"

She turns without waiting for an answer and limps away, spluttering on the smoke. Solma watches her go and wonders if begging Blaiz for a second chance will help. It probably won't. That's it, then. She'll be a squad recruit for the rest of her miserable life, which will be short and probably painful.

Earth! Suddenly, the reality of it overwhelms her and she clutches the sides of her head against a wave of nausea.

"Sol? Solma?"

Maxen is by her side, one hand on her shoulder and the other rubbing the small of her back. He grabs her arm as she sways, gradually lowering her to the ground, and holds her ash-coated hair out of her face as she is thoroughly sick.

"Okay," he says. "It's okay."

But it's not okay. None of it is. Solma wipes her mouth and reaches shakily for the water bottle clipped to her belt. It isn't there. She struggles to her feet to find Maxen holding out his own bottle. She takes it gratefully and drinks.

"I'll take the consequences," she says, handing back the bottle. "Just ... ask Blaiz to leave Warren and Bell out of this, yeah? It was my fault, I—"

Maxen's eyes soften and he squeezes her arm. "No," he says. "I'll fight your corner. He was attacked. It was a deliberate distraction—"

"Which I fell for!"

"—Which *any of us* would have fallen for because we love our families. I'll speak to Dja. He'll let you keep your rank. You're a good Sergeant and the villagers respect you, Sol. Dja knows that."

Solma presses the heel of her hand to her forehead, "But the boar—"

"Was not your fault. You did everything right and the thing charged. Trust me, alright? There aren't enough kids of the right age to replace you right now and, let's be honest, our new recruits ..." he shrugs and winks. Solma snorts a laugh. "Let's just say I reckon Dja'll be easy to persuade, alright?"

"Alright."

Solma doesn't feel better. Blaiz might be a good Steward but he is not the kind of man you cross. The memory of that nameless girl bursts into her mind again, striding into the unknown ... that single glance back, her face splashed with freckles ...

The flower ... the guilt ...

"What was he doing out of the bunker anyway?" Maxen says.

Solma blinks. "What?"

"Warren. Why did he come out of the bunker? He knows better than that."

Solma's breath catches. She could say it now, unburden herself. She lines the words up on her tongue, meets his eye. She can do this. It's a simple sentence. *We found a bee.* Four little syllables. The secret will be out in less than a breath.

But that's the problem, isn't it? It's been a secret since this morning. It's a secret that cost them the storehouse, their food. It's a secret Solma should have reported the moment the little thing had clambered from the soil. And she didn't. And Blaiz Camber can't abide secrets. Blaiz Camber knows everything that happens in his village. If he knows Solma left her post for something like this—

It won't matter how much Maxen fights her corner. She'll be walking out of the village just like the girl with the red freckles. And then what will happen to Warren?

She lets the words dissolve in her mouth and shrugs. "No idea."

It's beginning to frighten Solma how easy it is to lie. She watches Maxen's face, half-expecting him to arrest her there and then. But he doesn't. He just frowns.

"Well, you need to talk to him," he says. "He put the whole village in danger. I know he's only seven, Sol, but he mustn't do that again. If he does ... well, Dja'll have to punish him."

Solma's insides curdle. She nods, clasping her hands together to stop them from shaking. Punishments for kids and adults alike in Sand's End aren't kind. If they don't involve exile, they involve pain and humiliation. Blaiz can't tolerate insubordination. The thought of Warren's little, white back exposed and striped with flogging welts is enough to make Solma breathless. Maxen reaches out and brushes his fingers against hers, electrifying her. He leaves a finger-trail of soot across the back of her hand and when she glances up he's drawn closer to her, his eyes searching hers.

"You sure you're alright? Look, I can take you off duty this afternoon if you need—"

Solma shakes her head. "No. Olive's out of action. I'm fine." She forces a smile, which feels unnatural. "Come on. We got work to do. Let's assess the damage."

She tries not to think about the real extent of the damage, about how she's broken more laws this morning than in her entire life. She blinks, and the image of Warren being lifted from the ground flashes behind her eyelids. She remembers that black-gloved hand reaching for Warren's closed fists, for the precious thing they held.

Had they known?

She follows Maxen through columns of yellow smoke, picking their way through debris and still-wet blood.

All this chaos, Solma thinks, all this chaos because a bee crawled from the earth this morning.

ELEVEN

THE SUN IS WELL past its midday height before Solma
finishes morning duties, and she's only got half an
hour before Maxen expects her back. Her footfalls are
heavy as she heads home, picking her way through
the scattered debris of lives. Doors hang limply from
split hinges, or lay wrecked on the ground. Soot coats
everything. Every face Solma sees is grey with smoke
and battle-grim. People walk past her in a daze. The
storehouse is almost emptied and what little remains is
blackened and bitter with smoke. No one died, which
is a small miracle—Solma's a bit confused about it,
actually—but means there has been no reduction
in mouths to feed. Both the plough horses made it
through the battle ok, but one is still wild-eyed and
thrashing in his stable. Solma went to check on them
before the end of her shift, but there was nothing
she could do. She left old Piotr and the Field Master

barking orders while the poor animal screamed and kicked.

Somehow, though, the sky is still a vibrant blue through the haze of smoke. It's slow going on the way back home because people keep stopping her, grabbing her hand in both of theirs, asking, "Will it be okay? We gonna be alright?"

Solma smiles, pats their hands and says the Steward is doing everything he can, he won't let them starve, but it's important for everyone to pull together.

The people let out their breath and thank Earth for Blaiz Camber, and for her.

They hurry on, unaware of how their words make Solma's gut lurch. Because she didn't protect them, did she? She left her post. She saved her brother instead.

And now, they have a secret. Solma's never had one before. It's a constant pressure in her head. This is not good.

She finds Warren sat cross-legged a little way out from the house. He's found a patch of sun and he's peering at his open palms as that damn bee trundles across them, waving its antennae as if everything's fine.

She storms to Warren's side and looms over him, hands on hips. He lifts his head, squinting up at her silhouette. On his palm, the bee freezes, shocked by the sudden shade.

"What's this?" Solma demands. "Why d'you still have that thing?"

Warren blinks at her. He can tell she's angry and he doesn't understand why. She can see the puzzlement written all over his face.

She shouldn't shout at him. It's not his fault.

Only, it *is* his fault! Doesn't he realize what he's made her do? If he'd just stayed in the bunker—

"She was suffocating in there, Sol," he says quietly. "She needed sun and she crawled to the light. I tried to stop her, but people were looking and I couldn't get to her, I—"

"You gotta let it go!" Solma hisses. "You cost us the entire storehouse's supplies for a miserable little insect. It's gonna be dead in a week!"

She checks her voice before it rises enough to draw Bell out of the house, glancing over her shoulder to make sure no curious faces are watching. Everyone is busy with the damage, with hopelessness and fear. She and Warren are quite safe. Quite alone.

Solma folds her arms and scowls. "We got to tell Blaiz about this," she says. She knows exactly what Warren's going to say, knows he's right, but it infuriates her all the same.

"We can't!"

She can't deal with him right now! She throws her hands up in frustration, almost turns to go, but then changes her mind. He needs to understand what he's done, what he's made *her* do. But the look of shame and sadness on his face stops her in her tracks.

He blinks furiously, frowning at the little creature exploring his palm. The bee looks worn out, its abdomen pulsing for breath. Its fluffy amber stripes are coated with soot. It's hungry. And tired. And confused.

Solma sighs, lets all the tension and frustration and fear escape in that one, heavy breath. She unhitches her rifle and lays it on the grass, then crouches in front of Warren and cups her hands beneath his. Now they're both holding the bee.

"Warren," she says. "We've broken the law. You understand that, don't you? You know what happens when people break the law?"

Warren nods slowly without looking up. Solma squeezes his shoulder.

"We can't keep doing this. Let it fly away and we'll keep going like before, okay?"

Warren still doesn't look up, but this time he firmly shakes his head. "No."

Frustration spikes in Solma's chest again. She sucks in a breath. "Warren—"

"No!"

He doesn't shout, but the word hits her like a hammer blow. She stares at him open mouthed. He lifts his gaze, his green eyes hard and defiant, angry tears glistening in them. Solma sighs, knuckling tiredness from her eyes. A near miss with a monster-boar this morning and an attack on the storehouse means she could really do without a seven-year-old's tantrums. Not for the first time, the burden of being Warren's protector weighs so heavily around her neck she can barely breathe.

"Fine," she snaps, no longer trying to be nice, let him play about with that insect until he gets bored. Let the Steward catch him ...

That thought pulls her up short. How young is too young to exile? Will Warren become like that young girl, a child his village barely remember, a name on the fringes of someone's memory?

"Sol?"

She starts and looks down at her brother. His bright, meadow-green eyes soften her anger.

"Sol, you said she could save our village. She could get the world going again. We have to try."

Solma sighs. "We should've told Blaiz."

Warren shakes his head vigorously, lowers his eyes to the bee again. "Blaiz won't get it," he says. "Blaiz will try take her, just like the raiders did. He always wants to be in charge—"

Solma snorts a laugh. "Warren, he *is* in charge!"

"No, I—" Warren bites his lip, grappling for the right words. "I mean he won't let nobody else ... he don't ..."

He growl-screams in frustration and the bee in his hands lifts her antennae in question. Solma softens. She barely remembers the limits of being seven. She'd had her Ma and Dja back then to help her understand her own thoughts, but Warren only has her. What he senses is so much bigger than himself and he can't get it out.

She cups her hands under his again and watches the little bee as it runs its front feet over its face, cleaning. A thrill of something rushes through her. A hope, despite everything. She tries to swallow it down, clench it closed, but it won't be contained.

This little bee could be everything.

Or she could be the end of everything.

But the truth is, it's too late to go back now, isn't it? It's been a secret for almost a whole day. It's cost them the storehouse. Earth! It would be so much simpler if this little thing just flew away and left them alone!

"We got to help her, Sol," Warren whispers. "She needs a nest. She's really hungry. We have to help."

Solma pinches the bridge of her nose. "How can you *possibly* know this, Warren?"

Warren rolls his eyes. "She told me, didn't she?"

That pulls Solma up short. This is ridiculous. His games are going to get them both exiled.

"It's a bee, Warren," she snaps. "I know we ain't never seen one before, but I'm pretty sure they don't talk."

Warren fixes her with a withering look. "They *do*," he insists. "Just 'cos *you* don't understand them, don't mean they can't speak!"

Solma scowls with impatience. She glances at the sun and her phantom limb itches. She doesn't have time for this. The village is in tatters and they're both sat out in the open with the deepest, most illegal secret anyone has ever had in a hundred years. Why won't the damn thing just fly away?

"Enough, Warren," she says, rising and turning away. "I got to go. Maxen's expecting me."

"You don't believe me," Warren says sulkily. "You *never* believe me."

Solma sighs, hands on hips. "That's not fair, Warren," she says. "I believe you when you tell the truth."

"I *am* telling the truth!"

Solma whirls on him. "You're not!" she snaps. "Are you?"

Warren meets her eyes, his own full of steely determination. "Alright," he says. "I'll prove it. I'll ask her to fly twice round my head and land on your hand. Hold it out."

Solma raises an eyebrow.

"Go on!" Warren insists. Solma clenches her teeth. She doesn't have *time!* But something in Warren's face makes her huff out a breath and proffer her palm. She watches as he lifts the little bee up to his face, staring at it intently as it trundles across his fingers. It'll only take a minute or two to prove to Warren he's making up stories, and then ...

The little bee fires its deep, vibrato engine and lifts into the air. It hangs in front of Warren's face for a moment, then zooms in two circles around his head before cruising over to Solma. It hovers in the air at eye-level and Solma stares into its strange, jewel-like eyes. The little thing looks so alien, it's hard to imagine there's any kind of intelligence behind those eyes, but Solma can't help feeling the bee is challenging her.

See? She imagines it saying. *Not so clever now, are you?*

And then it lands on her hand, folding its gossamer wings and probing her skin with its antennae.

Solma stares, open-mouthed. She looks from the bee to Warren and back again. Warren smirks.

"See?" he says. Solma's too stunned to speak for a moment and can only nod her head.

"*Now* will you help her?" Warren demands.

Solma feels the village, the future, slipping from her fingers. But Warren ... and this bee ...

"Okay," she says. She lifts the little bee into the light and feels it— *her*—shiver with delight at the sun's strength. She smiles. Warren smiles back.

And Bell's voice rings out across the smoky grass-land.

"What on Earth're you two doing out there?"

They both start, snapping their faces towards her. Bell is stood beside them, fists on hips, thunder in her eyes. Like everyone else in the village, her face is smeared with soot but the ruddy glow of her cheeks blooms through the dirt. She radiates disapproval.

"I—" says Warren

"We—" says Solma.

Bell's eyes flick from one to the other and then down to Solma's hand. Solma isn't quick enough. She cups her hands together and pulls them to her chest, feeling the little creature buzz and panic against her skin.

But it's too late. Solma can tell from the look on Bell's face. She's seen everything.

TWELVE

SOLMA ONLY REMEMBERS SEEING Bell cry once. When Ma died. A lot of people cried that day, Solma included. Ma's death was ugly and sudden. Gored under the tusks of a boar, she'd held on until they carried her home, then succumbed in front of her children, the wreckage of her body seeping into the bedsheets.

Solma remembers that, more disturbing than the blood or the way her Ma's body twitched with pain, was the way that Bell had cried. It hadn't been pretty. Bell screamed as if she was being gutted, cradling the body of her elder sister and refusing to let go. Solma ran at that point, not to escape the death of her mother but to escape the way Bell's grief permeated every timber of that house. Even though she ran right out of the village, to the furthest orchard, and cowered amongst the withered saplings, she'd still been able to hear Bell crying.

But this time it's different. The tears creep softly down Bell's cheeks. She lets out one, gasping sob and then claps a hand to her mouth.

"Is that …?" she whispers.

Solma and Warren exchange glances. The bee shivers against Solma's fingertips, impatient and confused.

Solma uncurls her hands and the bee clambers out, her wings droning like an engine as she drives heat through her body. Her antennae twitch. Solma feels the delicate whisper-touch of the creature's feet against her skin.

Bell creeps forward, one hand still raised to her mouth, kneels down between the two of them and holds out her hands.

"Oh, Solma …"

The bee buzzes curiously and marches from Solma's hand onto Bell's. Bell gasps, tears pooling in her eyes again. Solma resists the urge to snatch the bee away, as if too many eyes might harm it.

"It's a—"

"—A buff-tailed bumblebee," Bell finishes, tears glittering on her cheeks as she smiles, "I only seen them in pictures. Earth! Ain't she beautiful? Strong, too, big for her species. Look at that fur! She's a fighter, this one. She could do it …"

Solma and Warren gape at her. Is this their flustered, fussing aunt who drives them both silly with exasperation? She's talking like a scientist, like something out of the past. Solma's barely heard Bell so much as mention the death of the flora and fauna that disappeared so long ago. And now she's crying over a bee. A—what did she call it?

A buff-tailed bumblebee.

The bee hums on Bell's hand, fanning her wings and twitching her antennae as if to say *that's me*.

Bell looks up sharply. "Have you told Blaiz?" she asks, her voice stern. Solma's heart is suddenly twice as heavy in her chest.

"Not yet, but—"

"Good," Bell says.

Solma's mouth falls open again.

"What?" she splutters, "But—"

Bell waves a dismissive hand, careful not to disturb the bee. "Secrets are sacrilege, the Steward must know everything. Yes, yes! I heard it all before. It's nonsense."

"I—"

Solma doesn't know what to say. That doesn't make any sense. Blaiz is their keeper, their savior, their—

Bell huffs an impatient sigh. She passes the bee back to Warren, carefully nudging the little creature onto his palm. She scowls at Solma.

"I thought your Ma and Dja taught you this," she says, shaking her head. "I trusted your Ma at least to tell you the truth. And you got to know, so you understand why this is important." She turns to Warren, "Has the bee fed?"

Warren frowns down at the tiny creature. "I fed her some sugared water on a spoon earlier, but ..."

He reddens as he realizes what he's confessed. Bell laughs. "I wondered what you was doing with a fistful of sugar. Right, I'll cut some lavender for her so she can eat properly. Will she fly away?"

Solma and Warren stare at each other before Solma sighs and shakes her head. "She hasn't yet," she says. "She seems to ... like Warren. Trust him. I dunno how that's possible, but she ain't behaving like a normal bee—" she stops. How would she know what a normal bee behaves like? "At least, I don't reckon she is."

"Hmm."

Bell watches Warren with a strange look on her face. Warren chews his lip.

"I called her Blume," he says quietly.

Solma snorts a laugh and squeezes Warren's shoulder. "War, you can't name a bee—"

She catches sight of Bell's face and shuts up. Bell simply smiles. "Good," she murmurs. "Blume. Fitting name for a queen. Come inside. I'll explain everything. And then—" she clambers to her feet, brushes down her apron and runs critical fingers through her hair, "—then you'll find her somewhere to build a nest. Come on, I got something to show you."

THIRTEEN

WARREN'S LEFT FOOT SWINGS against the table leg.
Thump. Thump. Thump. He twists his fingers together so furiously that Solma worries he might hurt
himself.

"Warren," she murmurs, draping her hand over his.
"It's ok."

Warren sighs and, for the tenth or eleventh time in as
many minutes, glances behind him to the windowsill
where a shaft of sunlight illuminates the clay pot Bell
placed there, filled with water and freshly cut lavender
flowers, and from which a tired and grateful Blume
feeds. She buzzes her wings, her tongue dipping into
the flowers.

"She's fine, War," Solma says, squeezing his hand.
"It's ok."

Warren shakes his head, chewing his lower lip.

"She didn't want anyone to know." He mutters.

"It was an accident."

"She just needs a chance—"

They both start as the cellar door creaks open and Bell bustles through, arms full of books. Solma's insides curdle and she bites her lip. Blaiz has never gone so far as to forbid the parents of Sand's End teaching their children to read, but he considers it a waste of time and he'd be disappointed to know of the hours Bell spent with Solma and Warren at this table, teaching them how to turn the strange, printed symbols into sounds and words. There are no schools in Sand's End. Most of the adults here haven't been able to read for generations and Blaiz has always said this is the way it's supposed to be. Letters don't sow seeds. Books don't pollinate crops. But they burn well in the long, winter cold. Blaiz would confiscate all Bell's books if he knew she had them.

Being able to read has helped her a lot as a Gatra and it's meant Maxen's let her take down the reports. Still, Solma's not exactly proud of Bell for bending the rules like that. She stares hard at the ground as Bell heaves the burden onto the table and they scatter across the old wood, and only looks up when Bell bustles back over to the cellar door to lock it. Solma risks a glance at the tomes Bell's brought out.

They aren't like the tattered old things Bell hides under the floorboards and only brings out to teach Warren his letters. These are ... different.

"Right," Bell says, locking the cellar and popping the key in her apron pocket. "Let's see what we have here."

She riffles through the volumes and Solma sees snatches of strange titles and beautiful color photographs.

"This is what you keep down there?" she says, carefully browsing through the books. Bell never lets her or Warren down to the cellar. Makes sense, now. "You should prob'ly hand these in to Blaiz—"

She stops at the thunderous look on Bell's face. "It's my house. And these're my books. They won't go to Blaiz, girl, and that's that."

Solma rolls her eyes and examines the exotic titles again. The books are beautiful. Solma doesn't think she's ever seen so much precious paper in one place. *Complete Encyclopedia of Alphorian Wildlife*; *Apiculture for Beginners*; *How Bumblebees Came to Alphor* and on and on.

Until Solma realizes something. Her heart kicks. "These were Ma's books."

Bell's eyes soften. "Yes. They were."

Solma pulls one towards her and opens the cover. Inside, in that spidery scrawl she remembers from younger days, is her mother's name: Leile El Gatra. Solma runs her fingers over the lettering, feels where the pencil has pressed into the paper. Her entire body pulses with grief. Ma wrote her name here. Ma opened this book and touched this paper, just as Solma is touching it now.

"Ah!" Bell exclaims. "Here it is!"

She smooths out the pages of the largest book so Solma and Warren can see properly. They stare, open-mouthed, until Warren laughs, all his tension forgotten. He presses his open palm onto the image that takes up most of the double-page spread.

"It's Blume!" he giggles. Bell smiles.

"Exactly," she says. "The common buff-tailed bumblebee, as it was then. Not so common no more."

Warren removes his hand and they both gaze at the image. It's hand painted, but beautifully accurate; a great bumblebee—just like Blume—rendered in full color as she lands on a pink flower. She's annotated too. Solma's eyes scan the strange language surrounding the bee, words she's never heard before: spiracle, ocelli, scopae. She runs a finger over the text and marvels.

"It's beautiful."

Bell tuts. "Yes, it is," she agrees. "But not the point. We already know she's beautiful. We got to figure out how to help her."

"Right!" Warren agrees, his tongue poking from between his teeth as he drags the book closer towards him. Solma rolls her eyes.

"War, I can't see if you do that—"

"It says they nest in burrows underground!" Warren exclaims, completely ignoring his sister. "Sometimes they use old rodent holes. What's a rodent? Once she's found a nest, she'll lay her eggs, and ..."

A strange look comes over his face. He sits back, dispirited. Solma blinks at him.

"What is it?"

Warren shakes his head. "She can't lay eggs," he says. "We ain't seen no boy bees. She needs a boy bee to make eggs."

Solma hadn't thought of that. She, too, slumps back in her chair, dispirited. She knew though, didn't she? She's been trying to tell Warren all morning that the bee won't survive. So why does this feel like such a blow?

"Well," she says. "That's it, then."

"It most certainly is not!" Bell snaps, hands on hips, cheeks ruddier than usual. "I didn't spend hours teaching you to read just so you can ignore what's in front of you. Go on! Research!"

Solma sighs. She's about to bite back but Warren looks close to tears. She reaches out and squeezes his shoulder. "Come on," she says, "Let's have another look."

It takes them less than ten seconds to find the little box of text that explains a queen bumblebee will have mated before she hibernates for the winter, that everything she needs to start a new colony is already tucked away in her body. Excitement renewed, they scan pictures of haphazard bumblebee nests with clusters of bee-built honey pots and diagrams of glistening bee larvae (Solma thinks they're disgusting but Warren scowls at her when she says so). There are lists of flowers that bees like to visit, the lifecycle of a nest—at this, Warren looks pained.

"You mean, she'll only live 'til the end of summer?"

Bell nods, unapologetic. "But she'll lay more queens, Warren, and those queens'll fly and mate and hibernate. If she lays daughter queens, she's done what nature intended."

Warren doesn't look convinced, and Solma clench-
es her jaw. Nature intends lots of things, she thinks.
Nature intended to take both her parents. Nature
sends drought and famine and destroys their harvests.
Nature nearly took Solma's other leg this morning.
Nature intends nothing but ill will to human beings.

Absently, Solma pinches the corner of the page and
lifts it to see what's next. Warren gabbles away beside
her as she examines the image overleaf. Her insides
twist again. With trembling fingers, she turns the page
so everyone can see. Bell and Warren both fall silent.

There's a color spread on this page, too. Bright reds
and oranges and the velvet black of smoke. It's a picture of a bumblebee nest in flames. Bodies of the tiny
creatures litter the outskirts of the image as an angry
man thrusts a spade into the nest, his face twisted with
hatred. The image spreads right across the page, falling
beneath clusters of text. In red ink across the top of
the spread, the title reads: *The Hive Wars*.

Warren and Solma stare at the massacre in silence.
Solma feels her brother's hot little hand nudging
against her own and she takes it. But it's hard to re-
assure him when horror has clasped her too. As one,
they stare at Bell, whose face is inscrutable.

"This is what I want to tell you," she says. "This is why I think you should keep Blume a secret."

She pulls back a chair and sits, clasping her hands on the table. "We're allowed to teach you a lot of history," she says. "But we're forbidden from teaching you this. You need to know that before I explain. What I'm doing don't just break village law. It breaks *provincial* law. But this—"

She glances towards where Blume has finished feeding and now shivers her wings happily in the sun.

"—this is bigger than anything. This could mean ... and you need to know. You need to understand why the insects and the birds disappeared. And it's 'cos of this. 'Cos of the Hive Wars."

Warren whimpers, his eyes glassy as if he's seeing something that isn't there. He shrinks back in his chair, tears sparkling in his eyes.

"Warren?" Solma clasps his shoulders, trying to bring him back. "Warren, what's wrong?"

Warren shakes himself and comes to his senses, clutching Solma's wrists. "I smelled smoke and ... there was burning. So much death." He shudders, his gaze drifting towards Blume. "That came from her," he whispers. "She remembers."

Solma should dismiss this as childish fancy, but she can't. The more she watches this strange little bee, the more she feels something vivid and important surrounds her. How can a bee possibly remember something that happened a hundred years ago? How can a bee possibly remember *anything*?

She clutches Warren's hand and says to herself that it's to comfort him, not because she needs comfort herself.

Bell waits patiently until they are both facing her again. Solma scrutinizes her aunt's face and thinks, for the first time, that this is her Ma's sister. Her Ma, who taught her to shoot before she turned eight, who told her there should never be pleasure in killing, even when that killing is necessary. Her Ma, who was endlessly hopeful. She settles down to listen.

"A hundred years ago," Bell says, "Alphor was a different place. It was green and the air was thick with living things. Clouds of insects gathered under the eaves of trees, honey bees gleaming in the sunlight. There was great colorful dragonflies as large as my fist. And birds! Birds in the skies. The air weren't never still, never silent. Not like now." She pauses, imagining. Solma almost reaches her other hand to Bell's but something stops her.

"People back then should've seen the signs," Bell admits. "The wildlife was already struggling. Many species of bee only survived because humans took control, built hives and used the bees to pollinate the land. Something was killing the insects. Pesticides, or the destruction of wild meadows or ... I dunno. But the bees were already dying, and nobody knew why. It was a strange time. But here's the thing; the provinces that had control of the bees became richer 'cos they were producing better food. Their workers got stronger, their harvest was better and they could grow and expand. The other provinces struggled. Almost all their work went into pollination because there weren't no insects to do it for them. Harvests failed, villages couldn't gather enough seed to plant the following year and communities starved." Bell shakes her head and tears glint in her eyes. "The richer provinces should've shared. But people are greedy when they have power. They hoarded their bees, set up chemical barriers to prevent them from pollinating foreign crops. And y'know what happened? Their bees started dying too. Every year there was fewer and fewer hives. And the poorer provinces got poorer and more desperate, until one day ... One day they had enough.

"It started in the south, with our province, actually. The villages got together and they marched. They felt, if they couldn't benefit from the insects, why should anybody else? And so the Hive Wars began. At first, it was just about invading other provinces and stealing hives. Rioters would attack richer villages and loot the hives, taking the bees for their own. But they didn't know what they were doing and many of the hives died. This only made the rioters angrier. And it stopped being about sharing the bees, and became about levelling the playing field."

Solma's heart gives a sickening lurch. "They started burning the hives," she whispers. There's no way to keep the horror out of her voice.

Bell nods a confirmation. "It started with the honey bees," she says. "Because they were the easiest to keep. But it soon moved on to other species too, bumble-bees and solitary bees. Wherever a bee nest was discovered, rioters destroyed it. The richer provinces fought back, sending in soldiers to raze poorer villages to the ground. On and on it went, for years, flaring up whenever there was a poor harvest or a richer province made an unfair trade deal. No one could stop it. And by the time we understood what we were doing, it was too late. The bees were gone, along with the butterflies, who'd suffered in the violence, and the dragonflies, and many others. And when the flying insects died out, the birds went. And when the birds went, lots of our land mammals died. And on and on and on until Alphor's soil dried up and the air emptied and there weren't no rich provinces no more. Every province was starving and it was all their own fault."

She stops, staring at the table, her fists clenched and shaking. Solma reaches out again, stops again. This is hard. It's hard to hear, even harder to understand or know what to do. And Bell looks so much like Ma, more than she ever has.

Bell takes a deep breath. "Make no mistake," she says, "We ain't learned our lesson. If Blume is seen, there'll be another Hive War."

Solma shakes her head before she can stop herself. "No," she says. "Blaiz won't do that, he won't—" she stops.

Wouldn't he? Suddenly, Solma's not so sure. He wants what's best for the village, doesn't he? But does he also want what's best for the whole of Alphor? And even if he does protect Blume, he could still exile Solma for secrecy. And Warren. And Bell now, too.

Bell waits, watching as Solma struggles with the weight of this secret, until she clenches her fists to stop them shaking.

"So what do we do then?" she asks, hating the childish whine in her voice.

There's a pause that lasts both a few seconds and a lifetime. Solma glances up and meets Bell's gaze.

"You found her," she says. "You and Warren. What do *you* think we should do?"

FOURTEEN

SOLMA CASTS A GLANCE at Warren, bouncing on his heels beside her, his face strained with concern. She lays a hand on his shoulder.

"Blume'll be fine, Warren," she says. "She'll be out in a minute."

Warren says nothing. He twists his fingers together, staring at the patch of earth behind Bell's house as if, with his eyes alone, he can encourage Blume to emerge.

By the time they'd finished reading and learning the previous evening, Warren had been adamant. They were not telling Blaiz. No way. Solma's heart bucks at the memory of it, and guilt trickles down her throat, but she'd agreed. She doesn't know why she agreed, but she couldn't get that picture out of her head, the one with the man driving his spade through a bee's nest, the fire, the little, charred bodies ...

So they agreed to keep it secret. For now. Even though it made Solma feel sick just thinking about it. Last night, it had been too late to begin searching for a nesting site. Blume's energy was waning and her lethargy sent Warren into fits of panic. Full of solutions, Bell scooped up the little bee and took her outside to the patch of lavender growing behind the house. It's a modest plant, painstakingly pollinated every year by Bell, for the sole purpose of harvesting cuttings that help Warren sleep. Last night, though, it became Blume's evening sanctuary and she clambered happily over the purple flowers, dipping her tongue—her proboscis, Bell called it—into the nectar. The three of them crouched around the plant, fascinated, and watched the little bee feed. It was as if she'd carried the memory of how to do this through her however-many-years of slumber. Knowledge passed down from her sisters and mother, a hundred bee-lifetimes ago.

When she was sated, she buzzed down to the earth and shuffled about, picking her way into the shadow of the plants. Warren panicked again until Bell explained she needed somewhere to sleep. With a finger, she pressed a hole into the loose soil and Blume crawled right in.

"Well, ain't much we can do before morning," Bell said, one hand on her nephew's shoulder. "Let's get some rest, eh?"

But Solma didn't sleep all night. Instead, she listened to the wind rattling at the loose windows. What if Blume was too cold? What if some hungry animal gobbled her up? *What if someone saw her?*

Interspersed with these thoughts were the recurring pictures of burning hives, land carpeted with dead bees, angry men driving spades into the Earth.

If we can't have them, no one can!

By the way Warren had fidgeted in the bed beside her, she doubts he got any sleep either.

Now it's morning and they both stand at Blume's sleeping spot, waiting for her to emerge.

The sun peeps over the horizon and a chill mist still hangs at ankle height. Warren shivers and hugs himself. There's a sharp crash from inside the house, followed by Bell swearing. Warren giggles nervously and Solma squeezes his shoulder again.

"It might be too cold, still," she says. Warren nods, though he doesn't look convinced.

"Yeah, and she was proper tired ..."

"We dunno how much sleep a bee needs ..."

"Maybe she found somewhere else ..."

They fall silent and stare at the little patch of earth. The sun warms Solma's shoulders. She grasps the strap of her rifle: scanning the ground. Then—

"Look!"

Warren points as the soil begins to move. He crouches, peering at the disturbance.

"Come on, Blume. Come on, you can do it ..."

Solma squats beside him, dizzy with relief as the bee clambers into the morning, particles of soil clinging to her black-and-gold fur. Warren reaches out his hands and Blume clambers aboard. His grin is huge.

"She's ok, Sol!" he whispers, proffering the bee as proof. "She's ok!"

Solma nods, hand over her heart to try and calm it down.

"Yes."

"Now," Warren says to the bee, "we're gonna find you a home!"

Solma's smile fades as the hugeness of their task stretches before her. Find a nest. Keep it alive. Keep it secret. Avoid exile.

How can something so tiny have sent such massive quakes through her life? Yesterday morning, Solma was a law-abiding villager, a proud member of the

Gathering Guard. Overnight, she's become a criminal.

She shakes that thought away as Bell emerges from the back door, dressed in her Fei uniform for planting duties. Over her shoulder, she carries a satchel with trowels and gardening forks poking out of it.

Solma shoves her hands into her pockets.

"Sure you don't wanna come with us?"

Bell smiles and shakes her head. "Better if only you two know where the nest is," she says. "Know where you're gonna look?"

Solma shrugs and glances down at Warren. He doesn't have any ideas, either.

"Somewhere there's flowers?" he suggests, and Solma's heart cracks a bit. She strokes red-gold hair from his eyes.

"There ain't any wildflowers, remember?" she says. "Flowers only grow if people pollinate them."

Warren's little face falls. "Oh."

He stares down at the bee and Solma thinks he's beginning to understand how impossible their task is. Maybe they *should* just tell Blaiz ...

"Why don't you try under that cluster of trees to the east?" Bell suggests, pointing out beyond the village to where an ash tree stands tall against the horizon, flanked by a couple of birches and some bramble bushes. Solma frowns.

"I'm sure I told Piotr to cut that tree down."

Bell raises an eyebrow. "Maybe it's a good thing he didn't," she says. "Anyway, I'm just saying it might be a good place."

Solma scowls. "I thought you *didn't* want to know where the nest was?" she snaps. Bell rolls her eyes and fusses with her satchel, handing Solma two cannisters of water. "One's for Warren," she says. Solma sighs.

"Obviously."

Bell ignores her. "Get off the path as quick as you can," she says. "Head past the orchards and steer clear of the watchtowers. And," she brandishes a trowel at Solma. "Take care of your brother, y'hear?"

She sets off at a steady stride, the satchel bouncing against her hip. Solma watches her go and wonders who on Earth this woman is now. Crazy Aunt Bell? Or the bee expert who came out of the cellar with all those books? She clings to her rifle strap as Warren shuffles up to her with Blume perched on his shoulder. Solma takes one look at him and laughs.

"The Bee Whisperer," she says, smiling.

She stops smiling as the truth of that hits her. If Warren's connection with Blume isn't some kind of

Whispering, what is it? This whole affair gets madder by the hour. She puts an arm on Warren's shoulder—the one that doesn't have the most precious creature known to humanity perched on it—and winks at him.

"Let's get this done, eh?"

They head east out of the village, trying their best to look normal as the planters emerge from their houses and head to the fields. Warren cups Blume close to his chest, hushing her as the bee buzzes in protest.

Solma has covered every inch of village territory during patrol, she's sure of that. She knows every wire fence, every watchtower, every tree in the managed forest. Trudging through the unmanaged land out to the east of the village is not her favorite thing, but it's not unusual. Grass particles burst up into the air as she kicks her way through the growth, feeling the cold touch of dew-ridden shoots skim her ankle. Her blade keeps getting tangled in the damp threads of grass and she wrenches it free so that it comes away fringed with greenery. There's nothing out here. No flowers. There are barely any left in the whole of Alphor. Flowers must be deliberately grown and managed with pollenbots. There was a time when the village was rich enough to do that, but not now.

No flowers. No food for a hungry bee.

She pinches the bridge of her nose against a sudden headache. What are they doing?

Warren treats the whole thing like an adventure. He skips through the grass, which is almost up to his waist, plunging his feet into the growth and giggling as they disappear. Blume is, at turns, riding on his shoulder and buzzing eagerly ahead, flying down to examine patches of sheltered soil before zooming back to Warren. She draws lazy halos around his head. Warren talks to her constantly, jabbering away with utter certainty that she understands him. Which she actually seems to.

If Solma hadn't seen Blume's strange behavior for herself, she'd be certain that Warren is mad. But having witnessed it, she's now certain of something worse: her brother has a power never seen on Alphor. A power that could rival the Earth Whisperers. A power that makes this whole situation more terrifying. Because it won't just be the bees everyone tries to take, will it?

It'll be her brother, too.

She clenches the strap of her rifle tighter.

"C'mon, Warren," she mutters, lengthening her stride. She glances to one side, afraid they're being tailed, but there's no one. Of course there's no one. The planters are all in the fields by now, the orchard workers up tending the trees, and anyway, who else would be mad enough to turn off the path and strike out into the unmanaged grasslands in search of non-existent flowers? Solma's jaw clenches in frustration.

"Warren! Don't go too far ahead!" she calls, waving at him to come back. "Careful of the watchtowers ..."

They travel a wide arc away from the village, careful to avoid the busy orchards and the dark smudge of the watchtowers on the horizon. They traipse through clinging grasses and head south towards the managed forest. Nothing. No flowers. Only an endless desert of tough grass and bare soil.

After an hour, Solma's getting agitated. She tracks the sun as it shuffles across the sky and her eyes keep darting back towards the village. She's supposed to meet her squad in half an hour.

"Warren," she says, hating herself. "Warren, it's no use—"

But he's not listening. He squints into the distance, shielding his eyes while Blume whizzes round his head. Solma frowns.

"What is it?" she asks. "Warren?"

Warren takes off, haring through the grass with a triumphant shout that makes Solma wince.

"Warren!"

She lurches after him, tripping on the grasses. It's only when he stops under the shadow of the ash tree that Solma realizes they've ended up exactly where Bell suggested. A gentle breeze stirs the shimmering birch leaves. Solma leans on her knees to get her breath back.

"Warren ..." she stops, gaping.

"How can—" Solma stutters. "How did—"

Warren grins as Blume settles back on his shoulder, waggling her antennae. He slips his hand into Solma's and the pair of them just stare.

The cluster of trees shields this patch of land from the watchtower and, in their dappled shade, clusters of white flowers bloom. Their petals hang like bells. Blume shivers her wings and buzzes down to investigate. She lands heavily on one flower and the whole thing flops over under her weight. Warren lets out a guffaw, but Blume isn't disheartened. Righting herself, she tries again, this time powering her wings so the flower doesn't take her full weight. She dips her tongue into the bowl of petals and drinks. A little further out from the shade of the trees, there's a smattering of yellow flowers, too, and Blume, delighted, investigates these next.

Warren punches the air and throws his arms round Solma.

"We did it, Sol!" he cries.

"Yeah ..." Solma says, absently. She stares at the flowers, wondering if she's lost it completely. How has she never seen these flecks of white and splashes of yellow on her patrols? Of course, there's little reason for her squad to pass this shady cluster, but surely they'd know if flowers were growing wild on village land?

How did Bell know?

Warren shuffles closer to his bee, watching. Blume now has clumps of yellow dust packed on her back legs and is busy adding to her strange load. Warren glances up at Solma, frowning in question.

Solma shrugs. "Didn't Bell's books say something about them gathering pollen?" she says. "You read it to me." Warren's face clears and he nods, beaming.

"Oh yeah!"

Suddenly, Blume launches herself off her flower and buzzes to the base of a tree. She zigzags across the roots, droning excitedly. Warren scrambles round to see what she's doing and gasps.

Blume has landed in the dirt between two tree roots and as they watch she disappears down a tiny hole. They knock their heads together trying to see where she's gone. Warren clasps his hands together excitedly.

"I hope she likes it," he murmurs. Solma looks at him.

"Likes what?"

"Her new nest," Warren says. "It's perfect, ain't it? Bell was right!"

Solma scowls. It's annoying that Bell was right.

They peer at the dark hollow. Solma tingles with anticipation.

"How will we know—?"

"Shh!" Warren hisses. "Wait!"

Solma scowls but obeys. They seem to stand there forever, staring at the ground, until Solma feels restless. She glances over her shoulder, peering towards the watchtower on the horizon. Her patrol's in a few minutes. They need to go soon. If they're seen ... if they're caught ...

Then Blume's happy vibrato cuts through the silence and she emerges from the hollow, lifting into the warm air. She flies a lazy circle around the burrow. Then another and another, rising higher into the air with each pass. Solma frowns.

"What's she doing? Is she sick?"

Warren chuckles. "I don't reckon so," he whispers. "I bet she's memorizing. She's making a map of the burrow in her mind before she goes to get more pollen."

Solma frowns. "I don't think she's that clever, Warren," she says. Warren flashes her a furious look.

"How would *you* know?" he retorts. "Just 'cos you don't understand her or speak her language, doesn't mean she's stupid!"

Solma opens her mouth to protest, then closes it again. He's got a point.

Suddenly, Blume seems to feel she's done enough mapping and hums off towards the managed forest. They watch her go in silence.

"Right," Solma says after Blume's tremolo song fades into the distance. "Let's leave her to it, eh?"

Warren, of course, kicks up a fuss about having to leave Blume.

Solma checks the sun through the canopy of leaves. She doesn't have time for this.

"Come on, Warren," she says, trying and failing to keep the impatience out of her voice. "Please?"

There's a rustle and snap somewhere up ahead. They both freeze. Solma's rifle is off her shoulder in seconds and she's gathered Warren behind her. They peer between the trees, out into the long grasses beyond. Silence.

Solma is about to relax when a flash of russet catches her attention and she snaps her gaze round just in time to see a figure running in the distance, dressed in Gatra black, with a red braid bouncing against a rifle. Her gut twists.

"Who was it?" Warren whimpers. "Did they see?"

Solma swallows against a sudden lump in her throat, "It was Olive," she whispers. "And I don't know. She might've seen nothing, or ..."

She shoulders her rifle, lungs tight with worry. "... or she might've seen everything."

FIFTEEN

THE KNOCK AT THE door makes Solma and Warren jump. Warren whimpers and drops his spoon. Porridge spatters his knees. Solma reaches across the table and covers his little fist in hers.

"S'ok," she says. "S'alright."

The lies are coming more easily than the truth these days. But Warren isn't fooled. He fixes Solma with his meadow-green stare.

"It might not be," he whispers. "What if she told? What if—?"

The vision of Olive's red braid flashing as she ran from Blume's nesting site bursts into Solma's head again. She shakes it away.

"We don't know for sure ..."

Bell clatters something at the stove, making them both jump again.

"Is one of you gonna answer that?" she demands, "or've I gotta do everything myself?"

Solma glares as she gets up, giving Warren's little fist one more squeeze and wanders over to the door as the knock comes again. The one room of Bell's little house trembles under the impact and the sun clock sways on the wall. Solma draws in a deep breath and sets her face in what she hopes is an innocent expression. It's ok, she tells herself. It's been nearly six weeks since they found Blume a nest, and she's only been back once since. She's pretty certain no one except Olive saw them and, so far, Olive has kept her mouth shut ...

Not that the impossible bee is the only thing Solma has to worry about. That precious promotion she'd been so proud of six weeks ago teeters on a knife edge. Maxen delivered the news to her himself, the day after the raid. Indefinite leave with immediate effect. Steward's orders. Solma's heart spasmed painfully at the prospect and hurts still, every time she thinks about it. Maxen told her it would be fine, but Solma was never so certain. No patrols for six weeks, nothing but planting duties. It's been both boring and humiliating. At least she's barely had any contact with Olive in that time. One less problem to confront.

She pulls the door open a little too quickly and almost hits herself in the face. When she finally meets Blaiz Camber's strong, blue gaze, she sees a flicker of amusement there. She'd known it was him, of course. He's got that way of knocking that rattles the whole house. But seeing the Steward at her front door is doing all sorts of strange things to her insides.

"Steward!" she gasps. "We wasn't expecting you!" (A lie.) "What are you—can we—?"

She reddens and falls silent.

Wordlessly, Blaiz raises an eyebrow. Solma opens and closes her mouth a few times, searching for something to say. "There ain't no more to report at the orchards," she tries, her cheeks flushing with heat. "Piotr reckons he's tackled the rot. The Oritch've been reporting things straight away. I passed everything to Maxen."

Blaiz blinks. "I'm not here about Piotr or the orchards," he says. "Are you going to keep your Steward waiting on the doorstep all morning?"

The heat in Solma's cheeks spreads across her whole face. "No," she stutters. "'Course not."

She shuffles aside, catching her blade in one of the floorboards and stumbling as she gets out of his way. Earth! What's wrong with her?

Blaiz steps into the room, steel-capped boots ring-ing on the wooden floor. As Steward, he doesn't have a uniform color like the other castes, and he wears a loose leather waistcoat over a grey linen shirt and loose trousers, patched at the knees. He runs a hand over his shaved scalp, and his perceptive eyes drift across the room as he enters. His gaze snags on the unmade bed in the corner, which is no more than a large mattress and a heap of blankets, accommodating all three resi-dents. He blinks at Bell as she stands by the stove with a ladle in one hand and the kettle hissing on the fire behind her.

Blaiz smiles. "I would ask for some oat milk," he says. "But our supplies were stolen."

He turns and faces Solma, who forces herself to meet his gaze. The strength of his stare seeps into her blood. Her flesh prickles with sweat.

"Yes, Steward," she says, pouring as much regret into her voice as she can. "In the raid. I'm sorry."

Blaiz raises an eyebrow again. "I'm here to review your situation," he says. "You left your post."

Behind Blaiz, Solma sees both Warren and Bell flinch. Warren's brows draw into a frown and he opens his mouth as if to offer Solma defense, but Bell's hand lands on his shoulder and she gives a barely perceptible shake of her head. Warren scowls but obeys.

If Blaiz senses any of this, he gives no sign, only waits for Solma to reply. Solma searches his eyes. He knows the answer. He's put her on leave for this last six weeks, giving himself time to think over her position.

"Yes, Sir," she answers eventually, unable to think of anything else to say. "I did. My brother ... he was in danger and ...Sir, I couldn't leave him. They was trying to kidnap him."

Blaiz frowns. "They were trying to distract you," he says. "And it worked."

She can't argue with that. Not without admitting that Warren had something the raiders seemed to want. Not without disclosing what that something is.

Would that be so bad? Perhaps he'd forgive her secrecy if she admitted it now. Perhaps he'd be merciful.

She almost says it, almost opens her mouth and lets the whole story tumble out.

There's a clatter and a splash behind her. Bell swears. "Earth's *sake!*" she snaps, then, "Sorry, Steward. It's just ... Long days in the field, you know? Gets to us all. I was talking to Gerta about it the other day. 'Course, it weren't so bad back when she was a Fei ..."

Solma stares at her aunt as Bell bustles about, dropping to the floor with a cloth and scrubbing while she talks. She's blathering like an anxious teenager.

But her eyes never leave Solma's, and there's warning in them.

Solma snatches a glance at Blaiz as he waits for Bell to stop dithering. He's losing patience. It's obvious. That cool veneer slips ever so slightly, a vein twitching in his temple. For the first time, Solma notices differences between Blaiz and everyone else: he's thin, yes, but not as thin as many of the villagers. He's taller than most, fed well on larger rations. His eyes are not that watery grey Solma is used to seeing, his skin not puckered with freckles from the sun, hands not calloused.

But Blaiz isn't greedy. He can't lead from the fields or make decisions on a starved gut, can he? He is doing this for the village, surely ...

Solma thinks about that girl he exiled all those years ago, how she'd walked into the unknown and was never seen again. She was only a few years older than Warren is now, Solma thinks. And Solma's already deep into this secret. She swallows down the truth and hopes her shame doesn't show in her face.

Eventually, Bell runs out of breath and gets to her feet. Her cheeks glow pink, but the distraction has done its job. Solma sags under the weight of defeat.

"I fell for it, Sir," she says. "I'm sorry."

Blaiz's face relaxes, as if he'd expected this. "Luckily for you, my son is an advocate for your defense. He assures me you are a good fighter, that you were instrumental in ensuring our losses were not total, and that you would have done the same for any villager, not just your brother."

That's not entirely true, Solma thinks. But she's not about to argue the point.

"Yes, Sir."

"So," Blaiz continues. "I have agreed to let you keep your position. For now. As a favor to my son. And because I know you are honest and loyal. I know this was a mistake, so I will forgive you this once. For this one mistake."

He stares at her intently, his blue eyes unblinking. Solma's heart lurches. Maxen must have argued hard for her, risked his Dja's displeasure. But Blaiz's words feel flint-sharp and he's aimed them well. Still, relief floods Solma so fast it makes her dizzy. She lowers her gaze and nods.

"Thank you, Steward," she whispers.

Blaiz clasps his hands behind his back. Bell places a steaming mug of tea in front of him and he smiles, taking a seat. Bell hands Warren a cup of water, but she doesn't sit.

"I know you are loyal to our cause, Solma," Blaiz says, taking a delicate sip.

Shakily, Solma sits next to Warren.

"I am, Sir," she says.

Blaiz takes another sip.

"So I know you will help me with this if you can."

He pauses again, examining the contents of his mug as steam curls from within. Solma can't help herself. She leans forward. Blaiz fixes her with those eyes that see more than human eyes have any business seeing.

"I've had reports," he says slowly, "of most unusual sightings. They're impossible, of course, but I can't dismiss them out of hand. I expect you will find this laughable, but several planters and orchard workers have suggested they might have spotted an insect that looks like a bee."

He waits, letting the accusation hang in the air. Solma feels Warren kick her under the table and she gasps.

"R-really?" she stutters, affecting surprise. This is bad. The worst. This means an outright lie.

It's been getting so easy to lie, lately. But ... lie to the *Steward?*

Blaiz watches her, searching her face. Solma realizes her fists are clenched under the table and forces herself to relax, trying to control the tremble in her fingertips.

"So, you haven't seen this mythical bee yourself, Sergeant?"

It takes every ounce of strength Solma has to shake her head. "No, sir."

Blaiz is silent for a moment.

"Because," he says, after a while, "it would be miraculous if such a creature existed. And I'm sure you would tell me if you were aware of its existence."

"'Course," Solma agrees. How is it possible to lie to her Steward twice in a single breath?

Blaiz stares into his mug. "Good," he says. "Because I'm sure you understand what it could mean, a bee colony in our village. It could boost our riches, boost our status. And every other village in the province ... Earth, every other village in Alphor ... will feel the same. But if there are bees here, Sergeant—" he meets her gaze again, "—they are ours."

Solma lowers her gaze. She can almost smell the cloying smoke, feel the heat of the fires that burned across the world. She squeezes her eyes closed, and sees the man driving his spade into the nest again. The ground littered with bodies.

"Yes, sir." She whispers.

Blaiz examines her face and Solma tenses. She wonders if he smells her lie, hears the tremble in her every word. Blaiz sips the last of his tea.

"If there are bees," he says. "They will need to be monitored. Insects are tricky creatures, Sergeant."

Solma feels her skin prickle under that glare.

"They don't understand what's important," Blaiz continues. "They need to be regulated—"

"No, sir!" Warren interrupts. Solma jumps at his voice and whips round in her chair, glaring at him hard. She gives a subtle shake of her head, eyes wide with warning, but Warren hasn't noticed. His eyes are fixed on Blaiz.

"Actually, that's not true, they're—"

Bell knocks hard into the table, spilling Warren's cup of water all over him. Warren yelps at the sudden cold and Bell sets about scolding him as thoroughly as she can.

"Oh, for Earth's *sake*, Warren!"

Warren, both dripping wet and open-mouthed with confusion, begins to protest, but Bell bustles him out of his chair. He stamps his foot, frustrated by the injustice.

"It weren't me—!"

Bell barely leaves room for him to defend himself. Instead, she hounds him about his carelessness until Warren, teary-eyed with puzzlement, kneels with her on the floor to help mop up this latest mess. Bell spews another torrent of apologies at Blaiz and Solma turns away from the commotion, struggling to keep the fear off her face. Blaiz's eyes meet hers. They're full of triumph, glittering with something Solma can't put her finger on. He's clever. Warren's thoughtless outburst might be enough to seal their fate ...

A shout from outside makes everyone except Blaiz jump. Warren leaps to his feet and Bell grabs his arm before he can run to the window. She gives him a warning look, then turns away so Blaiz won't see her fear. But Blaiz is distracted. He strides to the window and leans out as villagers rush past, shouting and smiling. A flock of the youngest children totter by, banging on doors as they go.

"Come out! Come out!" they laugh and scurry on.

Blaiz smiles. "I believe the Earth Whisperers have arrived," he says. He drops a hand onto Solma's shoulder as she passes. "You are a loyal villager and a strong Gatra, Solma."

Solma wonders, briefly, how true those things are. She doesn't feel like a loyal villager. She doesn't feel like a strong Gatra, either. She just feels sick.

"I'm sure," Blaiz says quietly, "my son is right about you. You will keep me informed. And not a word of this to anyone. Especially not the Whisperers. You have made one mistake already, El Gatra. Do not let me down again."

Solma nods, not trusting herself to speak, and watches Blaiz as he sees himself out.

SIXTEEN

A YELLOW MIST HANGS at ankle height where dozens of feet have kicked up dust on their way by. Solma holds Warren's hand and they follow the laughter south. Her belly churns and her breath comes in short gasps. She can't help it, no matter how she tries. It's probably just relief that the Earth Whisperers have arrived (even if they are late, as usual).

Nothing to do with the raid, the bee, Blaiz's visit. Just plain relief ...

"Ouch!" Warren cries. Solma starts and glances down at him. "Sol, you're hurting me! Quit holding my hand so tight."

Solma loosens her grip. "I'm sorry," she mutters. "Come on, we'll miss them otherwise."

Warren breaks free and runs ahead and Solma quickens her own pace to keep up. Ahead, the villagers gather, clapping and stamping, jostling to get a better look. Solma clenches her teeth, irritated by how much the Whisperers are celebrated, despite turning up late and doing little to ensure a good harvest. Their arrival is hidden from view, and Solma realizes she wants to see, though it'll only be the same as every year: the line of sage Whisperers with their heads shaved, regardless of their gender, their bare feet treading carefully, their forest green robes swishing about their ankles, their hands clasped together as if in one of the old prayers. Though tinged with bitterness, her childhood memories pull at her and she runs faster, excitement building like it did when she was Warren's age, back when she saw the Whisperers as heroes, and ran to greet them with Ma and Dja.

She wishes so badly they were here.

Bell wouldn't come with them, which is not unusual.

"They're late," she'd said stiffly. "And I dunno why we always treat them like old world royalty. They got a job to do, same as everyone else."

Solma's inclined to agree, but her brother's big, green eyes were impossible to say no to. Bell turned back to her stove, muttering about how the last of the pork wouldn't salt itself. So, Solma quietly took Warren's hand and left her to it.

Now, though, she's glad she did. Even with Blaiz's warning echoing in her mind and the terrible fact that she's broken the law, the joy of the villagers is still infectious, pushing through her fear like some persistent flower.

Like a bee emerging after a hundred years ...

Solma reaches the back of the crowd and finds Warren stamping his little feet in frustration. "I can't see!" he rages. Solma chuckles and grabs him round the waist, hoisting him up onto her shoulders. He's getting heavy, almost too big for this now, but she shifts the strap of her rifle to make room and he sits as tall as he can. He throws his hands into the air and shouts with delight.

Because they've finally arrived. And their powers will wake the soil and the crop will grow. It has to. Solma clamps down on her distrust. They're here. They're late, but they're here. It's better than nothing.

The crowd parts and Solma gets her first glimpse of the Whisperers in a year. There are seven of them this time, dressed in long green robes with bare feet and soft smiles. They're a smaller band than last year, and younger, too. Their leader looks to be little older than Solma herself, with his head bowed, his hands pressed lightly together in front of him. His mouth works softly, whispering something. His skin is deep black and he's taller than any of the villagers, clearly from a province either more prosperous than Southtip, or more capable of coping. Behind him come six others, three boys and three girls, a mix of skin-tones and ages. The littlest, a boy smaller than Warren, clasps the lead rope of two stocky, tan ponies pulling a cart, heavily loaded and covered with sack-cloth. The oldest girl doesn't seem more than fourteen or fifteen. They all carry hemp satchels slung loosely over one shoulder.

Solma holds Warren's legs and squints against the glare of the morning sun.

There's one girl there, a girl whose pale skin splashed with freckles seems somehow familiar.

But when the girl looks up, her gentle gaze meeting Solma's, Solma no longer recognizes her. The girl's gaze drops and Solma shuffles back into the crowd so the procession can file past her to where Blaiz and Maxen are waiting. They're both smiling and clapping too, but more out of politeness, it seems, than excitement.

The lead Whisperer pauses before Blaiz, drops his hands to his side and meets the Steward's gaze. Blaiz holds out his hand in greeting.

"You're late, my friend," he says, smiling. There's a nervous titter in the crowd. The Whisperer stares at Blaiz's hand and then up into his face. He doesn't offer his own hand in reply.

"Our apologies," he says, his voice deep and rumbling. Solma can't place his accent, though it sounds western. "We have been chasing some ... strange rumors."

Blaiz drops both his hand and his smile at once. "With all due respect, Whisperer, our village cannot wait on rumor. We lost our stores in a raid six weeks ago and are struggling to trade for goods. Only the dedication of our Gathering Guard is keeping our people alive. We needed you sooner."

The crowd is silent now, no longer smiling. They shift uncomfortably and someone coughs. A child wails and its mother hushes it. Beside Blaiz, Maxen reddens and stares at his feet.

The Whisperer blinks, his face still a picture of serenity. He opens his arms and the six others he brought with him break from their single file line and come to huddle around him, their hands still pressed together, their heads bowed.

"We heard about your raid," their leader says. "We have brought some things ..."

The six others unshoulder their hemp satchels and reach within them. The youngest drops the ponies' lead rope and scuttles round the cart, uncovering the goods within. Heads still bowed, they reveal bread, salted fish and meat, produce from some of the surrounding villages. There's some seed, too, to help with planting. It isn't much, won't compensate for the loss if their harvest is poor this year, but the gesture is appreciated. The crowd bursts into generous applause until Blaiz, unsmiling, holds up his hand. Solma hoists Warren off her shoulders and grabs one of his hands so he can't clap. He wriggles unhappily but submits sensing the strange atmosphere as well. Something is happening.

"I have not yet had the pleasure of your name," Blaiz says to the leader. The vein in his temple twitches and Solma grabs the strap of her rifle to stop her hand from trembling. The lead Whisperer inclines his head.

"My group," he says, gesturing to the child-Whisperers around him, "call me Mamba,"

Solma gulps down a shudder. Taking the name of a snake is not unusual for Earth Whisperers when they are inducted. When a youngster is discovered to have Whispering ability, they step away from their village into a new identity, their power belonging to no-one and everyone. Solma knows Whisperers hold snakes in great reverence, close as they always are to the earth or trees. But Mamba is an unusual title; one of the deadliest snakes in Alphor, it is responsible for many deaths in the western provinces where it lives. Even the Whisperers treat it with caution.

Warren wriggles at her side. "Sol, you're squishing my fingers again," he complains. Solma loosens her grip and glares him into silence. He scowls, lower lips quivering in confusion.

Mamba presses his hands back into prayer position. "Perhaps you can help us," he says, bowing his head once again. "We have been tracking an ... unusual ... band of raiders: large, uniformed, well fed and fiercely armed. And far too quick to set things on fire."

Blaiz's vein jumps. "Pity you did not catch up to them before they decimated our village," he says, his tone accusatory. Mamba barely reacts.

"We thought as much," he admits. "We think they were after something. Something ... impossible."

Solma's gut twists. Her ears clang, which makes it difficult to hear anything important. She squeezes her eyes shut, trying not to see the raiders again; one lifting Warren high into the air as he kicks and clasps Blume to his chest, the other reaching out for his cupped hands, as if knowing what treasure Warren held ...

Blaiz's face is inscrutable. Beside him, Maxen shifts his weight and glances towards Solma. Their eyes meet and Solma pours her confusion into her gaze, hoping that Maxen will understand. He just shrugs.

The silence lengthens until Mamba gives a gentle smile.

"We would also like to test some of your young-sters," he says. "For abilities."

Blaiz's face darkens and Solma grips Warren's hand tighter, despite his protests. She doesn't know how they do it, but a Whisperer can always feel the pow-er of another Whisperer, even if it lies dormant in a young child. It's how they always find and whisk youngsters away, no matter how carefully their fam-ilies try to hide them.

"None of our children have shown an ability," Blaiz says curtly. "If they had, we'd have sent word."

None of the Whisperers say anything, but the al-most-familiar girl shifts slightly and clasps her hands together.

Blaiz glares, but stands aside and gestures for Mam-ba and the Whisperers to precede him along the path towards the village.

"Perhaps we had better take this conversation some-where more discreet," he says, his voice strained and displeased. Mamba hesitates briefly.

"My Whisperers are tired," he says. "And the ponies need water. May I request we rest before I meet with you? We will set up camp away from the village."

Blaiz looks put out, but agrees. He steps aside for the Whisperers.

Solma's heart squeezes. She almost lurches forward and cries for them to wait, but Maxen catches her gaze again.

"I'll tell you later," he mouths. Solma sways restless-ly, desperate to follow. This is about Blume, it must be. But how? And worry makes her cling to Warren tighter. Could it be his ability the Whisperers sensed?

Maxen stares at her hard. "I'll tell you *later*," he mouths again, eyes full of warning. Solma resists for a moment, but Blaiz and the Whisperers are already on their way to the Steward's house. The crowd begins to disperse. Solma sighs and nods, mouthing thanks at him. He offers her a small smile and she finds that gesture fortifying in a way she can't explain. Maxen Camber: honest as the summer is long. She feels a rush of affection for him and quells it quickly before it brings heat to her cheeks. Thankfully, Maxen doesn't see. He turns to follow his father. Solma takes a deep breath, turning back towards home ...

And freezes.

Because there is Olive, a fading bruise extending halfway across her face, glaring at her, mouth working slowly around that damn sugar cane.

Warren notices her and whimpers, squeezing Solma's hand. The surrounding noise dies away—villagers returning to their duties—until it's just the three of them. Solma rallies herself. It's not like she hasn't seen Olive since the day they found Blume's nest, albeit from a distance. But now, after that bizarre exchange between Blaiz and the Whisperers, Solma remembers Olive's flashing red braid disappearing into the tall grass. She meets Olive's gaze as the other girl's jaw rotates around her sugar cane.

"Hey, Olive," she says, trying and failing to affect nonchalance. "Wonder what that was about?"

Olive continues to stare. "You'd know," she says, green eyes hard with accusation. Fear flickers in Solma's belly, but before she can say anything, Olive turns and stalks after the crowds.

SEVENTEEN

THE FEI ARE BACK in the fields by the time Solma and Warren trudge home. The Aldren are installed in rickety old porch chairs, managing the Yuen. Solma frowns at the crude repairs the village has managed after the raid. Mismatched timber covers broken windows and new mud covers damage to the walls. Solma watches the village activity and feels somehow separated from it, everything blurry and muted. They head into the house where Bell is waiting at the stove.

"I'm starving!" Warren announces, and Solma's heart kicks, she knows he's not exaggerating.

Still, she rubs away a smudge of dirt on his chin and says, "No you're not. C'mon, Bell has fresh bread, I can smell it."

Bell glares at her. "I'd like at least one loaf of bread to last beyond the end of the day," she mutters, but as Solma helps Warren unwrap the rags from his feet, she sees Bell slicing the loaf. Steam curls from the knife and the soft scent of fresh bread oozes through the house, settling Solma's tight gut.

She flops into a chair beside Warren as Bell places a board of sliced bread in front of them both. Warren lunges for the thickest slice and crams most of it into his mouth before remembering his manners. He emits a muffled "Thank you," when Bell glares at him and devotes his attention to devouring as many slices as possible.

Solma picks at her own slice, chewing pieces slowly in the hopes that this might trick her body into feeling full. It never works, but she keeps trying.

Bell flicks her eyes towards the open door, checking for wandering eyes and keen ears, before she whispers, "Sol, did you go check this morning?"

Solma's stomach lurches and she abandons her bread on the table. She casts Warren a sideways glance and nods. "Still no sign," she says. "But I couldn't stay long."

Warren's gusto for eating falters. "You still ain't seen Blume?" he says, voice loud with panic. Solma kicks him.

"Ouch!"

"Speak quietly!"

Warren scowls as he rubs his knee and Solma, getting sick of these rolling waves of guilt, gives him the rest of her bread. Warren's knee magically stops hurting. He gobbles the steaming slice in a matter of seconds.

Bell cleans her hands on her apron. "I had another look at your Ma's old books," she says softly. "Queen buff-tails need to incubate their first brood. She's probably sitting on her eggs."

Warren licks his finger and dabs up a few scattered crumbs from the table, "Won't she get hungry?" he asks, "She was hungry all the time before she found her nest."

Bell smiles. "Almost as hungry as you always are!" she laughs. "Yes, she prob'ly will be. But she knows where my lavender is."

Warren doesn't look convinced.

"What I worry about," Bell says, more to herself than anyone else, "Is someone might see her. And after what Blaiz said, it sounds like they already have."

The three of them fall silent. They're each still in their own thoughts when the voice at the door makes them all jump.

"Already seen who?"

Bell drops a cloth and utters such an un-Bell-like string of oaths that Solma gapes at her. She crouches and makes a show of gathering her cloth but Solma sees how her face has colored. Warren scrambles from his chair and draws himself up to his full three-and-a-half foot height, glaring at the visitor.

"What do you want?" he demands.

At this Solma, finally turns towards the door. And stops.

"Oh," she says, tensing again. "Hello."

A boy and a girl stand at the door. The boy is Mamba. Solma bristles as she meets his unfathomably black eyes. His expression is hard and he holds her gaze, unyielding. Solma's hand twitches as she resists reaching for her knife. Tricksters and frauds they might be, but nobody harms a Whisperer. Solma settles for glaring at him.

The girl bows her shaved head and presses her hands together in the typical greeting of Earth Whisperers. The climbing sun catches on her spring-green robe and Solma sees threads of gold woven into the fabric. She stares, trying to stop her fists from clenching. What could these two possibly want?

The girl lifts her gaze and fixes her eyes on Warren. Solma sees the splash of freckles across the girl's face, the russet-red fuzz of her shaved hair, her green-grey eyes. It's the same girl she'd thought looked familiar when the Whisperers first arrived, and no wonder. With dappled skin and red hair, she could be from around here. But her posture, her stillness, her power are all Earth Whisperer. She searches Solma's face for a moment, as if she expects something, but whatever it is, she doesn't seem to find it. She sighs.

"I'm sorry to disturb you," she says. "My name is Cobra, and this is Mamba. We were hoping to speak with Warren."

Solma feels the air sucked from her lungs, the words a punch in her gut. She almost asks how Cobra knows Warren's name but that would be pointless. Whisperers always know more than they have any business to.

"He's seven," she gasps instead, clutching her belly in fear. "He's too old for your lot to take him. He ain't shown any sign of Whispering—"

Her protests fall still as Cobra's eyes meet hers again. "That's not true, is it?" the Whisperer says softly. "Don't worry, Solma, we only want to talk with him. You can come too. We're going for a walk."

Like hells, they are. Solma's hand grabs Warren's before she can stop it, her other hand reaches for her rifle strap.

"Where to?" she demands. "What for?"

Earth! Could they be after her brother? Solma's heard stories of villagers who have discovered power in their children and tried to hide them, to save them from being snatched away by these nomadic tricksters. But the Whisperers always know, and the children are always taken. Whispering belongs to everyone and no-one. It's the law of Alphor, though who wrote that law, Solma doesn't know. All she knows is she'll die before she sees them take her brother.

Cobra touches her palms together again, waiting in that confounded silence that Earth Whisperers all enjoy so much.

Warren squirms away from Solma, leaning towards the door. "Sol, I want to go—"

"No!" Solma snaps, more harshly than she'd intended. Doesn't he understand? She promised Ma and Dja she'd keep him safe. How can she do that if he's taken away by the Whisperers?

Beside Cobra, Mamba bristles. He places a hand on Cobra's arm. "Maybe this is a bad idea," he says, but Cobra doesn't respond. Mamba stares from Solma to Warren and back again.

"Come on, Co," he says. "I can come back and test the boy later. Why don't you go back to camp?"

Cobra says nothing, only shakes her head ever so slightly. "No," she murmurs. "No hiding."

There's a long silence. Warren stamps his foot in frustration and then tugs on Solma's sleeve.

It's Bell's voice that finally decides the issue.

"Let him go, Sol," she says softly. "Go with him if you must, but don't stop him. It ain't fair."

Solma clenches her jaw, still holding onto Warren's little hand. Of course it isn't fair. Nothing is fair. But ...

"Whispering is a precious ability," Cobra murmurs. "It doesn't belong to any one province or nation. It's a power to be shared equally. In this way, we maintain peace. If Warren has the ability, we must know."

The words ring in Solma's ears. Shared equally. Maintain Peace. She bristles, but something stirs in her mind at the same time: the smell of burning, bee bodies littering the ground ...

"Because of the Hive Wars," she whispers, feeling a flicker of satisfaction when both Cobra and Mamba glance up in surprise.

"Solma!" Bell hisses, but Solma ignores her. Whisperers work by their own rules.

"That's why, ain't it?" she continues. "We destroyed the insects 'cos we couldn't share. So now we gotta share the Whispering."

The surprise on Cobra's face only lasts a moment before it falls back into that familiar serenity, "Yes," she admits. "Although not every Steward is good at keeping that rule."

The memory of Blaiz's visit, only that morning, resurfaces in Solma's mind. Not a word, he'd said, especially not to the Whisperers. But he'd said that for their protection, surely? Because Whisperers can't be trusted. He'd said that so Warren could stay at home, so their family could be together.

Except ...

Solma releases Warren's hand and doesn't try to stop him when he leaps towards the door. He bounces to Cobra and takes her hand in his. She smiles at him. Stood together like that, their skin almost the same hue, their freckles match for match, Solma permits herself a small stab of jealousy. There really is something horribly familiar about that girl. Whisperers. Condescending fools. She'll be damned if Cobra's going to take her brother away from her. No way.

"I'll wrap his feet," she says. "And I'm coming, too."

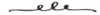

Solma curses as her blade catches in the grass again. She tugs it free and glares at Cobra's back. What was wrong with the path? Bloody Whisperers. Warren skips ahead, chattering to Cobra, who drifts effortlessly through the tangled, grassy wilderness, smiling at Warren the whole time.

Whisperers are so annoying.

Mamba, though, is different. He keeps separate from everyone, wandering ahead, then drifting back, then falling into step beside Solma to ask if it was necessary for her to bring that rifle. Solma scowls at him.

"I ain't gonna shoot you, if that's what you're worried about," she snaps. "We don't shoot Earth Whisperers."

Doesn't mean she has to trust them, though.

Mamba says nothing, but his gaze flickers towards Cobra. He strides ahead. Solma rolls her eyes and hitches her rifle higher onto her shoulder, glancing at the sun. Back on duty now, her patrol starts in an hour. With Maxen at his father's side, preparing the village for the Whisperers, it'll be Solma in charge today. This ridiculous escapade had better not take long.

Solma wipes sweat from her eyes. It's already sweltering. Among these grasses, there's no shade and the stillness of the air only adds to the oppressive heat. The Whisperers' ability to persuade the earth to yield will only get them so far without rainfall. And now, with the storehouse raided, they need a miracle.

Solma silences that thought before it can take hold. No sense panicking. Still. She can't stop the image of Olive's accusing face bursting into the forefront of her brain as she trudges after Cobra and Warren.

What was all that about?

You'd know ...

Had Olive told after all? It's been weeks and no one's come to batter down their door yet. Instead, they've had Blaiz, quietly bringing his accusation to their home, those blue eyes drilling into her, trying to breach her secret.

Solma fights through the clinging grasses. She's so lost in her own torment that she doesn't realize where they're headed until Warren shouts her name. She looks up and her heart squeezes.

It's been only a day since she last crept out to the ash tree to check on Blume, but there'd been no

sign of the bee and Solma left quickly, in case someone—Olive—was watching.

Now here she is again. The last place she wants to be.
She stares at Cobra and her brother, hand in hand, beneath the boughs of those trees, the site of her crime.

"Look where we are, Sol!" Warren says, beaming
and bouncing on his heels. He's forgotten himself.
He's about to say it, about to blurt their terrible secret
out in front of this complete stranger. He throws his
hand up into the air.

"It's—"

"Trees!" Solma shouts, cutting him off. "Yeah, I
know, Warren! It's a bunch of trees!"

She scowls at him, hoping he can read her warning,
but he's oblivious. He spins on the spot, arms out-
stretched.

"We came here a bit ago when we were looking for
... and we ..."

He realizes suddenly and stops dead, the smile gone
from his face. He stares up at Cobra like a puppy that's
been caught with its snout in the pie. Solma places a
hand on his shoulder and glares at Cobra, daring her
curiosity. But Cobra says nothing, and even Mamba,
who wanders between the trees, seems uninterested.

Solma's eyes narrow. Whisperers. They always know things. She doesn't trust this lack of curiosity.

Cobra inclines her head. Solma's beginning to find this constant deference infuriating. She's not bowing back, if that's what Cobra's after.

"It's beautiful here," Cobra says. "I can see why you like it. And a perfect spot for our test."

The pit drops from Solma's stomach. "Test?"

Cobra smiles. "It's very simple," she says. "Look, Warren, kneel down next to me and I'll show you."

Solma doesn't want Warren to kneel next to Cobra. Or be anywhere near her at all. Especially not here. Her eyes flicker towards the burrow under the nearest tree root. Blume might emerge from her nest at any moment and blow her world apart. But the nest is silent and by the time Solma's attention returns to Warren, he's squatting in the dirt beside the wretched Earth Whisperer, watching with wide-eyed fascination.

Solma rolls her eyes and unshoulders her rifle. "I'll keep watch, then."

Cobra blinks up at her. "For what?"

Solma gives her what she hopes is a withering look. "I—"

But it's a good question. What, exactly, is she expecting? The watchtower dogs keep redbears and sabrecats away and the only other thing to worry about is Olive. Who's been keeping the secret long enough, now, that it's her burden, too. Solma sighs and drops to her knees with Warren and Cobra, placing her rifle beside her. Somewhere in the shade, she thinks she sees Mamba trying to suppress a smile. She scowls at the soil.

"Fine," she says. "Come on, let's get this over with."

Whisperers do her head in. They're all so well-spoken, like something from the past, like they're looking down on folk who haven't had time to learn reading and writing so they can study the land they work. Solma's heard stories of Whisperer camps in the north where they've got whole libraries dedicated to the world they manage. Everyone knows Whisperers can read. Wouldn't it be nice to have that sort of time on your hands? And Cobra's calm smile and constant bowing is so annoying it makes Solma want to be sick ...

Or maybe that's from the fear of what she might be offering Warren. Solma can't decide.

"Ok, Warren," Cobra says. "Watch closely."

She holds her hands flat, like two shovels, and carefully presses them into the soil. She doesn't jab them into the earth, like Solma has seen Whisperers do before, but coaxes the ground to let her in. When her hands are into the Earth up to her thumbs she closes her eyes and breathes slowly. Suddenly, her eyebrows raise and she lets out a gasp, making both Solma and Warren jump. She begins to Whisper something. Solma can't be sure what it is. Since she was little, she's always imagined it to be a plea.

Please grow, little one, please grow ...

But she doesn't know, because she doesn't have that power. Watching Cobra, though, stirs something in her. She's not sure what, but it's an old feeling. And it hurts. It hurts enough that she sits back on her haunches and closes her eyes.

When she finally opens them, Warren is leaning forward, his little hands pressed against the ground as he concentrates. Despite herself, Solma leans in, too, watching the ground between Cobra's hands as it begins to lift, something beneath it trying to break loose. A little green shoot breaks the surface, unfurling delicate, papery leaves. It climbs towards Cobra as if she's the sun. When it is six inches or so, Cobra inhales deeply and withdraws her hands, examining the little plant in front of her.

"We don't want to give them too much," she explains. "Or you wear yourself out and the plant never learns how to grow on its own. All we do is wake them up and give them a head start."

She nods at Warren. "If you've got the gift," she says. "You'll be able to do this. It won't be easy and it'll make you tired, and you probably won't manage to push the plant to more than a couple of inches high, but we'll see it. You want to give it a try?"

Warren's grin is so huge it almost wraps around his whole head. He nods eagerly and Solma's heart feels like a loaded weapon.

"You don't gotta do this, Warren," she hisses. Cobra fixes her with a soft, green stare.

"This is more important than anything, Solma," she says. "Let him try."

Warren doesn't need telling twice. He nestles his muddy knees into the dirt, his little tongue poking from between his teeth as he shoves his narrow hands into the dirt. Far from the serene picture Cobra cast, Warren is a bundle of energy, desperate to please. His eyes move rapidly under tightly closed lids and his mouth trembles, anticipating the moment when his mind finds a dormant seed.

Solma can neither bear to watch nor bring herself to turn away. She's felt heartbreak before and recognizes its ache; the pain of watching someone moving away from you and being unable to follow. Warren's losing definition before her eyes, his edges blurring. Or perhaps that's just frightened tears. Solma wipes her eyes when she's certain no one's looking.

After ten long minutes, Warren sits back, deflated. He stares at Cobra, his little mouth turned down at the corners. "I can't do it," he whimpers. "It feels strange ... I can't ..."

He shakes his head. For the first time, Cobra seems genuinely surprised. She's gentle, though, which makes Solma hate her a little less.

"It's alright, Warren," she says. "Did you feel any seeds underground, even if you couldn't make them grow?"

Warren shakes his head and dizzy relief overwhelms Solma for a moment.

"No," Warren whispers. "I felt ... it felt like ... I don't know."

"Like silence?" Cobra suggests. Warren hesitates for a moment, then nods his head, looking confused.

Cobra almost seems disappointed and Solma fights the stab of smugness in her gut. Poor girl was only trying to help. Easier to say that now, though. Now that she *isn't* spiriting Warren away.

Cobra puts a quiet hand on Warren's shoulder.

"Never mind," she says as Mamba comes to join them, a frown furrowing his brow. "Well done for trying. Come on, let's take you home."

Warren clambers to his feet, despondent. Solma tries to squeeze his shoulder but he wrenches away. That hurts more, Solma realizes, than his success would have done.

They trudge home in silence.

~ A MOMENT ~

NONE OF THE FOUR figures heading home looks back. If they did, their gaze might have fallen on the spot where Warren knelt and tried to persuade the plants to grow.

The soil his hands touched begins to move, now that there are no people around to witness it. It bulges, something beneath it trying to push free. Gradually, whatever it is fights its way to the surface. But what emerges is not a plant. It's green, soft and covered in fine hairs, bright as a jewel and far more precious, with a dark, blunt head, two black eyes at the front and two rows of strange, pointed limbs. It undulates towards the sun, lifts itself into the light and takes in the world for the first time.

There isn't a name, anymore, for what this is. At least, not one that's used regularly.

But if Solma and Warren had seen it, and had rushed home to tell Aunt Bell, and had scrambled through her books to identify it, they would have found a picture of this tiny creature. They would have learned it was once called a caterpillar, and that, like the bees, no one has seen one for a long time.

They might also have seen a red-haired girl of Solma's age emerge from where she'd been kneeling in the tall grass. She creeps towards the trees, kneeling before the caterpillar, her freckled face shining with awe. They'd have seen her hoist her rifle out of the way and carefully offer the creature her hands, squirming as it clambered aboard. They'd have seen her transport it to the ash tree where it could not be crushed by an indiscriminate foot.

They'd have seen her stare back towards the village, and the four disappearing figures, waiting until they were far enough away for her to follow without being seen.

EIGHTEEN

AFTER A WEEK, EVEN Bell is fed up with Warren's moping. She shoves a plate of bread towards him, glaring.

"Will you eat, please?"

Warren groans and pushes the plate away. Solma's bread feels like sand in her mouth as she watches her little brother's head drop heavily onto the table. Torn between fear and annoyance, she kicks him in the shin.

"Warren, you gotta eat!"

Warren ignores her. Sometimes she thinks the sole aim in a little brother's life is to irritate his older sister. Warren can turn that into an art when he wants. Today, Solma is done with it.

"Eat your bread, Warren!"

Now, Bell is somehow on Warren's side again. "Don't shout at him!" she snaps. "He's just a kid—"

"*You* just shouted at him!"

"I did not," Bell says, with that infuriating superiority she has. "I gave him a stern command."

Solma opens her mouth, armed with an arsenal of retorts, when a voice at the open front door ends the argument. Probably a good thing, really.

"Sol?"

Solma whirls round, suddenly aware she hasn't combed her hair this morning and there are breadcrumbs on her chin. "Maxen!"

She scrambles to wipe her face then changes her mind halfway through and tries to smooth her hair, which means she just ends up swiping maniacally at her head. She desists and hopes the heat in her cheeks doesn't show.

Warren lifts his head from the table, enjoying his sister's odd behavior. A knowing smirk plays at the corners of his mouth. With immense difficulty, Solma resists the urge to kick him.

Maxen hovers at the threshold, waiting for Bell to invite him in. She doesn't.

"Hey, Maxen," she says stiffly, and begins to clear the plates away. She fixes Warren with a glare, pointedly pushing his plate closer before she carries the rest of the crockery to the sink, which is actually just a basin of water balanced on a crate. Solma watches her aunt wrestling the grease from the china and wonders if there is a real sink with pumping water at Maxen's house. Probably.

"I was wondering," Maxen says. "If I could speak with you?"

Warren giggles behind his hand and Solma does kick him this time.

"Ow!" he protests. "Sol, don't kick with your lucky leg!"

Solma kicks him again with her boot. "Better?"

Warren glowers and picks moodily at his bread. Bell hisses something at him and Warren bursts into tears.

"Yeah, sure," Solma says quickly. "I'll grab my rifle."

Anything to get away from her crazed family.

She kicks off her boot and grabs its laces. No point wearing it out further until evening patrol, and she likes to feel soil beneath her foot. She rushes Maxen from the house as Bell starts haranguing Warren again.

"Will you eat that bread!"

Solma shuts the door on Warren's wails and offers Maxen what she hopes is an apologetic smile.

"What's up?" she asks. Maxen's face doesn't seem able to settle on any expression and Solma feels her own gut kick. "Everything alright?"

Maxen grabs her hand and begins to pull her south, turning off the path into the unkempt grasses below the orchards, the same unkempt grasses Solma fought through a week ago only to see Warren fail spectacularly at his Whispering test. She can't seem to get away from this place.

The sun sinks, its lower edge kissing the horizon. It's cold this evening. Solma's arms prickle with goosebumps. She sees the cluster of trees silhouetted against a sky painted gold with evening. Why does everything bring her back here?

"Maxen, wait—"

He stops, still holding her hand. "You ok?"

"Yeah, I—" she can't think of an excuse and, in the long pause, she bends down to rub her knee.

"Lucky leg?" Maxen asks. "Is it slipping?"

Solma leaps on the suggestion. "Yes! Sorry," she says, "It's the cold. Can I adjust?"

She flattens the unruly grasses into a serviceable seat and flops down, unstrapping her prosthesis and making a show of examining it before she rewraps the cloth around her knee. Maxen sits down beside her and Solma flushes.

"I'm—" Maxen runs a hand through his pale hair and Solma is surprised to see his cheeks are also red.

His freckles disappear into his embarrassment. "Look, Solma, I'm really sorry about my Dja bothering you. I didn't know he was going to come and accuse you of knowing about the bees. I told him, if anyone would have reported such a thing straight away, it's you."

Solma ducks her head and hopes Maxen won't see the pain written all over her face. This is not going well. And as first dates go, it's awful.

Ah well, Blaiz has probably already chosen Maxen a wife: some nice daughter of another Steward in a neighboring village. No point tainting the bloodline with someone like her. This was over before it even began—

"Sol ..."

He's grabbed her hand. Actually grabbed it and is now holding it in both of his own. In her surprise, Solma yelps and drops her leg in the grass, but she doesn't pull away. Something tingles between her skin and Maxen's. The air smells thick with energy, like it does just before a thunderstorm, though the sky is empty as a desert.

Solma stares at her hand in Maxen's, and then up into Maxen's face. He's gazing at her earnestly, his white-blue eyes so intense she can't look away.

"I really am sorry," he murmurs. "You're so loyal and Dja ... well, sometimes when things are hard, he just sees enemies everywhere. It isn't your fault ..."

Solma doesn't say anything. She doesn't breathe, terrified as she is that the smallest movement might scare him away. His pale eyes lock with hers, searching her face. For what? Forgiveness? Or something else? Perhaps this isn't so awful after all ...

Maxen's eyes widen and his mouth drops open.

"Solma!"

Solma jerks her hands away. "What? What've I done?"

"No, Sol, stay still! Don't move!"

Solma freezes, fists clenched, ready, as always, to fight. For Earth's sake! Can't the world just leave her be for half an hour?

Maxen reaches a hand, slowly, towards her shoulder and Solma squeezes her eyes shut. It's some sort of scorpion, it must be. They clamber out of the dry earth this time of year. Or it's a biting spider, or a poisonous lizard. She braces herself, ready for the sharp stab of pain.

But instead, all she feels is the gentle whisper of tiny feet against the bare skin of her neck. All the fight goes out of her.

"Oh …"

That familiar buzz of wings fills the air as Maxen's hand gently pulls away from her, a little buff-tailed bumblebee on his fingertips. He stares at it, mouth a perfect O. He looks, Solma thinks, like he used to when they were both young. Hopeful. There's a throb of something that could be dismay in her gut. Or it could be the ache of hope that she's been so afraid of for the last few weeks. It's hard to tell.

The little bee shivers her wings again, clambering clumsily over Maxen's fingers. It isn't Blume. She's too small, her antennae are too short. Her fur is scruffy where Blume's was always sleek. But the feel of her little feet and the sound of her shivering wings … this must be the first of her daughters. Relief and fear wrestle for dominance in Solma's chest.

Blume is alive. There will be more bees …

Which means more chance of people seeing them.

Maxen's eyes flicker towards Solma's face.

"Solma, it's a bee!"

"I know."

"You don't look very surprised."

Solma's cheeks flush and she ducks her head, pretending to untangle her prosthetic leg from the grass. Blume's little daughter waggles her antennae and fires her engine, droning away. The air fills with the sound of her flight. Maxen watches her go as if he's watching the erratic progress of a young god. When Solma finally finds the courage to look up again, he's staring at her, his brows drawn together.

"You knew," he says. "Dja was right. You knew."

Maxen's eyes are hard with accusation. Shame, Solma's old friend, rises like a tide to fill her again.

"Maxen," she whispers. "I'm sorry. It weren't my idea. We got scared she'd being found, that others would come and try to take her ..." It all gushes out of her now, the dam of silence bursting and the secrets surging out to drown everything around her. But she can't stop. "And Warren ... I don't know, he got this strange connection with the bee, like he can hear what it's saying. We had to make sure they was ok. We had to help them get strong. I wanted to tell Blaiz, I really did. But then Warren got in trouble during the raid ... and he was looking for that damn bee ... I was so scared, Maxen, I can't let my brother be exiled ..."

She trails off, suddenly very tired. All this shame. All these secrets. And Maxen won't want to know her anymore. He'll tell Blaiz. And oh, Earth! Blaiz will exile her. And Warren, and Bell, too. Her heart kicks, her lungs are squeezed tight shut.

"Maxen, please ..."

He says something so quietly Solma barely hears him.

"What?"

"I said," Maxen repeats, meeting her eyes. "I won't tell Dja. Not yet. Ok? It was a reckless thing to do, Sol. But ... I can't see you exiled. I can't bear it. We'll find a way to tell him so you don't get in trouble. We'll figure it out. I promise."

There's a rush through Solma's body and she feels giddy, palms sweating. "Thank you," she says. "Thank you."

Maxen offers her his hand and she takes it. Clammy and hot as her own palms are, it's comforting to feel his skin against hers, to see her fingers intertwined with his, like her foreignness no longer matters. Like she belongs.

Maxen smiles at her. "A bee!" he says, and he sounds just like Warren did that first day. "A real bee!"

Solma can't help herself. She smiles, too. "Yes. And more than one. She'll have had babies by now. Hundreds."

Maxen's eyes widen. "Hundreds of bees!"

Solma laughs as he takes her other hand. "It's amazing," she says. "Unbelievable. Impossible—"

And the impossible things aren't over, because Maxen doesn't wait for her to finish speaking. He pulls her closer and then his mouth is against hers and the heaviness she's been carrying in her heart evaporates like summer rain. She thinks she hears bee song. Or perhaps it's her own blood buzzing in her ears. It doesn't really matter.

They huddle in the long grasses until Maxen eventually pulls away, turns his eyes towards the sun and says, "We should go."

Solma smiles, not trusting herself to speak. She secures her prosthetic leg, trying not to blush. It feels somehow intimate now, him seeing her tighten the straps, even though he's seen her do so hundreds of times before. They head back to the path, only releasing each other's hands when they join with the usual traffic of planters and farmers bustling at the end of the day.

A few minutes after they leave, the sun now disappeared below the horizon, the grasses rustle and a figure rises from among them. It's Olive, of course, with wet grass in her hair and mud clinging to her knees.

She hangs her head as she follows Maxen and Solma back to the village. The newly risen moon reflects in her eyes. She sniffs and wipes her hands angrily across her face. She's on patrol this evening. It won't do for people to see her crying.

~ BLUME ~

I WAKE IN A cluster of bodies, newly lain eggs under-
foot, fresh-hatched daughters squirming and begging
for food. Dawn calls us. Feel its scent-song pulling
at our antennae. Remember the warmth of sun on
my fur, the sweetness of lavender. Thought I'd miss it
when I went to nest, but other things take over.

My daughters—my *daughters*—scurry around me,
pressing pollen and nectar to me so that I will eat. Eat
and lay. That's the lot of a queen. Endless mother-
hood in the dark, only a few short weeks in the sun.

The thrum of my daughter's wings fills the nest.
They will fly, my daughters, and forage, returning
with stories of flowers and sunlight and fresh fields.

The nest busies as they wake, igniting their engines.
Gossamer wings flash in the rising sun. The world is a
bright circle at the end of a tunnel and in here is the
heat and scent of *bee,* of hatching eggs, busy daugh-

ters, nectar pots and rolled-pollen bee bread. I have work to do, too. So I drink deeply of the nectar. I will lay today, as I laid yesterday and will lay tomorrow. Egg after egg after egg, packed into a ball of fresh pollen, incubated by my adult daughters to give me time to lay more. Endless, endless daughters.

My sister-memories say nothing of this. Their lives were full of sun and nectar. But few of them were queens. All of them are dead, now.

My foraging daughters march up the tunnel towards the day, their scent full of hope, full of love for the sun. I turn my antennae towards them, drinking the last of their excitement. I set to a day of laying. Lay and lay and rest and eat and lay ...

The day crawls by and my daughters return, helped by their sisters to unpack half-full pollen baskets, all-but-empty nectar stomachs. The food is scarce and their scent, so full of hope when they left this morning, is now tangy with frustration. Their buzzing is lackluster and angry.

What is it? their sisters ask as they shake out their fur. *Where are the flowers?*

There are no flowers, the foragers reply. *We search everywhere but the land is dead.*

No flowers?

My heart shivers. I have laid dozens of daughters this morning alone and my eldest are telling me there are no flowers? I think of the lavender by the village. I think of the snowdrops and dandelions outside our home. I point this out. There *are* flowers! I've seen them.

My daughters flick their antennae. What would I know about it? I have been underground since they were born.

The snowdrops and dandelions are finished. The lavender is not enough to feed a colony. We need more.

How can I provide more flowers? I cannot talk with the soil or call dormant seeds to push towards the light. I am just a bee. A queen, yes, but what is she except an endless mother? I cannot give them flowers. But I know a human boy who can.

NINETEEN

THE BOAR IS UPON her and Solma can't get away. She scrabbles across the uneven ground, unable to find her footing. Her prosthesis is loose. Her body won't do as it's told. Sharp trotters stab into her. The boar's eyes are full of rage and it's saying—

"*Wake up, Solma!*"

Solma lurches upright, arms flailing. She swears viciously and catches Warren across the ear by accident.

"Ouch! Hey!"

He jabs her in the ribs again and Solma, still half asleep, feels the dream-boar attacking. She cries out, trying to work out where she is, until Bell sits up in bed and wraps an arm around Solma's shoulders.

"Shhh. It ain't real. You're alright. You're at home. It ain't here."

Solma fights Bell's hold, but only half-heartedly. Gradually, the room comes into focus; the uneven beams of the ceiling, the cracks in the windows, the watery dawn light. She relaxes into Bell, waiting for the fear to pass.

"Dammit, Warren!" she growls when her voice feels steady enough. She pulls away from Bell and glares at her brother, who retreats guiltily to the end of the bed. "You can't be so close when I'm ... dreaming like that! How many times I gotta tell you?"

Warren's lip trembles. "I'm sorry, Sol," he whimpers. "I forgot."

He rubs his ear where Solma caught it. It's a little red but otherwise undamaged. Solma clenches her fists to hide the tremble in her fingers. That damn boar! It's been years since she last dreamed of it attacking her, years since she relived the loss of her leg so vividly. Why now?

It doesn't matter why. She breathes deeply through her nose.

When it happened, Olive shot the boar six times to get it off Solma. She pulled Solma free. It's annoying how often Olive has saved Solma's life, especially as she's so snarky about it.

But what's worse is, in the dream, Olive isn't there. And Solma's screaming for her. *Olive! Olive!* But Olive never comes. The forest is empty except for her scrabbling in the dirt. And the boar screaming towards her ...

She shakes her head and presses her fingers to her temples, forcing the memories to the back of her mind. Foul dreams.

She fixes her brother with a stare she hopes isn't too furious. "Don't forget again," she says. "What's so important, anyway?"

Warren twists his fingers together as Solma straps on her leg. He chews on his words for a moment and then fixes Solma with huge, frightened eyes. Bell ushers them both off the bed so she can tidy the blankets. "I'll make tea," she murmurs, bustling towards the stove.

"I really am sorry, Sol," Warren says. He slips his hand into Solma's and the residue of her anger evaporates. She smiles.

"It's ok," she says. "I know you didn't mean to. What's so important?"

Warren chews his lip as his eyes flicker towards the closed front door. He leans in to Solma, "It's Blume!" he says in an exaggerated whisper. "She needs our help!"

Solma's gaze finds Bell's. Her aunt gives the slightest nod and sets the kettle boiling.

"What kinda help?" Solma asks, steering Warren to the table. Warren's eyes are huge with pre-emptive guilt. Whatever he suggests, Solma isn't going to like it. Blume has been underground for nearly two months, now. A hot spring is slowly building into a sweltering summer. Planting is done and the bees, so far, have kept to themselves, as if they know what trouble they will cause by being seen. She's been fine for two months. What can she possibly want now?

"She needs flowers," Warren says. "We gotta grow them for her."

Solma stares at him. "Warren ..." she touches his hand softly. "Flowers don't grow overnight. We can't make them outta thin air!"

Warren's small brows draw together and, with a stab of horror, Solma knows what he's thinking.

"Oh no, Warren. We ain't doing that."

He nods firmly as Bell places a steaming mug of tea in front of each of them. "We are, Sol," he says. "We got to."

Bell wipes her hands on her apron and folds her arms. "Got to what?"

Solma puts her head in her hands.

Warren says, "We gotta ask Cobra."

Solma expects Bell to fuss. She expects the usual ruddy-faced scolding. But there's none of that.

"Yes," she says. "Good idea."

Solma gapes. Warren's worried little face breaks into a grin so huge, Solma wonders how it fits on his face. She narrows her eyes at him.

"This *ain't* a good idea," she points out. "We agreed this was—" she glances towards the front door, digging her fingernails into her palms and hoping the spike of pain will give her courage. "We agreed this was a secret! I broke enough rules already and Blaiz *told* us not to say nothing to the Earth Whisperers!"

Bell raises an eyebrow, hands on hips, back to the Bell Solma knows so well.

"Your Ma ..." she begins, then stops. Heat burns Solma's face. She's on her feet before she knows it, fists clenched. Who does Bell think she is?

"My Ma *what?*" she snarls. She feels the anger contorts her face, feels how twisted and maniacal she looks but she can't help it. Even the flash of disappointment in Bell's face isn't enough to quell it. Her body throbs with volcanic energy.

There's a tug on her sleeve. "Sol?"

She glances down and there is Warren's face, soft and freckled and full of love, looking up into hers. "Sol, you ok?"

Solma forces one hand open and Warren takes it. "She didn't mean it, Sol," he whimpers. "That's not what she meant. Don't be angry."

Solma's missing leg aches. So does her head. Impossible bees, bad dreams, dead mothers. It's scrambling her mind until she can't remember who she is or what she ought to feel. She forces herself to sit, suddenly shaky and tired.

"Sorry," she mutters, not even looking at Bell.

Bell hands her a mug of tea. "I was just gonna say," she says. "That I reckon your Ma would've told the Earth Whisperers. We can trust Cobra."

Solma glares at her. "How do'you know?"

"I just know."

Solma rolls her eyes, "Whatever," and then feels daft for being so petulant. Bell says nothing. She turns back to the stove and begins scrubbing at some imperceptible stain. Solma gulps her tea, wincing as it scalds her throat. When she puts her mug down on the table, Warren is watching her.

"Come on, then," she mutters. "If we're gonna do it, let's get it over with. But just so you both know, it's a terrible idea."

Bell doesn't answer, doesn't even turn. Warren, though, leans forward and pats Solma's hand. "Don't worry, Sol," he says. "It ain't a terrible idea. It's a good one. Let's go."

They find Cobra and the other Whisperers south of the orchards. Solma's certain many households would offer shelter to the them while they're here, but the Whisperers themselves never entertain this idea. Instead, they've erected two canvas tents and are currently gathered around a small, controlled fire. Something that smells delicious sizzles gently in a pan. Every so often, one of the Whisperers stirs it. The two tan ponies are tethered nearby and graze peacefully. Two of the youngest Whisperers squat in the dirt, drawing shapes with sticks. The group have coaxed water out of the Earth and collected it in a metal basin. One of the older boys washes in it. He smiles and dips his head as they approach, apparently unconcerned by his nakedness. Solma feels Warren's hand squeeze her own and he wriggles, eager to make new friends, before remembering that they are there for grown-up matters. He desists his wriggling.

Cobra sits by the fire, deep in discussion with Mamba, but raises a hand in greeting when she sees them. Warren hurries across, leaning into her and gabbling into her ear. Solma hangs back, hand gripping the strap of her rifle. She scuffs her bare heel into the dirt.

Suddenly, Cobra is beside her, moving so quietly that her appearance makes Solma jump.

"Hi," Cobra says, smiling. Solma grunts and nods.

"She says she'll help us!" Warren says, bouncing. Solma's eyes narrow.

"What d'you tell her?"

Warren's grin falters but Cobra puts a gentle hand on his head. "He said you needed some flowers," she explains. "I think it's a great idea. Color in the Earth comforts the spirit."

Solma has to stop herself from rolling her eyes. It's such an *Earth Whisperer* thing to say. No one in this village needs their spirits comforted. They need their bellies filled. But, whatever. If it means she'll help ...

The boy washing in the basin clambers out, careful not to waste any water, and one of the younger Whisperers, a girl, darts over to take his place. She tugs off her green robe and steps gingerly in, catching Warren's eye and laughing. Solma nods towards the basin.

"We can wait," she says, unsure why she's so reluctant. "If you wanna bathe first."

Cobra glances over her shoulder and Solma thinks she sees the girl's smile falter a little. "No, it's alright," Cobra says. "I bathe privately, anyway." She straightens out her robe. "I felt a few seeds under the soil when we did your test, Warren," she says. "Why don't we head back there?"

Solma groans. That damn wild grass, that cluster of trees. Why does everything seem to end up dragging her back there?

"Co?" comes a voice from the fireside. Mamba stands and approaches. "You ok?"

Cobra nods, explaining about the flowers. Something passes across Mamba's face. "You want me to come with you?"

Solma's heart quickens. Is the whole world going to find out about the bees before the sun sets today? This is ludicrous! But Cobra smiles and shakes her head.

"No," she says. "Don't worry about me. Solma and Warren are good people."

Mamba frowns, though Solma reckons she sees fear in his eyes. Finally, he relents, whispering, "Be careful," to Cobra before he wanders back to the fireside. Cobra offers Warren her hand. He takes it and Solma scowls.

"We gotta be quick," she says, feeling how impatient her voice is. "I got a hunting mission this morning."

The thought sends a ripple of dread through her. *The dreams, the ache in her leg ...* But it's pointless worrying. The village needs feeding and the only food is currently snuffing about under eight hundred pounds of muscle and fury.

Flowers first.

They traverse the wilderness to the south. How is it, Solma wonders, that both Warren and Cobra can glide through these tangling grasses with such ease, while she fights for every inch? The grass seems to part for them but it grabs at her, wrapping around her leg and blade like hundreds of snakes. It's ridiculous. This is why grass needs to be *cut* and land needs to be *managed*, otherwise you can't move for all the wilderness.

By the time she reaches the ash tree with its honor guard of little birches, Cobra and Warren are already kneeling in the soil. Cobra's eyes are closed and she's scanning the ground with her fingertips. Solma unhitches her rifle and checks it, then positions herself on watch duty. There's not much she can do if a villager marches up to them and demands an explanation, but hopefully anyone looking over will see her, assume she's on official business and stop thinking about it.

"This better not take long," she mutters over her shoulder.

"Shhhh!" Warren hisses back. "You'll disturb her!"

Solma bites down a retort about minding his manners, mainly because it would make her sound too much like Bell. Seriously, though, where does this kid get his sass? From her, probably. She suppresses a smile and casts another glance at Warren as he watches in reverent fascination. Cobra digs her fingers into the soil, mutters, and the earth yields a green shoot. Warren is transfixed. When Cobra pulls away before the plant has fully matured, he squeaks.

"No, no! We need the flowers!"

Cobra smiles at him. "It'll flower," she assures him. "But we've got to let them do some growing on their own."

Solma grips her rifle a little too tight, her knuckles white. What now?

"How—how long will that take?" she asks. Cobra's smile disappears as she looks from Warren to Solma and back again.

"A week or so," she says. Warren fidgets desperately.

"We need them now," he says. "Today." He thinks for a moment and then adds, "Please."

Cobra is silent. Solma glares at her, daring her to ask, but her lungs are tight with fear. What do they do now? Warren's little face is too full of trust. He can't say anything. He mustn't—

But Cobra doesn't ask. She fixes each of them in turn with a long, unfathomable stare, then shrugs and pushes her fingers back into the soil. "Okay," she says, and brings the plant to flower.

It's beautiful; a tall central stem with bright purple flowers blooming along its length. It sways in a soft breeze, the open palms of its flowers seeking the sun. It's called viper's bugloss, Cobra explains as she brings up two more identical plants. Next, she grows a particularly tall plant with pink, bell-like flowers. Foxglove, she tells them, and don't touch it, it's poisonous to humans. Next comes a long-stemmed flower that blooms bright blue. Cornflower, apparently. And then a slightly shorter plant with a wide, blood-red flower. Poppy.

When Cobra finally pulls her hands free of the dirt, her eyelids droop and she sways on the spot. "Will that be enough?" she asks.

Solma stares at the ground. It's now a riot of color; pink, purple, blue, red. Earth knows how they're supposed to hide this from the village. And Cobra knows something. Why wouldn't she ask what they're up to?

Warren, though, doesn't seem to have the same concerns. He claps, his face glowing with delight. "It's perfect!" he announces. "She'll love it! I mean—"

"Warren!"

Solma's sharp voice makes him flinch, but it's too late. He stares guiltily up into Cobra's gentle face and Solma waits, heart frantic. She sees Cobra's mouth forming the question. They'll have to think of an excuse, which Cobra won't believe anyway. And Blaiz will find out and, oh, Earth! How long do exiled children last in the wilderness beyond the villages? A week? If starvation doesn't get them, raiders will …

But Cobra's question is answered before she has a chance to ask it. A familiar droning fills the air and a young bee, small and exhausted but unmistakably one of Blume's daughters, buzzes between them and lands directly on a poppy. Cobra's mouth drops open. Warren and Solma freeze, staring in horror. The little bee shivers her wings against the flower, her tongue probing for nectar. She drinks, then gathers sticky particles of pollen on her back legs. Nobody says anything. When she's finished with the poppy, the bee fires her engine and powers to the next plant; the foxglove. Delighted, she shoulders her way into the bell of the biggest flower until only her fluffy backside is visible.

Cobra watches, fascinated, and Solma sees tears glistening in the young Whisperer's eyes. "How ..." she breathes. "Oh my ..."

Something snaps behind them and Solma whirls round, rifle aimed.

"Warren!" she hisses, but he doesn't need to be told. He scrambles for the flower and cups his hand around the bee. "Go!" he whimpers. "Go! It ain't safe!"

This day just gets better, Solma thinks miserably. The bee, of course, hears Warren and obeys. She wriggles free of the foxglove and drones off towards the trees. Cobra follows her progress, open-mouthed, and then turns her flabbergasted face to Warren.

And that is when the person in the shadows becomes visible. It's Olive, of course. Her expression is thunderous as usual. Solma groans.

She sees Solma and stops, hooking her thumbs into her pockets. Her mouth rotates lazily around her sugar cane as her gaze travels over Cobra, Warren, the hundreds of flowers that have mysteriously popped out of the earth ... this secret is escaping. Solma can't contain it. It wants to be known, but the world isn't ready, and Olive is the last person Solma needs turning up right now. Look at her, standing there with that sneer on her face, sharp eyes seeing far more than they have any business seeing.

"Having a nice time?" she asks, voice dripping with sarcasm. Solma's jaw clenches.

"'til you showed up." She bites back.

Olive snorts. "Whatever. I just came to tell you Blaiz wants us at the council hall. We all been called."

Solma's gut squeezes. "Why?"

Olive shrugs. "How should I know? They never tell me nothing. A whole bunch'a Stewards from other villages turned up, demanding access to something and Blaiz says he don't have it."

Warren clambers to his feet and creeps to Solma's side, slipping his hand into hers. "Access to what?" Solma asks.

Olive glares at Solma. "They keep saying Blaiz is hiding a colony of bees."

TWENTY

THE COUNCIL HALL IS surrounded by milling bodies when Solma and Olive arrive. A Guard squad stands by the door, rifles ready. They try to hold back the curious crowd but none of them are older than sixteen and all are trying to issue orders to women who have seen them haring about as naked toddlers. Their efforts are ineffective.

A boy no older than twelve holds his hand up to an elderly woman balanced precariously on two walking canes.

"You can't come in here, Ma'am," he says.

"Ma'am!" the old woman cackles. "I changed your nappies more times'n I can count, Leo. You don't tell me what to do!"

Poor Leo's face burns beetroot as his squad-mates snicker and the old woman ducks under his arm while he's not looking. Solma unshoulders her rifle and re-turns Olive's thunderous scowl with one of her own.

"What?" she snaps. Olive rolls her eyes.

"Don't be foolish," she mutters. "Put your rifle down. Whatcha gonna do, shoot our own people?" she clicks her tongue and spits her chewed-up sugar cane into the weeds. Solma screws up her face. Disgusting.

"Everyone else's got their rifle ready," she says through gritted teeth. Olive barks a laugh.

"Oh Solma," she says, mocking. "Y'know that's the worst excuse in history, right?"

Solma's grip on her rifle tightens. It's ridiculous how Olive has this effect on her. She can't understand it, but the girl's like the detonator to Solma's inner bomb.

"You don't get to talk to me like that," she growls. She has more to say, but Olive lets out an impatient groan.

"Whatever," she snaps. "Do your job."

The crowd jostles and the poor kids on the Guard squad find themselves holding back grown men and women twice their size. Considering the elderly folk are malnourished to the point of starvation, some of them are surprisingly strong. Leo yelps as someone knocks him down and the crowd surges towards the door. Olive and Solma react without a word, struggling through the packed bodies to the front of the crowd. Solma hears Olive barking orders as they force their way to the front and she reiterates the message.

"Keep back!" she calls. "Stay calm, please! The crier'll bring news when the meeting's done. The fields won't manage themselves!"

The crowd calms a little at the sight of Solma and Olive, united at the entrance to the hall. Their squad have some sway over the villagers, Olive's mother being the community's only doctor and Solma the daughter of two respected villagers, but it's not enough to disperse the crowd.

"They're saying there's bees!" someone yells.

"Rubbish!" cries someone else and the jostling starts again. Olive and Solma brace for impact and this time, when Olive growls at her to disarm her rifle, Solma obeys. There are children in the crowd. And one of them is Warren. He's stood at the back with the Earth Whisperers, his hand in Cobra's, face stricken.

"Sol!"

Maxen appears behind Solma. "Where were you? Come on."

He grabs her hand and pulls her inside.

"Yeah, you're welcome!" Olive calls as she follows them. "It only took me an hour to find her!"

Inside the hall, the sounds of unruly villagers are muted. The candles on the walls barely penetrate the gloom and the garish wallpaper—peeling and blackened with mold—absorbs what little light the flames throw out. At the end of a short corridor, Solma hears raised voices. A lot of raised voices.

Maxen keeps hold of her hand. "It's starting," he whispers, his thumb stroking her palm. "You ok? You look ... I dunno ..."

Solma realizes she's trembling. She presses her free hand to her eyes for a moment. "Yeah," she says. "Yeah, I'm fine."

Maxen smiles and squeezes her hand. He's about to say something when Olive pushes past them. "Save it," she growls. "We got work to do."

She storms towards the main hall, muttering. Solma meets Maxen's gaze. He raises an eyebrow.

"D'you think she's ever happy?" Solma asks, exasperated. Maxen laughs.

"If she is, I've never seen it," he admits. "Come on."

The main hall is the grandest space in the village, but by the standards of other villages it is still a shabby mess. The windows are old and grimy. The ceiling slants and a series of warped wooden beams run across it, straining to keep the ceiling up. The floor is uneven stone and the whole place is dim and uncomfortable. Normally, it's drafty, a relief from the summer heat outside, but today it's so full of people that Solma and Maxen have trouble squeezing through to their posts. Their squad and two others are stood behind Blaiz, who is clean shaven, lounging on a rickety chair. His eyes flash dangerously as Solma takes up her position between Maxen and Olive. The vein in his temple twitches. Solma's gut tightens.

The other squads have unshouldered their rifles and hold them casually, ready to raise at any point. Solma doesn't like this. Why are they here? A threatening presence? A kind of army? She glances sideways at Maxen, but he stares resolutely forward. She looks to her other side and accidentally catches Olive's eye. Great. But Olive's usual scowl is gone. She pops another sliver of sugar cane in her mouth and chews ferociously, eyes darting across the assembled visitors. Her gaze flickers towards Solma's and, for a moment, Solma reckons they're thinking the same thing.

This doesn't feel peaceful. It feels full of threat.

Blaiz lifts his hands. He doesn't bother to stand and, though his expression is utterly livid, his voice is calm.

"Please!" he calls. "Let's settle and talk. How can my humble village help you?"

Solma scans the crowd and feels the base drop out of her stomach. At least six of the delegation are the village Stewards from the rest of Southtip Province. Their red-gold hair, sinuous bodies and pale, freckled faces give them away. But there are far more than six Stewards gathered in here. Solma sees the dark-skinned faces of the Heart Desert Province, the diminutive stature of the Landlock Province and the coal-black hair and eyes of the Westwater Province. Westwater Province: on the *other side* of Alphor. They must have travelled for weeks.

A tall woman with a silken scarf draped over her shoulders steps forward. Her face is grim, her hands fidgeting at her sides. With her, she has two young men. No, not men. Boys. Twelve years old, at most, armed to the eyeballs with vicious looking knives, crossbows, throwing stars and a pistol each at their waists. Solma's grip on her own rifle tightens.

The woman raises a hand and points at Blaiz, her finger as sharp and angry as any bullet.

"No secrets," she growls. "That was your decree, Blaiz Camber. No secrets among the provinces. We share this land. *You* said it would prevent another war.

And now we come here and find you have a hive all your own! What is this?"

Her words are caustic, stirring the moods of the other Stewards. A low muttering starts up and won't be quelled by Blaiz's raised hand. Beside Solma, the muzzle of Maxen's rifle raises a little and he shifts his stance. Solma does the same, transferring her weight to draw attention to the guns. She stares down at her hands, trembling against the black metal of her rifle. This feels so wrong, displaying their power by threatening violence. Over what? A colony of bees?

Except it isn't just a colony of bees, is it? It's the future. It's reliable harvests, surplus food, fewer graves to dig. It's hope. And look what that does. Solma realizes she was right to be so afraid of it. Look at them all!

The woman and her two boy-soldiers step back, smirking. Blaiz stands, his hands raised in appeasement.

"Friends!" He calls, and Solma thinks how unfriendly the crowd seem. "I understand your concern. We must work together on this. Sand's End village has not been secretly keeping a bee colony. In fact, we don't even know where the colony is hidden! I assure you that when we find it, its wealth will be shared."

Solma bites her lip and frowns at her feet, guilt gnawing at her insides. They're all here because the bee colony is hidden. They're angry because no one except her and Warren know where it is. What have they done? Blaiz was right, secrets are poison. She should tell him. She should have told him weeks ago.

"Don't lie to us, Blaiz Camber!" someone shouts. "If you find that nest, you'll claim it and make sure every new nest is in your territory! Why should we trust you? I say whoever finds that nest first gets to take it!"

A flare of agreement from the crowd. Blaiz raises his hands again but no one is listening to him anymore. Solma feels her heart wrung like the neck of a long-extinct bird. What's happening?

The mood darkens and now everyone's shouting at once. Blaiz steeples his fingers together and glances at Maxen. He nods.

Solma's lungs squeeze shut, but when Maxen gives the signal, she does as she's told. She marches into the crowd, bullying, shoving, threatening, until every Steward in that room is pushed out of the hall.

Under the high sun, their voices echo less aggressively, but the muttering hasn't stopped. Cold, accusing eyes glare at the Guard squad. This isn't over.

TWENTY-ONE

SOLMA JOINS HANDS WITH Olive and Maxen to hold back the restless crowd. The delegation of Stewards stalks down the path, their bodyguards prowling behind them. The crowd bellows and Solma's cries of "Stay back, please! Stay back!" have become mechanical.

She stands, churning the helplessness in her core into anger in the hope it might make her feel more powerful. It doesn't. The muscles in her neck strain as she yells. Tears prick at her eyes, too, which doesn't help. She feels like a naughty child. Stuck her hand in a fire and then cried when she got burned. This is all her fault. What does she do now?

The visiting delegates refused to go home, despite Blaiz's best efforts. They are setting up various camps around the village, staking out their own territories, posting guards and establishing makeshift boundaries. Sand's End village is under siege.

The seven Earth Whisperers stand on the outskirts of the crowd, the hems of their green robes now black with dirt, their heads bowed. When the visiting Stewards draw level with them, Mamba steps into their path. The Steward with the silk scarf snarls something at him but he doesn't react. His lips move but Solma can't hear what he's saying. The Steward clenches her fists but says nothing as she stalks past and Mamba stands, his body now slumped. Beside him, Cobra holds Warren's hand and moisture glisten on her cheeks.

Someone shoves Solma hard and she stumbles backwards, her hand snapping free of Olive's.

"Oi!" Olive barks, shoving back hard. "Watch it!"

The villager in question, unperturbed, screams obscenities and Olive, as usual, refuses to be outdone. Solma finds her balance just in time to be both appalled and grudgingly impressed by the imaginative abuse Olive spouts.

A hand squeezes her shoulder and she glances up to find Maxen by her side. "You ok?" He asks. She tries to smile but can't remember how.

Maxen clasps her hand. "You're bleeding," he says, thumbing a globe of blood from her lower lip. It stings and Solma winces, exploring the split with her tongue.

"Ouch," she says. Maxen's smile is mischievous.

"I bet you've had worse," he says, winking. Solma manages a laugh.

Olive's voice carries, loud and fierce, over the protests of the crowd. "Why don't you all just f—!"

Someone else's obscenity drowns her out at the key moment and Solma snorts. "We should help her."

Maxen shrugs. "She seems to be doing alright by herself. She always does. Strength of a redbear and attitude to match."

Still, they both turn and rejoin Olive in ushering the crowd home. Solma glances over to see how Ilga and Aldo are doing. They're trying to wrestle an old man into submission. Solma squints, but there's no mistaking it. It's Piotr.

"No!" he cries. "My orchards! It could save my orchards!"

Someone shoves him. "Shut up! You Oritch always reckon you're more important than us!"

Some of the other Fei join in the abuse and Piotr is jostled. His hands flail. Aldo fumbles with his rifle.

Piotr lurches forward grabs at the weapon. Solma's pulse quickens.

"Aldo!"

He doesn't hear her. Ilga shoves Piotr in the shoulder and he stumbles, hands grasping. Aldo doesn't pull his gun out of the way in time.

A shot blasts and the crowd utters a collective gasp, ducking their heads. Piotr yells and falls, staring in horror at the hand he'd wrapped around the barrel of the rifle. It's smoking, the flesh of his palm burned red and raw.

Solma breaks ranks with Olive and Maxen, hurrying to Piotr's side. Someone screams. Aldo blinks furiously, his rifle slack at his side. Solma grabs his collar.

"Help him up!" she snarls. "And get him to Roseann!"

She kneels by Piotr, hushing him, but the pain has dulled his senses. Solma manages to get him to his feet and wraps his undamaged arm over Aldo's shoulder.

"I'll deal with you later," she growls in Aldo's ear.

The rest of the crowd are easy to disperse after that but, by the time they're gone, the sun is almost at its peak. Solma squints up into the bright sky, the heat already stifling.

"Great," she mutters. "Half a morning's pollinating gone and our Orchard Master injured."

The Earth Whisperers disperse, too. Cobra, still clutching Warren's hand, approaches Solma with a shy wave. "We managed to fix some of the pollenbots," she says quietly. "Is there anything I can do to help?"

Behind her, Mamba hesitates, watching.

Solma twists her hands together and shakes her head. "Can you calm them all down 'fore they start hurting each other?" she says, hating the tremor in her voice. Cobra's green-blue eyes soften.

"Why don't I take Warren home?" she suggests. Solma throws up her hands.

"He can't go home, Bell's got field duty today! Earth! Why'd this all happen at once?"

Warren sways at Cobra's side. Tears glisten on his cheeks and he won't meet Solma's gaze. He's trembling all over.

He shouldn't have seen that.

"Someone needs to look after him," Solma mutters, panic flaring. It can't be her, she's on patrol. Where can he go?

Cobra holds up a hand. "We'll look after him," she says, "I'll take him back to camp. Come find us later."

Solma opens her mouth to protest. The last thing she wants is her brother spending time with Whisperers. But Warren looks distraught. His eyelids begin to droop. He's in shock.

"Ok," she says, grudgingly. "Don't take your eyes off him."

Solma watches Cobra lead her brother away. Mamba joins them, taking Warren's other hand. They talk to him softly, looking for all the world like the perfect little family.

Solma presses her fists to her temples.

"I don't know what to do," she gasps. "What do we do?"

Maxen sets his rifle on the ground and grabs both her hands, his pale eyes meeting hers. "It's ok. Stay calm. We need to protect the nest, yes?"

Solma nods. Yes, he's right. The nest first. Keep the nest secure and there is nothing for any of them to fight over.

"Ok, I'll do that."

"I'll come with you," Maxen says, retrieving his rifle from the floor.

Solma hesitates. But Maxen's gaze is soft, full of concern, both so like and so unlike his father's. And he's kept quiet until now, hasn't he? He's had her back, just like any Gatra would.

Only he's not Gatra. He's Steward-caste. He's Blaiz's son.

Trying to keep this secret has been like trying to hold the wind with her bare hands. Impossible. Now their sleepy village is ground zero in a turmoil Solma can't control. There's no way they can win this, even with Blaiz's clever words. Other villages are richer, better equipped. Other provinces have stronger weaponry. One girl and her rifle cannot keep Blume's colony safe.

Earth! Why didn't she persuade Warren to let that little bee fly away when she still had a chance? Why *wouldn't* Blume fly away?

Maxen touches her shoulder, making her jump.

"Sol?" he says, and his voice stills the roiling fear in her head. "I can help. I want to help. You can't do this on your own, not anymore."

His fingers trace down her arm and he holds her gaze, his own full of determination.

"Ok," she says. Maxen smiles at her.

"Wait here," he says. "I gotta grab my ammo ration first. I'll be right back."

He hurries off. Solma hugs herself close for a moment and then busies herself with helping Olive usher away the children. Unchecked by parents, they've wandered over to witness the commotion. They mill about, ducking away from Solma and Olive's grasp and refusing to be herded away. Olive loses her temper and terrifies most of the younger ones into submission. Eventually, the older kids get bored and skulk off to find trouble elsewhere.

"Someone ought to cuff summa those kids round the ears," Olive mutters when the job is done. She hooks her thumbs into her belt and stretches out her back. Solma frowns.

"Remind me never to ask you to watch my kids when we're older," she shoots back. Olive laughs.

"We'll not make it to kid-making age, Sol," she says. "We're in the Guard, remember?"

Solma opens her mouth to retort but thinks better of it. She's too tired for Olive's needling today. She flops onto the floor and unclips her leg, rearranging the cloth wrapped around her knee. It's snagged on her trousers.

"Dammit!" she snarls. Olive rolls her eyes.

"Stop fussing," she sighs. "Here."

She kneels in front of Solma, tugging the cloth free and unwrapping it. She hands the bundled cloth to Solma and settles down beside her.

"Thanks," Solma says grudgingly. Olive confuses her sometimes. She saves Solma's life but can't say anything kind, and then she'll patiently help Solma unwrap her leg. Strange girl. Solma wishes Olive would make up her mind whether or not she likes Solma. This constant pendulum-swing between friendship and rivalry is exhausting. But Olive's been like that since her Dja died: sullen, snappish and lonely. Solma feels a stab of sympathy when she thinks about that. It wasn't nice for either of them, watching their fathers die. It changed them both.

Olive is silent while Solma reattaches her leg. After a while, she says, "Don't show Maxen the nest."

Horror wriggles up Solma's spine. "What nest? What you on about?"

Olive groans and slaps Solma's arm. "Don't," she says. "I know about the nest. And I know you know that. You saw me watching."

"Spying!" Solma shoots back, casting a furtive glance over her shoulder. Olive reddens.

"*Watching*," she insists. "I didn't mean to. I just—look, it doesn't matter! It's not safe anymore. You can't show him."

"He's trying to help!" Solma snaps. "Earth knows we need all the help we can get. The nest ain't safe."

"It weren't safe before, Sol!" Olive growls.

Solma turns on her before she can stop herself, "What d'you know about it?" she demands. "All you do is tell me I'm wrong and I'm not good enough, make me feel small and childish! And now you come and reckon I should take your advice? Shove off, Olive!"

For a moment, Olive's face is full of hurt and dismay. It takes Solma by surprise. Olive doesn't get hurt. She either shrugs off insults or bites back with one ten times more insulting. This new, vulnerable Olive is confusing. But then Olive's expression hardens again and Solma is back on familiar ground.

"Fine," Olive snarls through gritted teeth. "Do what you want. I don't care anymore. But you'll regret it."

She grabs her rifle and stalk towards the village, not even bothering to look back. Solma watches her until she disappears, then swears violently to herself. That girl.

Maxen reappears and helps her to her feet. "Right," he says. "Let's protect that nest." He offers her his hand.

Solma takes it. Now on her feet, she glances down the path again. But Olive is gone, and there's no taking back what's been said. She smiles at Maxen and puts Olive out of her mind.

"It's this way," she says.

TWENTY-TWO

THE LIGHT IS FAILING by the time Solma heads home, eyelids drooping from exhaustion. When she'd shown him the nest, Maxen peered at the tiny, almost-hidden entrance to Blume's burrow with a critical expression.

"This it?"

She nodded.

"You sure?"

Solma raised an eyebrow. "Well, it's where we put her down and she went underground and now there's loads of other bees around. They gotta have come from her."

Maxen stroked his chin. "Ok," he said. "Good. Now we can protect it." He glanced up at the sun. "We're late for patrol ..."

Patrol had been awful. Aldo, suffering from grass fever, was more squinty than usual, sniffling and sneezing to the point where Maxen sent him home to rest. Olive sulked the whole way round and, when they passed by the orchards and asked after Piotr, the Oritch workers told them his burned hand wouldn't move properly. There'd been tension between them and the Fei since the meeting. Worse than that, more trees had died. Solma ordered them to dig the dead trees up and mark off the contaminated soil.

"It won't contain itself," she'd said as the workers grumbled. "We got to take charge of these things."

She'd said it mechanically, the same way she'd always said it. But the sound of those words out in the air had suddenly felt hollow. Was that true anymore? Had it ever been true?

Solma watched the workers digging, her gut twisting inside her. When their patrol concluded at the edge of the planting fields, Maxen grabbed her hand and smiled at her. "Don't worry," he whispered before turning and heading back home. Solma felt the smile pulling at her mouth as she watched him go, but then she'd caught Olive's eye, full of warning and ... what else was that? Hurt? Well, how was it Solma's fault if Maxen liked girls who were cheerful, occasionally? Olive wasn't doing herself any favors.

They'd parted ways without a word.

But Solma can't get Olive's face out of her head. The hard set of her mouth, the crease in her brow, the glimmer of sadness in her eyes that Solma couldn't read. Her stomach rolls until she feels sick and stops, leaning against the mud wall of a darkened house to get her breath back.

"I've been looking for you," says a voice in the dark. Solma jumps, automatically aiming her rifle. Blaiz emerges from the gloom between two houses, hands held up in mock surrender. He's smiling. It's not a nice smile. Solma lowers her rifle, wondering why she feels so exposed.

"Steward," she says. "I didn't see you ..."

"No," says Blaiz, lowering his hands. His strange, unpleasant smile widens. "I didn't want you to see me."

Solma tells herself the chill in her gut is just from the night. The gooseflesh on her arms has nothing to do with Blaiz's threatening words. Blaiz advances, never taking his eyes from hers.

"I've watched you all your life, Solma El Gatra," he says, spitting out her name. Solma bristles, but Blaiz is still talking. "Look at you! So eager to fit in, aren't you? But we both know you never have. All that lumbering height. You'll be towering over everyone in the village by the time you're ready to settle—if you live that long." His eyes seem full of pity, but his voice is cruel. "We both know your Dja's blood runs strong in you," Blaiz says. "He was the same, always wanted to prove that he could be one of us. But he never was, was he?"

Solma's rifle drops to her side. Her hands tremble. Who is this man? This is not her Steward, her protector. Why is he speaking to her like this?

"Dja ..." she gasps. "Dja was loyal, he ... he trusted you. He believed in you."

Blaiz laughs and shakes his head. "You're a foolish girl, aren't you?"

Solma stares. "Wh-what?"

"I said," Blaiz growls. "You're a foolish girl. Aren't you?"

She can't have heard him right. This must be a mistake. Solma gazes at him, open-mouthed, waiting for everything to make sense.

Blaiz's smile disappears. Solma stumbles backwards despite herself and her shoulder blades smack into the wall of the house behind her. Still Blaiz prowls closer, but now Solma has nowhere to go. Instinctively, she makes to raise her rifle.

But this is the Steward. *Her* Steward. What is he doing?

Blaiz approaches until he's inches from Solma's face, his hands on the wall either side of her, trapping her. His eyes lock onto hers. Grey. Hard. Shrewd.

"Where are the bees, Solma?" he whispers. "I know you know."

Solma shakes her head vigorously. "I don't."

"You do," Blaiz insists. "And you also know that keeping it from me is treason. I'll forgive you, Solma. If you tell me now, I'll forgive you."

His eyes are lightless pools and Solma can't read them. It would be a relief to confess it now. The secret is a thorn festering in her heart. She so wants to tell the truth.

But this man doesn't look like the fair, kind Steward she's used to. He's twisted and angry. Incapable of forgiveness.

The vision of the red-haired girl flashes again in Solma's mind, glancing back before she disappears into the unknown. Exiled. Gone. Blaiz did that to her, knowing it would kill her.

As Solma speaks, it's Warren she thinks of. And Bell. And the tentative hope of the bees. She takes a breath, steadies her voice. "Blaiz," she says, quietly. "I dunno where the bees are."

Blaiz's laugh is cruel. He bares his teeth and there's no longer even the ghost of pity in his eyes.

"Just like your Dja," Blaiz hisses. "In the end, he was a traitor, too. Too busy protecting his precious beetles, trying to bring back the birds with your aunt!"

Solma's breath snags in her throat. "With ... with Bell?"

Blaiz isn't listening. "He tainted your whole family. And you're tainting this village, Solma El Gatra. I'll find the bees, with or without you. And when I do, Solma ... when I do ..." He doesn't bother to finish the threat. It hangs in the air between them.

Solma's heart thunders in her chest. Her mouth is a drought, her lungs a hurricane.

But somehow, *somehow*, she finds a nub of calm. She digs into it, holding tight, keeps her face as neutral as she can.

"I dunno where the bees are," she says. "I'm honest and loyal, Blaiz. I promise."

Blaiz's face contorts into something horrifying. He draws breath, but before he can speak, candlelight flickers in the window of the house and the front door opens.

Olive and Dr. Roseann appear at the door. Roseann rubs sleep from her eyes, her hair unkempt. But Olive looks like she hasn't been to bed yet. Solma stares. She hadn't realized she'd been right outside Olive's house the whole time. Relief and dread battle in her gut.

Earth, she's tired.

"Everything alright, Steward?" Roseann asks. She lifts the candle a little higher so that its light falls across Blaiz. In an instant, the monster is gone and Blaiz's looks human again. Solma blinks, wondering if she'd imagined that snarling beast. Blaiz backs away from Solma, smiling.

"Yes, thank you, Doctor," he says, "the Sergeant was just reporting the day's events. She's heading home, now."

"I'll escort her," Olive offers. She steps outside, not even bothering with her boots. "I'm sure you're tired, Steward."

A flicker of concern passes across Blaiz's face and his eyes linger on Roseann for a moment. He nods.

"That's a good idea," he says.

"Yeah," Olive agrees. "Solma's our best Sergeant. The villagers trust her so much. There'd be uproar if anything happened to her, wouldn't there? We gotta keep her safe. From the other Stewards."

Her eyes never leave his, a clear challenge. Solma gapes. What's happening?

The Steward's expression hardens, but he inclines his head and turns, stalking into the gathering dark and leaving Solma with her back still pressed against the wall.

No one says anything for a few minutes.

Solma finally finds her voice. "Thanks," she whispers. Olive shrugs.

"D'you actually need me to walk you home?" she asks. "Only I'm tired. And trouble follows you everywhere."

Solma rolls her eyes.

"Whatever," she grumbles. "I'll be fine. Go to bed."

Olive disappears into the house without another word and Solma is left with Roseann's apologetic smile.

"'Night then," the Doctor says.

"Yeah," Solma replies, staring at her hands as they shake uncontrollably. "Night."

The door closes, the candlelight is extinguished, and Solma is left alone in the dark.

TWENTY-THREE

SOLMA IS STILL SHAKING by the time she gets home, but the sound of Warren crying jolts her. His wails are desperate and loud even through the closed door. Solma doesn't think, just shoulders the door open, snapping the top hinge clean off. She bursts into the dim room, brandishing her rifle, expecting some invasion from foreign soldiers or a visiting Steward.

But the room is empty except for Warren, Mamba and Cobra, all of whom yelp upon Solma's ridiculous entrance. Warren dives under the table, Mamba steps in front of Cobra with his fists raised and Cobra, apparently not as peaceful as she would have Solma believe, grabs and brandishes a kitchen knife. She drops it in the bucket with the rest of the dirty crockery when she realizes it's only Solma.

"It's alright," she says, smiling. "We don't mean any harm. We're just comforting your brother."

Warren crawls out from under the table. The shock of Solma's entrance wears off him quickly and he resumes his crying, face contorted with misery.

Solma snaps the safety on her rifle and props it by the now broken door. Bell's going to kill her later. Speaking of which ...

"Where's Aunt Bell?" she asks. "Can't she help with this?"

She flops into a chair and unclips her prosthesis. Bell hates having it on the table but Solma couldn't care less today. The end of her lucky leg, just below her knee, itches something awful and she unwraps the cloth to let it breathe. Now that she isn't terrified for her brother's life, the confusion she felt towards Blaiz resurfaces. That can't have just happened. It must have been some sort of mistake ... she glowers at the table, thoughts whirling.

Mamba shuffles his feet, staring at Solma as if she's a wild animal, which Solma finds a little hurtful. This is *her* home after all. And he's a Whisperer. Untrustworthy, tricksters ...

According to Blaiz. Blaiz, who's just cornered and threatened her in the dark.

No, that can't have been what happened. Solma pushes the thought aside and turns her attention to her brother. He needs her.

"Come here, Warren," she says. "It's ok."

She beckons him over and hugs him close, despite his wriggling.

"What happened?" she demands, glaring at Cobra.

Cobra either doesn't pick up the insinuated accusation or chooses to ignore it. She goes to the fire and stokes it, placing the full kettle on top to boil before she comes to sit down.

"Bell's gone to Dr. Roseann," she explains. "Warren's been suffering with panic since the meeting at the council hall. We've tried to comfort him but it hasn't helped. Bell's asking for herbs to help him sleep."

"No!" Warren wails, pounding Solma's arm with his fists. "No! I ain't taking them! I won't! You ain't listening to me!"

Solma grabs hold of his wrists and holds them, careful not to squeeze. "Warren. Warren! Stop. It's ok. We're here. We're listening."

Warren trembles in her grip, his red face shining with tears and snot. Solma slips off the chair and kneels in front of him. "It's ok," she says. "Tell me."

His puffy eyes blink away tears, searching the cracks in the floor as if the answers might be hidden there. "I ..." he says. "I ..."

But whatever it is, he can't find the words to explain. He stamps in frustration and misery overtakes him again. He clutches the side of his head and wails, as if a terrible noise is deafening him. Solma clenches her jaw, his desperation leaves deep grooves of pain in her heart.

"Warren ..."

She tries to rub his shoulders but he squirms away and Solma has to stop herself from scolding him. She's never been good at this bit of being a big sister. Fighting off half a dozen raiders to save his life? Easy. But comfort him when he's crying? It would be simpler facing that Earth-forsaken boar again.

Warren hugs himself, pacing.

"Warren?" Solma says. He ignores her. She's about to say his name again, more sharply, when Cobra kneels beside her. Solma tenses, but Cobra's demeanor is soft, placating. She means no harm.

"Warren," she says gently. "It's ok to cry. Come and sit here. I want to tell you something."

"Co," Mamba says, an edge of warning in his voice. Cobra dismisses him with a wave and Mamba bristles.

That boy is always expecting a fight, Solma thinks. She glares at him and is surprised to find him meeting her gaze and matching it with a force she didn't think Earth Whisperers were capable of. She looks away.

Warren hesitates, peering at Cobra through swollen eyes, before he relents and goes to her. He cuddles into her lap and she wraps her arms around him. Solma says nothing, afraid that if she opens her mouth, the stab of jealousy will make itself known.

"I ... dunno how to t-tell you ..." Warren gulps, trying to wipe tears from his eyes and only succeeding in smearing them around his face. "I c-can't make the words right ..."

Cobra squeezes him tight. "I know how you feel," she says. Warren wriggles, angered.

"No you don't!"

Cobra lets him struggle a bit and he eventually settles down, leaning into her shoulder and sniffling. Solma reaches out to stroke his hand, willing Bell to hurry home with those herbs.

"Did you know, Warren," Cobra murmurs, "That when I was born, everyone thought I was a boy?"

"Cobra!" Mamba hisses. Solma is about to tell him to shut up, but when her eyes meet his, it's not anger she sees there, but terror. His fear fizzes in the air like a raw nerve and it disarms Solma completely. What is he so afraid of, this almost-man who names himself after Alphor's deadliest snake?

Cobra gazes at him and shrugs. "They're good people," she says. "I told you. We can trust them."

Something stirs in Solma again: the sense that there's a memory hidden away in her somewhere. She can almost grasp it, but it evades her. She shakes her head. It's been a long day. She's too tired for this.

Mamba's expression doesn't change and Solma wonders what he thinks she and Warren might do. Warren stops crying and frowns at Cobra.

"Why'd they think you were a boy?" he asks.

Cobra smiles wryly. "Well, why did everyone think *you* were a boy when you were born?"

Warren shuffles his feet and blinks up at her, embarrassed. Cobra squeezes his shoulder.

"It's hard to know who people really are when all you've got to go on is what they look like on the outside," she says. "Don't you agree?"

Warren thinks about this for a moment, then spreads his hands wide as if the answer is obvious. "You could just ask," he suggests.

Cobra laughs and Solma chuckles nervously. She catches Mamba's eye again and sees the other Whisperer relax. But only a little. She resents the insinu-ation. Sand's End is more open minded than many other villages. Blaiz would never exile someone for liv-ing their own way or loving their own way. As long as they do their duties and produce kids when the village needs them to, no-one cares who people choose to be or who they make a home with. It's a bit different for the Steward-caste, but it always has been. Marriages for them are alliances between villages. But it's never mattered for plain old Gatra or Fei or Oritch. It just so happens that there aren't many people who *want* to live their own way in the village right now. That's not Blaiz's fault. Sand's End is a safe place. And Mam-ba can stop looking at her like that. Like she doesn't know the half of it. Solma's fully aware what it's like to be an outsider, so he can stick his eyes back in his head.

"I always felt a bit like people didn't really see me," Cobra explains, "like who I was and who everyone else saw were two different people. It was so hard to ex-plain back then, but it felt like I was muted. I couldn't fully connect with the world and the people around me. My parents could see that I felt different right from when I could walk and talk. But the truth is, I didn't understand what I was feeling and I couldn't explain it to them. I used to cry and rage just like you, right up until I finally understood who I was."

Warren stares at her. "Really?"

Cobra nods and strokes a lock of hair from his face. "Really. So you see, I understand how you feel. I really do. D'you want to try explaining again? Solma and I are right here. We're listening."

Warren's eyes flicker between Solma and Cobra. Understanding dawns on Solma and she reaches out and grabs Warren's hand.

"It's ok," she says gently. "It's ok. I think ..." She can't quite believe she's going to say this, but perhaps it's the right thing to do. Perhaps Blaiz isn't right about *all* Whisperers. Perhaps Cobra isn't so bad. "I think we can tell her."

She casts a sideways glance at Mamba and wonders if they can tell him. Don't tell the Whisperers, Blaiz had said. But Mamba looks more fearful than threatening, and the pair of them already know something.

Warren's frustration overwhelms him again. "I don't know *how!*"

He begins to sob and Cobra hugs him close, hushing him and stroking his hair.

"She's in my head!" Warren whimpers. "She's all ... it's just so much noise!" He clutches his head again and shakes it so furiously Solma's frightened he'll hurt himself.

Solma grabs his hand and squeezes. "We'll tell her together," she says. "Shall I go first?"

Warren peeps at her from underneath Cobra's chin, eyes puffy. He nods.

So Solma explains, haltingly at first, about Blume crawling out from the soil in the planting fields. Warren tries to interject.

"I sort of ..." he mutters. "I sort of ... I don't know! I heard her underground. I told her *hello*. And it's like ... like she heard."

This is news to Solma.

"You *heard* her underground?"

Cobra's expression doesn't change. "Go on," she says.

Warren taps his forehead. "She's in my brain," he says. "I can ... sort of ... smell it. She's afraid. All her fear is like ... like ..."

Solma's heart kicks. *Smell?* Is this what he's been struggling with these past months? It must have overwhelmed him.

She watches him now, as Cobra strokes his back gently. "It's ok," she says. "Tell me more."

They explain, talking over each other sometimes, how they helped Blume find a nest, how Blaiz came to them, demanding answers. Cobra's face darkens at this but she says nothing. Neither she nor Mamba look surprised. Solma feels a flutter of concern in her core. They should be surprised by all this. Why aren't they?

Warren wipes the last of his tears away. "When you ... when we ... did the Whisperers' test," he whimpers. "I did ... I did feel something but I didn't know how to explain it."

His face crumples again and Cobra reaches out and catches his hand before the tears can return. "Warren," she says, her face alight. "Warren, that's amazing. It's ok. I understand. Oh Earth! This is incredible!"

"What?" Solma snaps. "What? What's incredible?"

She wraps an arm around Warren and draws him close, despite his protestations. Cobra glances over her shoulder at Mamba. Her smile is huge and when Solma steals a glance at Mamba, she sees the fear in him has been replaced by astonishment. Her heart kicks. Cobra's figured it out, hasn't she? She's worked out why Warren's special. They'll take him from her, they'll—

"He can hear the insects," Cobra breathes. "Underground. I don't know how. It makes no sense, but that's what it is! They're waking up because they can hear him. It's ... I don't know. It's a new kind of Whispering I've never heard of before. I *knew* I sensed something in him! He might be the answer, Solma. He could have the ability that heals Alphor."

Mamba lets out a short laugh and covers his mouth. Somethings glisten at the corner of his eye. Is he crying? "That's ... but how?" he asks, his voice reverent as he watches Warren.

Solma feels sick. She clutches her belly and tries to return Cobra's elated smile. Warren's gaze flickers between the two of them, frowning.

"So ..." he says. "I *am* an Earth Whisperer?"

Cobra laughs. "Of a kind," she says. "A new kind."

"This means he's got to go with you, don't it?" Solma whispers. It hurts even saying it. "'Cos of his power."

Cobra's smile falters. She's about to speak, but at that moment, Bell returns, brandishing a bundle of herbs. She scowls at the broken door.

"Who's responsible for this?" she barks. "Solma?"

~ BLUME ~

PACKED CLOSE. MY DAUGHTERS' bodies shiver
around me. I feel the thrum of eggs under my abdomen. We sleep, a huddled mass of bees. I smell their
dreams. Fresh flowers, heat at the tips of their antennae. Soft, sweet scent of new eggs, the long tunnel to
outside.

I flex my wings, shift my antennae, find the daughters whose nightmares smell like fresh venom and
singed fur.

*Flowerless deserts. Smell of burning. There are no
other bees.*

It stings, smelling their nightmares. I pull my antennae back, the tips tender with their pain. I do
not dream except through my daughters, through the
memories of my sisters. Mother bee. Not a maker of
memories but a keeper of them. My daughters don't

call me queen like the human larvae boy does, they call me something he might translate as *time traveler.*

Because I am from another lifetime ago. I am from a hundred lifetimes ago. And I remember there being millions of us, air full of bee song. I remember fields of flowers. I remember dancing through the air, any number of males on my tail. I remember choosing the fastest, the strongest, the bravest. Because I could. Because there were many.

But in my daughters' nightmares, we are the only ones. Apart from us, the air is empty of buzzing. Apart from us, the air is empty of everything.

I am awake now, shivering my wings to keep warm. So, of course, I sense it first.

A tremor shakes the nest. Tense, antennae stretched, feeling for danger. Around me, daughters stir. A frightened hum echoes around the nest cavity. The air is sharp, tinged with bitterness. It drowns out everything. All I smell is hunger.

And then the wall of the nest bursts and there is a monster there, scooping my daughters into its cavernous mouth and crunching them into shattered bodies and loose fur.

My pheromones scream. My daughters' scents scream, too.

We are dying, we are dying. And I don't know what to do.

TWENTY-FOUR

WARREN SCREAMS AND SOLMA bursts upright in bed. The thin blanket slides onto the floor and, beside her, Bell wakes, too.

"Warren! Shhh, Warren!"

It's Cobra's voice. Solma hadn't realized the Whisperer was still here. She wonders if Mamba is here, too, unwilling as he was to let Cobra out of his sight. Solma shuffles to the edge of her bed and fumbles for her leg, accidentally catching it with her elbow. It clatters on the wooden floor.

"Earth's sake, Solma!" Bell growls. Warren screams louder, and suddenly there is sense in his cries.

"*It's eating us!*"

Horror uncurls in Solma's belly. She can't breathe. Where's her leg? The sound of his terror ricochets around her brain and she thinks she can hear bee tremolo underneath. How is that possible? She needs to get to him. *Where is her leg?*

A candle flame hisses to life and suddenly Solma can see. She squints against the brightness, snatches her leg and glances up to see Warren clutching the sides of his head, fingernails digging into his flesh. His back arches, his leg kicks, face red with pain and fury. Tears stream down his cheeks. He screams while Cobra tries to stop him hurting himself.

"*It's eating us!*"

No time. Solma lurches from the bed, leg still in hand, and kneels beside Cobra. Mamba is nowhere to be seen but Bell hurries over with a damp cloth and tries to press it to Warren's forehead. He fights her.

"Warren! Warren!"

He screams again. Solma cups his chin in her hands and tries to stop him from bashing his head against the floor. He moans, his terrified gaze meeting Solma.

"The nest, Sol!" he gasps, and bee-terror buzzes in Solma's head again, as if she can hear Blume's fear echoing through Warren. "You have to go! Now!"

Solma doesn't move. "But—"

"We've got him," Cobra says, snaking her arm underneath Warren's shoulder blades and cradling him. "It's ok. I know what he's going through. We call it a forceful projection. His mind is so linked to the life he's nurtured he feels everything." She fixes Solma with a hard, determined stare. "You can't help him here. Whatever's happening to Blume, you need to stop it. Go!"

Solma snatches her hunting belt from over the back of a chair. Something nags in the back of her brain.

"Where's Mamba?"

Cobra shakes her head, attention returned to the writhing Warren. "Went back to camp. There's no time! Go!"

It seems to take an age to get her prosthetic leg on. Her fingers shake and Bell helps her wrap the cloth properly. Solma scrambles for her boot, not bothering to lace it up before she stumbles out the door, pulling it shut behind her. She expects lights to flicker in the neighboring houses, the whole village awoken by Warren's shrieking. But the village is dark and silent, Warren's screams muffled by a bracing wind that worries the windows. His shouting could be a trick of the weather. Except it isn't.

Something's not right. Where's Mamba? Solma feels a tug of fear at leaving her little brother with a Whisperer. But the nest ...

She shakes her head, trying to rid her brain of the echo of bee-fear, unhooks a torch from her belt, winds the charging handle and flicks it on. The light is poor, so she winds the hand pump a few times, hoping it'll last. Briefly, the light flares brighter, before giving up and sinking into a yellow pool on the ground. Solma gives up and sets off at a run, despite the darkness. Moonlight helps to light her way, but barely. She races south and turns off the path, battling the unruly grasses until she sees the shadow of the ash tree. There's a noise in the distance, now. A kind of shuffling, snuffling, clawing. Solma lengthens her stride, swearing as her blade snags in the grass and she trips. She throws her hand out to catch herself.

And someone else grabs it.

She lurches upright, grabbing for her rifle. "Who's there?"

"Shhh! It's me!"

Solma lifts the torch. The yellow light illuminates Maxen's face, pale in the gloom and streaked with dirt.

"What's happening?" Solma demands as they jog towards the nest. Maxen matches her stride. "I don't know," he says, "I heard something, so I came out to look."

"The nest's being attacked!" Solma hisses.

She breaks into a run, swinging her rifle off her shoulder and slamming the safety off. Maxen's voice drifts from behind.

"Sol! Wait!"

No time to wait. No time for anything. She reaches the cluster of trees, skidding in the damp grass, and squints into the dark. "Where is it?"

She's still muttering to herself as Maxen appears beside her.

"Sol—"

"Shhh!"

She puts a hand on his chest to silence him, turns her head to better pick up that strange sound. That shuffling, clawing, snuffling. That underlying buzz of panic.

Something snaps in the undergrowth and Solma focuses on that sound: shuffling, clawing, snuffling. She turns, aims, fires.

Something squeals and a dark shape shudders and collapses. Solma stumbles over to it, aiming her torch-light at the ground.

It's chaos. Great gouges have been torn into the earth, exposing the hollow underneath. Bee bodies lay scattered like the remains of a battle, half crunched and torn. Larvae writhe and shudder, ripped from the safety of the nest, and the tiny, ovoid pots the bees have made and tenderly filled with nectar spill across the grass, leaking their precious cargo.

Horror hooks Solma's throat and she falls to her knees, aiming her torch into the mess of the nest. She peers inside.

There's still activity in there. Bees scurry about, buzzing angrily, gathering the remaining larvae and pulling them back into the safety of the hollow. Thankfully, the attacker barely had time to break into the center of the nest, so the damage seems superficial, salvageable.

And there, in the center of the mass of bee bodies, fiercely guarded by her daughters, is Blume. Alive. Unharmed. Solma feels wetness on her cheeks and smears the tears away with her sleeve as Maxen kneels beside her.

"Is it gone?" he asks. "Are they dead?"

Solma shakes her head. "No, it's okay. It's okay. We got here in time. Here, help me."

She tucks the long grasses around the exposed side of the nest, shoring it up with fallen leaves and twigs. She packs earth around it and hopes it will be enough to let the colony recover. Blume is still alive. That must count for something. But she'll have to get rid of the bee bodies, hide them somehow, and the nest will have to be watched. As often as possible.

It's not good news.

"What was it?" Maxen asks, getting to his feet. "What caused it?"

Solma shakes her head. "I dunno ..."

She swings her torch around, training it low, until it catches something. Solma hears labored breathing, the yelps of something still alive. Her heart lurches. She shuffles closer, rifle held loosely in one hand. "Maxen? Maxen, look! Oh, Earth—"

It's a moon badger. She's not seen one in years and thought they'd all migrated further north as the summers had become hotter over the last few years. But there's no mistaking it. The cream stripe dividing its face is dark with blood and the fur on its flanks is matted and wet. It tries to scramble away as Solma approaches but its back legs don't work and its long prehensile tail is lifeless. Solma's eyes fall on the dark patch growing on its belly, the wetness spreading across the ground. It bares its teeth one last time.

Poor thing was only hungry. Solma's cheeks are wet again, but this time she doesn't wipe them dry.

"I'm sorry," she whispers. For some reason, it's Ma's face that bursts into her mind, her mother's words ringing loud and fresh in her head.

Sometimes the killing is necessary, Sol. That's what it means to be in the Guard. It's necessary, but it's still horrible. You should feel every bullet you put into another creature. Feel the guilt. Never enjoy death. Never.

Solma never has. Boar after boar she's shot and dragged home to feed her village. She's shot desperate redbears when they've wandered too close during winter and threatened the children. She's shot people, too. Raiders and attackers.

And every thrust of the knife, every bullet forcing its way into flesh, returns to her now. She aches all over, watching this creature die. It was only hungry. Only hungry like they all are.

But it can't have this nest. Solma reaches out and strokes the soft fur behind its ears. "I'm sorry," she says again, her voice catching. "I'm sorry, but I can't let you. Forgive me."

The creature blinks slowly at her, the tension in its shoulders fading. It lets out a small, sad moan.

"I know," Solma says, unsheathing her knife. "It's over now."

She jabs the blade into the back of its neck. It twitches once, then falls still.

It's difficult to do in the dark, but they manage to carry the body a fair way from the nest and hide it at the edge of the forest. Solma sprinkles it with dirt to disguise the bullet wounds and hopes a scavenger will find it before anybody else does. That's another question she really doesn't need people asking. When they're done, she straightens up and realizes she's covered in badger blood.

"I can't ..." she holds her hands out helplessly. "I can't go home like this."

Maxen stares at her as if he's seeing her for the first time, this tall girl with outsider features and blood on her hands. He hesitates, then sighs and pulls a bandaging cloth from his hunting belt.

"Here," he says, dabbing the worst of the blood from her skin. She stands numbly as he cleans her up, gently turning her hands over so he can mop blood from between her fingers.

"Poor thing," she murmurs. Maxen raises an eyebrow at her.

"You've killed things before, Sol," he says. She glares at him.

"Yes," she growls, "To *eat*. To *survive*. That was ... different."

Maxen says nothing, just cleans up her other hand.

"Why was it out here?" Solma asks. Maxen remains silent, so she presses on. "We haven't seen any for ages. Why now?"

Maxen finishes cleaning her up and tucks the bloodied bandage back into his belt, where it hangs over his hips like a dead thing. He shrugs.

"Does it matter?" He asks. "It's dead now. Come on, we should—"

But Solma's not listening. There has to be a reason, doesn't there? It can't be a coincidence. She aims her torch down, squinting at the darkened ground. "Maxen! Look!"

They both kneel and peer into the torchlight. Is that ...? No, it can't be. Solma reaches out to touch the pale crumbs littering the grass.

"Bread?" she asks, turning a crust over in her fingers. "But, who—?"

Maxen turns. "There's more here, look. A trail ..."

The crumbs are scattered in a neat line. They follow it clumsily, losing it sometimes and having to double back to find it again. But there's no mistaking where it leads: all the way from the forest to the cluster of trees where Blume built her nest. Solma stands for a moment, staring once again at the massacred bees.

"Someone led it here," she says. "Someone led it here to destroy the nest. They know where it is and they ..." she turns on Maxen, fury twisting her face. "Why would they *do* that?"

Maxen's face is grim. "Who would want it to belong to no one?" he whispers. "Who would want to keep everything equal by making sure we all have nothing?"

Solma stares at him. "No. No ... they wouldn't do that. They *couldn't* do that ..."

Maxen takes her hand, not looking at her. The sky lightens in the east, a thin band of dawn peeping over the horizon. The surviving bees stir, buzzing and repairing. She hopes.

"You think the Earth Whisperers did this?" she mutters. Maxen says nothing, but his silence is enough.

"We should clear up the trail," he says. "Before anything or anyone else finds it."

TWENTY-FIVE

SOLMA'S TOO FURIOUS TO care that she's terrifying
the Earth Whisperer children. She bursts into their
camp, ignoring their tears. The sun's barely up and
the village is just stirring. Solma doesn't bother with
ceremony. She unhitches her rifle from her shoulder
and snaps off the safety, stopping just short of aiming
it at Mamba.

"Give me back my brother," she snarls.

She'd stormed home after saving the nest, expecting
to find Warren there, expecting to confront Cobra
and throw her out. But neither Cobra nor Warren
were there. There was only one place they could be
and Solma marched straight here.

Mamba blinks, nonplussed. He's a good liar, Solma
thinks. She'd almost believe the alarm in his eyes if
she didn't know the truth. The younger Whisperers
scurry behind their elders for safety. A little girl with

orange eyes sobs loudly. Mamba crouches beside her as she reaches up for his comfort.

"He's with Cobra," Mamba says quietly. "He's safe—"

"He was never safe with you lot!" Solma hisses. "Where is he?"

Mamba scoops up the whimpering girl, his gaze unreadable.

"Cobra?" he calls. "Bring Warren here, please."

A tent flap curls inward and Warren bounces out, followed by Cobra and, to Solma's surprise, Olive. Warren sees Solma and runs to her, smiling. His face is still messy with last night's crying and his hair is disheveled, but he's no longer panicked or tortured by bee-pain. He grabs her wrist and gazes up at her.

"It's ok!" he whispers. "I felt her. She's alright. They're fixing the nest."

Solma glares him into silence and the smile fades from his face. "Get behind me, Warren," she growls. Warren hesitates, eyes darting to Mamba and Cobra. Solma feels her hackles rising like a wild dog. "Now, Warren!"

He starts at her ferocity and obeys, peering out from behind her hip. "What're you doing, Sol?" he whispers. Solma ignores him.

Mamba still holds the child, but Cobra has reverted to that infuriating tranquility, palms pressed together. She's not fooling anyone. Lying, two-faced hyena! It takes all Solma's self-control not to aim her rifle at them right now. It's Olive who steps forward, arms folded. She raises a critical eyebrow.

"I'd stop now, Sol," she sneers. "If I were you."

Solma bares her teeth, "You ain't me," she snaps. "So you can shut up. Why're you here anyway?"

Olive's expression darkens. "That ain't none of your business."

A realization strikes Solma so forcefully she almost reels backwards. She can't believe she didn't see it before. It's so obvious!

"You!" she exclaims. "It was you, weren't it? You and them!"

For the first time since they've known each other, Olive looks perplexed. "What?"

But Solma can see it, that glint in her eye, that curve in her mouth. She's in on it. "I shot the badger," Solma snarls. "And Maxen and I cleared up the trail. We're guarding the nest every night from now on. So you can forget trying that again."

Olive scowls. "Sol, you're such an ass—"

"Don't!" Solma says, finally unable to stop herself aiming her rifle at the three of them. She feels a mild and guilty thrill of satisfaction when Mamba and Cobra shuffle backwards. Good! Let them fear her. How dare they? It's so obvious now Solma thinks about it. Where had Mamba gone last night? They'd tricked her. And she'd fallen for it. She glares at Mamba.

"Your name," she snarls. "Deadliest snake in Alphor? It *suits you,* you slimy—"

But Olive steps in front of her, shielding the two Whisperers and glowering Solma into silence. Her rifle is unshouldered, her red braid burning bright in the rising sun.

"Back off, Sol," she says, very quietly. "You're making a mistake."

"You reckon everything I do is a mistake," Solma snaps. Heat rises in her cheeks and there's a tell-tale burning in her eyes. She blinks it away. She mustn't cry. Can't be so pathetic in front of Olive. She tightens her grip on her rifle. "I know what you did."

Olive lets out a snort. "I'm doing what's right, Solma El Gatra," she bites back, "But you go ahead, make yourself feel big and strong with your rage and your naïve loyalty. I can't be bothered with you anymore. You can get lost for all I care!"

"I'll go in my own good time," Solma snarls through gritted teeth. At her feet, Warren whimpers and makes to run back to Cobra. Solma grabs his wrist. Tight.

"Ouch! Sol, you're hurting me!"

He squirms but she doesn't let go. "You don't come here again," she growls at him. "You stay away from these traitors, you got it?"

Warren frowns. "Sol, they're not traitors—"

"Yes, they are!" Solma snaps, shaking him so he whimpers with shock. She forces herself to calm down. It isn't his fault, is it? He's too young, too trusting. He's never known how to survive. This just proves it. She glares at him. "They lured the badger to the nest, Warren," she says. "You're precious Whisperers and Olive. Get it? They betrayed us!"

It's Cobra's voice that cuts through the madness. Hardly more than a whisper, but her words strike something in Solma nonetheless.

"You'd know all about betrayal, Solma," she says. Solma hesitates. Something in the back of her brain stirs. She stares at Cobra, at those green eyes ...

But Mamba steps in front of her, scowling, and the moment is gone. Solma pulls Warren's wrist until he stumbles after her, wailing in protest. Olive says something but Solma's ears roar too loudly for her to hear what it is. "Shut up!" she snarls. Warren's wriggles become more forceful.

"They didn't!" he protests. "You're hurting me! Let go!"

She doesn't. She's not letting go of him. Not ever. He's too precious to relinquish to these traitors. She holds him tight and turns, fixing Cobra with a venomous glare.

"If you come near him again," she says, her voice dangerously quiet. "I won't hold back. D'you understand? I don't want to hurt you, but I will. And you should leave. All of you."

She turns and marches away, dragging Warren behind her. He fights her, his protests becoming angrier, until he starts uttering swearwords Solma didn't think he knew. She scolds him and keeps marching. Olive's face burns in her mind but she doesn't look back. It's too late to look back.

TWENTY-SIX

WARREN STOPS WRIGGLING AND directs his energy into complaining. Loudly.

"Sol! Let go! I hate you! Get off!"

Solma ignores him. She knows she's holding his wrist too tightly, but she can't loosen her grip. It's all falling apart. She'd promised Ma and Dja to keep him safe and now the Whisperers are trying to take him away. Solma has to stop herself from tightening her hold on him at the thought. Panic and fury compete in her gut so her body pulses with adrenalin. She can barely see, but she knows where she's going. She marches into the village, ignoring the children who implore Warren to come and play.

When she turns up the first path, Warren is quiet. Solma feels him tensing as the realization hits him, and he starts struggling with renewed vigor.

"No, Solma, no!" he cries, sobbing. He writhes and punches her hip. His fists are so small his attack barely registers. Solma glares at him.

"It's the only way, Warren!" she snaps. "We should'a done this from the start!"

It seems so obvious now. How could she put her faith in the Whisperers? Traitors. All of them.

Ahead, the Steward's house comes into view. It's easily twice the size of any other house in the village, with a row of solar panels on the roof and glass in the windows instead of shutters. It's the only house in Sand's End with these luxuries and Solma wonders why she feels a pang of dread when she sees them. That doesn't make sense. Blaiz is their Steward. He needs electricity and warmth more than the rest of them. She shakes the feeling of foreboding off and quickens her stride.

Warren throws his head back and wails when he sees the house, prying at Solma's fingers, begging her to let him go.

"No! You don't understand!" he yells. "You don't get it! He'll kill her, Sol! He'll kill her!"

Solma shakes his wrist. "Don't be such a child!" she snaps. "He won't!"

Earth! She sounds like Bell. Suffocating and over-protective. She knows she's hurting her brother, knows her fingers are tight enough to leave bruises on his wrists, but she can't help it. Fear is a pack of wild dogs at her back, driving her on.

This is all so wrong. It's so wrong and she's so helpless.

When they reach the door to the Steward's house, it opens before Solma raises her hand to knock. And there is Maxen, in his Guard uniform with his rifle gleaming on his shoulder, boots freshly polished.

He stares at her. "Sol?"

"I got to speak to Blaiz."

Warren gives up fighting at the sight of Maxen. He stands miserably at her side, his wrist limp in her grip. Maxen stares between them. "Yeah," he says. "I think you do. Come in, then."

He steps aside. Warren resists at the threshold and Solma attempts kindness.

"Come on, Warren, it's ok."

He glares at her with such a sense of betrayal that Solma gives up and tugs him roughly through the door. He's trying so hard to get away from her. He's too young to understand. One day, he'll get it. One day, he'll look back and know she did it to protect him.

She can live with his hatred for now. As long as he's safe.

She swallows the bitter taste of guilt and follows Maxen down the long corridor. She's never been in Blaiz's house before. It's huge. A veritable mansion. With rooms. Every house she's ever been in is just one room, with curtains and cloth hung haphazardly across the ceiling to afford a crude privacy. This has doors upon doors. It has locks on the doors, and some of the rooms even have electric lights.

Solma tries to keep the astonishment off her face, but there are rugs on the floor and the windows have proper glass in, some of them are framed with curtains. So many riches. She'd never realized …

"Sol, please," Warren sobs. "Please."

She clenches her jaw and ignores his whimpering as best she can. Maxen pauses outside a closed door. "He's in his study," he says finally. "I'll let him know you're here."

He goes to knock, but before he can, Solma reaches out and snatches up his hand, surprising them both. Maxen turns to her. They are almost the same height, Solma slightly taller. She can look into his eyes almost without tilting her head and she holds his gaze now, questions gathering at the back of her throat. He searches her face and his hand closes around hers, his thumb stroking her wrist.

"You ok?"

She nods, then changes her mind and shakes her head. His expression softens and, before Solma can protest, he gathers her against him and gently kisses the top of her head. "You're doing the right thing," he says. "I promise. I'll help you."

Solma breathes him in; the earthy, musky scent she's so used to, that she must smell of too, from days working in the Guard. He smells like safety. Like home. The fragrance fortifies her, so that when he eventually lets go, she feels strong enough to stand on her own.

"Ok. I'm ready."

He knocks and a muffled voice on the other side says, "Enter." Maxen opens the door a fraction.

"Wait here," he says, and slips inside, pulling it closed behind him. Solma shifts her weight from leg to leg, waiting. Warren shakes his head, face red and shining with tears.

"Please, Sol," he begs. "Please."

Solma kneels beside him, loosens her grip on his wrist. She wipes his tears and finds a ragged cloth to clean his nose. He resists, pushing her away. Patience, she tells herself. He doesn't understand.

"I'm sorry, Warren," she says. "But I got to. To keep you safe, d'you understand?"

He shakes his head again and fresh tears pour down his cheeks. Solma gives up and stands. She transfers her grip from his wrist to his hand and squeezes it. He's her little brother. He's lived this long because of the sacrifices she's made and one day, he *will* understand that. It's not his fault. It's not either of their fault. They stand outside the door to Blaiz's study, listening to the muted conversation within. Warren's hand is limp in hers. They wait.

The door creaks open and Maxen peers around it.

"He'll see you straight away," he says, pale eyes glistening as they meet Solma's. "You're doing the right thing."

He stands aside. Solma makes sure to hold her head high as she enters Blaiz's study, Warren in tow. The room is like nothing Solma has ever seen. At least half again as big as Bell's entire house with a burgundy rug thrown across the center of the floor. The window is large so the room is well lit, even without the electric light on Blaiz's desk. And the desk is vast, awash with heaps of papers that Blaiz seems to have written on once and then had no need to reuse. She can't help herself. She gapes. She doesn't remember ever seeing such wealth before and had no idea it existed in her village.

Blaiz sits behind the desk on a tall-backed wooden chair, frowning. Stubble shadows his jaw and his pale eyes—the same blue as Maxen's—are hooded. He beckons Solma forward without looking up and snatches a document from his pile as if it is nothing. As if the paper deserves no reverence but is simply a fact of life. It crumples a little under his thumb and Solma almost whimpers at the damage. Blaiz doesn't notice. When he places the document down, the crease left by his touch is still there. Solma clenches her fist to resist the urge to smooth it. She mustn't touch it. Her hands are grubby with work. Grubby with guilt.

"Hello, Sergeant," Blaiz says, meeting her eye. Solma blinks, and the memory of his twisted face, inches from hers, flashes behind her eyes. She forces it back. It doesn't feel real. Perhaps it wasn't.

"Hello, Sir," Solma says. Warren whimpers and wriggles in her grip. Reluctantly, she releases him. He glares at her and rubs at his wrist but says nothing. His eyes dart around the room, to the windows, the door now closed behind them with Maxen stood in front of him. He's looking for escape. But there is none. Solma tastes that bitter guilt again. She can't do this. Maybe she should just go.

Maxen catches her eye, gives her a small smile and nods.

"Go on," he mouths.

She gazes at him a little longer, drawing strength from those pale eyes. He's right. She must. She takes a deep breath and turns to face Blaiz.

"Sir, I know where the nest is," she says, quickly, so that the words don't stick in her throat. Behind her, Warren whimpers and clutches his head, fresh tears springing from his eyes. Solma plunges on. She won't turn back now. This is the right thing. The Whisperers never deserved her trust. And if Solma's honest with herself, that hurts. It hurts because she dropped her guard. It hurts because she should have known better. Never again.

"I know where the nest is," she says again, "and I reckon the Earth Whisperers tried to destroy it."

And Olive, she thinks. But something holds her back from saying that.

"Maxen and I managed to save it. But it's in danger. I know the secret is forbidden but you can't exile us."

Blaiz stares at her with eyes like needles. Solma flinches before she can stop herself. She holds his gaze as best she can, hoping she looks brave. Hoping she doesn't look like the helpless, childish wreck she feels. Warren's whimpers intensify and become open sobs. Solma reaches back to squeeze his shoulder but he worms away from her, glowering. Blaiz steeples his fingers together, his eyes unblinking. He seems to look right through her.

"And why," he asks steadily, "should I not exile you, Solma El Gatra, Traitor of Sand's End?"

The words cut like bayonets and Solma flinches. He doesn't mean it. He's just angry. She's not a traitor, not really, she just wanted to do the right thing.

Her eyes flicker to Warren. This is a gamble. Can she do this? If she does, Blaiz might punish Warren. If she doesn't, he'll definitely punish them both. This is the right thing.

"'Cos Warren can control the bees," she says. "If you want the nest, you need him. And if you need him, you need me. I can keep him and the nest safe."

Blaiz barely moves but Solma sees a tendon in his jaw twitch. "How do we keep the location secret from the other Stewards?" he demands.

"No Gatra patrol there during the day," she says. "I'll do covert patrols in the area as if it were a usual

Guard route. At night, we post hidden Guards to watch it."

Blaiz rubs his chin with the back of one hand, thinking. He glances towards the door where his son stands in silence.

"And you vouch for her, do you, Maxen?" he asks. "If you do, know that you are responsible for her."

Solma's gut twists. She resists the urge to sneak a glance behind her and read Maxen's face. But she doesn't need to. He doesn't hesitate.

"Yes, sir," he says, striding to her side. He places his hand on the small of her back. Solma's rush of relief is dizzying.

"Good," Blaiz says. He stands and stalks round his desk. Solma stiffens, holding herself to attention, but Blaiz bypasses her altogether and kneels in front of Warren. Warren backs away, green eyes sparkling with fear. He's stopped sobbing now, but tears still leak from his eyes. He stares at Blaiz, clouds of confusion crossing his face.

"You can control the bees, eh?" Blaiz says, his voice a low growl. Warren says nothing. "So the Whisperers were right. You do have power. I thought as much. But you're ours, Warren, and we'll not let that treacherous lot have you. If you can make the bees work for us, we'll keep you and your sister safe."

Warren blinks, droplets clinging to his lashes. He stares at Blaiz, then up at Solma. He looks so tired, his little hands balled into fists at his sides as he drops his gaze to the floor. Blaiz stands.

"The glasshouse produce is coming into season," he says, "and we don't have many pollenbots left. Direct the bees to pollinate there." He turns towards his desk, then pauses for a moment, thinking. "And Warren?" He says, not turning around. "They must move discreetly. I'll direct my Guard to destroy any bees they think might lead enemies back to the nest. Is that clear?"

The words hit Solma like a punch in the gut and she clutches her belly, fighting nausea. He can't mean that. Surely he can't. Solma searches his face, waiting for some sign that it's just a warning, just to scare them. But he appears sincere.

Warren doesn't look at Blaiz. Instead, he lifts his eyes to meet Solma's, his gaze full of grief.

"Yes, Sir," he whispers, still glaring at his sister. "It's clear."

TWENTY-SEVEN

RAISED VOICES CARRY FROM the center of the village. Raging, frightened. Two of them are voices Solma recognizes: the croaky tone of Piotr and the high-pitched wailing of his younger sister, Gracie. The other voices are unknown, though the clip of a Westwater accent and a desert twang catch her ear. Solma nudges Maxen's arm.

"Let's go," she says.

Maxen sighs. "Everyone's going mad," he grumbles, but he squeezes her hand before they head towards the commotion. Maxen glances back over his shoulder. "Aldo's in charge," he says. Olive looks thunderous but doesn't reply. What's the likelihood she'll start bossing around the other two the minute Solma and Maxen are gone? She never was good at following orders. Solma pauses for a moment to fix Olive with a hard scowl but Olive only glares back harder. Solma

rolls her eyes and leaves it be. Olive is treading dangerous ground and she knows it.

The voices from the village grow bolder, with
threats and posturing clearly becoming the odd shove.

"Don't you touch me!"

"I'll do what I like!"

"Then I'll make you sorry!"

Solma's exhausted just listening to them. It's happening so often now that she can barely muster the
adrenalin she felt when it all first started. Now, it just
makes her tired. It's always over the same thing: the
visitors think all of Sand's End know about the bees.
All of Sand's End think the visitors should shove off
home. It's a never-ending cycle of scuffles, home in-
vasions, property destruction and, occasionally, full
blown fights. Last week, Solma and Maxen had to
persuade elderly Gerta that pointing a hunting rifle
straight between the eyes of a visiting Steward was not
going to sort this out. That it might, in fact, make
things worse. Solma's known Gerta all her life. She
sat on the woman's lap as a child and listened to her
stories. Gerta helped Bell nurse Solma after she lost
her leg. She's a peaceful woman. Yet there she was,
hunting rifle cocked and ready as if she would blast
the visiting Steward straight to hell without a second

thought. Maxen's right. Everyone's going mad. Solma's not sure how long this can go on for. Nearly two months of it and she's worn out.

Two weeks ago, someone slashed open a Northtip Province tent. Then a rock was thrown through a village window, splintering the shutters. Then a couple of village children went missing. Everyone was frantic for twenty-four hours before they were found happily playing under guard in a visitor's tent. Then there was an attack on one of the Stewards ... Solma can't even remember how that started or ended.

There are squabbles between the villagers, too. The Fei are still angry with the Oritch over Piotr claiming first access to the bees. Two days ago, the Oritch turned up at their fields to find some of the new saplings slashed and uprooted. Solma can't rule out that it was the Sand's End Fei that did it.

She squeezes the bridge of her nose, willing the ache behind her eyes to go away. The aim had been to avoid another Hive War. But she doesn't seem to have managed that.

They've caught the fight early this time; it's still all shouting, squaring shoulders and each side measuring the other up. By the looks of things, Piotr's picked a fight he has no hope of winning. His eyes dart frantically, searching for an escape that won't end in him losing face. He cradles his injured hand to his chest and it makes him look small and frail. When he catches sight of Solma and Maxen, his face floods with relief.

But the three soldiers he's squared up to look less impressed. They're huge, draped with weaponry and snarling like redbears. They're in a uniform of sorts but they don't look like Gatra. They're wearing dark grey shirts with matching combat trousers and thick, heavy boots. Expensive boots. Wherever their loyalty lies, they are well provided for. Their heads are shaven and ...

... and Solma recognizes them, recognizes the vicious curve of those knives, the pistols.

She recognizes the man who turns to face her, with violet eyes and a flame inked above one eyebrow ...

She stifles a gasp and forces her face not to react as he bares his teeth. Solma can still see him snatching Warren up in one arm, lifting him bodily from the ground. She can still see his fury and frustration as the blade of her knife pressed against his throat. She'd let him go. She'd let him go and now he's back.

Solma unshoulders her gun and snaps the safety off.

"Go back to your Steward," she growls, "and there will be no further trouble."

Beside her, Maxen hesitates. Piotr and Gracie shuffle backwards, somehow managing to place Solma and Maxen between them and the soldiers. Solma barely notices. She can't break her gaze away from the violet-eyed man.

Raider, she thinks. Renegade. Thief. Murderer!

"Who're you with?" she demands. Maxen glances at her sideways.

"Sol ..."

Solma ignores him. "Who," she says again, her voice heavy with fury, "are you with?"

The violet-eyed soldier sneers. "What you gonna do, little girl?"

Solma reacts before she can stop herself. Knife unsheathed, she kicks her blade-foot against the man's knee and brings her knife up to his throat as he drops to the dirt. His two friends unsnap pistols from their holsters. Solma has a barrel pressed to the nape of her neck and another at her temple but she doesn't care. Maxen shouts something. Gracie screams. Solma barely hears a thing. She can see nothing but the violet-eyed man, glowering from where he kneels in the dust. His hands are held out, surrendering, but his expression is raging.

"Remember this?" Solma snarls. "Been here before, ain't we?"

The violet-eyed man says nothing. Solma leans in until her face is inches from his. The enemy guns track her.

"Who," Solma repeats, her voice just above a whisper, "are you working for?"

The man's lip curls and he opens his mouth to answer.

"Vulkan!" One of his friends warns.

The violet-eyed man hesitates. He smiles. His canines gleam, animal-sharp. "We're on the same side," he sneers. "*Little girl.*"

Solma presses the blade a little harder against his throat and sees a bulb of red bloom above the steel. The violet-eyed man sucks in a breath and his fellows cock their weapons. Solma could kill him. It would be so easy. The tiniest change in pressure, a soft flick of her wrist.

But the violet-eyed man raises his gaze and meets Solma.

"You don't wanna kill me, Solma El Gatra," he says. "Remember? Remember the look on your brother's face?"

Solma feels the breath punched from her lungs. He knows her name. He remembers Warren. His eyes ... Who is this man? He's no-one, Solma tells herself. He's a murderer, a raider. He's better off dead. Better off spilled onto the ground where he can't burn and steal. Where he can't snatch her little brother away.

She angles her wrist to slice him open.

"Sergeant!" Maxen barks. "Stand down!"

Solma freezes. The warning in Maxen's voice is clear but the violet-eyed man grins at her, wolfish in his glee. Still, it would do no good to kill him. The thought of bleeding him makes Solma queasy enough that her anger melts away.

For the second time, she removes the blade of her knife and stands back. "Go back to your master," she snaps. "Stay outta the village. Leave our people alone. *Vulkan.*"

She has his name, now. And she'll remember that face, those eyes. Vulkan gets to his feet, wiping blood from his throat with the back of one hand. He examines the scarlet smear on his knuckles and grins. "Your people," he says, laughing nastily. "They don't look like your people, little girl."

Anger bubbles in Solma again but this time it's Maxen who steps in. He aims his rifle between the man's eyes. "Leave my Sergeant," he orders. "And leave my village. This is your last warning, or I'll shoot you and your friends. Clear?"

The violet-eyed man glares, but he backs down. His friends holster their guns and the three of them turn and trudge away, not even bothering to glance back. Solma is tempted to follow them but Piotr faints before she has a chance and Gracie drops to his side, clutching his face, yelling his name. Vulkan goes out of Solma's head.

"I'll get Olive," Maxen says. He turns to go but Solma stops him.

"No!"

She grabs his arm, holds him back. He stares at her, puzzled.

"Piotr needs a doctor, Sol," he says. "What's wrong?"

Solma gazes at him, imploring him to understand without her having to explain. Because Olive is with the Earth Whisperers. Because Olive is angry with her.

Because she can't bear to see the girl's face, ask for her help, knowing that Olive helped attack the bees.

That betrayal still cuts deep, though Solma has no idea why. She hates the idea that she might need Olive's help but that's not a good enough excuse.

"'Cos—" she splutters. "'Cos Dr. Roseann is busy with all the nonsense we've had. Piotr's fine, he just needs somewhere to rest. Let's get him to Gerta. She'll look after him."

Maxen tenses and, for a moment, Solma doesn't think he'll yield, but then he sighs and touches her face. "Good thinking," he says, smiling. "Alright. C'mon, help me lift him."

TWENTY-EIGHT

SOLMA IS UNNERVED BY how light Piotr is. He hangs in their arms like a child's doll. Still, it takes them fifteen minutes to carry his body, suspended like a bridge between them, to Gerta's house. When they arrive, Solma's breath is ragged, her face filmed over with sweat. They lay him down and Solma props his head up with her food pack. Gracie cries Piotr's name, trying to shake him awake. As if that will help. Solma bats her away, more impatiently than she'd intended.

"He needs rest," she says, trying for compassion and managing exasperation. Gracie glares.

"I know what he needs," she snaps. "And you done enough."

Solma blinks. She's about to retort but puzzlement overtakes the hurt and she ends up just staring. What on Earth is Gracie talking about? Solma has done nothing that hasn't been for the village, for the protection of her brother and their people. And yet Gracie stares with eyes hollow as bullet wounds. Hateful. Accusing.

Maxen raps his knuckles on the door and Gerta croaks from within.

"Who's that now? Wait a minute ..."

The door pulls inwards. Solma opens her mouth to explain. And freezes.

It isn't Gerta at the door. It's Cobra. Who looks equally surprised to see Maxen and Solma.

Her eyes meet Solma's and her gaze hardens. "What do you want?" she says. Her voice is quiet but edged with something fierce. Solma does not like that tone.

"What you doing here?" she demands. "Get out! This isn't your house!"

"No," Gerta growls, shuffling into view and leaning heavily on her stick in the doorway. "It's my house, and Cobra is my guest. So you watch your tone, young Sol. I landed you plenty smacks when you were little and I ain't afraid to do it now, rifle or no." She wraps her free arm around Cobra's shoulder and the gesture is so familiar that Solma's anger is shaken from her. How does Cobra know Gerta? And why is she in Gerta's house?

Cobra says nothing. Her green eyes search Solma's face, her mouth turned down. Her head looks freshly shaved, Solma thinks, and her skin shines as if just washed. Her green robes are spotless and there's fresh stitching on one of the sleeves. Solma's eyes narrow.

"Don't you dare, Solma El Yuen!" Gerta barks. "You leave Cobra alone!"

Solma's jaw clenches. "It's El Gatra, now," she says, trying and failing to keep her voice steady. "I've been in the Gathering Guard for four years, remember? I'm not a Yuen anymore."

Gerta's mouth twitches and Solma wonders if she's being laughed at. Daft old woman. Solma hasn't been a child for a long time now. She's been patrolling the village territories, hunting wild boar, fighting raiders. She lost her leg for this village and its people. She deserves some respect.

But before she can say anything, Gerta hugs Cobra and kisses the top of her head. She whispers something into her ear and hands her a small fabric bundle, knotted at the top, that smells faintly like Dr Roseann's medical kit. Why is Gerta giving Cobra medicine?

Cobra kisses Gerta's cheek and accepts the bundle. "Thank you."

She presses her palms together and glides out of the house without looking at either Solma or Maxen. Solma rolls her eyes. Infuriating. Affecting that ridiculous air of peace when she's the one who lured the moon badger to the nest. If Gerta knew ...

But she doesn't. And there are more pressing matters.

Gerta's eyes fall on Piotr, who lays blinking and murmuring, not knowing where he is. Gracie mops his brow with the hem of her grubby dress. Gerta sighs.

"Exhaustion," she says. "And malnutrition. And dehydration. And lack of sleep. And the trauma to his hand. Why've you brought him here? He needs Dr. Roseann."

Solma reaches down to scratch her leg before remembering it isn't there. Her nails drag against the prosthesis but the itch remains. She desists. Gerta's eyes narrow.

"You do that when you're nervous, girl," she says. "What'ya got to be nervous about?"

Solma opens her mouth, then thinks better of it and closes it again. She feels Maxen staring at her, eyes full of questions, but she refuses to meet his gaze. Gerta grunts and shuffles aside.

"Better bring him in then," she says. "But you be quiet. Your brother's sleeping."

"Still?"

Solma's gut twists. She'd left him sleeping nearly five hours ago, after a long night soothing his nightmares. Is he sick? He can't be sick.

Gerta raises an eyebrow, "Yeah," she says. "Still. I dunno what Blaiz has got him doing, Solma, but it's driving him nuts. You need to have a word with that Steward of yours."

Solma scowls as she and Maxen steady Piotr and guide him into Gerta's house.

"He's your Steward, too," Solma points out. Gerta barks a laugh and says nothing.

Piotr's head lolls and a thread of drool hangs from his mouth. Gerta closes the door and firmly directs Gracie to sit in the rocking chair. "Get yourself some tea," she says, waving an absent hand at the pot. "You sit still and you be quiet, you hear?"

Gracie nods, cowed.

Piotr crumples onto a heap of straw and blankets Gerta keeps laid out under the window. They cover him with a scratchy blanket and he falls into a more natural sleep. Gerta places a bucket and a cup of water by his head before easing herself onto a rickety stool. "He needs sleep," she says. "Like we all do."

Solma says nothing. There's nothing to say, is there? Instead, she leaves her rifle with Maxen and pulls back the curtains around Gerta's bed, where she left her brother before her Guard shift. Warren sleeps fitfully, curled into a tight ball with his fists clenched beneath his cheek and his eyes searching under closed lids. He mutters something Solma can't hear. Every so often, his finger twitches or his foot kicks. He is anything but peaceful. He fights in his dreams just like he fights when he's awake. Solma brushes a lock of red-gold hair from his forehead and feels the grime on his skin. His eyes are sunken craters. His cheekbones prominent, mouth a pale flower.

He's so small. So weak. He can't do this anymore. But Solma can't think of a way around it. Blaiz is relentless with him; issuing orders about where the bees should be, what they should pollinate and the paths they should follow to avoid being seen. Warren protests but Blaiz just gets impatient with him, reminds them both that, if they don't like it, they can find another village.

Warren had screamed and cried at first, stamping his little feet and wailing that they *would* find another village! Just Blaiz wait and see! But he doesn't understand, does he? He doesn't know what those wastelands are like. He doesn't know how hostile other villages can be.

He just got angrier when Blaiz laughed.

But these last few weeks, he's not been angry anymore. He's been exhausted. He whispers Blume's name in his sleep and when he wakes, he pushes Solma away. He doesn't want her, he says. He wants Cobra. Cobra understands.

But how is Solma supposed to explain? That Cobra isn't who he thinks she is. That Cobra betrayed them.

Maxen appears beside her, shoulder to shoulder, so that no one can see him take her hand. He casts her a sideways smile. "He ok, you think?"

Solma tastes something bitter and gulps. She doesn't trust herself to speak, so she nods. Decisive. Yes, he'll be fine. He's got her. She'll take care of him. Maxen squeezes her hand. "You need a minute?"

Solma hesitates, but Maxen seems to know. He always knows. He nudges her shoulder gently with his own and she finds herself smiling softly at him. He's a good person. A good soldier. He'll make a good Steward one day, too.

"I'll take first watch," he says. "Come take your shift in an hour, ok?"

He squeezes her hand again before letting go and handing her rifle back. He nods to Gerta and leaves without another word. Gerta watches him go, eyes narrowed, then turns accusing eyes on Solma.

"Sneaking around with the Camber boy, are we?" she says quietly. Solma's eyes flicker towards Gracie before she can help herself, but the woman is, once again, kneeling by her brother's side. She doesn't appear to have heard. Solma shakes her head firmly.

"We're just friends," she says, "And you ain't my minder anymore, Gerta, so back off."

Gerta affects hurt and taps her stick against the ground. "Huh. Don't mind me then, little Sol. Never mind an old woman nearly five times your age who might have a bit of life experience to share. Go your own way then. See if I care. Ain't no matter to me if you get exiled, running around with Steward-caste. He'll have a wife set up ready for him, y'know."

Solma scowls. "I know," she says.

Truth is, she hasn't thought about that in a while. Gerta's right, though. The other castes can set up home with who they want from their own village, but a Steward's son marries a Steward's daughter, regardless of his wishes or preferences. She and Maxen are never going to be together. Not really. Not if Blaiz has anything to say about it.

Gerta stares at Solma for a moment longer before she hobbles to the stove to reheat the kettle. She shoos Gracie away from Piotr, commanding her to sit still or go away. Gracie whines but subsides when Gerta towers over her, brandishing her stick like a sabre, and tells her to shut up or she'll get a thorough smack on the behind. Gracie shuts up.

Solma props her rifle by the bed and wets a cloth in the sink, returning to mop her brother's grimy face. He stirs at her touch, his eyes cracking open.

"Sol?" His voice is croaky with exhaustion and thirst. "Sol? That you?"

She winks at him. "Yeah," she says. "Sleepy head. You feel better?"

Warren thinks about it, laying still while his mind and body return to the waking world. For a moment, his eyes are bright in their sunken craters and his face is empty of worry. But then the world hits him again and Solma sees the weight settle on him, suffocating him. His little face crumples and he moans, rolling away from her. She rubs her palm against his back but he pushes her off. Irritation flares in her throat but she swallows it down, determined not to get cross with him again. He's too young for all of this. He doesn't understand this is the price they pay for safety. He'll get it one day. He'll look back and realize she was only trying to keep him safe.

There's a sharp knock at the door, rattling the windows. Solma jumps and her hands reach for her hunting knife before she can stop herself. She stares at the door, where a shadow shifts across the seam of light beneath. Solma's heart squeezes. Gerta hobbles over, calling for whoever waits beyond to be patient with a tired old woman. But Solma knows who it is. It doesn't matter which house she rests Warren in, which old woman she hides him with, Blaiz always finds them.

TWENTY-NINE

He steps wordlessly into the house without greeting Gerta or even looking at her. Gerta grunts her disapproval but says nothing as she closes the door. Blaiz's eyes are furious, his fists clenched. He scans the room, the vein twitching in his temple, until his gaze lands on Solma and Warren.

"Everyone out," he says, voice dangerously quiet.

Gerta begins to protest. "This is *my* home—"

"And my village," Blaiz interrupts, "so get out."

Gerta glares but does as she's told, hobbling to the door and holding it open while Gracie wakes Piotr and helps him out. They both cast fearful glances at Blaiz as they pass. Solma feels a thrill of irritation at the way they look at him. But watching him now, commanding a room with such selfish ease, she wonders why. Somewhere in the back of her brain, a memory of Blaiz flashes: snarling as he traps her against a wall, words full of venom, eyes full of hate. He looks like he could be that man again now. She ought to stand, but Warren clings to her, cowering behind her shoulder as if he can hide from his Steward.

Blaiz waits until the door closes before he lifts a hand and opens his fist. Warren whimpers.

"Please," he murmurs. "Please."

Blaiz says nothing. He stares at them as they gaze at the dead bee on his palm. It's small, but healthy looking, aside from the fact it's dead. Its antennae folded back over its blunt head, multifaceted eyes dull and lightless. Its wings are crossed quietly over its back. There's a tiny ball of pollen still packed against one leg. It had been on its way home, ready to deliver its precious cargo.

And now it's dead in Blaiz's hand.

Could've been anything, Solma tells herself. Could've died of exhaustion, flown into a window or been caught by a gust of wind. Blaiz might've just found it, already dead. He probably scooped it from the ground so no one else would see it.

But in the deepest corner of her heart, Solma knows that isn't true.

"I told you," He growls. "To guide them wide of the village. I told you, if I saw one, I'd kill it."

Warren begins to sob, his little hands covering his face. Solma resists the instinct to hug him close. Somehow, such a show of love doesn't seem right in front of Blaiz. Instead, she squeezes his shoulder and rises off the bed so that she's stood between her brother and this tyrannical man she's supposed to trust.

She *did* trust him. She chose him over Cobra and Olive and the Earth Whisperers. It was the right thing to do. It still is. But she can't take her eyes off the dead bee in his hand.

Blume's daughter. A tiny piece of a whole organism. She almost expects the little thing to thrum to life at any moment. A silent bee feels an unnatural thing.

"Where did you find it?" she asks, quietly. She realizes her hand is still on the hilt of her hunting knife and, with great effort, forces herself to release it. Blaiz sneers.

"Skulking about the entrance to a glass house," he says, "as if it had all the time in the world. Stupid creature. I told you, Warren. They weren't to linger. You've disobeyed me."

Solma takes a breath, ready to defend her brother. She expects him to wail, to curl up in a fetal ball and hide beneath Gerta's blankets. But he doesn't. She feels him bristling and glances back to find he has clambered to his feet. His face shines with tears but he's stopped crying. Instead, his eyes are furious, little body shaking. He steadies himself, leaning heavily against the bed. Solma bends down to support him but he squirms away, glaring hard at Blaiz. There's something in his gaze she's never seen before. Those meadow-green eyes, usually glittering with hope, are suddenly hard and furious and ...

... and *hateful.* Solma's breath catches. Her brother is growing up. He's growing up and she can't bear it.

"I ain't disobeyed you," Warren says. His voice trembles, but with anger rather than fear. "I told them what you said. But I can't control them. It ain't like Solma said. They ain't ... they ain't pollenbots. They're *creatures.* They're just trying to live!"

Blaiz brandishes the dead bee. On his hand, the corpse topples onto its side, revealing the legs clutched up underneath it, as if in pain. Warren clasps his own belly and moans, but he recovers before Solma can intervene. Again, he squirms away from her arms. He hasn't looked at her this whole time. His eyes, gleaming with animosity, never leave Blaiz's. Solma's stomach weighs heavy as lead.

Earth! She was only trying to protect him and look what she's done. He's so full of hate. It rattles in his breath, gleams in his eyes. She's afraid that he'll turn that furious gaze on her, too.

Blaiz neither notices nor cares. He closes the gap between them and holds the bee inches from Warren's face. "This one didn't do a very good job of living, did it?" he growls. "Don't be so naïve, boy! You have no idea what's at stake! You think I'm going to let any other village find our bees and take them from us? I'd rather see the nest destroyed than let that happen!"

Solma bristles before she can help herself. She's drawn breath to fight back but the tiniest touch on her arm stops her. She looks down to find Warren's fingers wrapped gently around her wrist. He doesn't look at her, still, but his meaning is clear. Calm down, he's saying. There's no use in that. She stares at him. Since when did her brother start comforting *her*?

"They ain't our bees," Warren whispers. "They belong to themselves. I'm doing my best."

Blaiz clearly wasn't expecting this. For a moment, the anger vanishes from his face and he stares in astonishment. But the moment is gone so quickly Solma wonders whether she imagined it. Blaiz's face twists again and his fingers close hard over the body of the bee, crushing it. Warren winces but says nothing.

"You are treading on dangerous ground, you two," Blaiz growls. "You broke so many rules. The only reason you are still here is because of what *he*—" he jabs his finger into Warren's chest, "—can do. If he can't do it, you're gone. You hear? I'll see you thrown out of this village like the garbage you are. I've done it before."

Solma barely hears what he's saying over the hammering of her own pulse. His voice becomes distant as her mind rushes with faraway images.

A girl with flame-red hair and a splash of freckles, looking back before she walks away. Solma had watched it happen and felt her world fall apart. She was terrified for that girl. Why was she so frightened for a girl whose name she can't even remember?

The girl ... the flower ...

But with Blaiz sneering, brandishing the body of a dead bee, she can hardly think straight.

"And," Blaiz snarls, unaware of the storm in Solma's mind, "I'll see to it you'll be shot on sight if you come within two hundred yards of any village, not just this one."

His spittle peppers Solma's face. There's foam at the corners of his mouth, his eyes huge and wild. He's losing it, Solma realizes. That control he's so good at, he's losing it. And, Solma thinks, she has no idea what this man is capable of.

THIRTY

Maxen's hand traces Solma's collarbone. She snuggles into the crook of his arm and closes her eyes. His breath warms her cheek as he plants a kiss there. With her eyes closed, Solma concentrates on the smell of the grass. It's so tall, now, rustling in the breeze. Just beyond is the ash tree, flanked with its honor guard of birches, where Blume's nest is hidden. Every so often, a small shape emerges from the shade, buzzes in circles around the trees and then zooms off like a tiny shooting star. Solma hears them drone past and her heart kicks with both joy and dread. She hopes the little worker bee finds her flowers. She hopes Blaiz doesn't find the bee first.

Harvest is underway. The orchards are bursting with so much fruit that Solma hardly believes her eyes whenever she patrols them. And there are tomatoes in the glass houses. Hundreds of them. It doesn't feel right that a single nest of bees has brought such riches to their village. It feels like cheating.

And the other Stewards are still here, stalking through the plentiful fields on the lookout for the secret they know is there. The Earth Whisperers patrol the fields, too, their hands clasped together in that ridiculous imitation of prayer. But Solma knows what they're doing. They're no better than the Stewards. Hypocrites. Traitors. Solma takes a deep breath to calm herself.

The village feels more alive this year. There's hope amidst the tension. But the tension is still there, like a snake in the shade, deathly patient.

Solma left Warren sleeping fitfully that morning, argued with Bell again, and took the long way to her post to avoid passing Blaiz's house. She's avoided Blaiz since he showed her and Warren the dead bee a month ago. That incident has ... confused her. And Solma's not sure she's ready to face that confusion yet. She feels Maxen kiss each of her closed eyelids and smiles.

"You need some sleep," he whispers. "I can take tonight's watch if you want?"

Solma shakes her head. "No," she says. "Your Dja would know. He don't like me."

Maxen chuckles. "Dja's got a lot to worry about," he points out. "He doesn't like anyone. But he needs you. And he knows the villagers respect you."

Solma says nothing. What is there to say? Can she tell Maxen that his father cornered her in the village as the sun was going down and told her she was a traitor? Would he believe her? Would he believe that his Dja marched into an old woman's house and brandished a dead bee? Solma's brow furrows. Blaiz is a good man, she's sure of it. At least, he used to be. She's not sure anymore. Every time she tells herself that he's her Steward, that he keeps them safe, she remembers his twisted snarl as he'd told her she was just like her Dja ...

... her Dja and his precious beetles, he'd said, trying to bring the birds back. Earth, her head is a mess. Maxen's right. She *does* need to sleep. But she can't. Not until this whole thing is over.

Whenever that might be.

Maxen kisses her softly. Solma feels warmth trickling through her body and lets herself not care for a moment. She lets herself kiss Maxen back. This is a good thing. This is one good thing amidst the chaos and madness and impossible things. He pulls away and smiles at her.

"I hope your Dja didn't see *that*," Solma says, grinning. Maxen shrugs.

"So what if he did?"

She laughs and punches him lightly on the shoulder. "You ain't the one he'll punish!"

Maxen wraps his arms around her and holds her close. "Nah," he says. "I won't let him."

Solma raises an eyebrow. "Like you'd have a choice!"

"Hey, shut up!" he says, feigning hurt. Solma laughs harder and he quiets her with another kiss. She lets herself be silenced, lets herself settle into the grass and drift into the moment. She wants, however briefly, not to be Solma the Soldier. She wants to be Solma the young woman. Just for a little bit.

But the sun is climbing quickly, its warmth on Solma's skin a reminder that their time is stolen. Eventually, Maxen pulls away from her and, shielding his eyes, squints up to check the sun's progress.

"Second patrol," he says. "I gotta go."

Solma nods. Pointless arguing. "How's Olive been?"

The words are out of her mouth before she has time to wonder why she wants to know. She's barely seen Olive this past month. Maxen has kept them apart, posting them on different patrols and assigning Olive mainly to village peacekeeping duties, which she must hate. Besides, most of Solma's time these days is spent here: hiding in the grass, guarding a bee colony that no one knows is there. Maxen glances at her in surprise.

"She's ... ok," he says. "We've been keeping her busy, away from the Earth Whisperers."

Solma shakes her head, mouth turned down in disgust. "We should throw them out of the village," she mutters, her fury surfacing again. "Traitors."

Maxen suppresses a smile. "You know we can't do that," he says. "They're free to go where they choose. We can't throw them out."

Solma rolls her eyes. "Yeah, but while they're watching us, who's watching them?" she points out. "Who's stopping them taking things for themselves? Or keeping secrets? Or destroying bee nests?"

Maxen raises an eyebrow. "This really isn't a conversation we've got time for right now, Sol," he says. "Look, you sure you don't want me to take this watch? You can take second patrol and be done in an hour. You could get some sleep after. You look like you need it."

She hits him playfully on the arm. "I look fine!" she protests. "And no. It's my watch and my responsibility. I promised your Dja."

Even mentioning him sets her gut writhing. She clutches her belly without thinking but Maxen doesn't notice. He plants a last kiss on top of her head and gathers his rifle, brushing dust from the trigger guard.

"I'll come get you this afternoon, then," he says, smiling. "Don't fall asleep."

She throws him a withering look, but at the sight of the mischief in his grin she stifles a laugh. "Go on!" she chuckles. "Before you're late! I'll see you later."

He winks at her and sets off towards the village. Solma watches him for as long as she dares before she turns her attention back to her duties. She grabs her prosthesis from the grass beside her and straps it deftly to her knee, making sure it's secure before she shuffles onto her belly and readies her rifle. She scoops a mound of dirt together to prop its muzzle on and tugs the charging handle to check the load. Everything's in order. Now she just watches, waits and hopes that nothing happens.

She lowers one eye to the sight and lines the cross hairs up with the cluster of trees. Her body aches. Her eyelids droop. She shakes herself, shifts her position so that her hip is pressed painfully into the ground, hoping the discomfort will keep her alert. Now all that's left is to watch and wait and hope.

—*ell*—

Something crunches in the grass and Solma jerks awake. Stretched out above her is a ceiling of deepest blue and the sinking sun makes her squint. It takes her a short moment to work out where she is and that the thing digging into her shoulder blade is a loose stone.

She's laying in the grass. By the cluster of trees. Guarding the nest.

And she fell asleep.

Adrenalin kicks the grogginess from her and she scrambles back into position, adjusting her rifle and peering through the sight. How long has she slept? One arm is numb and she feels the imprints of stone and grit on the side of her face. Last she remembers, the sun was still creeping higher into the sky and now it's beginning to dip towards the horizon again. Earth, it's been hours!

Trembling, she scans the trees. Anyone could have been and gone in that time.

She wills her pulse to be quiet, sure that it's raging so wildly that anyone sneaking around will feel her heartbeat through the ground. But the nest site is quiet. The trees mutter softly in a hot breeze. The dry grasses rattle. Distant shouts from the harvesters drift through the static air and Solma feels herself calming.

It's ok. No one snuck past, no one else knows the nest is here—

A shadow moves between the trees and Solma's body is alight with adrenalin. She hooks her finger over the trigger, glares down the sight. Something moves from the cluster, keeping low, silhouetted against the bright sky. It stumbles twice, recovers, sprints from the nest site, a hand raised to hold onto a hat. Its movements are darting and fluid in a way that Solma recognizes. Her heart tightens.

But it couldn't be the same figure from the raid, could it? That's impossible.

She swings her rifle round but the high grasses make it impossible to line up a shot. Could she shoot anyway? There's no doubt it's a human being. A human being wearing clothes not typical to Sand's End. A human being with hair like hers, tall and strong, a stature typical of the western provinces.

The figure disappears over the horizon and Solma's on her feet, rifle slung over her shoulder, pelting after it. She catches glimpses as the figure dodges through the grasses. Earth! These painful grasses! They cling to her legs. She's never mastered moving through them and now they grab at her so tightly she tumbles forward, landing heavily and smacking her chin on a sharp stone. A wet hotness trickles down her neck.

She glances up in time to see the figure stop, turn back, catch her eye. It's a boy. Only a boy, perhaps a few years younger than she is. But he's tall, dark haired, with a tooth missing at the front and the pockmark scars of a childhood pox disease puckering his cheeks. And he has a tattoo. A flame inked just above one bright, violet eye. Solma stares at him, *raider*. But he's so young. So much younger than the raider she twice spared.

And looks so much like him. So much like Vulkan.

He sees her and grins.

"Ha!" he shouts, as if he'd just won a silly bet. "We *knew* you had bees!"

He turns and darts off. Solma untangles herself from the grass and clambers to her feet, staring in dismay at the distant visitors' camp, towards which the kid runs.

~ BLUME ~

THE AIR CHANGES. I feel it in the scent of my daughters, the smell of the loam, the heat. We grow older. My eggs are cared for differently when the daughters come home. They're fed something richer. Some of them are nurtured tenderly and, when they hatch, they're fat and glistening. They will be future queens.

Others are a kind of bee I only remember seeing once before, on my mating flight. For the first time in my life, I have sons. They flaunt their broad wings, puff out their bright fur. They smell of musk, of strength and possibility. They smell, like my princesses, of the future. But they make my other daughters anxious. They're angry, buzzing dissent. They feel betrayed.

We won't feed these brothers! They buzz. *They are lazy! They are greedy!*

Where once the bee song in the nest was harmonious, now I hear discord, smell the key-change of their anger, the way it permeates into the walls of our burrow. I catch some of them trying to lay their own eggs. Traitors! I reprimand them. I kill some of them. How dare they?

Their sisters drag the bodies out of the nest to keep the place clean. But the growing rebellion poisons the air. It stings my antennae. Once, I was their mother. I was their creator, their time-travelling marvel. Now I am their tyrant. They buzz of mutiny.

I am attacked, one morning. A daughter approaches and I think she brings food, but she brandishes her sting, venom glinting on its tip. She is strong from numerous foraging flights, powered by anger, but I am larger than she is, and strong from relentless laying. I am her mother. I kill her swiftly because I have mercy. Her sisters carry her out and I lay more eggs. I lay eggs to try to placate my daughters, but then the eggs hatch into sons and my daughters grow more hateful.

The nest is ending. I can feel it. This glorious world I built for us when I was young, it's falling apart. It hurts, this ending, though I knew it was coming. My joints are stiff now. Age dulls my senses. My air sacs shudder as I draw breath. How quickly I've grown old!

I feel the fear in my daughters that it's all been for nothing.

Because where are the foreign princesses for my sons to court? Where are the foreign sons for my daughter queens? My daughters don't want their brothers as mates. They want fresh, strong males to fly them. They want new blood to pass on to their own daughters.

The nest is dying and there are no others. My princesses will die unmated, and we will wink out of existence. I imagine the future flower song, the perfume-melody of new buds calling for attention. And there will be no bees to answer.

Because we are the last. I understand that now.

We are the last, unless the boy-who-speaks-bee can give us one final miracle.

THIRTY-ONE

Solma skids into the village, her blade-foot kicking up dust. She'd hoped to arrive before the news but raised voices and a gathering crowd tell her she's too late. She makes it to Bell's house before any violence starts. Bell is at the front door, both hands on Warren's shoulders, frowning down the path towards where the villagers congregate. Solma glances at Warren and her insides twist painfully. Earth, he looks tired. His sunken eyes with their drooping lids, his cracked lips slightly parted, his limbs heavy with exhaustion. He gazes at Solma as she jogs towards him and she sees fear sweep across his eyes.

"They've been spotted, Sol," he whispers. "I'm sorry. I tried. I really did. I tried to tell them but—"

His little face crumples and Solma kneels in front of him, cupping his face in her hands, hushing him gently. "It's ok, Warren. It ain't your fault."

No, it's not his fault. Because it's all hers. She did this. And now she needs to fix it.

"What're they saying?" she asks. She's looking at Warren, but it's Bell who answers.

"Oh, all the predictable nonsense," she snaps. "There's talk of marching on the nest, digging it up. Some are talking of burning it so others can't get it. Others threatening to kill anyone who tries that. Oh great! Now the Earth Whisperers have turned up."

Solma whirls round, peering towards the growing crowd. The shoving has started, and people throw their fists in the air. The violet-eyed boy stands in the middle of the group, shouting.

"I know where it is! I've seen the nest!" he cries. Someone boxes him across the head and he slumps in the dirt, out of Solma's eyesight. The visiting Stewards are here, too, their bodyguards brandishing all sorts of weaponry.

"We ain't kept no bees!" Someone cries in a deep, croaky voice. It's Gerta, shaking her walking stick with all the ferocity of a Guard Sergeant. Solma's almost proud of her, of her toothless snarl as she faces up to one of the tallest men Solma's ever seen in her life.

A tall man with violet eyes. And a flame inked above his eyebrow. Solma's heart punches. The violet-eyed boy is on his feet again now and, yes, Vulkan's huge hand rests on the boy's shoulder.

His son. It must be. The boy points at Gerta and laughs. His father strikes Gerta in the temple with the hilt of a knife and the old woman crumples to the floor like an empty sack. Her walking stick clatters against packed earth. Solma unshoulders her rifle and darts towards the fray. There's more shoving, now. A punch thrown. Weapons drawn and aimed.

"You knew! You knew about the bees and you hid them from us!"

"We ain't got no bloody bees!"

"Liars!"

"They're ours anyway. Get your own!"

Solma is vaguely aware of Mamba and another Whisperer in the middle of the chaos, their arms spread, imploring peace. No one listens. Someone kneels by Gerta, stroking wiry, grey hair from the old woman's face, checking her pulse, rummaging in a shoulder bag for water and bandages. It's Cobra. Solma falls into the dirt beside her and their eyes meet. There's that familiarity again, that moment where Cobra's gentle, freckled face stirs a distant memory. But then Cobra speaks and the moment is gone.

"Here," she says, thrusting a bandage into Solma's hands. "Press this against her head."

Solma does as she's told. Gerta stirs beneath her hands and she hushes the old woman softly. "It's alright. It's Sol."

"Sol ..." Gerta croaks. "Where's ... where's Kobi?"

Solma frowns. "Who?"

She glances up, wondering if Cobra knows what the old woman is talking about, but Cobra's head is bowed, her cheeks red, wetness on her eyelashes. Solma wants to ask, but something stops her. That memory floats closer to the light this time and Solma almost catches it.

Kobi. A young girl looking back over her shoulder. Walking into the wilderness ...

"You're not pressing hard enough!" Cobra barks. She slaps Solma's hand away and takes over. Solma lifts her hands in surrender.

"I was only trying to help—"

"Well don't!" Cobra snarls. She glances up, her face puffy with crying. Her gaze is hard, furious, sad. She gestures towards the fray, still growing around them. "This is what happens when you try to help! You can't see what's right in front of you, can you? Wake up, Solma!"

Anger bubbles under Solma's ribcage. She stands, glaring at Cobra, rifle clutched in both hands. Ignorant girl! What did she think would happen when she tried to destroy the nest? How can she blame Solma for this ridiculous mess? She opens her mouth to say something when a shot rings out, shivering the air. Solma ducks instinctively, aims her own rifle towards the noise. There are a few yelps of surprise and the fray dies down. The weapons lower, the villagers and the visitors back away from each other. Stood in the epicenter, pistol raised and smoking, is Olive, her other hand on the shoulder of the orange-eyed Whisperer girl, whose lips tremble. Olive bares her teeth.

"Go home," she growls. "All of you. Now."

The crowd hesitates. Solma can tell they're sizing each other up, wondering if their collective strength is enough to disobey Olive. Solma doubts it. She smiles for a moment before she remembers she's furious with Olive and forces her face into a frown.

The crowd parts and a visiting Steward strides to face Olive. It's the woman with the silk scarf. She's at least half a head taller than Olive and gets close enough so that she can look down at her, their noses inches apart. Solma bristles before she realizes what she's doing and almost steps in, knife in hand, but someone grabs her arm. She glances down to see Cobra holding her wrist, eyes imploring. Solma scowls and wrenches her arm free, but it's enough to stop her diving in and starting the scuffle anew.

The Steward grins down at Olive, teeth bared like a predator. "We'll go home," she murmurs. "When your pathetic little village gives us its bees."

Olive cocks her pistol and presses it up under the Steward's chin. There's a gasp from the crowd and the Steward's guards brandish their weapons again. Olive either doesn't notice or doesn't care.

"Don't think I won't," Olive snarls. "'Cos I will."

Solma believes her. She clutches her belly to quell the churning inside it. Could Olive really shoot an unarmed woman? Except ...

There's a flash of steel at the woman's hip and Solma sees with a kick of her heart that the woman is not unarmed at all. The steel winks in the sinking sun. The Steward's grin widens and Solma sees, as if the whole world has slowed down, Olive's eyes widen in sudden realization.

Someone roars and Solma realizes that it's her. She's running, her knife discarded in the dirt, rifle raised. There's no time to stop the upward arc of the Steward's knife as it drives for Olive's gut, but Solma runs anyway, barreling into Olive in time to shove her free of the knife's path. Heat rips through the flesh just above her hip and she gasps through her teeth, but adrenalin dulls most of the pain. She turns, her body working without thought, and drives the barrel of her gun into the Steward's shoulder, dislocating it. The Steward yelps like a child and drops her knife, stumbling backwards into the dirt. She clutches her damaged arm, glaring up at Solma with rage in her eyes. Shock ripples through the crowd and the Steward's bodyguards rush forward, sickles raised.

By that time, though, Solma has her rifle aimed squarely at the Steward's chest and Olive is on her feet, pistol pressed between the eyes of one of the bodyguards.

Yet again, everyone freezes.

"I said," Olive says, her voice dangerously quiet, "go. Home."

There's a moment's resistance in the crowd, but the injured Steward gets to her feet with the help of one of her guards and, with a venomous glare she struggles away. The rest of the crowd follow, leaving only Mamba and Cobra, both knelt beside Gerta as she gradually comes to.

Olive lowers her pistol. "You didn't have to hit me that hard," she says, rubbing her shoulder where Solma barreled into her. Solma rolls her eyes as she retrieves her knife from the ground. Her hip throbs and when she looks, there's a slash across it, bleeding profusely. The wound is wide but shallow. Nonetheless, blood seeps into her trousers. She presses a flat palm to the injury and glares at Olive.

"How do you manage to be so infuriating all the time?" she snaps. "Oh, and you're welcome, by the way."

Olive scowls. "I had it," she grumbles. "You didn't need to throw yourself at me like that."

Solma glares at her. "You didn't," she says, pointing at her bloody hip, "And I did."

They stare at each other for a brief, eternal moment. Solma doesn't think she's held Olive's gaze this long before. There are dapples of amber and blue amidst the green of her eyes, and the freckles over her nose only just disguise the crease between her brows. But there's something beyond fury in Olive's gaze today. Something deeper. Solma can't quite tell what it is but finds herself wanting to comfort Olive.

Which is ridiculous.

Olive maintains her furious glare only for a second before she relents. "Yeah, alright," she admits. "I didn't have it. Thanks, or whatever."

Solma dips her face to hide the smile she can't quite suppress.

"Where's Maxen?" Olive asks.

Solma shrugs. "Dunno," she admits. "Maybe at the campsite, managing this nonsense."

Almost as one, their eyes turn towards Gerta as Cobra and Mamba help her to her feet. She leans heavily against Cobra, one withered arm thrown over the Whisperer-girl's shoulders. Olive sighs.

"Let's patch up your hip," she mumbles. "Here."

She kneels at Solma's side and works deftly, tearing Solma's trousers a little so she can clean the wound. Solma winces, though Olive is surprisingly gentle, spraying the wound with antiseptic before she applies a bandage. She presses the dressing flat and Solma feels the pain dull under the pressure.

"You'll still need to see Ma so it don't get infected," Olive grumbles, shaking her head. "Damn reckless thing to do." Solma rolls her eyes.

"Better a sliced hip than a dead Olive," she points out. "Despite everything you've done."

Olive meets her gaze and raises an eyebrow. Solma expects a retort but Olive just shakes her head again and gets to her feet, packing up her med kit.

"Whatever," she says. "I'll help get Gerta home."

Solma nods.

"I better go to Blaiz," she says. Her eyes meet Olive's in time to see the flash in the other girl's eyes. Was that *fear* Solma just saw in Olive? It can't be.

"Sol," Olive says, a tone in her voice that Solma's never heard before. "I know you hate me or whatever. I know you think I did something bad—"

"You *did* do something bad!"

"Just, shut up a second, would you?" Olive snaps, throwing her hands up in exasperation. "Earth! You're so *sanctimonious* all the time!"

Solma sighs. Here they go again, bickering like red-bear cubs over a morsel of meat.

"Look," Olive says, trying and failing to keep her voice level. "I know you think you gotta report to Blaiz, but I'm asking you not to. Please. For the sake of—everything. For the sake of those bees."

Solma can't help herself. She punches Olive, hard. Olive staggers back, surprised.

"Ow! Hey!"

Solma shakes her head. "Just—" she grits her teeth. "Just *shove off*, Olive!" she snaps. She tries not to storm when she marches away but it's impossible and she feels how petulant she must look. Honestly! The *cheek* of it. For the sake of the bees ... Really? As if Olive could've cared less what happened to the bees when she helped the Whisperers bait that badger.

So no, Solma will not do as Olive asks. Instead she marches furiously straight up the path towards Blaiz Camber's house.

THIRTY-TWO

THE DOOR TO BLAIZ's magnificent house is thrown
open and the porch is empty of guards. Solma thinks
the worst when she arrives. She grabs her knife and
drops to a semi-crouch, creeping across the threshold,
eyes darting towards the shadows. She half expects a
foreign assassin to make themselves known at any moment. But the corridor is empty, and the floorboards
creak menacingly under her weight.

When she reaches Blaiz's office, the door is ajar and
a dim, yellow glow comes from inside. Someone riffles through papers, muttering under their breath.
It's Blaiz. Solma recognizes the cadence of his anger.
She imagines him, teeth bared, canines glinting in the
candlelight, a vein jumping in his temple. She closes
her eyes. And there he is again, looming out of the
darkness, trapping her against the wall of a house.

She needs to stop this. He's her Steward. He's not a monster, he's just trying to protect them. He's trying to keep them alive.

She sheaths her knife before knocking on the door.

"What?" Blaiz's voice from within is caustic.

Solma jumps as she pushes the door open. It whines on aching hinges and Solma winces at the noise. Blaiz's office is a state. There are papers all over the floor, crumpled and torn. Solma can't stop her mouth from falling open. Blaiz shuffles through the documents on his desk, carelessly casting folders aside as he searches for some unknown treasure. His fingers ruck up edges, smudge the ink. How can he be so thoughtless with something so precious as paper?

Solma stares at the chaos and wonders who this man is, so hurried and destructive. He glances up and his gaze hardens.

"What do you want?"

Solma flinches at the venom in his tone but forces herself to straighten to attention. "Sir, the nest's been found."

Blaiz rolls his eyes and returns to his frantic search. "Are you an idiot? I know that. Get out."

Solma freezes, staring. He knows? Then what on Earth is he doing?

"Sir—"

"Oh do shut up, Solma!" he snaps, slamming his palms on his desk so that papers crumple beneath them. "You failed, do you understand? You kept a secret, and then you lied, and then you let someone discover the nest. I've got no time for this. You're done. Your whole family is done. I'll exile you as soon as I've dealt with this mess, so you can all pack your things."

Solma's breath snags. Blood hammers in her ears and fear floods her vision. Exile. The thought is like losing her leg all over again. She feels the stab of hunger, the ache of injury, the rasp of hopelessness already. She and Bell and Warren, stumbling through the wilderness until they die of exposure, or starvation, or run into a raiding party.

Warren ...

The thought of him perishing out there galvanizes what little courage Solma has left. She squares her shoulders. "There's still time. We can save the nest—"

Blaiz barks a cruel laugh. "Save the nest," he sneers. "Don't be such a child, Solma. The nest will have to be destroyed. Harvest is here and we've no more use for the bees. They're a liability now. I'll dig it up first thing tomorrow. Dammit! Where are those plans?"

Solma stares at him open-mouthed. "But—" she splutters. Blaiz fixes her with his cold, cruel gaze.

"But what?" he demands.

The words ricochet around Solma's head. She feels the flames of the last Hive Wars licking her heels, the stab of iron and steel into the soft earth, ravaging the bee colonies until there was nothing left but a litter of bodies. She feels the whole continent falling into poverty all over again. Can't he see that? Can't he see that this is a chance to make things right? Her mind is a firestorm of doubt. She is aflame with it, burning until she can't take it anymore.

"You can't destroy the bees," she hears herself say, her voice thick with anger. With betrayal.

Blaiz doesn't even look up. "Yes I can," he says. "They belong to me."

It's like a bullet, that statement. Solma reels from it. Is this what Warren's been trying to tell her? What Bell's been trying to tell her?

She hadn't realized, at the time, why they'd wanted to keep the bees from him. But she can see it now. He's like a wild dog defending a kill he's just made. He'd rather destroy it than see it taken. He'd rather no one had that power than have it stolen from him.

Warren was right all along. And Bell, and Olive, and Cobra, and ...

A sudden gut-punch of fear. "Where's Maxen?" she asks before she can stop herself. Again, Blaiz doesn't look up.

"He's busy," he growls. "With things that don't concern you."

Solma bristles, her hand on the hilt of her knife again. She takes a step forward. "Where is he?" she demands. "What've you done with him?"

Now Blaiz does look up. He sees her, battle-ready, knife half drawn. And he laughs.

"I haven't done anything with him," he snarls. "Get out of my house."

Solma hesitates. Tears of fury prickle in her eyes. She bites them back, forces the anger into her gut where she lets it build. This man is not her Steward. This man is chaos and destruction. And Solma has bigger concerns than him, now. The word *exile* beats in her brain like the clatter of a war drum. She leaves Blaiz's house, trudges back up the path towards home. The village is stirring again, like a monster waking from a deep sleep.

Solma gazes in the direction of the orchards, where some of the foreign Stewards camp. There's activity there, too. They're preparing to march on the nest. Preparing for war. And in the meantime, Solma must prepare her family for exile.

THIRTY-THREE

WARREN'S VOICE DRIFTS THROUGH the open door when Solma arrives home. He's frantic and for a moment, Solma can't handle it. She stands outside, back pressed against the wood-and-mud walls, and crushes her eyes closed. She's so tired. Sleep pulls at her mind like kite strings, beckoning her somewhere far away, a more forgiving place.

Warren had a toy kite once. She'd made it for him after she'd been accepted into the Guard. Scraped pigskin stretched across a couple of whittled sticks. It wasn't like the colorful kites she's heard about in other provinces. And it was heavy, needed powerful winds to keep it even vaguely airborne. But Warren loved it. He loved it, he said, because Solma had made it for him.

What had happened to that kite? Tangled in a tree, probably. Lost somewhere. Whatever happened to it, it's gone now. Like the hope she'd had of keeping him safe, like the hope of the bees, like home.

Solma shakes herself. She hitches her rifle and steps inside. Bell glances up at the sound of footsteps, Warren clutching her skirts, tugging her apron, wailing his head off.

"You're not listening! I need to—Sol! It's really important—"

As soon as he sees her, he's at her feet, grasping her hand. She twists free. "Not now, Warren."

"But—!"

"I said, not now!"

Her voice shocks him into silence and the guilt surfaces again. It isn't his fault. She softens and cups his chin. "I'm sorry, Warren," she says. "I just ... there's a lot to deal with. Tell me later, ok?"

Clouds of concern drift across Warren's face. "We ain't got time to—"

Solma turns away. He doesn't get it. He's too young. Sometimes, she wishes he'd grow up like all the other kids, take responsibility for once. She's tired of him being too young.

Bell's hands are on her hips. "Where you been?"

Really? They're playing this game again, are they? Solma pinches the bridge of her nose and bats Warren away as he grabs her arm. "I went to see Blaiz," she mutters. "I was doing my job."

Bell looks as if she might say something more, but then her frown deepens and she thinks better of it. She wipes her hands on her apron and heads to the stove.

"Tea, I think," she says. "Warren! Stop pestering your sister!"

Warren throws his hands up in frustration. "But I got to—"

"No, you don't!" Bell barks. "Behave!"

Warren stamps his foot, uttering a short, sharp scream. He kicks out at nothing. "But—"

He is ignored. His wailing falls into the background as Solma drags herself to the table and flops down. She can take five minutes. Five minutes to bend under the weight of the world, to gather her courage and break the news to her family while everything they've ever known shatters around them. The chair creaks as she sits. She glares at the table, eyes tracing the grain, until Bell slides a steaming mug in front of her.

"Drink."

Solma shakes her head. "I ain't thirsty."

"I'm not interested," Bell says. "You look exhausted. You look ill. Drink."

Solma rolls her eyes and, for once, Bell says nothing about her attitude. She just watches as Solma takes the first tentative sips. The tea is warm, infused with lavender and an array of other herbs. Soft aromas drift around Solma's face and she breathes them in, feeling how they soothe her. At least a little bit.

Bell waits until Solma drains the mug. Outside, the chaos builds. Warren stands by the door, peering out. He bounces on his toes, then runs over to pester Solma again.

"Sol! Sol! I need to tell you—"

Bell shoos him away and he wails, beating his fists against the wall in frustration. They leave him to his tantrum. At least he's occupied. Still, Bell waits. She waits until Solma finally glances up and their eyes meet. She searches Solma's face and her expression hardens.

"You don't need to say it," she whispers. "It's ok. I know."

Solma's face finally crumples. "I'm so sorry," she gasps, choking on tears. "I tried. I really did. I tried to keep us all safe and do the right thing and I failed."

There's a whisper of cloth, a creak of wood and Bell's arms are around her. She can't remember the last time her aunt hugged her like this. Not the tight, excitable hug of pride, not the firm touch of the Bell she's used to, hardened by suffering. This hug is all-encompassing. It's gentle and soft and compassionate, the kind of hug Ma would have given her. The kind of hug that tells Solma it's ok to fail. It's ok to be weak. She can't be everything to everyone all the time and that's ok.

She sighs and lets her head fall against Bell's shoulder, lets the sounds of conflict from outside, the sounds of Warren's tantrum, melt away into a muffled nothing in the background.

"You didn't fail, my girl," Bell says. "That man has been after me and mine since … well, for a long time. You did what you could. And we'll cope. We're tougher than you think."

She kisses the top of Solma's head and releases her, brushing the creases out of her skirts. "How long we got, d'you think?"

Solma shrugs. Even that simple action feels like raising a mountain. "He wants to march on the nest," she sighs. "We got time to pack, at least."

Bell nods, "Right," and begins bustling.

Solma sinks into her chair and closes her eyes. If she could just sleep … but Warren is in front of her, his little fists thumping her knees. "Sol!" he begs. "Sol! We can't let him march on the nest! Please—"

Solma leans forward with as much patience as she can muster, holding him at arm's length. "We can't stop him, Warren," she says. "There are too many. It's not just him, is it? They're all after it, and—" she bites her lip. "Remember the book? The book says that at this time of year the new queens will fly. Maybe a few of them might get away. Maybe some of them will start new nests and—"

Warren wriggles free and brings his fists down on the table, so forcefully it reverberates through the floor. Her mouth falls open in shock.

He turns on her, face flushed with anger. "You're not *listening to me!*" he screams. "I'm trying to tell you! She's calling me!"

Solma splutters before finding her voice. "Who?"

"Blume," says Bell before Warren can answer. She's stopped what she's doing and come to join them, a hand on Solma's shoulder. "He's talking about Blume."

"Yes!" Warren throws up his hands, his exasperation plain. "There are no boy bees, Solma! There are only her sons and her daughters and it ain't enough! She needs boy bees from another nest!"

It takes a moment for this information to sink in. Solma blinks and suddenly the heaviness in her doubles, so impossibly vast that it threatens to suffocate her. Her lungs contract, her heart shivering like a bee's wings.

"We need to find another nest!" Warren says, green eyes huge and desperate.

Solma stares at him. The whole world is muffled. "There ain't another nest," she whispers. "They'll all die. They were all going to die right from the start. It's all ... it's all been for nothing."

It's all been for nothing. And finally, Solma lets the weight of it overwhelm her. She drops her head into her hands and sobs rack her body. The tears won't stop. Because all of this, all the fighting, the secrecy, the fear. All the hope ...

It's all been for nothing.

~ A MOMENT ~

BELL CLOSES THE FRONT door out of respect for her niece's grief. Still, Solma's sobs carry on the air. There aren't many people left in the village to hear her: most have gone with Blaiz to march on the nest with their shovels and self-righteous anger. Only the youngest, the oldest and the most cautious remain, hiding in their houses. They are no longer hopeful. They are afraid. All of them.

Except one.

Olive leans against the wall of Bell's house with her arms folded, listening to Solma's inconsolable weeping. She winces at the sound as if Solma's despair causes her physical pain. Her fingers flex in and out of fists. There's nothing she can do for Solma here. There is no enemy to fight, no creature to shoot, no physical thing in front of which she can place herself to shield the girl who both infuriates and fascinates her. But she had caught Bell's eye as the door closed. Bell's a good person. Brave. Olive likes her. More than that: Olive *respects* her, which is something she can't say about many people. Bell had stared at her for a long moment, then nodded, as if giving Olive permission, and promptly shut the door.

That gave Olive everything she needed. With a grunt of dissatisfaction, she pushes away from the wall and checks her weaponry. Her rifle is loaded and strapped across her back. She shunts a new magazine into her pistol, checks both her hunting knife and her multi-knife are where they should be. She tightens the laces on her boots, scrapes her mane of red hair back into a braid and pulls a hood over it. Her body buzzes. She's ready. Everything is broken: all the people she loves are broken and she'll be damned if she isn't going to find a way to fix it. Or die trying.

She squares her shoulders, unclips her pistol from its holster and marches out of the village, towards the nest of impossible bees. She knows where it is, of course. She's always known. And Solma will likely never know how many nights Olive snuck out of her house and sat guard under the ash tree, how many moon badgers she's chased away from the site, how many times she's used knowledge her Ma bestowed on her to lay a chemical boundary around the nest, deterring predators.

Yes, Olive knows the nest. She's sat in wonder as the first fingers of dawn brushed the nest's entrance, as the first of the day's bees trundled into the light, fired their engines and droned into the morning. She's felt the whisper of bee feet on her palm and been utterly charmed. It's a kind of rapture Olive has never felt before.

And for the first time in Olive's life, she'd wept with *happiness* at the delicate touch of such a life against her skin. Hope is tenuous as a cliff edge. Sticky as goosegrass. Olive thought she'd expunged every last atom of it when her Dja died. She hadn't realized a tiny particle had clung to her all this time.

Olive has decided she likes hope. She's watched Warren be emboldened by it, watched Solma try not to give in to it, watched the village cautiously embrace and then lose it. Humans, Olive thinks, are fools.

And Blaiz, most of all. A clever man who can see nothing in this hope but the possibility of his own gain. How many such men have ravaged the Earth? How many played their part in making Alphor what it is now?

Well, screw him, Olive thinks. Blaiz always underestimated her, and that's how she likes it. Blaiz will get what's coming to him. Olive promised that the day her Dja died. She's no fool. She knows who's responsible.

She heads into the wild grasses, going only a few meters before she dips down and moves on all fours. She's spent so much time in this grass that she understands it now in a way Solma never mastered. Holstering her pistol again, she moves carefully so as not to draw attention. She keeps her head low. She knows where she's going. As she draws near, she risks peeping above the fringe of grass.

She can't get as close to the nest as she used to, but the sight of it affords her some relief. She half expected smoke and screaming, the crushed bodies of bees littering the ground. But the nest seems unharmed. In fact, Olive spots bees zooming back and forth from the cluster of trees, their fur gleaming gold in the sun.

It doesn't take Olive long to realize why the nest has been undisturbed. It's under siege.

Blaiz and the villagers got within a hundred meters of it and have so far defended their position, but the other Stewards have surrounded it too, each with their own makeshift fortress constructed from sandbags, barbed wire and scavenged wood. A few have come prepared, with steel sheeting to reinforce their positions.

Olive scans the horizon and counts seven fortresses in total, spread in a wide circle around the nest site. Blaiz has established a position north of the nest, just below the orchards. Olive watches the activity between the barricades and grits her teeth. There's Blaiz. There's the other members of her Guard squad and every other desperate person she'd expected to see following their deranged leader into a pointless fight. But it's not only Southtip Province that are after the bees. She recognizes colors and insignias from all across Alphor. News of these bees has travelled far. She's curious enough to wonder how that happened but dismisses that line of thought quickly. Knowing why won't change the situation.

She scans the no-man's land around the nest and spots the shapes of three bodies strewn in the grass. One, she recognizes: it's Piotr. His mouth and eyes are open, as if in shock. He stares sightlessly back towards the village and Olive eyes the bloody wound in his back where a shotgun pellet ripped through his spine. So Blaiz tried to get closer, did he?

Or maybe he didn't. Maybe he sent Piotr—poor, terrified Piotr—into the no-man's-land to test his rivals. They clearly didn't disappoint. Olive allows herself a few, precious seconds of grief. Piotr was a good man. Hard-working, honest. Blaiz will have told him it was safe and Piotr will have believed him. Blaiz is a snake. Olive has a bullet in her magazine just for him and she'll take pleasure in expending it.

But Piotr isn't the only casualty. There's a boy, too, no more than twelve or thirteen years old, with an arrow in his eye. And a woman from a rival province with a hole in her temple. This is why the nest is still intact. No one will let anyone else get closer. Olive wonders how long she has before it turns to chaos. Someone will get impatient. Someone won't care how many lives it takes to secure the power. What's the betting that someone will be Blaiz?

Olive lowers her head and clenches handfuls of dirt in her fist. Greedy. Selfish. Thoughtless. People like this make her so angry she wants to scream. But she doesn't. Instead, she bites her teeth together and hisses her frustration, quietly. That'll have to do for now. She slips away from the nest site, crawling back through the grasses until she is far enough away to risk standing without being seen. She expects Blaiz will wonder where she is, why she hasn't marched with the rest, but she doesn't care.

Instead, she unclips her pistol again and heads south, towards the woods. She has an itch of suspicion that needs scratching; an itch that began the moment she found the caterpillar after Warren's failed Whispering test. If she's right, then this hasn't been for nothing. If she's right, there is still hope.

Just before she reaches the forest, a flash of white catches Olive's eye. She stops, tenses, turns.

But what she sees fills her with wonder rather than dread. A whisper of feet against her arm. She glances down in time to see the creature that lands there, with its long antennae waving, its thorax fluffy with dark fur. It presses its delicate, white wings together, resting for a moment, before it flutters into the forest.

It's a butterfly. Small and white and alive. Olive knows enough about butterflies to wonder if it used to be the caterpillar she so carefully placed on the trunk of a tree. It could be ...

But regardless, the sight is enough. There is hope.

And despite the danger of great, curved tusks and raging muscle, Olive doesn't hesitate as she heads into the woods alone. Because she's thinking of Solma's face, she's thinking of what Solma will say if it turns out Olive is right. She doesn't hesitate because Solma needs her not to. There is hope. There has always been hope.

THIRTY-FOUR

AFTER A WHILE, SOLMA's sobs subside. Her eyes
prickle but she's got no tears left and a thunderous headache looms in her forehead. Bell plies her
with tea, holding it to her lips when she's too tired
to raise her own arms. She fights at first, swears at
Bell (who is uncharacteristically patient) but the tea
is warm and soothing, calming her hammering mind.
She stops fighting and accepts the help. After a while,
Bell switches from tea to cool water and slides a bowl
of soaked oats across the table.

"Eat," she says.

Solma tries, but her stomach churns and her hands
barely have the strength to grip anything. She's so
tired. Tired enough to miss her Ma, which she hasn't
admitted to herself for a long time. She wants to be
Warren's age again, curled up in Ma's arms, Ma gently
stroking her hair, singing. Ma wasn't much of a singer.

Dja used to tease her for it, but Solma never cared. She loved it because it was Ma. She misses it so much.

Her face crumples again but no tears come. Bell reacts wordlessly, rubbing her back, murmuring something that Solma barely understands. She sits beside Solma and begins to feed her, one spoonful at a time. Solma eats. Slowly, at first, nausea ebbing and flowing in her gut. She forces herself to chew, swallow, chew, swallow. Eventually the headache fades, the nausea dulls, Solma's body settles into the exhaustion she's used to. Just the right side of bearable. She finishes the last of the porridge and sits back in her chair.

Warren slips silently into view and sits cross-legged at Solma's feet. He places a tiny hand on her blade foot and peers up into her face.

"Sol?"

Solma tries to tell him she's ok but her throat is raw from crying, despite the tea. In the end, she manages to smile at him. Bell cleans her hands on her apron.

"Right," she says. "I guess we better get packing."

"For what?" Warren asks, and Solma's grief threatens to overwhelm her again. How is she supposed to explain to her gentle, hopeful little brother that she's failed him? Where does she even start?

Bell's expression softens. "Warren, we've been—"

"Exiled," Warren interrupts, to everybody's surprise. "No, I know *that*. I mean, where we going to go? We got to pack right, don't we?"

Bell and Solma stare at him. Sometimes, Solma thinks, her brother is tougher even than she is. Bell's eyes twinkle with a mischief Solma hasn't seen for years.

"You know what?" she says. "Now that we're officially enemies of the village, I don't see any harm in telling you the truth anymore. Maybe it'll give you some hope."

Solma sits up straighter in her chair. "What truth?"

Bell winks at her. "Come here and I'll show you," she says. "Come on, Warren."

"Have you ..." Solma whispers. She can't believe this. "Have you been keeping secrets?"

Bell laughs. Properly laughs. She throws her head back and the sound is deep and delicious, right from her ribcage. Solma's never heard her laugh like that before.

"What you gonna do, my girl?" she chuckles. "Report me?"

A grin tugs at Solma's mouth and she lets it show.

"There are secrets within secrets you've no idea about," Bell continues. "Secrets I kept safe in honor of your Ma and your Dja. But I think it's time you knew. Come on."

She fumbles in her dress pocket and produces the key to the cellar. "Ever wonder why you're not allowed down here?"

Solma stares. The truth is, she *hadn't* wondered. How had she never wondered? It's just always been the case. Bell goes into the cellar, Bell locks the cellar behind her, Bell keeps the key. She even sleeps with it on a cord around her neck. Solma's never wondered because it's always been that way. The cellar is out of bounds, just like secrets are illegal and bees are impossible.

Now, she kicks herself for accepting that so easily. Now, she *does* wonder.

She gets to her feet and Warren hops up beside her, slipping his hand into hers. She gazes at him and he's smiling. He's smiling in that way he used to, before all this happened. *That's my sister*, his little face says. *That's my sister and I'm so proud of her*. Solma's heart constricts. She squeezes his hand. He squeezes back. He's forgiven her. And suddenly, exile doesn't seem so bad. Whatever they meet out there, they'll face it together.

"Ok," Bell says, slipping the key into the lock. "You need to know there's no turning back from this. Once you know the truth, that's it. Understand?"

Solma hesitates. But what's she got left to lose? There's no turning back from this anyway. Blaiz isn't her Steward anymore, if he ever was the man she thought he was. Maybe he'll change his mind. But she doubts it. Maybe Maxen will try to persuade him—

That's a point. Where *is* Maxen?

She'll never see him again. The grief builds but she forces it down. That was never going to happen anyway, was it? A silly, teenage dream. She must push it aside. Forget it, like she should have from the beginning.

Still—

"We're ready," Warren says. Bell turns the lock and Solma is still thinking of Maxen as she follows her aunt and brother down the stone steps and into the gloom.

Bell unhooks a battered old torch from the wall, pumps the handle and flicks the switch. A half-hearted beam of light flutters to life. Solma and Warren huddle together at the foot of the stairs while Bell fusses in the dark, swearing under her breath as she trips over something. Eventually, she manages to light five or six candles and spreads them around the cellar so that there is just enough light to see by. She beckons Solma and Warren forward, hands Solma another torch and gestures around the room.

"Take a look," she says. "I'll explain when you're done."

Solma raises the torch and sweeps it around the room, still holding Warren's hand. Light falls against walls lined with fold-out tables, books thrown open with hasty notes scribbled through them. There are more books on shelves nailed to the walls, diagrams of animals Solma has never seen before, glass jars containing strange things. Solma shuffles to one shelf and picks up such a jar, peering at the treasure inside. It's almost like a leaf, but deep black and, when Solma plays the torch beam on it, it shows a blue iridescence.

"What's this?" she whispers.

"A feather," Bell says softly. "A magpie feather. They were a flighted bird. This is what's called a primary. Birds used them to fly."

Solma's heart jolts as she turns the jar in the light, staring in wonder at this strange thing. It's so unlike the messy feathers she's seen on the burrowing ground birds or the chickens they trade for in other villages. This is a work of evolutionary engineering, developed to defy gravity.

Another impossible thing.

Solma places the feather carefully back where she found it and begins to scan the open pages of the books. There are layers of dust on some of them, the pages are cracked in places and Solma is scared to turn them in case they disintegrate. But she hungrily reads what's on display.

... the common kingfisher would sit in tree branches above running water, darting down to catch fish ...

... flying insects were the main food source for swifts and swallows ...

... many fruiting trees relied on insect pollinators to produce ...

Warren slips out of Solma's grasp and runs off to stare at an enormous painting of an insect with the most glorious set of purple wings.

"A butterfly," Bell explains. "They died out shortly after the bees."

Solma half-listens to Warren's chatter as she moves around the room, scanning page after page. She's moved on from the encyclopedias and atlases and now reads the hand-scribbled notes tucked inside pages or left in haphazard piles. She had no idea there was so much paper in her own home. She's afraid to touch it, afraid to mark it in any way. But there's no doubt about one thing.

The scribbles she's reading are in her parents' handwriting.

Most of it is formulas, codes of some kind that Solma doesn't understand, and then a few notes about climate, habitat and food chains. Something clicks in Solma's mind. She remembers Blaiz's face, twisted with anger, inches from her own.

Your Dja ... Too busy protecting his precious beetles, trying to bring back the birds ...

But this isn't just her Dja's handwriting. It's Ma's, too. She turns slowly away from the books and notes and shines the torch at little trays filled with tiny seeds. She scoops a few into her palm and lets them run through her fingers, soft as silk, then reads the labels on each of the trays. Her heart thunders. Poppy. Borage. Cornflower. These are all old species. No one bothers with them anymore. Beneath the bench with the seed trays is a crate filled with other seeds. Huge ones. There's a name for them, Solma thinks. What is it? *Bulbs*? She kneels and peers at the label. Crocus. Tulip. Snowdrop. Her jaw drops open. She stands and trains the torch beam on Bell, who waits quietly in the middle of the room.

"The flowers by the trees," she says. "You knew they were there."

Bell nods. "I did."

"Because you planted them."

"I did." Bell smooths her skirts and clasps her hands together.

Solma's scared to ask the next question, but it needs to be asked. She takes a breath. "Did you know the bees were coming back?"

Bell chuckles. "How could I know that, girl?" she says. "No, I didn't. I'm just hopeful. I been planting flowers by those trees every year. This year, I'm glad I did. Now, are you ready?"

Solma clenches and unclenches her fists, but her hands are steady. She nods. "Yeah," she says, her heart a wild bird in her ribcage. "But I think I know what you're going to say."

Bell smiles sadly, her eyes glitter. "Come here, then," she says, unfolding three wooden chairs.

"This is Ma's and Dja's, isn't it?" says Warren, scrambling up onto the first chair and swinging his legs. Bell puts a hand on his knee to still him.

"Yes," she says. "Your Ma's and Dja's, and mine, and Dr Roseann's and her husband's."

Solma gives a small, involuntary squeak as she sits down. Olive rarely speaks about her Dja. Solma had so wanted to talk to her after both their fathers died, but Olive went quiet and sullen. There were questions at the time about whether it had been the same illness that took them both. Solma vaguely remembers the tang of panic infecting the village air. Could this be an outbreak? But no one else got sick like that. Ever. And eventually, the fear subsided. People spoke reverently of both Solma and Olive's Djas. They were tragic deaths, it was said, terribly sad, but nothing more.

Now, Solma glances around this cave of treasures and wonders if that's true.

"What were you doing down here?" she whispers.

Bell raises an eyebrow at her. "You already know that."

There's a long silence. Solma's pulse throbs violently in her head. She pinches the bridge of her nose. "You were working to bring the insects back," she says. "And the birds. But how—"

"It was a foolish hope at first," Bell admits, shaking her head. "We thought perhaps we could assimilate genes from preserved specimens with still-living fauna. Your Dja brought some incredible knowledge from wherever it was he came from. Sciences from the old world. Your Ma was fascinated. So was I. It took us a long time learning, but we reckoned we might be able to heal some'a the hurt our ancestors did to Alphor a hundred years ago. Only, we didn't have the equipment we needed. I mean, look at this place!" she gestures around them. "Poor lighting, dust, fold out tables. We didn't have the facilities necessary for that sort of work. That dream was over before it even began. But ..."

She twists her skirt in her fists, biting her lip against some memory. Solma waits, frowning. Once again, she's mentally kicking herself for being so incurious all her life. She's been so focused on survival, so bent on protecting her brother, that she failed to consider what he actually needed protection *from*. Or who.

"But what?" Warren presses, gently stroking Bell's hand. Solma smiles. Look at him. Despite everything, despite the fear, the lies, the betrayals—*her* betrayal—he is still gentle with people.

She underestimated her poor brother. And time and time again, he's forgiven her. She feels a rush of love for him and Bell. She doesn't deserve their forgiveness, but she has it anyway.

Bell takes a trembling breath. "We began to see signs of fringe life," she says. "The more we looked, the more we found. It was difficult, because we had our planting and our village positions to attend to, and we knew Blaiz would not take well to what we were doing. So work was slow, secret. We believed we'd found dormant life underground. We thought if we could revive this life we might stand a chance of repairing the eco-system. Your Ma believed that the insects were the basis of everything. Revive the small life, and you persuade the larger life to come back. If we could stir the insects from their sleep, we could revive the birds, and perhaps some new animals would take the place of the bird-eating mammals that died out. We knew it would be a long process. We knew we might not live to see the end of it, but we wanted to try. For you. For your children and their children." She shakes her head. "Humans have made so many mistakes. Killed so many creatures, either through fear or anger or plain negligence. We never bothered to look where we were treading." She snorts a mirthless laugh, her brows drawn together in consternation "And your Ma and Dja and Roseann's husband ... and me ... we tried. We tried to make it right. But ... we were prevented."

Solma sits forward. "Prevented?"

Bell stares avidly at her hands. Her cheeks flush, but not with embarrassment or shame. Solma sees tears glittering in Bell's eyes.

"Oh Earth," she whispers. She knows what's coming.

"What I'm about to tell you," Bell murmurs "Is going to be hard to hear."

Solma's heart is a thunderstorm. Its every beat sends lightning blasting through her. She doesn't want to hear this, but she can't *not* hear it. This is the thing that Blaiz covets so badly, the thing he hoards like men once hoarded bees and money and power.

The truth.

"Your Ma's accident gave Blaiz an opportunity," Bell says. "I don't believe he arranged her death. Not entirely. But he reassigned her to a new squad just as we were getting close to a breakthrough. A team he knew was loyal to him. When your Ma was caught by that boar, no one helped her. No one shot the thing, no one tried to drag her free. Not until it was clear her body was beyond repair. Then the animal was destroyed and dragged home, along with your Ma. I think Blaiz was waiting for something like that to happen. I think he counted on it. Roseann did her best to save her, but she knew, like we all did, what happened.

"Still, the rest of us carried on trying, in your Ma's name. I don't think Blaiz expected that. That's why ... that's why your and Olive's Djas both ..."

She stops, her head in her hands. A sob jolts her body.

"We don't know exactly what he used," she whispers. "But something ... some poison or other ... by the time Roseann and I realized what had happened, it was too late. We were looking for a sickness, treating for fever and pain. We never imagined ... never imagined poison. We had nothing to prove it, neither. But ..."

She glances up, eyes red and raw already. A single tear draws a track down her face.

"Blaiz killed your parents. I'm certain of it. He killed them to shut down our work. He killed them to keep power. I should have told you years ago, but I wanted to keep you safe. But safety is irrelevant now."

Solma stares. She doesn't know what she expected to feel, but this puzzled and paralyzing numbness isn't it. Warren nudges her hand and slips his own into it. She squeezes his fingers in hers.

So this is it: the truth, in all its ugliness. This is the way greedy men smash the world. This is the way it really works. And Solma is repulsed by it. She wants to be sick. She wants to scream, to rage, to fight.

But she's prevented from doing any of that, by the insistent knock at the door upstairs.

THIRTY-FIVE

SOLMA WANTS IT TO be Maxen at the door, which is why she flies up the stone stairs to open it. She *expects* it to be Blaiz, which is why she hesitates before reaching for the handle.

But it's neither. Bell and Warren hurry to her side as Solma wrenches the door open.

It's Olive. And Dr. Roseann. And Gerta, for some reason, resting her hand lightly on Cobra's shoulder. On Cobra's other side, with his hand in hers, is Mamba. They stand in a solemn line and behind them are the other five Earth Whisperers, unsmiling, their hands clasped together. They stare expectantly at Solma. The orange-eyed Whisperer girl steps forward and looks up at her with a frown.

"You going to let us in, then?" she asks. "We're here to help."

Solma's jaw slackens in surprise. Beside her, Warren beams.

There's a heavy silence. Cobra's gaze meets Solma's.

"There won't be room for all of you inside," Bell says matter-of-factly. "Pick your representatives and come in. The rest of you can wait out here. I'll see if I can find some refreshments ..."

She steps aside, but Solma notices how her eyes meet Roseann's. A kind of energy passes between them.

"I'll wait out here," Roseann says, unshouldering a leather bag. "These kids could do with a medical check."

She kneels and start rummaging through her supplies, beckoning over a gangly boy who approaches with a limp.

Olive grunts something and marches inside, followed by Cobra and Mamba. Cobra pauses at the door and gazes back at Gerta, who shakes her head with a gap-toothed grin.

"Nah, I'll stay out here m'girl," she says. "You bin alright without me these few years, you'll be alright in there. I want to chat with your friends 'bout what they can do for my herb garden ..."

Cobra gives a small smile, and squeezes Gerta's hand. Solma feels a stab of something like jealousy and hates herself for it. Still, once the door closes behind the four of them, she stands squarely between her family and their unlikely guests.

"What're *you* doing here?" she growls.

Mamba bristles but Cobra touches his arm and he quells. Olive, who's no stranger to confrontation, mirrors Solma's stance.

"Came to help out, didn't we?" she says.

Solma's jaw tightens. She can think of a whole host of things to say to that. Most of them are not very polite and all of them are untrue. Because they *do* need help. Solma just isn't sure she wants it from this lot.

"Why should I trust you?" she demands, "after what you did?"

Olive rolls her eyes. "Here we go," she sighs. "Go on then, Sol, what is it you think we've done? Let's get it out in the open so we can explain what an utter fool you've been and get on with the rest of our lives. Well?"

Solma opens and closes her mouth a few times, but the righteous certainty she'd felt drains away. Could she have made a mistake? Well, yes. She's made many. This wouldn't be the first. It probably isn't the last either. She steels herself for yet another emotional battering.

"You led the badger to the bees," she says, hating how small her voice is. "You sided with the Earth Whisperers. You tried to destroy the nest."

Behind her, she feels Warren gasp. She hears Bell groan with sudden realization and now, with everything that's happened today, she understands how that sounds. Olive raises an eyebrow.

"You didn't do that, did you?" Solma says. Guilt—her old friend—floods her again. "Oh Earth! I'm such an ass."

"Yep," Olive confirms. "You are."

"I never thought—"

"No, you didn't."

"I should've—"

"Yeah, you should."

Solma clenches her fists. "*Alright,* Olive, I get it! You can shut up now."

To her surprise, Olive does, indeed, shut up. When Solma risks a glance, she sees Olive isn't wearing her usual expression of disdain. She hardly looks angry at all. She's watching Solma with ... what's that in her eyes? Pity?

Solma looks away and tries to hide the heat in her cheeks. A hand brushes her shoulder. Despite the lightness of the touch, Solma starts and turns to find

Olive standing beside her. "Look Sol," she says, chewing her lip. "I know I ain't the easiest of people. I ..." she sighs through her nose and scans the ceiling, as if the words she's searching for might have escaped up there somehow. "I just ... people are hard and I say what I think and it comes out wrong. But I ain't no traitor, ok? I looked out for you. I just wanted ... I just wanted you to get it right."

Solma pulls away and glares, though when she thinks about it, it's more out of habit than actual anger. "I thought I *did* get it right," she mutters. "I thought ..."

"I know what you thought," Olive interrupts, her voice unusually gentle. "I get it, Sol. You had good intentions. It's just you trusted the wrong person."

Trusted the wrong person.

Solma's heart lurches like a stumbling horse. She feels her breath tighten and now she's staring past Olive, past Mamba and Cobra towards the door, as if desperately believing, *hoping,* it will fly open and he will be standing there.

"Where's ..." she whispers, hardly daring to ask. "Where's Maxen?"

Olive's gaze hardens and Solma thinks she might snap or sneer. But she doesn't. She simply glares at the floor. When she speaks, her voice is low and bitter, but not derisive. Not cruel. It's full of hurt. "Where do you *think* he is?" she asks.

And it all makes sense. It's been there, lurking just beyond the light this whole time. The truth. Earth! How Solma hates its bitter tang.

Because of course, it was Maxen. She remembers stumbling into him in the dark on the night of the badger attack, the dirt on his face ... what had he said?

That he'd heard something. Heard what? Solma remembers the wind masking Warren's cries. She'd heard nothing, not until they'd got right up to the nest itself. So what was it Maxen heard? She hadn't even asked. She'd just believed him. Oh Earth, she's been such a fool. He'd convinced her it was the Whisperers she should blame, and all the time, it was him ...

"No," she hears herself say, shaking her head. She doesn't know why she's denying it. It's so obvious. "No, he wouldn't."

But he would. And he did.

He's played her. He's taken her affections and used them to undo her. She wonders, bitterly, how persuasive Blaiz had to be to get Maxen to trick her like that. She hopes Blaiz had to use all his slimy, manipulative cruelty to recruit Maxen. But somehow, she doesn't believe that. Maxen will inherit the Stewardship after his father, won't he? The spoils of the father will be passed to the son. And Solma gave them exactly what they wanted.

She ought to break down again, to sob over that false love. But she cried herself out this morning and all she feels now is this pulsing anger calcifying in her gut. This is how a world dies, she thinks, how an entire species signs the deeds to its own death. They keep making the same damn mistakes as their parents. Over and over, like the pull of the seasons. Inevitable as gravity, and she fell into that same trap.

Well, not anymore.

She lifts her head, clenches her fists, stares Olive in the face. "Whatever happens," she growls, "Whatever you decide to do, you leave Maxen to me. My knuckles have his name on them from this moment on."

And to her surprise, Olive grins. "Only if I can hold his arms back," she says, and grabs Solma's hand. Solma freezes, but Olive's touch isn't what she expected. Fierce, yes, full of purpose, with the catch of calluses on her hand. But it isn't possessive, rough or demanding. Olive's touch says, *I'm with you*. It says, *I got your back*. Solma finds it's not at all unpleasant.

It's Warren that shatters Solma's newfound strength.

"What about the bees?" he whispers. "Blume needs boy bees. Her daughters are gonna fly soon and they need to mate before they go to ground, or there won't be any bees next year. What do we do?"

Solma's hand drops out of Olive's. She'd forgotten about that. For a moment, she'd almost let herself hope. What a childish thing to do. She shakes her head.

"Forget it," she mutters, "There ain't any males, are there? It's just one nest. None of it matters anyway." She closes her eyes. Earth, she's so tired! She's tired of fighting, tired of trusting, tired of hoping. It all ends in disaster anyway.

Olive punches her in the arm.

"Ow!" Solma protests, punching her back. "What was that for?"

Olive smirks. "Someone's gotta jolt you outta your self-pity," she says. "Don't you trust me?"

"Not really, no," Solma grumbles, rubbing her arm. Olive rolls her eyes.

"Look, Sol," she says, "pack it in, ok? We got something to show you. Come on."

She hoists her rifle onto her shoulder and heads to the door. Solma hesitates, her eyes flickering towards Cobra and Mamba. They've not spoken a word, only stood in stony silence and watched. Their faces are inscrutable. Solma frowns, but it seems pointless to tell them she's sorry again. She *is* sorry. Sorry she's hurt them, sorry she put her faith in men like Blaiz and Maxen. But she hasn't earned their trust. Not yet.

Mamba's hand is on Cobra's shoulder. It's not a possessive touch, more that he's ready to push her behind him at any moment. He looks at Solma as if she's some kind of predator. Which she probably deserves.

"Oi!" Olive barks, pausing at the open door. "You lot coming, or what?"

Mamba gestures for Solma to go first. "After you," he says, in a tone that suggests he'll stab her with her own knife if she tries anything. Solma tries not to take it personally and fails. She holds out her hand for Warren and he takes it. They both stare at Bell, who shrugs.

"There's some Whisperers' kids out here that need feeding," she says. "You two go. I'll be there when it matters."

Solma nods and follows Olive. They leave the door open behind them and, when Solma glances back, she notices Gerta whispering something in Cobra's ear. The old woman passes Cobra another little packet of medicine. Solma's eyes narrow. Something nags at the back of her brain again but she's not sure what. And Olive is calling. Hope stirs again, like an impossible creature burrowing up from deep underground.

THIRTY-SIX

WARREN SKIPS AHEAD WITH Cobra. He chats animatedly to her, just like he did all those months ago when she first appeared. Solma's eyes narrow as she watches but she says nothing.

They're heading out of the village, taking a roundabout route towards the wilderness so those holding Blume's nest under siege won't see them. They're going to the woods. Solma's absent leg itches at the thought and she stomps through the grasses, trying to distract herself. Why would anyone head into these woods if they didn't have to? But of course, Olive is right up in front, striding into the shadows as if there weren't monstrous animals lurking within, as if nobody had ever died in these woods. Solma clenches her fists around the hilt of her knife. Her knuckles tremble.

Beside her, Mamba glances down at the knife in her hand. He frowns and shakes his head.

"You people never learn," he mutters. "Something goes wrong, you grab straight for a weapon."

Solma scowls at him. "Says the boy who named himself after Alphor's deadliest snake?" she shoots back. "Blaiz always said your lot were double-faced. You name yourself after poisonous reptiles that hide in the grass and wonder why people don't trust you?"

Mamba laughs, which Solma had not been expecting. Her hand loosens around the knife hilt.

"Alright," Mamba says, "A little lesson in Whisperer customs, yeah? Do you know how we choose our names?"

Solma shrugs. "I always figured you just ... picked your favorite snake?"

Mamba rolls his eyes. "Wow. Ok. Sometimes, Solma, it's a good idea to not just assume stuff. Snakes are as important as any animal to the ecosystem. They help keep the population of mice and rats under control and they, themselves, are food for bigger predators, which some other provinces hunt for game. But lots of people don't realize this, and they get scared of them. Human beings are rubbish at that: we destroy what scares us, or what we don't understand.

Whisperers often rescue snakes from under the shovel-blades of angry or frightened villagers. Sooner or later, as a Whisperer, you get bitten. We choose our names based on the first snake that bites us."

Solma stops dead and stares at him. "You got bitten by a *mamba?*" she gasps. "How're you still alive?"

Mamba keeps walking, which forces Solma to jog a few paces to catch up. When she glances at him, he's grinning.

"No one really understands it," he admits, "but snake poison doesn't affect us the same way it does ordinary folk. I was sick for a few days. I hallucinated a lot, but I survived. I've seen five-year-old Whisperers walk away unharmed from adder bites. Mamba poison is potent though, so there are very few mamba-named Whisperers."

Solma nods, staring at her brother as he chatters to Cobra.

"What about her?" she asks quietly. "How'd she get her name?"

Mamba frowns. He's silent for a few minutes, then says, "High Savannah Province. We went to one of the border territories where a village found a nest of cobra eggs. They were hatching and the villagers all gathered to destroy them. Our Cobra? She walked straight in amongst the villagers and knelt by the nest, waiting for all the youngsters to hatch. Then she put out her hands and asked them to slither up her arms. I don't know how many times she was bitten. Five, maybe? Or six? But she barely flinched. She carried those baby snakes around her arms and neck, miles from the village, and set them all free. She was ill for days afterwards. Vomiting, dizziness, insomnia. I've never known a Whisperer suffer so many bites all in one go. But she never complained. She said to me, 'If I die, I die doing the right thing.' ..." He shakes his head and turns away, though Solma has already seen the tears glistening in his eyes. "She's braver than you'll ever know, our Cobra. She's overcome so much."

He's silent again and Solma doesn't know what to say. She thinks of that peaceful girl, carrying an entire nest of frightened baby snakes to safety, never blaming them for biting her, never hurting them back. She thinks how little time or patience she's afforded that girl, and it fills her, once again, with shame.

"So," she says quietly, "You save the snakes. I had no idea."

Mamba wipes his eyes and nods. "Once we've got our name," he says, "we tend to stick with rescuing or relocating that particular snake. It's another way we guard the ecosystem: protect the creatures human beings destroy."

Solma thinks for a moment. "Like bees," she whispers.

"Like bees," Mamba agrees. "People misunderstand us. Like they misunderstand snakes, the world and each other. It's not us who're double-faced, is it Solma?"

Heat floods Solma's face, but she deserved that. She releases the hilt of her knife. "No," she murmurs. "It's not."

They fall silent, traipsing through the grasses so that only the swish of greenery and the sound of Warren's chattering permeate the quiet. Olive waits on the outskirts of the woodland for the group to come together, then fixes them with a steely glare.

"Keep together," she says. "And keep alert."

Solma rolls her eyes before she can stop herself. "You're Sergeant now, are you?" she snaps. Olive raises an eyebrow.

"You can be Sergeant if you want," she says. "Lead the way."

She steps aside and gestures for Solma to go ahead. Solma hesitates, gritting her teeth. "Alright," she growls. "I obviously don't know where we're going, so …"

She glares at Olive, expecting the other girl to say something sarcastic, but Olive doesn't. She simply shrugs and takes the lead, unhooking her pistol from her belt. Solma sees Warren slip his hand into Cobra's. They smile at each other and Solma scowls. Jealousy seems childish given what they're facing, but she can't help herself.

And there's that strange nudge at the back of her mind again when she sees Cobra grin, a memory trying to wriggle its way to the surface. Solma shakes her head and tries to focus.

They pick their way along the edge of the wood, avoiding the deeper, darker center, for which Solma is grateful. Although she's faced wild boar many times, it isn't something she relishes. Gradually, the ferns give way to modest plants and flowering vines that Solma has never seen before. That's not the only change, either. It happens so gradually that Solma doesn't even notice until the sound of it is so obvious it stops her dead.

Buzzing. *Bee song*. The deep, glorious tremolo of many gossamer wings trembling in the summer air.

Olive stops too, as if on some strange instinct, and glances back at Solma.

"Is that—" Solma gasps. Olive nods, a half-smile tugging at her face.

"Yeah," she says. "Bees. And I think they're males."

Solma's heart squeezes. But it's not the terrible tightness of fear or the punch of self-doubt or the thrum of guilt. This time it feels like a warm hand holding her steady. It hasn't all been for nothing, after all.

Warren laughs, his meadow-green eyes awash with light. He darts ahead of Olive and rounds a cluster of brambles so that Solma can no longer see him. She panics for a moment before his delighted voice drifts back to them.

"Look at them all!" he squeals, "Look, Sol! Look!"

Solma's face is doing something strange and she realizes she's smiling hugely. Olive grins, too, and the hardened, cold girl that Solma knows is transformed into someone gentle, open, *young*. Sometimes she forgets that she and Olive are both just about to turn seventeen. In the old times, they would be on the cusp of womanhood, though they both left the luxury of childhood behind long ago. There's a flash of youth in Olive's eyes now and Solma finds herself thinking Olive is quite lovely when she's happy.

Mamba and Cobra smile too. Hand in hand, the two Whisperers scurry ahead and Solma and Olive follow. As they skid round the brambles, Solma stops dead and stares, mouth open.

Olive laughs. "I'd close that," she chuckles. "You wouldn't want any to get in there."

Solma shuts her mouth but her wonder persists. Because they're in the middle of a little clearing, where sunlight illuminates the forest floor and the vine flowers turn their pale heads towards the light. Warren stands in the middle of the clearing, his arms spread, laughing with glorious, childish glee. He spins in a circle.

"Look, Sol! Look!"

Surrounding him, are bees upon bees upon bees.

Some of them hang in the air, their delicate wings catching the light. Some adorn the nearby flowers, clambering over the petals and drinking the sweet treats within. Some rest on vine leaves or tree trunks, or wrestle each other for prime spots in the sun.

Solma hardly believes what she's seeing. This is impossible. But then, bees always were, weren't they?

The engine of the natural world, the soul of the planet that had long seemed dead. Yet here they are.

Solma feels a whisper on her shoulder and glances down to find a little bee has landed there, folded his wings neatly over his fluffy back and is now cleaning his antennae. He's big; similar in size to Blume, and alert. His multifaceted eyes glitter with life, his fur is lustrous and full. He's strong and healthy. Solma slowly raises a hand and encourages him onto her finger. He shuffles onto her palm and explores a little, before deciding she's not a flower and firing up his wings. He lifts into the air with a deep, rumbling vibrato and joins his brothers in flight.

"This ..." Solma whispers, "is ... amazing. But how—"

Olive stands at her side, pistol in its holster, hands in her pockets, as relaxed as Solma has ever seen her.

"Well," she says, "Your brother's gifted, right? I been scooping insects from his footprints, Sol. He's waking them all up. Not just bees, either. I seen caterpillars, beetle larvae, hoverflies, sawflies ..."

Solma stares as Olive reels off more and more impossible creatures. She doesn't know whether to be more shocked that Olive has known about Warren for so long, or that Olive actually seems to know *quite a lot* about creatures that have been extinct for a century.

"... So it stands to reason," Olive continues, "that Blume won't be the only queen he woke. It's just she was the only one he *felt*. He nudged her mind into wakefulness, and she nudged him back. But she was just the first, Sol. I found three other living nests when I went beyond the forest. Found a whole host of dead ones too. Some were diseased, I found one that looked like a moon badger got it. There was another one where the bees were all behaving weird and there weren't no males coming from it, so I let it be. But a few of them made it through the summer."

Solma listens to Olive and feels a kick of shock at the thought. All those dead nests. All those failed queens, and yet Blume made it. Despite everything, Blume made it through the summer and now her daughters need mates so they can fly into the wilderness and carry the hope of their species to next spring. And Solma may have ruined that. She may have handed Blume's future to Blaiz. Her gut clenches at the thought. She can't let that happen.

"Ok," she says. "So now we have male bees. There's hope. What do we do now? Could Warren call the princesses out of Blume's nest? We can send them far away from here, across Alphor. If there are going to be more bees next year, Blaiz can't control them all. It doesn't really matter if he snatches Blume's nest as long as the new queens have mated. Right?"

Olive doesn't look convinced, but it's Cobra who speaks.

"It matters," she says. She speaks quietly, but it still makes Solma jump. Cobra's eyes are wide and earnest, demanding attention. "It matters that Blaiz thinks he can take whatever he wants. It matters that Blume's daughters live free from human control. We should fight for that nest, Sol. If we don't, this war will begin again next spring, and it'll continue for years. Blume's daughters will fly free. They *must.*"

Solma can't really argue with that, but she resents Cobra. "What would *you* know about Blaiz Camber?" she snaps, wondering why she still feels a need to defend the man that tricked, betrayed and exiled her.

Cobra raises an eyebrow. "I know everything about Blaiz Camber," she growls, baring her teeth in a show of anger that takes Solma aback. "And you were there, Solma. *You saw.* You saw and you chose not to remember. You've been choosing not to remember since the day it happened, and I bet my life that it's because *he* told you to forget me. He told you to forget, and like the obedient little pup you are, you did."

Solma frowns, shaking her head. "What—"

"Kobi Pre Yuen," Cobra whispers, and suddenly, the gates in Solma's mind open, and the memory is there. And Solma remembers the truth in all its awfulness.

THIRTY-SEVEN

SHE WAS NEARLY TWO years younger than Solma, but it hadn't mattered. She was one of the few kids who didn't look at Solma with wary disgust, who didn't call her mud-haired or death-eyed or make fun of her lumbering height. Because, it turned out, Kobi was different, too. They were both trying to fit in and that was how they found each other.

Solma was almost ten and Kobi, eight, when they first properly met. They were both still Yuen, though Solma was old enough to do field work with Bell and her Dja. But Solma's Ma had just died and everything about work seemed so pointless. She just wandered listlessly across the fields, trampling the seedlings, until the Fei dragged her back to the village and dumped her with the Aldren, telling her not to come back until she was ready to work. Not that she cared. All she wanted was her Ma back. She ached every night, missing that warm, soft touch. She cried often and her baby brother, still an infant, screamed so much with desperate hunger. Between them both, the house was always full of rage and sadness.

Solma's Dja fell sick, and only got sicker. Bedridden, he could barely muster enough energy to feed himself, let alone look after his children. Aunt Bell was so preoccupied with planting and keeping the baby alive she had little time for young, grieving Solma. So Solma was handed to Gerta most days and left to play on the old woman's porch.

But of course, she didn't play much. Not with enthusiasm, anyway. She missed her Ma. She was afraid for her Dja. There was talk of *disease* in the village and Solma knew that Olive's Dja had fallen ill as well. Olive, already silent and moody at the best of times, was even more so, now. She didn't stick up for Solma and chase off the other kids like she used to. That hurt: that Olive had left her to the meanness and the grief.

At night, during what little sleep Solma snatched, she dreamed of everyone she loved falling sick. She dreamed of the curtain-drawn darkness, the sour stench, the pre-emptive silence of disease. She woke sobbing every night.

It was this Solma that first met Kobi when she, too, was delivered to Gerta's door one morning by a frazzled mother late for planting. Both children were exempt from field work for a short while, though Solma never did find out why Kobi had been spared.

Solma had little interest in playing, or in anything really, but Kobi wasn't pushy. She sat with Solma, cross-legged in ragged dungarees, and twirled her twin-braids around her fingers, watching Solma quietly. Her hair was the kind of flame red that should be impossible, her eyes bright and intelligent. She had clever hands, too.

And Solma learned that afternoon, just how clever Kobi's hands were.

"Want to go outside?" Kobi asked, caressing Solma's hand. "I can show you something amazing. But you got to come outside."

Solma was tired. She didn't want to go outside. She only wanted to sleep. But she liked Kobi, and she hadn't yet grown out of her curiosity.

"Ok," she'd said. She took Kobi's hand; the pair of them trotted outside, giggling at Gerta's throaty calls to *stay near the house!*

They didn't stay near the house. They were just kids, and the sun and the grass called them. They disappeared into the morning and Solma smiled and laughed for the first time in months. This was exciting.

They crouched in the tall grass. Above, pale clouds scudded across an otherwise clear sky. Kobi had shown Solma her miracle: a flower, drawn up from the earth, spreading its white petals before their eyes. Solma watched in utter fascination. She'd never seen a flower before. Solma grew up in a world where plants had to be pollinated by hand, where the wild was devoid of color and the air was empty of life.

And yet here was Kobi, giving her the gift of the impossible. A wild, fresh flower.

"It's called Whispering," Kobi said. Solma felt a pang of regret. She knew what this meant. Her new friend would disappear soon, stolen into the unknown when the Earth Whisperers came to claim her. Whisperers belonged to no village, they were servants of humankind. But Kobi was already eight, and her powers were strong and controlled. She should have gone with the Whisperers already.

"I'm not allowed to go," Kobi said. "When the Whisperers come, I have to hide."

"Why?" Solma asked. Kobi smirked, proud of herself in that way only eight-year-olds can be.

"Blaiz says," she admitted. "He wants to keep my powers for the village. So I have to be a secret."

That word sent shockwaves through Solma's heart. Secrets were forbidden. She'd known that since she could walk and talk. All secrets belonged to Blaiz. Blaiz protected the land, and secrets were a threat. A secret was punishable by exile. And here was Kobi, keeping one as if there was nothing to be afraid of. Keeping one because *Blaiz told her to.* It didn't make sense.

Still, it was fun growing flowers in the long grasses, exciting to watch Kobi persuade the plants to flourish. Solma felt special that Kobi trusted her with this secret.

Almost a year passed. Kobi's miracle, it turned out, was not just in bringing the plants to life, but in bringing Solma to life too. Solma's Dja died in that time, slipping into the silent dark. He didn't respond when Solma tried to shake him awake one night. He was cold under her tiny fingers. Now orphaned, Solma cried often in anger and confusion. Bell tried to comfort her, but her own grief left her impatient, and a persistent and active Warren took almost all her time.

So it was Kobi that nourished Solma's soul through that darkness. It was Kobi that made Solma laugh, despite herself, and then stroked her hair and told her it was ok as she cried. When the other children were cruel to Solma, it was Kobi who shielded her from the meanness and told the bullies to leave her alone, using such vivid language that Solma herself had covered her ears. Kobi's flowers grew in the long grasses beyond the village, and they grew in Solma's heart. Kobi turned Solma's grief into a meadow. Every flower a memory of her parents. They built worlds for themselves among Kobi's Whispered flowers, charging through the undergrowth, flapping their arms, pretending to be the fabled flying birds from long ago. Kobi taught Solma that wings were not impossible and Solma would lay awake at night and love Kobi so much that it was a physical ache in her heart.

Solma never knew when it started, but Kobi's pride in her secret began to fade the following spring. Something in her changed. She spoke about her power differently.

"It doesn't belong to us, Sol," she said. "It's for everyone."

Solma frowned. "But I thought Blaiz wanted to keep it?"

"He does," Kobi admitted, her eyes serious. "But he shouldn't."

Solma gasped. Nobody questioned the Steward. Everything he did, he did for the village. He was their savior and guardian and leader. It hurt her heart to hear Kobi talk about him like that. But it happened more and more, until one day, Kobi said something that brought all of Solma's grief boiling back to the surface.

"I got to leave. I got to find the Earth Whisperers. I belong with them."

"No!" Solma screamed. "You belong with me! You're *my* friend! You're not allowed to leave!"

Kobi was gentle, but unyielding. She held Solma's hand, such wisdom and compassion in those eight-year-old eyes. "I'll always be your friend," she said. "You could come with me. We could go together."

When Solma thinks back on this now, standing amongst the bees and facing the girl Kobi has become, she's ashamed to admit she never considered leaving. No one left, not on purpose. Leaving meant death. Leaving meant starvation and hopelessness.

So Solma had stamped hard on Kobi's foot.

"I *hate* you!" she cried and ran. She ran even though her tears blurred her vision and she wept so hard she could barely breathe. She ran back into the village, her bare feet kicking up dust.

She remembers now. She remembers what she did next with a thud of horror and shame. She'd run straight to Blaiz's house.

How old had she been at the time? Just shy of eleven? Not old enough to consider what she was doing. She'd half expected Blaiz to turn her away. He didn't make a habit of listening to tearful children who'd fallen out with their friends. But he did that day. Perhaps because he knew the friend she was tearful over was Kobi, perhaps because he had a suspicion about why.

He had put a hand on her shoulder.

"Those Whisperers, they're nothing but traitors and tricksters. You've been brave, Solma. You're honest and loyal. Not like them."

It took less that twenty-four hours for Blaiz to exile Kobi, claiming she had stolen rations from the storehouse. Greedy, he'd called her. Selfish. He knew the Earth Whisperers were on their way, knew she planned to reveal herself to them. He was getting rid of her before then. The village gathered at the western edge to witness her departure, and Solma's heart coiled like a snake in her ribcage. She'd felt a horror she couldn't contend with, but Blaiz's words echoed in her mind as she watched.

Honest and loyal. Not like them.

She'd expected Kobi to be dragged out by the Gathering Guard, her parents screaming, her face puffy with crying. But when Kobi emerged from her house, she did so unaided, and her face, though pale with fear, was dry. Her flame-red hair hung loose and she had a pack slung over her shoulder. It was such an undramatic exit that the villagers started to drift away after a while, bored by the lack of spectacle. Blaiz stayed though. He stayed and watched as the door to Kobi's house closed behind her and the sound of her mother sobbing drifted through the open window, as Kobi hugged Gerta and accepted a small bundle of medicine from her, medicine that Kobi explained would help her to be the girl she wanted to be when puberty started. Gerta dug her stick into the dirt as Kobi set off towards the horizon, her mouth a thin, angry line.

Blaiz stood beside Solma, a hand on her shoulder.

Honest and loyal.

And then Kobi turned and stared straight at Solma. That splash of freckles across her face, those bright, curious green eyes. One last look at the friend she had loved, and then she walked off into the unknown. Solma thought she would die out there, as so many had. She'd cried then, bitter, shameful tears that coated her face and blurred her vision. Blaiz's hand was still on her shoulder.

Honest and loyal.

"She's a traitor, Solma," he'd said as he turned to go. "They're all traitors. Forget them. Forget her."

And, to Solma's shame, she did.

THIRTY-EIGHT

SOLMA REELS AT THE memory. She touches her face and her fingers come away wet. Her breath catches. She lifts her eyes and meets Cobra's—Kobi's. There she is; the friend Solma had driven away, a truth so painful she had locked it away in some cobwebbed corner of her mind.

But she remembers now. She remembers it isn't Cobra who's the traitor. It's her. All Kobi wanted was to live free, as the Whisperers should. She hadn't wanted to be in Blaiz's power. But Blaiz didn't accept that. If he couldn't have Kobi's miracle, then no-one could.

A year later, or perhaps less, Kobi's parents left the village. They'd said, at the time, they were searching for a better life. But Solma realizes now that they were searching for Kobi. And what was the bet Blaiz had given them that little push? Solma has no idea what happened to them. Most likely, they died out there in the wilderness, just as Solma thought Kobi had.

It all suddenly makes sense: Mamba's furious defense of Cobra, his distrust of Solma and Warren, his refusal to let his friend out of his sight. She's been so blinkered. So stubborn and incurious.

And now Blaiz is doing it again. He won't stop. Something new burns in Solma's core. It takes her a while to understand what it is, mixed with shame and horror and fear. But as its smoldering turns to a firestorm in her heart, she recognizes it at last.

It's fury. The rage of the misused. Blaiz didn't care about her. He didn't trust her. He tricked her.

The inferno inside her is so searing hot that Solma is sure the others must be able to see the glow of it in her chest. She gasps for air, her face twisted with anger. Her eyes don't leave Cobra's.

"I remember," she whispers. "I remember everything."

Cobra's eyes soften. She takes a tentative step towards Solma until she is close enough to hold Solma's hand. Solma gazes into the soft, patient eyes of the friend she'd betrayed and forgot. Her face crumples.

"I'm sorry," she gasps. "I'm so sorry. He tricked me. He tricked me and I—I *let* him."

Cobra squeezes Solma's hand. "He did trick you," she whispers. "He's tricked many people, and the ones he couldn't trick, he killed or exiled or scared into submission. Solma, you had my forgiveness the moment I met Mamba and the other Whisperers in the wasteland. I knew, then, what he'd done to you. Now you forgive yourself. It's time to make Blaiz pay."

Solma blinks and it's as if she's emerging from a cocoon she hadn't realized she'd spun for herself. The rules of the world have shifted. Cobra steps back to Mamba's side and Olive takes Solma's hand. Solma glances at their intertwined fingers and thinks how constant Olive has been. How unfailing, how patient.

"I should'a listened to you," Solma admits. "I should'a trusted you. I dunno now why I didn't, I—"

"Because I'm a pain in the ass," Olive says, grinning. "That's why. Look, Sol, we can do all the apologies later, okay? Right now, we got a job to do. So, this is what we got. We got an army of Whisperers. We got a kid who can talk to bees. We got a bunch of greedy Stewards trying to own something that don't belong to them and we got right on our side. What we don't have is time, so what we gonna do?"

Solma studies Olive's face, then Mamba's, then Cobra's. Finally, her eyes fall on Warren, stood patiently between them with a bumblebee on each shoulder, two on his head and one trundling across his palm. He looks so at home with these impossible creatures, a million miles from the frightened, delicate child she'd thought him to be. He is not weak, he is compassionate. And for once, Solma realizes that his compassion won't be his undoing, it will be his making.

He examines the bee on his hand.

"They're waiting for new queens," he explains. "That's why they're all here. They're ready to mate. Once the new queens fly, Blume's nest won't—won't matter anymore." His voice cracks a little and Solma remembers their research at Bell's table six months and a whole lifetime ago.

"She'll be old now, Warren," she whispers. "She'll be ready."

Warren nods and swallows down his tears. "I know," he says. "But we got to get the new queens out before anyone gets the nest. If the new queens fly and mate, they'll burrow underground after and sleep through winter. They'll be safe."

Solma nods. "Can you call them from here? Maybe we can get the queens safe before we deal with Blaiz."

Warren closes his eyes, holds his breath, then lets it out in a disappointed sigh. He shakes his head. "Too far away," he says. "I got to be in the village, at least. But it'll be better—I'll smell louder to them—if we're right by the nest."

Solma blinks at him. She decides not to ask what he means by *smell louder*. It must be a bee thing. She trusts her brother. She should have trusted him from the start.

"Ok," she says. "What do we do?"

She glances from Cobra to Mamba and finally, to Olive, across whose face a smile slowly spreads. "I got an idea," she says, her eyes alight with a mischief Solma's never seen before. She's still holding Solma's hand and she squeezes it now. It feels so natural for Olive to be holding her hand, like they should have been linked like this forever ago. Solma smiles.

"What's the idea?"

"It's mad," Olive admits. "But Blaiz won't never see it coming."

Warren grabs Solma's other hand. "Sounds perfect," he says, smiling. Mamba and Cobra step forward to join the circle. Solma's courage surges. She isn't alone now. It isn't only her shoulders carrying the weight. This is wholeness. This is how it should be. They hold each other steady, strength flowing between their linked fingers. Then they let go and turn towards the village. After all, they have a job to do.

THIRTY-NINE

MAXEN MOVES CONFIDENTLY AROUND the barricaded camp a hundred meters north of the bee colony. He patrols a line of villagers dressed in every caste color, armed with a haphazard array of weaponry, who crouch, trembling, behind corrugated iron and grain bags. He looks like a soldier, as if he's made for this. Solma can't believe she never saw it in him. She lowers the binoculars and scowls into the dirt.

"Pig," she snarls, "Bastard."

She spits a few more insults until even Olive blushes beside her.

"Alright, Sol," she whispers. "We get it."

Solma catches her eye and Olive grins. For once, Solma doesn't bristle. Instead, she feels Olive's hand brush hers and its invigorating.

"Are the others in place yet?"

Olive holds her hands out for the binoculars and lifts them to her face. Laying on their bellies in the grass is not, in Solma's opinion, the best way to stay unseen, but Olive was adamant that she's hidden from Solma enough times that she knows it works. Solma decided not to ask.

"Mamba's signal is up," Olive mutters, handing the binoculars back. Solma peers in the general direction Olive indicates and sees the stalk of a sunflower, beyond the cluster of trees, that wasn't there before. It trembles in the soft breeze. Solma slowly swings the binoculars round to the south and sees two more sunflowers behind the barricades of the invading Stewards. A fourth creeps up directly to the south.

"Four in position," she confirms. Not for the first time, her gut twists like snakes. "Warren needs to wait 'til we start."

"I know," Olive agrees.

"He can't go in too early, they'll see him."

"I know, Sol, I—"

"It's really important. He can't put himself in danger."

"Sol!"

Solma starts, but Olive's hand is on her wrist. Solma stares into her face. Her *friend's* face. Feels weird to think of Olive that way now, but Solma's beginning to realize that Olive has always thought of Solma as her friend. As more than her friend. And Solma finds it doesn't unsettle her. Actually, she quite likes it.

"Sorry," Solma says. "I just—"

"I know," Olive murmurs. "I get it. He's your brother and you want to keep him safe. But Sol, you seen him this summer. He don't need our protection the way you think he does. Trust him, yeah? He's a smart kid."

Solma hesitates a moment, then nods. Olive's right. She needs to trust Warren. To trust the right people for a change.

Olive twists round to glance behind them without lifting her head above the grass. She's wrapped a green and brown bandanna over her bright hair and smeared soil over her face. But wisps of orange-red hair have worked loose of their binding and now cling to her cheeks and forehead. How has she not noticed Olive's harsh, wild beauty before? She realizes she's staring and looks away before Olive notices.

"Ma and Gerta are in place," Olive confirms.

Solma nods. "Good."

Gerta is in no shape to fight anything larger than a shrew and, as the only doctor, Roseann needs to stay out of harm's way. She'd not been happy about that, and Solma had got first-hand evidence of where Olive inherited her temper from, but it was Bell who'd grasped Roseann's hand and told her this was the right thing. The right thing for Leile and Sten—Solma's Ma and Dja—and the right thing for Olged—Roseann's husband. Olive's father. Solma hasn't heard their names spoken for such a long time. It was like a flame sparking to life in the darkest corner of her heart.

For Leile and Sten and Olged. For hope and truth. For the impossible.

So Roseann agreed. She'd offered Bell her pistol but Bell only smiled and brandished her rolling pin. "I'll be alright with this," she chuckled. It sounded ridiculous, but Solma knows Bell will be fine. That woman is terrifying even when she's not wielding kitchen utensils as instruments of war. And for once, Solma is glad Bell is with Warren. She'll keep him steady until it's time for him to do his part.

They can do this. They *have* to do this.

"There he is," Olive growls, and Solma is thrown back into the present. She takes the binoculars Olive passes to her and puts them to her face. Yes. There he is. Blaiz Camber, stood to attention behind the barricade with a pistol at his hip and a wicked knife strapped across his back. If he's here, then it's time.

"Okay," Solma says, fighting against the tremble of adrenalin in her voice. "This is it."

Olive unholsters her pistol, aims it in the air and fires. The agreed signal. The sound cracks against the pale sky, rattling through Solma's body. In the distance, she sees the men and women in the makeshift fortresses flinch and swing their weapons round, trying to locate the source of the shot. There's shouting from some of the barricades to the south. Blaiz, though, stands predator-still, glaring towards the spot where Solma and Olive are hidden.

"He knows," Solma whispers.

"'Course he knows," Olive snaps. "That's why we gotta act fast. Come on!"

She's on her feet in seconds, running, shooting, yelling. Solma's right behind her, chasing Olive into the fray, roaring as loud as her lungs allow. Blaiz and Maxen pause behind their barricade, eyes snapping towards the noise. Solma sees the flicker of recognition in their faces: the concern and guilt in Maxen's, the fury in Blaiz's.

Someone fires a shot and it goes screaming over Solma's head. She flinches but doesn't break her stride.

Olive roars something unrepeatable and returns fire. There's a muffled cry from beyond one of the barricades and a flurry of activity. Solma pushes on. The grass tugs at her bladed foot but she doesn't let that slow her. Get to the nest. It's the only thing that matters now.

Barked commands echo through the still autumn air as it dawns on the Stewards exactly what Solma and Olive are trying to do. More shots, but only a few. No one wants to waste ammo. A boy with a viciously curved knife clambers over one barricade and rushes them. Olive's own knife appears in her hand. She blocks the boy's downward slash, kicks him hard in the groin and relieves him of his weapon, leaving him wriggling on the ground. They barely stop for breath.

And then they're under the ash tree, crouched amongst the shimmering birches and back-to-back over the nest site, weapons raised. The Stewards have abandoned all pretense now. The siege breaks as bodyguards, soldiers and ordinary folk pour from beyond their makeshift fortresses, rushing the two young women who now hold the nest.

"Come on," Olive growls through gritted teeth. "Come on!"

But nothing happens. The ground trembles under the angry feet of rushing attackers. Olive swears. Solma wrenches the charging handle on her rifle and reloads it, raises it to her shoulder. She aims and it's Blaiz in her sights, marching at the back of his makeshift army of farmers, his face twisted in rage. Funny how clearly Solma sees it now, how he uses his own people as his shield. They've never been anything but a tool to him. She hooks her finger over the trigger, gets ready to squeeze.

If she's going to die here, she's taking that monster with her ...

But suddenly her sight fills with greenery. Thick, wild brambles climb from the earth, looping and arching in a long, sharp wall around the nest site. Around Olive and Solma. Solma has just enough time to see the on-rushers skid to a halt, mouths open in awe and confusion, before they disappear behind the thickening bushes. The bramble-barricade grows in both height and depth until it is at least seven feet in all directions, so wild and thick that Solma can't see beyond it. Its gleaming thorns grow unnaturally long, and drip with a clear poison. Solma shudders. The Whisperers have outdone themselves. True to their word, nothing will get past this monstrous growth.

It muffles the voices beyond, trembling as bullets are fired and lost in its depths.

Olive lowers her weapons. "That was close," she says, wiping blood from her cheek. Solma's heart kicks. She hadn't even noticed Olive was hurt. She lifts a hand to the other girl's face.

"Let me see."

But Olive shrugs her away. "Don't fuss," she growls. "I had worse. *You* had worse! We got a job to do. That bramble wall ain't gonna hold forever."

Solma fights the snarl of irritation in her gut. Olive is always going to be difficult. But she's the one who's here, at Solma's side, risking everything. She's always been the one who risks everything for Solma, facing wild boar and spiteful Stewards alike. So, for once, Solma finds she can let it go.

"Yeah," she says. "Ok. Where's Warren?"

"I'm here," says a voice behind them. They both turn and there he is, barefoot and small and calm, with Bell at his side. Already, the bees respond to his presence. A few emerge from the burrow, antennae waving in greeting, and fire their flight engines. They hum into the air, circling their human visitors curiously. The deep vibrato of their wings almost drowns out the shouts of frustration from beyond the bramble wall. Their black-and-gold fur catches the sun. Solma holds out her palm so one can land there. The little creature's feet settle against her skin and the bee runs her front feet over her face, cleaning. She's so beautiful, Solma thinks, like a living jewel. She takes off again, her wings vibrating the air in deep, delicate bee song. They hover around Warren, landing on him as if he is some precious flower they're desperate to be near. He smiles at their touch. It's all he needs: to be near his bees, to feel their strange, fragrant language fill his senses and hear their peaceful drone. Solma watches him.

"You ready?" she whispers. "Can you hear her?"

Warren closes his eyes and nod. "She's there," he murmurs. "She's listening."

The cries from beyond the wall change and the brambles tremble and reel. Olive grits her teeth. "They're trying to chop through!" she snarls. "Warren, we gotta be quick."

Warren's eyes are still closed, his hands outspread. A frown creases his brow.

"Can't rush ..." he mutters. "Something wrong ... she says ... it ain't time. She says her daughters ain't ready."

Olive rolls her eyes. "Well tell them to hurry up!"

"It don't work that way!" Solma snaps. "We got to be patient!"

The cries from beyond the bramble wall grow more purposeful now. The growth slows as the Whisperers try to compensate for the damage. They'll be through, soon ...

Olive's hard, frightened gaze meets Solma's. "We don't got *time* to be patient!" she snaps. "Brace yourself!"

They turn as one to face the wall again, back-to-back, weapons raised. This time, Bell is with them, her rolling pin in one hand, a bread knife in the other. "I'll be damned if that slug of a man is taking my niece and nephew!" she rumbles, and Solma allows herself a small smile. She likes this Aunt Bell: Aunt Bell the scientist, Aunt Bell the warrior and rebel.

Warren's little face tightens with concern. "It ain't time," he insists. "I can't ... they won't come out ..."

A sudden cry of triumph cuts the air and Solma's eyes snap up in time to see the smoke. They're burning the brambles. She scans the ground, desperate to find the source of the blaze, but the smoke is everywhere, drifting in thickening clouds into the still, blue sky. And Solma can't find the source.

"No!" Olive cries.

The fire takes hold with unnatural speed, swallowing the bramble wall, even as the hidden Whisperers desperately try to call new growth. Solma lifts a hand in front of her face as the heat reaches her: hotter than any fire she's felt before. She's reminded, suddenly, of the speed with which the storehouse took to flame and a terrible thought occurs to her ...

She shields her eyes and squints towards the crumbling wall, where great gaps are being burned into the greenery, and ...

Yes. There. Solma's heart squeezes as if between the teeth of a predator. Because there, stood beyond the perimeter of the wall, with their arms raised and muttering furiously under their breath, are a man and a boy dressed in black. A man and a boy with violet eyes, grinning horribly. Vulkan's purple gaze meets Solma's and holds it. His mouth moves quickly, muttering. *Whispering.* The boy by his side does the same.

And as they mutter, the fire grows hotter. And as the fire grows hotter, their terrible smiles grow wider.

FORTY

THE SMOKE FORMS A thick screen around the nest site, obscuring the sky above. Bees droop out of the air, confused and subdued. Olive barks something. Warren shouts frantically. But all Solma's attention is consumed by those violet eyes, that malicious grin, those outspread arms.

He's making the fire.

Vulkan and his son are making fire without spark or tinder. They're making it with their minds. They're *Whispering* it. How is that possible?

A memory flashes in her mind: a childlike figure kneeling by the storehouse, and seconds later it was on fire ...

But Solma barely has time to consider that now, because the flames devour the bramble wall and there's nothing shielding her or Olive or her family from the onrush of desperate men and women. They surge from all directions, faces smeared with ash and blood, dirt and tears. Their mouths twist in hate, brandishing their livelihoods as weaponry: kitchenware, shovels, hatchets and secateurs. They look monstrous, fire and smoke reflected in their eyes. Solma step backs and feels her shoulder blades meet Olive's.

What now?

Bell clutches Solma's arm, rolling pin raised, her face grim. Olive bares her teeth and lifts her pistol. Warren huddles between the three of them, trembling, bees gathering around him. Solma glances at him and their eyes meet. His are determined. Seven-years-old and he looks ready to fight.

Solma sets her jaw and turns to face the invaders. And there, beyond the violet-eyed Fire-Makers, his face contorted in hate, is Blaiz, leading his villagers against her. Her friends, her squad, everyone she's ever known, he's made them want to kill her.

"We can't win this," Solma realizes aloud. "We can't—"

"Yeah?" Olive growls. She holsters her pistol and draws out a second knife from somewhere. "Well, I'll be damned if I ain't gonna try."

Her gaze flickers towards Solma's, green eyes gleaming with ferocious determination. There's no one Solma would rather have by her side, no one she would trust more with her life and the lives of her family. She sets her jaw.

"Together then," she says.

She shoulders her rifle, too. No point in guns now: there's too many of them and Solma doesn't want to shoot her friends. Two or three shots ring out as the village charges and the invaders converge on the nest site, but that's all. Ammo is precious and at close quarters, a shovel is just as effective. Solma unsheathes her hunting knife. Blood roars in her ears, drowning out the battle cries from all around her.

"No one gets near the nest," Olive barks. "Unless they kill us first!"

She darts backwards to avoid the swing of an enemy hatchet and thrusts out her leg, slamming her foot into the assailant's knee. There's a crack, a grunt of pain, and the young fighter goes down. Olive snatches his hatchet from his hand as he falls and turns her weapons on the next invader.

A rush of air and the sound of shouted insults hits Solma full in the face. She dodges left in time to avoid the swinging blade of a shovel. It takes her a moment to recognize the face of her attacker, warped with rage.

It's Aldo. Aldo with his sniffles and his squint, now baring his teeth as he tries to bludgeon her.

"Stand down!" Solma barks, though she's not his Sergeant anymore. Aldo ignores her.

"Those bees're ours!" he screams, lifting his shovel for another swing. He's no fighter though. Solma waits until he's thrown all his weight behind him, his weapon at the highest point of its swing, then jabs her elbow into his gut, throwing him off balance. He grunts and trips, shovel falling from his hands. His head strikes something as he topples and he lays still. Solma doesn't have time to feel sorry.

There are too many of them. And now they're surrounded. Someone grabs Solma by the hair and she yells, but Warren kicks them in the shin.

"Get off my sister!" he screams. Solma jerks round, knife raised, ready to defend Warren, but the attacker clutches at her face and screams, claws at her eyes, stumbles backwards. Solma recognizes her, too. It's Gracie. Gracie whose brother lies dead only meters away. Solma stares in confusion as Gracie thrashes in the grass, until a little worker bee wriggles free from between her fingers and flies back to Warren. Solma's mouth falls open.

"What the—"

"They sting," Warren says, fists clenched, twenty or thirty bees orbiting him like furry satellites. "And when they do, it hurts."

He opens one palm and a few of the bees break away, humming into the fray. Solma hears shrieks of confusion as they land and jab their poisonous weaponry into sensitive places: eyelids and throats, behind ears, between fingers. These creatures Solma had always thought of as such helpless unassuming beings are suddenly living bullets.

Solma watches in disbelief. "It don't hurt them?"

Warren shakes his head. "No," he says. "They got stings like daggers. And they're defending their nest."

He opens his other fist and more bees dart off into the chaos, their flightpath marked by screams of pain and confusion. Despite herself, Solma grins and turns in time to disarm a child with a kitchen knife.

Bell has a heap of bodies at her feet, all of whom have alarming injuries. She bares her teeth and swings her rolling pin. Amidst the chaos, her war cry rings out like a berserker call.

"You should be *ashamed* of yourselves!" she rages, and Solma almost laughs.

But no matter how many Solma takes down, how many the bees blight or Olive breaks or Bell bludgeons, they keep coming. Village after desperate village, no longer bothered about fighting each other, all focused on getting to the nest. There are too many. They can't possibly—

And then something strange happens. The onrushing attackers suddenly lose their footing, trip or can't seem to balance their weight. Solma readies herself to defend against an Oritch swinging a pair of secateurs but he falls flat on his face before he gets within striking distance. Suddenly, the villagers are no longer focused on Solma and her little group, but staring at their feet, hopping backwards, swinging their weapons at the ground. Solma stares down.

The grass ...

The grass knots itself together in thick, sticky ropes and grabs the feet of their attackers. It holds them fast by the ankles, tugs them until they fall, snatches at their feet and whips at their calves and shins.

Solma meets Olive's gaze and Olive grins. "You didn't think Cobra and her lot would let us down, did you?" she says. "Come on! Keep at it!"

Solma turns back to the fray, slamming her bladed foot into the belly of an attacker she doesn't recognize and leaving him to the mercy of the long grass. "Warren!" she cries. "We need those queens out! You need to get them to fly!"

No answer.

Solma disarms a child only a little older than her brother. She grabs the girl by the collar and pulls her close, snarling, "Go home!"

She throws the girl aside and glances up, expecting to see Vulkan and his son right where they were before ...

But they're gone. And so are Blaiz and Maxen. Solma's heart kicks. She whips round, knife raised, scanning the smoky horizon for those familiar, sneering faces. Nothing.

There's no time for this. Whatever Blaiz is planning, he won't hesitate.

"Warren!"

But when she turns again, Warren isn't behind her. His bees drone frantically above the nest, panicked and undirected. A few of them flock to Solma, as if sensing her fear. She feels their feet whisper across her fingers.

Two shots ring out, so loud the air trembles. Solma flinches and grabs Olive's hand. Her gaze darts around the madness, searching for the source. The tangle of attacking bodies falls silent, subdued by the vicious grass and the gunfire.

In the sudden stillness, Solma sees Blaiz, silhouetted against the smoky horizon, with Maxen at his side. Flanking them are Vulkan and his son. And held between them is Warren. Her brave, brilliant brother, with a gun pointed at his head.

~ BLUME ~

THE GROUND STOPS RUMBLING, but the air thickens with the scent of aggression. My daughters huddle around me, scrambling to tend their princess-sisters. They should be ready by now. My tired body tells me so. My air sacs struggle to circulate. My wings are heavy, my thorax muscles slow. I'm far older than a bee has any business being.

But I cannot die yet. Not until my daughter-queens fly. My time-travelling young, ready to go to ground, burrow and overcome the bee-killing winter. I hear him calling us from above: the boy-who-speaks-bee. His scent is full of fear and anger. He calls us and the fragrance is so strong my daughters flock to the nest entrance. But there's danger above. We sense it. It smells so strong our antennae ache. He's calling, but we cannot risk our princesses. Even so, they clamber over each other, wings a-tremble, congregating at the burrow's mouth.

And then something changes in his messages.

Wait, he says. *Hold.*

We are under siege. Predators converging on our sacred ground, their fury rumbling through the earth. But he's there. He knows what to do. My daughter-queens must fly before the monsters tear open the nest. If my daughter-queens fly, I've done my work. I can die exalted. I'll die a good queen. A good bee.

I strengthen his scent with my own. *Wait,* I say. *Hold.*

There's urgency in his scent, and my daughters are a-quiver. Poison gleams on their stings. They are ready for war. They are old, too, my daughters. Not as old as me, but I haven't laid worker eggs for a long time. They have nurtured princes and princesses for the last suns. They are exhausted. But they won't let the nest die yet. Not until the daughter-queens fly.

Not until the predators above rip us open, crush our bodies, spill our honey and bread. Not until every one of us lies twitching in our own death throes will my daughters give up.

We have too much to lose. We will give our breath and blood and bodies to our future queens.

So we hold. We wait for the boy's final call.

We are ready for this. We are ready to die for it.

FORTY-ONE

SOLMA FREEZES. OLIVE'S HAND holds hers but she barely registers. The battleground has fallen silent and every eye fixes on Blaiz and the boy he holds captive. Some stare in horror, others in rage, but more stare in puzzlement. Who is this kid? What power does he have that Blaiz thinks shooting him might end all this?

They don't know.

"Give up, Sol!"

It's Maxen. With a thrill of anger, Solma realizes Maxen holds the gun. Maxen, whom she'd trusted with her deepest secrets, Maxen, to whom she'd given her fear and vulnerability. Arrogant, two-faced pig!

Solma's hand tightens into a fist and Olive grunts in pain as Solma's fingers crush her own. She doesn't complain though. She just holds Solma back.

"Wait," she growls. "Assess. Don't do anything daft."

Sound advice, but irritation ripples through Solma all the same. She grits her teeth, watches.

"You can't win!" Maxen says. "Please, Sol! Please back down. This is for everyone. Those bees belong to us. They're ours. Let Dja take them. You know it's the right thing to do."

There's a grumble of anger amongst the army, but no one stirs to violence yet. Many eyes turn on Solma. They watch her. They wait.

"For me, Sol," Maxen pleads. "For me."

And Solma snaps. Maxen can go to hell. He betrayed her. And now he's pointing a gun at her brother. Solma meets his gaze, those pale-blue eyes that she had sought refuge in for many months now seem cold. She searches them, far away though he is, for any sign of affection, respect, love.

There's none. He played her. He played her and now, faced with her, he doesn't care how it hurts, doesn't care for her fear and heartache. He's his father's son. Solma feels a cocoon forming around her heart, hardening it.

She knows better now.

"You gonna protect the nest, are you?" Solma barks. "Gonna nurture it? Keep it safe? Manage our future?"

She sees him flinch, cast a nervous glance towards the villagers who've frozen meters from her and the others. But it's Blaiz who speaks this time. "Of course we are," he says, voice silky as honey, deceptive as venom. "What else?"

Solma laughs bitterly and the sound carries, sharp and spiteful, through the smoke. "What else?" she echoes. "You gonna tell them who led a badger to the nest, Maxen? Who tried to kill our bees? You gonna tell them what you told me, Blaiz? If you can't have the nest, no one can. It's got to be destroyed, you said. You gonna tell them that?"

There's a quiver of uncertainty in Blaiz's face. Solma sees a few of her villagers lower their weapons, mutter among themselves. They cast furtive glances in Solma's direction. Solma flushes.

But when she meets the eyes of people she's known all her life, it's not suspicion she sees in their gaze, but a dawning of truth. There are Aldo and Ilga, staring in confusion, Aldo still nursing the bruise Solma gave him. There is Gracie, face streaked with tears and a nasty swelling above one eye. Her gaze flits between Solma and Blaiz as she tries to work out who to trust. Solma remembers what Olive said the evening Blaiz cornered her.

Solma is respected. Solma is loved. They trust her, here. Even though they just tried to kill her, they're listening to her. She stands a little straighter.

Blaiz's face contorts. "Enough of your lies, Solma!" he barks. "The village knows everything I've done has been for its protection. Haven't I fed you all year upon year? Haven't I built trade with neighboring towns? Haven't I saved us from drought and flood and famine?"

The murmuring again. It's all true. Blaiz looks after them. Solma hears the puzzlement in their voices. The invading forces are losing patience, stirring again.

She has one chance to stop this. But what can she do? She's just one person. Just one voice amongst this violence.

But Blume was just one bee. One bee burrowing up from deep underground, carrying the hope of her species. One bee who built a queendom, exposed a tyrant, transformed a dead village into a paradise of plenty. One bee who needs a champion to clear the air for the future. So her species can live how they were supposed to live, nurture and govern the land as they have evolved to do over millennia.

One bee was enough to make a difference.

Solma doesn't realize what the sensation on her face is at first, until the familiar sound of bee tremolo breaks the silence. The bee's feet are gentle, its antennae search her, its wings whisper across her face. She freezes, not wanting to frighten it. And in that moment, her eyes meet Warren's.

Her dear little brother. He looks so frightened. His lip trembles and his face is grimy with tear tracks. But his meadow-green eyes are so determined. He stares at Solma and whispers something. Solma can't make it out, but his lips look like they are saying, *Trust me,* and then, *Listen.*

Trust him. She can do that. She looks at him, quivering with terror but still determined to fight. He's just a kid, seven-years-old, but he doesn't beg. Doesn't struggle. He trusts her. And it's time Solma repaid the favor.

She closes her eyes. Listens. And, somehow, like an echo from Warren's mind, she senses the bee's truth.

Firestorm in the storehouse ... a black-gloved hand reaching for Warren ... No villagers died that day ... a moon badger in the dark ... Maxen ...

She reels under the weight of it, staggering. But the truth is there, in the bee's quivering wings, the whisper of its feet. Of course. She sees it now, in all its twisted ugliness. It's been there all along, she just refused to accept it. The truth is there. And it smells like flowers.

Solma opens her eyes, glares at Blaiz and Maxen Camber.

"You gonna tell them how you knew about the bee all along?" she snarls. "How you been watching Warren's power since before he even knew he had it? How you paid the raiders to attack our village so they could kill the bee? I thought it was odd that we killed twelve of them and they didn't kill none of us! 'Cos you ordered them not to!

"You knew from my parents the insects might return. You knew Warren would be the one to wake them and you reckoned you'd keep the bounty all for yourself, didn't you? You gonna tell your people how you paid Vulkan and his boy to attack us, and then they burned the storehouse down and took our food? And look! Here they are, now! Setting fire to us again! You ain't our leader, Blaiz. You're our jailer! And the bees ain't yours. They belong to themselves. Let them go and they'll benefit us all. You can't have the nest, Blaiz! I won't let you!"

She gasps at her own brazenness. But it's true. She'd rather die than let him near it. She'd shoot the man she once called her leader rather than let him take this treasure.

She expects him to deny it, to make pretty words and persuade his villagers back to his side. For one terrible moment, she sees him turn to Maxen and thinks he might order him to shoot.

But the voice that calls out isn't Blaiz's. Or Maxen's. It comes from one of the invading Stewards.

"The raiders ain't working for him!" she shouts, confused. "They can't be! They're—" she stops and Solma sees fear flood her face. Another Steward pipes up.

"*You* paid them? That's impossible—"

And a third. "They can't be working for either of you—"

A murmur sweeps the army. Solma catches sight of the two Fire-Makers, their smiles faltering. The son takes a step closer to his father, whose face is thunder. Blaiz glowers at them.

Beside Solma, Olive barks a cruel laugh. "They've played you all, you bunch'a cowards!" she cackles. "You all paid them, didn't you? Desperate, greedy tyrants! You all paid them and look where it got you?"

There comes a sharp cry, followed by another and another. Someone raises a knife. Someone else raises a hatchet. Weapons swing. People fall. But this time, the violence isn't aimed at Solma and her friends. They're fighting each other. Solma watches the men and women of her village muttering, raising their weapons, and turning towards Blaiz.

"Traitor!" someone yells.

"Liar!" cries someone else. The desperate villagers turn and barrel towards their leader. Solma's heart kicks. *No.* Because she sees the look on Blaiz's face. She sees him turn towards Maxen, give the order.

Maxen hesitates. His grip on the gun slackens as he stares at his father. So Maxen doesn't really want to shoot a kid. It's not enough to absolve him, but it brings Solma some small relief. A tendon stands out on Blaiz's neck. He roars this time.

"*Shoot him!*"

Maxen raises the pistol.

Solma screams, but her feet won't move. She can't get there in time. There are too many people, too much smoke, too much violence.

Blaiz turns to Vulkan and the boy, whom he still believes are under his command. "Burn the nest!"

Solma watches Maxen struggle with himself—he's not his father yet. Still, he loops his finger over the trigger. Warren closes his eyes, his mouth working, saying something ...

And the air is full of bees.

They're everywhere: hundreds of them, their battle-buzz thundering with new fervor. Solma's body tightens at the sight of them, and Olive's hand tenses in hers. Bell lets out a grunt of surprise and stumbles backwards, her rolling pin still raised, but when Solma glances at her, it's an expression of awe, not fear, that she wears.

"Well, I never ..." she murmurs, and then her voice is drowned out by the bee's war song.

The effect on the army is immediate. A scattering of yelps breaks their silence, and there's a stampede as they scramble to get away. A few are stung on the elbow or shoulder as they retreat, but they're not the bee's main focus.

Solma watches, astonished, as the bees rise in a vortex, making ever bigger circles around the nest, gathering height and numbers. If she closes her eyes, if she listens hard enough, she can just hear the language of their song through Warren.

Killer! Killer! Save the young! Save the boy!

Then, like a living arrowhead, they surge towards Blaiz and Maxen. Their wings shimmer despite the smoke, poison gleams on their stings. Maxen's face falls at the sight of them but Blaiz's twists with anger. He shouts something but his voice is overcome by the deep, rumbling vibrato of the bees. Solma thinks that, through the haze, she sees Vulkan lift his hands.

"The nest!" she cries. "He's gonna burn it!"

But the bees don't respond. Solma swears, watches in horror as they overwhelm Blaiz and Maxen. A shot rings out, then another, but the bees, themselves, are bullets. They cling to Blaiz's face, Maxen's throat and wrists. They sting and sting and sting. They don't let up, despite the screams, despite the fingernails clawing them off skin. Maxen drops his gun and staggers away. Blaiz drops to his knees, his movements dull and spasmodic. Free, Warren darts from under them and races to Solma's side.

Olive, deprived of people to fight, stands dumbly and watches as smoke drifts from the nest burrow.

"Warren!" Solma exclaims, hugging him close. "We have to stop them! They're burning the nest!"

"It doesn't matter," Warren says. It takes Solma a minute to decide whether she's heard him right. She holds him at arm's length.

"What?"

"It doesn't matter," Warren says. Tears stream down his cheeks but he's smiling. "Look."

He points to the ash tree, whose roots shelter the bee nest. Solma squints at it, then her eyes widen.

"Holy—" Olive starts to say, but Bell's hand on her shoulder silences her. Bell's eyes are full of tears, her rolling pin hangs from a limp hand as she stares at the trunk of the ash.

On which dozens of bees are gathered, shivering their wings. They're big, big as Blume was when she first emerged, with lustrous fur and long antennae and the future in their bellies.

Queens. Blume's daughter-queens. They heard Warren's call after all.

A flicker of flame curls out of the old nest and Solma's heart squeezes.

"But Blume!" she whispers. Warren shakes his head.

"It's ok, Sol," he says, taking her hand. "It's her time. She's old and look at her daughters! She did it, Sol. The new queens'll come up next spring and make new nests."

Solma nods but can't bring herself to speak. She watches the orange flames consume the nest. The burrow entrance collapses, releasing a puff of smoke as the heat is contained inside, burning what's left of

Blume's home. Burning Blume. That bee. That impossible, brilliant bee.

She'll never know the extent of what she's done.

"Look, Sol!" Warren says. He raises his hands just as Solma looks back to the ash. The new queens lift together, their gossamer wings shining with promise. In a long stream they disappear south, towards the gathering of males waiting at the edge of the forest. To freedom.

Solma watches them go, squeezing Olive's hand in a mixture of triumph and sadness. She closes her eyes and tries to embed the sound of bee song into her memory so that she will remember it during the winter silence.

But it will be back next year. If Blume's daughters have any of her tenacity, there will not be another hundred year wait for the sound of bee-song to fill the summer skies.

FORTY-TWO

Solma doesn't flinch at the sound of someone knocking at the door. She and Warren have almost packed. Not that they have much in the way of belongings. Bell rummages in the cellar, gathering the books she doesn't want left behind and the bags of seeds she's kept hidden down there all this time. They don't have long before they'll be forced to leave, and Solma and Warren both agree that, when they step out of the village for the first and last time, it will be on their own terms.

The flight of the bees had ended the conflict. With the nest burned, there was nothing to fight over and though there were shouts of betrayal between the warring Stewards, the appetite for battle was gone and the villagers returned, crestfallen, to their homes. A few, headstrong voices called for Blaiz's blood, but as the numerous bee stings had driven him into a coma, there seemed little point in that. His unconsciousness made it easy for other Stewards to label him the villain and call an emergency convention, during which they would decide what to do about him, what to do about Sand's End ... and what to do about the bees. They're there now, in the council hall, shouting and bickering while their people pack down their camps ready to return home. Solma clenches her jaw at the thought. Whatever they decide, one thing's for certain. There's no way she's letting any one of those greedy Stewards take control of the bees. She'll fight them with every last ounce of strength she has.

Vulkan and his son have vanished, which Solma finds worrying if she lets herself think about it. It means they're still out there, with those devastating powers, beholden to no-one.

Maxen has taken residence in Blaiz's office. Solma hasn't seen him since Blume's last daughters chased him off her brother, but somehow she no longer feels a need to throw her fist in his face. She's seen his soul with her own eyes and she doesn't think she'll ever make him understand how he's hurt her. She hopes the vicious bee stings that now mar half his face will cause him even an ounce of the pain he's caused her.

They'll leave scars, those stings. Good. It'll mark him as an enemy of the bees, as *her* enemy.

The villagers accept his authority for now. As Solma knows, people sometimes take a long time to accept how thoroughly they've been played. But Solma has heard dissent among the people, seen the bitter looks they throw at his back as they walk past, noticed how they're a little slow to step out of his way nowadays. Well, let him lord over his little kingdom while he can. Solma has more important things to deal with.

Like her exile. It still holds and Maxen has not reversed it, which says everything that Solma needs it to say. Treacherous pig. He has, however, extended said exile to include Olive and Roseann. Solma expected some dry, wicked quip from Olive when the news was delivered to them, but Olive only rolled her eyes. "Ugh, what a pain in the ass," she grumbled, and set to packing. Solma thought she might have seen Olive smiling as she began folding up her things.

No one has seen or heard from the Earth Whisperers since the battle. So, when Solma turns now and sees Cobra and Mamba standing in their doorway, she jumps with surprise.

"You're here!" she says, pointing. Cobra smiles.

"Well spotted," she says. Warren laughs and runs to Cobra, wrapping his arms about her middle. She hugs him gratefully and ruffles his red-blonde hair. "Hello, brave one," she whispers. "I'm sorry about your bee."

Warren withdraws, his face serious. "She weren't my bee," he says softly. "She was always her own bee. But she was my friend. I'm sad she's gone, but she had a long life for a little bee. And her daughters will be back next year."

Cobra nods and lifts her gaze to meet Solma's. "But you won't?" she asks. Solma shakes her head and turns back to her packing.

"No," she says. "We won't. Don't know where we'll go yet, but we clearly aren't welcome here anymore. Not that I *want* to stay, knowing what I know."

"That's ..." Mamba says hesitantly, "actually why we're here."

He looks cross about it, clearly not his idea, but he'll go along with it because of Cobra. Solma gets the impression he'd do anything for her.

"What d'you mean?"

Cobra's smile is so wide Solma thinks it must meet around the back of her head. Her green eyes sparkle. "Well," she says, "Technically, Warren is a Whisperer. A new kind of Whisperer. He'll need teaching. This isn't over. When the bees return next spring, we'll need to be ready for more greed, more squabbles, more attempts to control nests. And they'll need flowers. Wildflowers, like Alphor hasn't seen in a century. Warren's powers will be needed more than ever."

Solma's whole body tingles. She stays stock still, terrified that moving might scare Cobra into changing her mind. Could this be happening?

"And," Cobra says, still grinning, "We could do with a couple of guards to protect us from raiders. And most of us are only children, so a doctor would be a wonderful help."

Solma raises an eyebrow. "And Aunt Bell?"

Cobra laughs. "You think I'd leave her behind?" she chuckles. "I'm addicted to her cooking, and the others will be, too. So, what do you think? Want to come with us?"

Solma's heart lifts like the gossamer wings of a spring bee.

"I'll have to ask Olive," she murmurs.

"No you won't," comes Olive's voice from the doorway, making everyone jump. "Olive says yes. Are you *still* packing, Sol? How long does it take?" She grins, squeezes past Cobra and Mamba and strides to Solma's side, leaning over and delivering a kiss onto

Solma's mouth. She's utterly unashamed about it and Solma doesn't quite know how to handle this new thing. It feels a little like betrayal, like somehow she's still answerable to Maxen, but Olive's been clear: what will be, will be. Solma calls the shots. They'll just ... see where this takes them.

And in the darkness after the battle, the night Solma knew would be the last she spent in her own home, she found herself picturing Olive's face and smiling.

Dr Roseann hovers by the door. She shakes hands with Mamba and greets Cobra warmly, calling her Kobi, asking after her health. Solma ducks her head, hiding the shame in her cheeks. Apparently, lots of people remember the tenacious, red-haired little Kobi. Now that Blaiz's offences are clear, no-one believes that she's a thief any longer, and they've made their acceptance of her obvious. Only Solma seems to have wiped this wondrous person from her memory, driven as she was by belief in someone who, in the end, didn't deserve it.

"Come on, Sol," Olive says. "You're dawdling. We can have this all packed in five minutes if you stop being so fastidious about it."

She grabs the shirt Solma's been carefully folding and stuffs it into a bag. "Hey!" Solma exclaims. Olive ignores her. Nothing new there.

Bell bustles from the cellar with an armful of books, all of them something to do with insects. "Figure we'll need these!" she says, wrapping them in hemp cloth. At the doorway, Roseann scowls. "Well, *you're* carrying them," she says.

Solma expects an audience to their departure, but there isn't one. The village needs prepping for winter. Repairs must be made to houses damaged in the various fights and there are bodies to bury. Half the village are down by the edge of the forest, laying the dead to rest. The other half are at work in the fields and orchards or fixing things. Nobody has time to witness the exile. Nobody cares.

Solma and her little band of fugitives trek to the edge of the village's territory, carrying their meagre belongings. Bell natters to Roseann at the back of the group, while Roseann responds with monosyllabic grunts of acknowledgment. She and Olive are so alike.

Solma watches Warren scurry ahead with a little backpack bouncing on his shoulders. His arms are outspread and he buzzes like a bee, meandering through the long grass, engrossed in his game.

They meet Cobra and the Earth Whisperers at the western edge of Sand's End village. The Whisperers look a little the worse for wear, with a few of them sporting bandages or deep bruises, but they're smiling and chattering.

The Whisperers let up a cheer when they see Solma's little party and one of the tan ponies even tosses his head in welcome. Cobra hugs Warren tight.

"Ready to go, Beekeeper?" she asks. Warren grins.

"Never thought I'd hear that word spoken in my lifetime," Bell huffs as she catches up to them. "Least of all about my nephew! The last beekeeper of Alphor …"

Warren wrinkles his nose, eyes sparkling. "I don't reckon I'm the last, actually," he says, with that confident, matter-of-factness that only seven-year-olds can muster. "More like the first."

He's going to say more, but one of the younger Whisperers smacks him on the arm. "You're it!" she announces, and hares off into the distance, giggling. Warren doesn't even think. Determined not to be outdone, he charges off to fulfil his duty as dedicated chaser.

Solma and the others fall into step with the Whisperers' troupe, heads bowed, prepared for a long hike. The conversation is quiet, but optimistic, with discussions about where they should go next, which villages will need them through the winter, where they might find trouble. They talk, too, about practical things: where they will set up camp tonight, how far they will need to walk tomorrow, where they might find help and supplies. Solma listens to these plans, to the names of far-off places, and her heart kicks with fear and excitement. This life is going to be hard. Her eyes search for and find Warren, scurrying about with the younger Whisperers. Can he do this? Is this enough to keep him alive? Solma doesn't know yet. Olive laces her fingers with Solma's and kisses her shoulder gently. "Thoughtful, are we?" she asks, raising an eyebrow. Her jaw rotates lazily around her sugar cane and, for once, Solma doesn't find it irritating.

Solma nods. "Yeah."

She doesn't say anything else. She doesn't need to. Olive holds her hand, still, but lets her muse. Lets her mourn and worry and hope in silence. Her presence, once grating, now feels reassuring. Whatever comes charging out of the unknown, she knows Olive will have her back.

She's still thinking this thought, still smiling, when she takes the step that carries her the furthest from Sand's End village, from home, she's ever been in her life. And she doesn't even notice. She's too busy trying to trace the drone of bee song she hears somewhere above her: a single bumblebee, drifting through the still autumn air, the sun gleaming off her black-and-gold stripes. One of Blume's children? Solma can't tell. She lifts her hands, hoping the little bee might deign to land on them, but she doesn't. She's intent on other things, like finding flowers to feast at before she goes to ground. Solma and the little band of wanderers are irrelevant to the newly-mated queen. She has flowers to drink at, a winter to survive. These humans? They're unimportant.

Solma watches her erratic path through the autumn air, her tiny body briefly silhouetted before she disappears and her song falls quiet. Sleep well, little bee, Solma thinks. She'll be listening for the first tremble of their song next spring.

THANK YOU!

Thank you so much for reading my story. I hope it gave your hours of joy and made you laugh, cry and think. It means so much to me that you've made it this far and invested time and energy in my story. Thank you.

I have one more small favour to ask. It would mean so much to me if you could head to the place you purchased your copy of the book and leave a review. Just a few lines to say what you thought of the book and why you might recommend it would help other readers to find it. Reviewing the book on Amazon, Kobo or Goodreads would mean so much, but even a post on social media or telling a friend about it can help spread the word to others who might love this book, too.

Thank you!

WANT TO READ MORE?

Did you enjoy reading this book and want more by the same author? You can get a free e-novella by signing up to my Readers' Club. Scan the QR code below to sign up.

After a few welcome emails, you'll receive updates, deals and exclusive stories and content from me every month. It would mean so much to me to have you as part of my readers' club. I look forward to seeing you there!

LEARN MORE ABOUT THE WORLD OF SILENT SKIES!

Do you wan to see a map of Alphor? Do you want to know what Sand's End looks like? Would you like to see character profiles and read about why I wrote this series? Scan the QR code below for all this and more about the world of Silent Skies.

You'll also find some interesting facts about bees and some information on how you can work to protect them.

ALSO BY REBECCA L. FEARNLEY

Keep an eye out for the next two books in the trilogy, coming soon! Check out my Amazon author page to keep an eye on new releases.

Or head to www.rebeccafearnleywrites.co.uk.

The Hive Child

Bee Song in a Burning Meadow

THANKS TO ...

Any writer will tell you that a book doesn't get written without the support, faith and guidance of many, many people. I'll start with those who've made this book the physical thing that it is. To my editor, Lara, thank you for your brilliant and thorough feedback and for showing such faith in the story. Thank you to Jeff from Curiosity Press for always replying to emails so quickly, being so helpful in finding me my editor and proof reader and just generally being super efficient. Thank you to my wonderful cover designer, Stefanie, at Seventh Star Designs, for your beautiful artwork in which this story lives.

Thank you also to my wonderful writing group, Lou, Georgia and Daisy, who've beta read this book and continued to push me to be the very best writer I can be, cajoling me through my fear and celebrating my successes. Thank you to Lucy, Carly from Limb

Power and Dave Goulson for your sensitivity and accuracy readings. Thank you to my ARC readers, who raced to read this book before publication so they could get reviews up for launch day. Thank you to the wonderful Sue, librarian at one of my residency schools, who has championed and supported me for years now, and without whose help, I'm not sure this book would have been finished!

Thank you to my family. To both my parents, who've remained stalwartly certain that I will succeed in my lifelong writing dream and have supported me in every way possible. Thank you to my brilliant siblings for listening to me cry, panic or celebrate down the phone and talk round in circles when I was feeling particularly overwhelmed. Thank you to my partner and life teammate, David, for your constant patience, faith and reassurance. I know you've had to tell me it will be fine a million times. I almost believe you now.

And lastly, but by no means least, thank you to you, my readers. The people who breathe life into this story. I hope it touched your heart. I hope it made you dream. My story continues to live on through you, and for that I am truly, deeply grateful.

ABOUT AUTHOR

Rebecca has been obsessed with two things her whole life: stories and animals. Luckily, they go together well. Rebecca writes fantastical tales, filled with unusual creatures, strange magic and strong protagonists. She's performed poetry all over the country and her collection, Octopus Medicine, was published by Two Rivers Press in 2017. She lives in Reading, UK, with her partner, her bunny, Cleo, and her parrot, Maya.

Printed in Great Britain
by Amazon

79035333R00274